*The People
We Hate
at the
Wedding*

The People
We Hate
at the
Wedding

GRANT GINDER

FLATIRON
BOOKS
NEW YORK

This is a work of fiction. All of the characters, organizations, and events portrayed in this novel are either products of the author's imagination or are used fictitiously.

www.flatironbooks.com

The Library of Congress Cataloging-in-Publication Data is available upon request.

ISBN 978-1-250-09520-6 (hardcover)
ISBN 978-1-250-15491-0 (international edition)
ISBN 978-1-250-09521-3 (e-book)

Our books may be purchased in bulk for promotional, educational, or business use. Please contact your local bookseller or the Macmillan Corporate and Premium Sales Department at 1-800-221-7945, extension 5442, or by e-mail at MacmillanSpecial Markets@macmillan.com.

First Edition: June 2017

10   9   8   7   6   5   4   3   2   1

FOR CLARE O'CONNOR

PART ONE

Brothers and sisters should never
be in the same family.

—CHARLES M. SCHULZ

Alice

Christ, Alice thinks, staring at the envelope, these invitations must have cost a fucking fortune.

Her phone buzzes against her desk, and she picks it up before it has a chance to ring twice.

"So, how much?"

It's Paul, her brother.

"Hold on." Alice scrolls down the website for a stationery company called Bella Lettera that she heard a coworker gushing about yesterday. Buried below a hundred pictures of dainty thank-you cards and save-the-dates, she finds what she's looking for: a pink-and-white pricing table for wedding invitations.

"I've only got about five minutes," he says.

"I'm going as fast as I can." She squints at the screen. "Why are you in such a rush?"

"I've just—I'm at work, okay? I've got shit to do."

"You're the one who was begging to talk last night."

"Yeah, and you said you were busy, just like I'm saying I'm busy now. So . . ."

She wasn't busy; that had been a lie. When she got home last evening, she'd had grand plans of going for a run in Laurel Canyon—plans that were effectively squashed when she checked her mail and found, among the catalogs and bills, an invitation to her half sister Eloise's wedding. She opened a bottle of white wine and dealt with the bills first—or perhaps *dealt* is too strong, too ambitious a word. Really, she just stared at the crushing amounts her creditors were demanding. Then, when she was good and drunk, she leaned forward and ripped open the invitation, giving herself a nasty paper cut in the process.

"Shit," she'd said, and stared at the dot of blood on her finger as she waited for the sting to register. A few moments later, once the cut had got her satisfyingly angry, she shoved her finger into her mouth and sucked on it, cringing at the metallic taste: her blood, she thought, the stuff that filled her body, was nothing but a fistful of pennies.

Returning to her couch, she sat down and stared at the mess of paper in front of her. As a rule, she doesn't believe in omens. She never reads her horoscope, and she thinks Fate is just the name narcissists give to Coincidence. Getting caught in a traffic jam, winning the lottery, dying in a plane crash: it's all just the slapdash workings of chance. Things happen, and things don't. Still, though: slicing your finger open on your sister's wedding invitation can't be a good sign.

Paul says, *"Hello?"*

"I'm here, I'm here."

She skims down the table's columns: foil, no foil; card-stock type; multiple colors.

"So how much did they cost?"

"Okay." Alice drums her fingers across her desk. In the cubicle next to her, the phone rings. "Let's see. We think it's two-ply paper, right?"

"I think so," Paul says. "I've got it right in front of me. Thick and nice as shit."

"Yeah, I've got it right here, too."

Alice picks Eloise's invitation up off her desk. The paper is full and cottony, halfway between papyrus and a quilt, she thinks. And if she looks closely enough, she can see details she missed last night: wisps in its pulp, places where it's been *hand* pressed—all sorts of little irregularities that add up to a hefty price tag.

Paul says, "Okay, so we can agree on two-ply?"

"Absolutely." She traces her half sister's name. "How many colors are we dealing with?"

"I was just going to ask that," Paul says. "I count three: gold, silver, and that terrible, shitty English-seaside blue."

Alice liked the blue when she first opened the envelope; it had reminded her of the peonies her mother used to grow in their garden in St. Charles.

"Right," she says. "Three colors. Do we think it's letterpress or foil stamping or what?"

Paul's breathing finally slows down. "So, Mark and I were talking about this last night. He originally thought it was letterpress. But, I mean, if you look closely, you can pretty *obviously* see the foil."

Alice closes her left eye and squints at the name of the groom: *Oliver.* The elegant *O* glints under the office's fluorescent lights.

"Definitely foil," she says. "And we estimated how many?"

"I'd say two hundred fifty. That bitch knows a lot of people."

"I think that's probably reasonable." Alice reaches for a pen and a Post-it, jots down a few numbers, and performs a series of mental calculations. "So, we're looking at about eighteen hundred, but that just covers the invitation, program cover, and program panel." She scrolls down to the site's next table. "For response cards, and the save-the-dates we got a few months ago, and menus, and all of *that* shit, we've got to consider another . . . looks like about fifteen hundred."

"So we're up to about thirty-three hundred."

". . . and then envelopes are going to run another seven hundred, at least."

"Okay, so four thousand. Anything else?"

Alice does a quick inventory. "No, I think that's it."

"We'll throw in an additional five hundo, because it's Eloise, which brings us up to forty-five hundred dollars," Paul says. "And you're sure this website's legit? Like, it's analogous to something El would use?"

"Totally." Alice lowers her voice to a whisper. "The girl I overheard talking about it is a *real* fucking snob."

"Okay, good. So: *forty-five fucking hundred dollars on invitations.* Absolutely ridiculous."

Alice examines her invitation again. "At least they came out nicely."

"Well, they *better have* for nearly five grand."

"You're acting surprised."

"Aren't you?"

"No," Alice says. "We knew it would cost her at least that much. We just wanted to be justified in our disgust."

Paul says, "It's blood money, is what it is."

"You're being a *little* dramatic."

"Am I, though? Our entire childhood, her dad's funneling cash into some trust fund for her, just because he feels guilty over what he did to Mom."

"He's her father. That's what rich fathers do. They give their daughters money." She adds, though she knows she shouldn't, "And speaking of Mom, you should really give her a call, you know."

"I'm not getting into that, Alice. Do you hear me? I'm *not* getting into *that*. Anyway, we never saw a cent of that money."

"It wasn't ours, Paul. We didn't deserve any of it."

She wants to believe herself.

Paul scoffs. "We went to a public school that looked like it was out of some D-rate John Hughes movie; she went to school—elementary school through high school—at Collège Alpin Beau Soleil in Switzerland. We spent our fucking summers in Tampa. She spent hers in Santorini."

"Yeah, well. Still. I'd much rather have had our dad for a father any day."

"Me, too," he says.

Alice tosses the invitation down on the desk. "I can't remember the last time I thought this much about a piece of paper. You're at least going to go, aren't you?" she asks, once she's sat back down.

"Probably not," Paul says. "Mark and I were already talking of plans that weekend."

"The wedding isn't until July eleventh."

"And?"

"And today's the first of May."

"So what's your point?"

"What life-changing plans could you possibly have made over two months in advance?"

In the background on his end she hears a gentle roar: a leaf blower, or a passing truck.

"We're talking about going camping with Preston and Crosby. In the Poconos."

Alice plants her elbows on her desk and cradles the phone against her shoulder. "I'm sorry," she says. "Did I hear you right? I couldn't have. I actually couldn't have. Because what I *thought* you just said was that you were going to *miss your sister's wedding* to go *gay camping* in the Poconos."

"Half sister," Paul corrects.

"I can't believe this." She pinches her eyes shut and wards off the beginnings of a flash migraine.

"I can't just drop everything every time Eloise decides to smother us with her own happiness, Alice. I have a life, you know."

"You're implying that I don't."

"I didn't say that."

"You didn't have to. That's what makes it an implication."

There's a pause. Alice bookmarks the Bella Lettera website, un-bookmarks it, and then bookmarks it again before finally closing the window.

She says, "Please tell me you'll be there."

"I need to think about it."

"*Paul,*" she says, trying not to plead. "*Tell me you'll be there.*"

"I have to go."

"PAUL."

"Alice, I'm leaving now."

She leans forward and lowers her voice to a whisper. "So help me God, Paul, if you hang up on me I'll fucking come for you."

Alice hears Paul sigh dramatically, and the line goes dead.

Paul

"What's your anxiety level?"

"My God, this is disgusting."

"Yes, I imagine it is."

"No, but *really*. This is absolutely repulsive. It's like you can actually *see* the disease. There, look, right next to my pinkie finger. Syphilis, crawling around, having a grand old time."

This time Paul doesn't answer. Wendy shifts her hands along the flanks of the garbage can, but she doesn't let go. Earlier, during their first session of the day, she'd kicked the steel bin away after five agonized seconds and Dr. Goulding, Paul's supervisor, had demanded that Wendy pick up each piece of trash with her bare hands. Three banana peels and a maxipad later, she lost it. Fell to the ground and started pounding her fists against the pavement. She wailed so hard and so loud about the pervasiveness of germs that a group of patients inside took breaks from facing their own fears to huddle in one of the clinic's broad bay windows, where they looked on, mouths agape. The only thing that got Wendy up was when Paul, playing the nice guy to Goulding's bad-cop shtick, had leaned over and said, "You're doing great, Wendy—just think of how filthy the ground must be."

Now, he hears himself ask again: "What's your anxiety level?"

"A nine? A nine point five? A nine point nine?" She pinches her eyes shut, and Paul watches the metal fog up around her fingers as she grips the can tighter. "What's higher than a nine point nine?"

"A nine point nine nine, I'd guess."

"Can I go to two decimal places? Can I go to nine point nine nine?" Sweat beads in the shallow grooves of Wendy's temples, and tears balance just beneath her eyes. Paul lets his gaze fall back to his clipboard: this is the part he hates the most, the moment right before the panic begins to slowly subside, when the patient seems so sure that fear and her own frenetic synapses might cause her heart to burst. When Paul, despite his knowing better, is blindly certain that, through some violent act of empathy, his own heart might burst as well.

"You can say it's a ten, you know," he says.

"No, I can't."

"If it feels like it's a ten, you should say it's a ten."

Wendy shakes her head. In the sun, the roots of her blond hair are streaked with dull glints of gray.

"I can't handle a ten. If I say it's a ten, then I can't handle it. I want to handle it."

Paul tries to keep a straight face—Goulding throws a fit whenever one of his caseworkers reacts emotionally to something a patient says—but he can't help it; he grins as he jots down "9.99" on a line marked COMPULSIVE FEAR AND ANXIETY CONTROL. He likes Wendy too much. Despite the fretful disposition, the need to wash her hands until they are blistered and red, the insistence on using a fresh toothbrush each night, there are other parts of Wendy that exist free of her compulsions, parts that Paul finds soothing: the frayed collars of her polo shirts, the chipped pearl earrings she wears every day. The creamy scent of the Yves Saint Laurent perfume that trails her around the clinic. All of it adds up to a sort of faded WASP aesthetic, like she's been plucked from a year-old Talbots catalog. She reminds him, more or less, of the mothers of his wealthier friends from college. The sort of women who didn't *visit* campus, but instead *dropped by*; who insisted on buying him dinner and laughing at his jokes; who always offered him a hopeful—if not entirely sober—form of kinship. He often catches himself imagining that Wendy could be his own mother, if his mother were, actually, someone else entirely.

She showed up at the clinic two months ago, at the forefront of a week-long rush of about a hundred other prospective patients. They'd all seen Goulding on *Good Morning America* ("Which time?" he asked each of them; behind his clipboard, Paul rolled his eyes), where he had been invited to discuss his latest book, *Torturing Your Way to a Peaceful Mind*. It was the third volume in a vague and loose-ish series. The first two, which had been required reading in the Master's in Psychology program at New York University, where Paul had studied, were titled *Killing Your Obsession* and (rather distastefully, Paul thought) *Murdering Your Compulsion*. Wendy, like most of Goulding's patients, claimed to have pored over each one multiple times, her highlighter poised ready in her gloved hand ("I'll make sure to tell the doctor," Paul had said, smiling. He didn't. He never did). The raves over Goulding's literature during initial patient interviews never come as a shock to him or any of the other caseworkers—all three books have been runaway hits, thanks in no small part to their incendiary titles and shocking methods.

More conservative members of the psychotherapy community consider Goulding a maverick when it comes to the treatment of obsessive-compulsive disorder. (In the January edition of *Psychology Today* that Paul had leafed through at the dentist's office, he had somewhat gleefully scanned a two-page spread in which a cadre of noted analysts likened Goulding to famous villains, ranging from Iago to the Joker. Then he remembered that this was the same Goulding who signed his paychecks, and he traded *Psychology Today* in for an old issue of *Vanity Fair*.) There are other therapists practicing similar treatments—in fact, Paul interviewed with another institute outside Boston two weeks before finishing graduate school—but none of them push the boundaries of exposure therapy quite as sadistically far as Goulding does. At those clinics, so far as Paul understands, the sort of immersive practices that Goulding champions are looked at as a final resort—a last-ditch effort desperate doctors try when cognitive behavioral therapy and drugs don't work. And even then, it's a matter of the patient being told she can't wash her hands before dinner; never would she be asked to molest a trash can.

"Can I take my hands away from this filthy thing now?" Wendy asks.

It's hot for May, even here, in the leafy suburbs of Philadelphia's Main Line, and the overripe scent of garbage is causing Wendy to pull a face.

Paul shields his eyes from the sun; Goulding forbids his caseworkers to sport any sort of eyewear. "Is your anxiety still at a nine point nine nine?"

"I've still got fucking Ebola crawling under my fingernails, haven't I?"

Paul stifles a grin a second time: he loves it when Wendy swears. She throws so much strength behind her *fucks*, her *shits*, her *damns* that the rest of the sentence is often left breathless and anemic. She looks down and blushes.

"Then no," Paul says. "You can't take your hands away just yet."

She quickly counts to five and then says, "How about now? Can I let go *now*? I feel much better."

"Your knees are shaking, and you're still sweating."

Wendy looks down at her legs—tan, crosshatched with shadows of varicose veins.

"Think of all those germs," Paul adds, following Goulding's script. "Think of all those germs crawling all over your body, and you're still alive."

"This isn't living, kid."

"Just hang on a bit longer." He stops himself short of agreeing with her. "You're doing great."

He watches her roll her eyes, and he thinks back to when he was first hired, nearly two years ago (God, he thought, could it *really* have been that long ago?). He'd just been awarded his master's degree, and he was more or less pure hearted and well intentioned; his actions and decisions were dictated by a sense of goodness and purpose. Or, at least, that's what he likes to think, now that he has the luxury of hiding behind hindsight. Regardless, the fact is that he had told himself that he believed in the work that Goulding was doing, and that was the important thing. It was controversial, and had a decidedly avant-garde bend, but still he believed in it, which made it the right job to take. Over the past five months, though, he's been having a tougher time convincing himself that he made the right decision. That purity that he felt, that blithe sense of goodness, has given way to a sort of flailing confusion, a rudderlessness that causes him to sneak cigarettes when Mark's out of town, or drink more whiskey than he should.

"All right," he says, "you can let go."

Wendy rips her palms away from the bin and begins wiping them against her shorts, leaving greasy fingerprints spotting her thighs. When she's done and her face is red and wet, she thrusts a palm out to Paul.

"The Purell?"

Paul folds his arms. "Not quite yet."

"You've got to be fucking kidding me."

He follows the script: "Wendy, I want to remind you that you're here voluntarily. You can leave whenever you want."

Wendy mutters another breathless obscenity and looks down.

"You people are more awful than Al Qaeda," she says.

He's been told worse. Hell, he's agreed with worse. He thinks that maybe, even though Mark's home, he'll have a cigarette, anyway. He'll close the door and light some cloying, lilac-scented CVS candle so Mark won't be able to smell the smoke from down the hall (he will, though; he inevitably does).

There are other reasons why he took the job. Reasons that are less righteous and more logistical, reasons that require less moral acrobatics. Namely: it was the only offer he got. Actually, no, that wasn't entirely true.

He deserved more credit than that. Revised: it was the only offer he got *in the Philadelphia metro area.* There were any number of other gigs he could have applied for back in New York, jobs that a few of his professors had pushed him to go after. They would have been more traditional in nature—a counselor at a high school in Brooklyn; an appointed caseworker in the Wellness Center at NYU—but the pay would have been fine-ish, and the hours comfortable. And besides, they would have allowed him the opportunity to actually *help* people, which is why he decided to forgo the sort of lucrative careers his friends were pursuing and instead become a social worker in the first place. Most important, Paul wagers, none of them would have required that he choke back an uncomfortable, guttural hybrid of laughter and tears while he watched some Daughter of the American Revolution bear-hug a trash can. But Mark had wanted to move to Philadelphia. He had presented Paul with no other option, really. Had said, in that coolly pragmatic, multiclausal way of his (which invariably made Paul feel slightly hysterical, no matter the context): "I'm going, and I'd love for you to come, but if you didn't, I'd understand, and I'd wish you the best of luck." Days later, over drinks at a basement bar on West Eighth Street, Paul's graduate school friends, newly minted social workers with names like Anita and Deidre, had begged him to more closely examine Mark's statement. They pleaded with Paul to confront the mixed messages that were inherent in phrases like "I'd wish you the best of luck" and the tinge of narcissism behind sentences that began with "I'm going." Paul had drained his glass of Cabernet and promised that he'd heed their warnings and give Mark's ultimatum some thought. Really, though, he left the bar and laughed. Therapy is as flawed a system as anything else, he thought to himself as he descended the subway stairs and started to make his way back uptown. More flawed, actually. More fucked. The only facts therapists have to base their conjectures on are the ones supplied to them by their patients— men and women who are, by their own admission, screwed up. And from that perspective, the whole process seems so cockeyed and subjective that you can count on it being about as reliable as a Ouija board. Which, okay, fine, is probably what drew him to the practice in the first place: facts terrified him, and objectivity he found cripplingly claustrophobic.

But in this case, in *this* case, facts are on his side: Mark wasn't being narcissistic, or intentionally convoluted—he was being practical. He'd just finished his Ph.D. in behavioral economics at Columbia, where his dissertation on risk aversion and rational decision-making among the native Sami tribes of Swedish Laponia earned him not only the department's highest honors, but also an assistant professorship offer at the University of Pennsylvania, where he'd caught the eye of the chair of that school's economics department. It was an opportunity too good to pass up, and Paul knew this. He was happy to support Mark in it, even if his support wasn't directly requested or expressly needed.

Besides, things had been going well: two years in they had finally moved in together, with Paul surrendering his studio on West Tenth Street in order to take up in Mark's one-bedroom in Morningside Heights. And despite the horror stories he'd heard about the first six months of joint habitation ("just wait—you'll learn things you can't unlearn about him"), they had settled rather flawlessly into a predictable domesticity. A bliss, even. And so moving with Mark south, to Philadelphia, on account of some new, incredible job, was hardly an act of manipulation or narcissism, despite what Anita and Deidre and their forty-thousand-dollar theories professed. Paul had made a rational, self-possessed decision—and if working at Goulding's clinic was a secondary outcome of that decision, then that was something that was entirely his choice and his doing.

And this is something he tells himself over, and over, and over again.

"So what now?"

"Pardon?"

Wendy stares at Paul. Her arms are stretched out in front of her, zombie-esque, and she has her fingers spread so far apart that the thin webbing separating their bases looks translucent in the sun.

"You said there was something else we were doing today," she says, with a tinge of impatient dread in her voice. "So, what is it?"

"Right." Paul sets his clipboard down on the grass and checks his watch: four fifteen in the afternoon. Behind him, twenty yards back, the porch of the clinic's main building—a blue-and-white colonial revival—is darkened by shadows. Bugs, energized by the heat wave, buzz around the campus's outdoor lamps. Paul swats a mosquito away from his right ear.

He says, "Okay, first, though, how are you feeling?"

"I was just molesting a trash can."

"Yes, I know. But *how are you feeling?*" Paul notices that Wendy hasn't reached for the gloves she usually wears once he's told her to let go of the bin. He can see her thumbs poking out from the pockets of her shorts. "Where's your anxiety?"

She throws him a look—they've both lost count of how many times he's asked her that question over the past few hours—but then her face softens. She thinks.

"A seven, maybe," she says. "It's lower."

"Okay." Paul nods, encouragingly. "That's good. That's very good."

Wendy smiles, but it fades quickly. "So, what's next?"

"Before I tell you, I need to remind you again that you're here voluntarily. No one is forcing you to complete any component of this treatment. Participating in any and all parts of Dr. Goulding's form of exposure therapy is done entirely on your own accord. If at any point—"

Wendy interrupts him by raising an ungloved hand. Paul can see a few telltale raw, pink spots where she burned her fingers with scalding water while washing herself. She says, "Save your breath. I read the waiver."

"Okay, then," he says. "I'm going to need you to take off your shoes."

She looks down at her white Keds.

"But this grass—"

"It's got a lot of dirt in it. I know."

She looks down again, then slowly slips out of each shoe, leaving the laces tied. When she sets her feet down on the grass she does so gingerly, arching the balls of her feet upward so that the only parts of her touching the ground are her toes and heels. In the back pocket of his jeans, Paul's iPhone vibrates and he reaches instinctively to silence it. It's the sixth time today that it's rung. The first time the call was from an unknown number bearing an Indiana area code—some telemarketer, he figured, wasting away behind a desk in some nameless office park. The five remaining calls came from his sister, Alice, and he dutifully ignored each one. Eloise, their half sister, was getting married—and in *England,* no less. There'd be expensive hotels where he'd be afraid to touch anything, and embroidered cloth napkins, and a reception at some estate straight out of *Masterpiece Theatre.* He'd told Alice once already that he *sure as fuck* wasn't going, and he suspects that's what she wants to discuss. So far, she's left two messages—the first politely asking to speak, the second threatening him with physical violence if he failed to call her back. Now, it seems, she's switched to a strategy of pure harassment.

"Is that it?" Wendy asks. She's still balanced on her heels and toes, and now both her hands are gripping the hems of her shorts, which she pulls higher and higher up her thighs.

Paul says, "It's not."

"Then . . ."

"I'm going to need you to step into the trash can," he says.

Wendy doesn't say anything.

"You can use my shoulder to balance yourself, because I realize it'll be a . . . a big step. But I'm going to need you to climb into the trash can."

"I can't do that." Wendy shakes her head.

Paul says, "Then you don't have to."

This, he admits, is off-script. If Goulding were here he would've insisted that Paul pushed harder before offering a way out, and ostensibly for good reason. But with Wendy—well, with Wendy.

He slaps at another mosquito, this one on his neck.

"Remember, this is entirely voluntary. You don't have to do anything that you don't want to do. If it's too difficult, you can walk away, and we can suggest some other treatment options. You don't have to do it."

"Yes, I do," she says.

"You really don't, though."

She glances up at him. "You know how much I'm paying for this bullshit? To crawl into a goddamned garbage can, and with no refund policy, no less?"

"It's expensive because—"

"You do. You do know how much I'm paying. So don't go saying I don't have to do this, because you and I both know damned well that I do." She adds: "Besides, I'm getting sick and tired of washing my hands. Every month I spend as much money on soap as most people do on car insurance. And if I burn away any more skin from my fingers the only thing I'll be left scrubbing is bone." She stares down at her hands. "So I have to do it, all right?"

Paul nods and takes a step forward. Now he is standing directly beside Wendy. Her Yves Saint Laurent mixes with the sourness of overripe cabbage. She grips his left shoulder and, bearing firmly down on him, lifts one leg into the steel bin. She stands like this for about a minute—one leg in, one leg out—catching her breath, repeating wordless mantras to herself. Paul still supports her, and as he feels her weight on him, he thinks of what else he put in the trash can earlier that afternoon: half a roasted chicken, week-old mashed potatoes from the clinic's kitchen, the assorted contents of waste bins from three different women's bathrooms. There is more, he knows—stuff that he pulled out of the Dumpsters behind the clinic that morning—but he prefers not to think about it. Because here is Wendy, who forked out over twenty thousand dollars just for the privilege of lowering her second leg into that mess. Paul sucks on his teeth: How much would someone have to pay him to stand in a trash can in suburban Philadelphia? It would have to be a lot of money. Too much money. And unlike Wendy, he is someone who has a relatively healthy relationship with germs. Sometimes he can't even be bothered to wash his hands after taking a piss.

He sucks on his teeth harder. Flattens out his grimace into a straight face.

"How you doing?" he asks.

She doesn't answer, and he looks down into the bin. A half-eaten Big Mac has split apart, and bits of orange cheese and beef cling to her calf.

"You'll be here for twenty minutes," he says, returning to Goulding's script. "And in that time I want you to imagine all of the possible germs and all the possible diseases that you're standing in right now, and that are touching your bare skin. As they come to you, say them out loud. I'll be recording them here, on my clipboard. Do you understand?"

Wendy takes her hand away from Paul's shoulder and lets it lie limp against her side. Still, though, she is silent.

"Wendy," he said. "I need you to tell me that you understand."

She doesn't, though. She keeps her lips pressed shut and her gaze fixed forward. After a minute or two, she shifts her right heel; something beneath it pops, and she begins, quietly, to cry. Paul looks back toward the clinic's main facilities, where a few lights have flickered on. He licks his lips and reaches into his pocket. Discreetly as he can, he works his fingers into a clean latex glove. Then, using his clipboard to shield himself from any observing eyes, he reaches out and takes hold of Wendy's hand, which he gives a good, firm squeeze.

Alice

May 3

She pokes her head beneath the stalls to make sure the bathroom is empty, and once she's sure she's alone, she turns on the faucet farthest from the door, takes a Klonopin, and throws some cold water on her face. She does this a few more times—filling the cup of her hand, letting the frigid splashes sting her cheeks and hang from her eyelashes—before she turns the water off and ventures a look in the mirror. There have been days when she's looked worse, she tells herself, tilting her chin left and then right. But then, there have also been days when she's looked a hell of a lot better. Her skin, which two days ago sported an early-summer tan thanks to a Sunday spent in Santa Monica, now looks red, blotchy. And her hair—God, if all the men who've called it "honey" could see it now. A bucket of dirty dishwater, hanging limply to her shoulders. She leans in closer and pulls the skin away from her eyes. Miraculously, they're fine: still that pale shade of blue. Free of the red spiderwebs you'd expect if you hadn't slept the night before (she didn't) or hadn't spent the last nine hours staring at an Excel spreadsheet (she has).

The door swings open and Alice jolts; she stands up straight and makes like she's drying her hands. Nadine, the new hire in marketing, smiles at her shyly and disappears into one of the bathroom's two handicapped stalls. Alice stares up into the fluorescent light above her until she sees spots, and when she hears the toilet flush, she leaves.

Back in her cubicle, she drums her fingers lightly on her desk and compulsively checks for new e-mails, of which there are none. Slyly, she rolls her chair backward and cranes her neck so she can peer down the long row of cubes, past the neon THINK BIG! sign, and into Jonathan's glass-enclosed office at the northwest corner of the floor.

He's on a call: she can see him standing, wearing his headset, arms gesticulating fluidly, his white shirt unbuttoned to show just enough of his chest. Behind him, the Hollywood Hills, with their quilts of mismatched houses, are obscured behind a screen of smog. In half an hour, Jonathan will flip a switch and a vanilla scrim will slide over the windows, blocking that same view ("It saves energy," he told her once. "Gotta think green"). Then he'll emerge from his office, navy blazer hooked over his shoulder, and saunter over to her cube. He'll knock lightly on the squat gray wall, as if there's a door to open, and ask her if the status reports for the Beijing accounts are ready yet (or maybe he'll ask for the Paris accounts, or the Rome accounts—it all hinges on where she's asked him to take her to dinner). She'll tell him it will be another fifteen or thirty minutes, depending on how much gussying up she thinks she needs before meeting him downstairs in the parking garage. (Time which, over the past eight months, has become less and less important, mainly because she likes to see what she can get away with: if, between cocktails and appetizers at Mélisse, he'll still want to slide his hand under the table and up her skirt if she decides to forgo eye shadow and blush. Even today, when she looks halfway like shit, she promises herself she won't reach for the tube of lipstick rolling around in her desk drawer.)

The whole charade has reached a point of predictability—honestly, at this point, Alice is shocked they haven't been caught—but that doesn't bother her; the Thrill of the Illicit wasn't the reason she started fucking Jonathan, anyway.

It was more the ever-changing power dynamic that first drew her to him, the idea that at one moment he might be screaming at her in the middle of a meeting for missing a deadline, and forty-five minutes later she'd be pinning him down against the shotgun seat of his Alfa Romeo, riding him to the precipice of climax, but never actually allowing him to come. She thinks of what Paul told her when she asked him what he liked most about having sex with another man; he described this feeling of being challenged, and the anticipation that at any moment the balance of control and dominance could shift.

At the time she accused him of being a gay misogynist (she was a junior in college and exclusively reading Susan Sontag); she said he was implying that a woman was expected to exercise docility in the bedroom, and only men—two men, for that matter—could be sexually aggressive. And while she still sort of agrees with all that (she continues to flip through *Styles of Radical Will* every now and then), she now understands a little bit more of what her brother had meant. Looking back, she's lost count of how many times at UCLA she had some half-drunk frat boy lying on top of her, squashing her tits as he pumped his doughy thighs to an awkward beat. Each time she'd wanted to do something to shake things up—roll on top of him and hold him down; work a finger up his ass, just to the first knuckle; something, anything, to break the monotony of being controlled. Whenever she did, though, the guy would freak out. Would rip himself out of her and stand abruptly, protesting that he wasn't into whatever it was she was trying to do to him, professing with slurred consonants how he was just looking for a nice girl (the implication being that a nice girl is something Alice is not). And while admitting so is a massive disappointment, things haven't changed much in the twelve years since she graduated. Despite their claims of sexual adventure, their organic diets, and their liberal voting records, the men Alice has encountered, at least until Jonathan, have all been beleaguered with the same redundant hang-ups. A bunch of perpetual eighteen-year-olds who, in the safety of their own darkened rooms, jack off to the nastiest shit they can find online, but who, once the lights are flipped on, squirm at the idea of eating her out.

"How are those Tokyo accounts coming?"

Alice looks up to see Jonathan smiling.

"Twenty minutes," she tells him, perhaps a bit too flatly. He winks at her, nevertheless, and saunters toward the elevator.

She glances down at the clock on her computer screen: it's nearly five o'clock in L.A., which means it will be coming up on eight in Philadelphia. If he isn't home by now, then something has happened. He boarded the wrong train and ended up in the middle of New Jersey, or drowned in one of the two rivers that run through the city. Knowing Paul, either option is plausible. How long has it been since she tried him last? She looks at the clock again: ten minutes since she tried his cell, twenty-seven since she called the landline in the apartment, when Mark answered and told her that Paul wasn't home yet. If Mark picks up again, she'll likely get an earful. Or not an earful, exactly. But he will do that thing where he explains to her *again* that Pauly isn't *home,* but that he's expecting him to walk in the door any *minute,* and in the meantime, is there anything *he* can do to *help.* And it will all be said in that lilting, condescending tone that he managed to pick up at Columbia and that she and Paul have too much fun imitating whenever they happen to be on the same coast.

The phone rings once, and she hears the receiver on the other end click.

"Alice. Thirty minutes. Right on time."

"Mark, I—"

"No, no. It's fine. He's here. Hold on."

Needing something with which to busy her hands, Alice reaches into the drawer for her lipstick. She holds the tube out in front of her, letting it roll back and forth across her palm.

"Yes?"

She hears him crunch into something hard. A carrot. He always eats while talking on the phone. He could be having a conversation with the Queen of England, and he'd still have half a goddamned Twinkie stuffed between his cheeks. It drives her nuts.

"You're home late," she says.

"Am I?"

"It's after eight there. And Mark said you got out of work early."

"Did he?" A pause. "We-*ell*, sometimes the train takes a while."

"Don't do that," Alice says. "Don't do that *we-ell* thing. It's irritating. It makes you sound like Mark."

"What's that supposed to mean?"

"You know exactly what it means. It's that same voice we—"

"Is this why you were so desperately trying to get ahold of me? To berate me?"

Alice takes a breath and closes her eyes and calms herself by trying to determine whether she can hear the traffic building up on Wilshire.

"Al?" Paul says.

"I'm here."

"So is that why you called?"

"You know that's not why I called, Paul." She sets the tube of lipstick on the desk and spins it in a circle, watching it as it pinwheels.

"I already told you: I'm not going to that wedding."

Alice pivots. "That's not why I called, either."

"Yeah, right."

"It's not," she says. "I called because Mom's been trying to get ahold of you."

Paul is quiet for a moment, and in the background she can hear the soothing monotony of *All Things Considered*.

Then, Paul spits: *"Donna?"*

"Yes. And for fuck's sake, can't you just call her Mom?"

"No, I can't."

Alice's cell phone vibrates against her desk, and she rolls her chair over to it. On the screen blinks a message from Jonathan—*Ready when you are =)*—that she quickly deletes.

She says, "There's got to be a statute of limitations on these things."

"On what?" Paul says. "Being some frigid cunt?"

Alice pinches the bridge of her nose. In the Relaxation Station, on the other end of the floor, a pair of interns start a game of Ping-Pong. "We're not talking about this right now. I didn't call to rehash this."

"You still haven't clarified why it is, exactly, that you're calling."

"Yes, I did. I said that Mom's trying to get ahold of you."

"And that's it?"

More crunching. A new carrot.

"She would appreciate—and *I* would *really* appreciate it—if you called her back."

"But I haven't—"

"Paul, can you please swallow before you speak?"

He coughs gutturally. Alice rolls her eyes.

"Better?" he says.

"Much."

"Good. In any event, *as I was saying,* I don't have any missed calls from her, so she couldn't have been trying that hard."

Alice thinks for a moment, considering the most strategic way to frame what she has to say next.

"She—she got a new phone," she offers, weakly. From here, she knows, it'll all be downhill.

"Well, good for her. Surely the number's the same, though, and I would have seen it if—"

"I'm sorry, I should have been more specific. She got a new phone *with an Indiana area code.*"

"Well, that makes absolutely no sense. Why would she—" Paul stops himself for a moment, and Alice waits for him to jam the pieces together. "Oh my God. Oh *my God.*" She bites her lip hard, just short of drawing blood. "She drove to Indiana to get a phone without a Chicago area code so *I wouldn't know it was her who was calling me.* You're kidding me, Al. *Please tell me you're fucking kidding me.*"

In the Relaxation Station, a Ping-Pong ball bounces off the table and into a planter filled with bamboo. One of the interns throws his paddle against the wall. Alice lowers her forehead to rest against her desk.

"I don't know what to tell you," she says.

"This is . . . this is unbelievable. I mean, just when I think that woman has written the *book* on passive-aggressive manipulation."

"She just really wants to talk, I guess."

"We-ell, *evidently*, Alice." She cringes. "Do you know what even *about*?"

"I'm assuming the wedding."

"Tell her what I told you: I'm not going."

"Why are you being so difficult about this?" she says. *"Eloise is getting married."*

"So?"

"So she's our *sister,* Paul."

"Half sister. And I haven't spoken to her in over a year."

Alice says, "Yeah, well. Whose fault is that?"

Her phone, now directly next to her head, buzzes again. Another message from Jonathan. This one less playful than the first: *Where are you??*

"Look," she says, "I've got to go. Do whatever the fuck you want. Just—it wouldn't kill you to call Mom back, all right?"

The waiter reaches forward and begins pouring a hot green liquid over the Dungeness crab. Through the steam Alice sees Jonathan looking at her. He raises an eyebrow, and she smiles before letting her eyes fall back down to the bowl, where the broth soaks its way into the crab meat, dyeing the flesh a shade of mossy green. "Sea bean porridge" is what the waiter calls it, and Alice is forced to admit (always silently, always to herself), that she doesn't have the first clue what a sea bean is. Hadn't been aware, really, that the sea produced beans *at all*—though, thinking about it now, as she watches the waiter bow slightly and vanish, she supposes it makes sense. The ocean is full of all sorts of crap she's never stopped to consider: weeds, strange pink blossoms sprouting from coral reefs, translucent fish lurking in bottomless trenches, and—now—beans. Green little pellets that she imagines taste like everything else she's eaten this evening: salty, and with a trace of gritty canned fish—sardines coated in sand. The trout roe with peas and lemon curd. The tuna with kale oil and quince. Despite the different ingredients, it's all the same. It all has that flavor she can't help but associate with the Gulf Coast of Florida, with those horrible smells that assaulted her in places like Pensacola and Panama City and Fort Walton Beach, where her father used to drag her and Paul and their mother (but never Eloise) on vacation every summer so he could fish for tuna, and which, metaphorically, couldn't be farther from Babél, the restaurant on Wilshire and South Wilton where she currently sits, staring at a trio of critically lauded, Japanese/neo-Nordic fusion dishes.

Discreetly, she looks at her phone. Thirty minutes ago, she checked in to Babél on Facebook. This is nothing new: she always checks in to the restaurant when she's out to eat with Jonathan. She likes the comments the postings garner, the jealous pleas for tips on getting a reservation, the requests for pictures of her food. More than anything, though, she appreciates the subtle message it sends to her half sister: a reminder that Eloise isn't the only one who can eat at pricey restaurants, that Alice belongs here just as much as she does.

Scrolling through the twenty-three "likes," she searches for her half sister's name. When she can't find it, she slips her phone back into her purse, irritated.

The waiter returns, this time with two servings of *uni*. Each one is balanced on its own slate slab and drizzled in almond milk. The man bows, and Jonathan lunges forward with a set of red lacquered chopsticks. Alice looks away.

"You don't want any?" he asks. A blob of orange clings to the left side of his mouth.

"No, you have it," she says. "I'm full."

She knows she's being difficult, and watching Jonathan sheepishly reach for the second piece of *uni,* she feels contrite; she wants to apologize, to say that her brother is being characteristically difficult, which has thrown her into a dark mood—and yet, every time she opens her mouth, the only thing she's capable of producing is some other dismissive comment, some other bitchy remark. Worse, inevitably, Jonathan will foot the bill: Alice can hardly afford drinks at a place like Babél, so he'll have no choice but to throw down three hundred dollars to eat disgraced puddles of raw sea urchin while the woman sitting across from him more or less ignores him. And even though he knows all this—he oversees her department's budget—he still, through some divine inspiration, manages to put on a good face. Manages to reach beneath the table and squeeze her knee between courses; manages to smile at all the right moments as he shovels bites of *uni* into his mouth.

She drains her glass of wine. She's chosen this place, which she wagers makes things doubly bad. At the time, of course, it had seemed like a good idea: she'd read about it in the *Times* and *L.A. Weekly* and on at least four of the ten restaurant blogs she had bookmarked at work. She had googled the menu and had been impressed by its absurd prices and foreign ingredients—exotic fishes and spices, frivolous vegetables whose shapes and tastes and provenances were total and complete mysteries to her. She had clicked through the interior pictures she found online and, upon seeing the careful balance of reclaimed wood, brushed steel, and poured concrete, felt the strange arousal she often experienced while flipping through catalogs from Room & Board and travel brochures from American Express. In short: she used the same process to find Babél that she uses to find any of the other overpriced restaurants in Los Angeles to which she asks Jonathan to take her. It's a process that she previously thought served her well—how else would she have been able to develop an opinion on the proper consistency of sweetbreads?—but that now, in the dim lighting of the restaurant, strikes her as transparent and mildly pathetic. It smacks of her seventeen-year-old self, who lied about the books she'd read and who felt crippled and uncouth whenever Eloise corrected her over a mispronounced word. The same sort of girl who'd brag to her friends about being able to distinguish between champagnes, but who'd never tell them she grew up sharing a bathroom with her brother.

She checks her Facebook post on her phone again. Still nothing from Eloise.

She thinks: What a bitch.

She wants a pizza. That's what she really wants. She wants a fucking pizza.

"You want to talk about it?"

Jonathan has just ordered another ninety-dollar bottle of wine. She wanted to tell him not to, that it's an unnecessary expense, but not enough to actually stop him from doing it.

"Talk about what?" she says.

"Whatever it is that's upsetting you."

Between them, the sea bean porridge cools and its oils begin rising to the surface, forming tiny, shimmering pools. Alice watches them as she considers Jonathan's proposal to talk, which is something that's been happening more and more frequently. Up until a few months ago, their relationship found comfortable footing on a foundation of adventurous sex ("the sort of sex that I'd want to watch," Alice once said) and outrageously expensive meals. Lately, though, Alice finds herself craving the types of conversations she initially forbade herself from entertaining: these exchanges when, in the afterglow of sleeping with Jonathan, her body still slick with his sweat, she'd tell him a small secret of her life. Her admissions have been nothing significant, at least not thus far. Nothing about Mexico City, for example, or the mess she left when she fled that terrible place. Still, though, they've been admissions. Minor additions to the long list she lays bare for him of unsatisfactory ways her life has unfolded. About how she hasn't read all the books she claims she's read, or how she's insecure about the fat behind her knees.

"My brother's really pissing me off," she says.

Jonathan wipes his mouth with his napkin and returns it to his lap. "Paul?"

"Yes, Paul."

The waiter swoops in with the fresh bottle of wine, and Jonathan tastes it, swishing it around in his mouth theatrically.

"Why's he pissing you off?" he asks once the waiter leaves.

"Because he's refusing to talk to my mother."

"*Still?* That seems a little childish."

Alice takes a swig of her wine and realizes only after she's swallowed that she's finished off half the glass.

"It is," she says.

"Hasn't this been going on for a while?"

"Three years."

"Jesus."

"And like I told you the other night, I'm meant to play peacemaker—"

"That's—"

"Which, as I'm sure you can imagine, gets a little exhausting."

There is a brief silence, a space in which the clinking of glasses around them grows louder, and Alice worries suddenly that she's said too much.

Jonathan leans back in his chair and sets his hands on the table. She stares at his knuckles. The tops of his fingers are tan, moisturized, and look a solid ten years younger than the rest of him, which already looks unnaturally young.

He says, "And this is all about your dad . . ."

"Yes," Alice says. She tries, unsuccessfully, not to be flattered by all that Jonathan remembers about the events of her life before he knew her.

"Paul didn't like the way that Mom handled my dad's death."

She swallows the rest of her wine, briefly considers waiting for the waiter, but then thinks twice about it and pours herself a second glass.

He runs a hand through his sandy hair. "I know I said this before, but I'm sorry . . . about your dad having passed, I mean."

Alice waves a hand in front of her face, which is something she always does when she tells someone about her dad and the person reacts in the way people are supposed to, with sincere condolences. She's never been good with obligatory compassion; she imagines batting away words like *passed* as if they were flies.

"It's fine," she says. "I mean, that's nice of you to say that, but it's fine. It happened nearly three years ago, anyway."

Jonathan opens his mouth, hesitates a moment, and says, "You still haven't told me how it happened."

"I haven't?"

"No. I mean, I knew your dad died and that's the reason you were out of the office, but . . . you've never told me how."

She swallows another mouthful of wine. She considers what to say, what might elicit a greater share of his sympathy: *Murdered in cold blood. Abducted by the Taliban. A plane crash. Some Southeast Asian budget flight that disappeared somewhere near Malaysia.*

"Gallbladder cancer. Real curveball, right? I mean, *who gets gallbladder cancer?* Actually—I can tell you, if you're curious. Less than five thousand people a year in the whole United States."

"That's awful."

"It's an anomaly, at the very least."

Jonathan shifts in his seat. "And they caught it . . . late?"

"That's the thing," Alice says. "With gallbladder cancer, you never really know. Or, that's not entirely true. You do know, when they finally tell you. It's just that, up until then, it's not something that they routinely *check* for, and the signs and symptoms aren't exactly the same as getting a lump on your tit, you know? Harder to tell that anything's wrong, and all that. Anyway. Yes. They did catch it late—by the time they diagnosed him, the thing had already set up shop in his liver. And by that point the only thing we could do was keep him comfortable and high enough so he wasn't in too much pain."

It's a rehearsed speech (though one that, until now, she's avoided having to deliver to Jonathan), not in the sense that she's practiced it in front of a mirror, but rather in that she's given it before—to friends, coworkers, countless first dates who ask *what happened.* At first it was uncomfortable—she rarely wanted to say it any more than they wanted to hear it—but then a shift happened, some hardening of nerves, and she actually managed to mine a sort of perverse joy in recounting the details of her father's death. It's avoidance, she knows—she is averting some core emotional issue that she needs to deal with. Paul, with his bullshit master's degree, has told her as much, and the truth is, he's probably right. For the time being, though, avoidance seems to work for her. It isn't fun—*fun* isn't the word for it—but it is distracting, and distracting is enough. She likes testing how much she can prevent herself from feeling, how long she can keep remorse at bay.

She imagines that someone else is telling the story, as if she, Alice, is watching some simulacrum describe the death of someone who had her father's name, and who had her father's disease, but who, aside from those two inconsequential details, is a complete stranger. She thinks how she'd judge the abilities of this impostor, this made-up version of herself: how well she played with the tones of her voice, how she milked compassion from her audience. This, she tells herself, is a trait she inherited from her father. While Paul prides himself on his emotional hysterics—his keen sense for holding a grudge, for painting himself as the family's black sheep—Alice has her dad's knack for maintaining a corpselike calm.

She remembers when he went in for stomach pains and, a week later, the doctors told him he had three months. Her mother was crying so hard that she wasn't able to drive home from the hospital. So Dad asked her to get into the backseat so he could drive—there was a Cubs game starting in twenty minutes. Alice, who had come home to be there for the test results, had sat next to him on the couch for nine interminable innings. They finished a twelve-pack of beer and half a pack of Marlboros. During the game's recap, she asked him if he needed anything and he told her to make him a ham sandwich.

She catches a reflection of herself in Jonathan's eyes, and wonders, briefly, if she's coming off as a bitch.

"You think I'm heartless," she says. "For what it's worth, I also go to a support group. Something to help me deal . . ."

"Is that where you go on Tuesday afternoons?"

"You've noticed?"

He smiles. "I like to keep tabs on you."

Alice smooths her napkin across her lap. "This is humiliating."

Beneath the table he grabs her hand. "Look, I think we all deal with shit like this in different ways."

She appreciates his diplomacy and squeezes his hand.

"Thanks," she says.

"Anyway." He's still holding her hand. "Your brother and your mom . . ."

"Oh, right," she says. "He doesn't approve of how Mom handled it all. So he's not speaking to her."

"And how did she handle it?"

"Another story that's too long."

"And your mother wants you . . ." He trails off.

A strand of hair tickles Alice's chin, and she hooks it behind her left ear. "To somehow make things right, I guess? It's all because of Eloise."

"Oh, right." With his free hand, Jonathan reaches for the bottle and pours himself another glass of wine. "The Wedding of the Century."

He sips and smacks his lips.

Suddenly self-conscious, Alice gently pulls her hand away and sets it in her lap. "I'm sorry," she says. "You've heard all this before. I don't want to bore you."

"You're not."

Alice chews on the inside of her lip. "Well, I'm sort of boring myself, to be honest."

"We can talk about something else."

"Would you mind?"

"Of course not. What do you want to talk about?"

"Anything," Alice says. She reconsiders: "Or, no, not anything. Talk to me about big data."

The corners of Jonathan's mouth twitch as he tries to suppress a grin. "You don't want to hear about that."

"Sure I do. You know how much I love the story."

And so he begins recounting his own personal history, or mythology, which, by this point, has become so familiar to Alice that she occasionally has to fight the urge to interrupt him and correct facts that he so endearingly fudges. He narrates his first few years after Stanford, when he held jobs at a handful of fledging start-ups, all of which ended up folding on account of (according to Jonathan) their inability to "procure and creatively interpret substantial masses of incongruent data." Then there was the pivotal trip to Australia (Jonathan says that he started in Sydney, though from past tellings of the story, Alice knows that he flew into Melbourne), where, *totally by chance,* he met Vishnu Goyal (*the Vishster!*), a Berkeley grad who'd just fled Google, and with whom Jonathan shared any number of acquaintances back in the Bay Area. They bummed around together for about a month, hitting Brisbane and the Great Barrier Reef, staring at the sunburned faces of Ayers Rock, until, on January 2, they found themselves at a bar in Auckland, hatching a plan for what to do with the rest of their lives.

"We just saw a need, I guess you could say," Jonathan says. "Just . . . this space for a company that could collect and interpret data the way that we do. Sure, there were a few big data companies then, but they still seemed to be stuck in the past, you know? Using metrics like page views and click-throughs. *Prehistoric* shit, really. No one was thinking as far out of the box as we were." He takes a sip of wine and smiles. "Anyway. The rest is history that you already know."

Alice considers what this means: how, in eight years since he started the company, Jonathan has turned Think Big Data from a two-man shop into one of the tech industry's leading big data firms. (Vishnu sold his shares in the company a few years ago for a reported thirty million after some shrouded dispute with Jonathan over a contract that he, Jonathan, had accepted from the NSA. *Moral disagreements* were the words that Alice had heard thrown around. She doesn't know many more details of the argument—Jonathan doesn't like to talk about it—but his friendship with Vishnu seems to have emerged from it unscathed. They still send each other holiday cards and meet, occasionally, for dinner.) The company's client pool ranges across fields (hospitality, retail, governmental) and across continents. (Diplomatic issues are currently preventing them from doing the sort of work in Russia that Jonathan had once envisioned. He's working on it.) She knows that *Ad Age* and *Forbes* have both run profiles of him, and she has heard how he's often invited to speak on panels whose names too often incorporate some iteration of the phrase *What's Next?* He's told her how he doesn't own a single item of clothing—not even a pair of shorts—that hasn't been custom tailored. How he doesn't have to vacation in spots like the south of France or Santorini or Fiji anymore because he can afford the places that no one's heard of yet.

Typically, confronting unchecked privilege sends her into a rage, a downward spiral that begins with frustration over the moral wrongness of global inequality and ends with (*and she knows this is bad*) a sort of solipsistic meditation on all the nice things she can't afford, but others (read: *her sister*) can. Or, it's not that she can't afford them—she's making more money than she ever has before, so to blame her current monetary chaos on sheer lack of funds is, frankly, letting herself off easy. The real problem is that, lately, the only way she's been able to quell this financial anxiety is through acts of flagrant consumption, these binge sessions of buying expensive dresses and handbags and (in one terrible case) a new Prius—things that she doesn't need, or even really like, but that nonetheless temporarily fill some shapeless void; that remind her that she has the same right to entitlement as everyone else, even if it's put her twenty thousand dollars in debt. Curiously, though, when Jonathan talks to her about his life she doesn't resent his wealth. She suspects, sheepishly, that there are two root causes for this: (1) more often than not, he's spending his money on her; and (2) she's in love with him.

He smiles at her. His teeth are stained red.

You can't call him arrogant, Alice thinks. Or, you can, but to do so wouldn't be fair. *Arrogant* is a tag reserved for people who are profoundly certain and aware of how far their accomplishments set them apart from others. Jonathan, meanwhile, still has a sense of being in awe of himself, as if he's just as surprised as the next person by what he's actually pulled off. Watching him talk, watching his hands move, she's reminded of Paul as a kid, before he became jaded and self-conscious, when he liked to construct elaborate forts out of sheets and pillows and unbent hangers. He'd wake her up early on Saturday mornings and pull her into the living room and point at the thing he'd built, the whole time scratching his head and laughing, bewildered by his own genius.

"Should I keep going?" Jonathan asks.

"I'm not stopping you, am I?"

He grins.

They started sleeping together last September: two years after her dad died, and six years to the day after the disaster in Mexico City. At that point, Alice was still considered a newish hire; she'd joined Think Big five months earlier, after having spent almost five years doing sales for a hospitality start-up that sold consumer insight to hotels. The jobs were similar enough (in both cases she convinced people to pay absurd amounts of money for access to information that she herself didn't understand) and toward both of them she felt the same lukewarm ambivalence—which, she knows, is what makes her so good at what she does. Doing what you love for a living: what a terrible mistake. That was one of the many hard-earned lessons she gleaned from everything that happened in Mexico. The second you slap a paycheck onto a passion, something changes. The stakes become too high. No, Alice thought, better to get yourself involved in something comically dull, something in which you feel zero personal investment. That way, you have no qualms about taking risks, because if you end up losing everything, it was never very much at all, anyway.

She stabs at a piece of crab floundering in the green porridge. It's too soggy, though, and slithers away from her fork.

She didn't make the decision to sleep with him the first day on the job, though it couldn't have come long after. Still, she likes to remind herself that he was the one who made the first move. That isn't to say she didn't go out of her way to lay the groundwork. But still, he was the one who reached across that line, who took things from hypothetical and phantasmic to real and messy, which is, as far as Alice is concerned, the point that actually matters. It happened on a Tuesday—or, at least that's how she remembers it. They'd been flirting for the better part of the morning on Ding Dong, the company's intra-office instant messaging platform (she pinged him first, she admits), with Jonathan telling her the sort of lewd and sexualized things he hadn't had the guts to say in person. She played along, laughing and occasionally rolling her eyes, right up until the point where he told her that he wanted to fill her up with his Big Data. Then, with smug satisfaction, she said—in as matter-of-fact a way as possible—that she needed to go to the supply closet.

She knew, obviously, that he would follow her, but there was some part of her that was still surprised when she heard him sneak through the door behind her. She turned around and saw him standing there, grinning like an eight-year-old, his body framed by shelves filled with pens and staplers and red Post-its shaped like cartoon lightbulbs.

"I just came to get some paper," she said. "The printer in the Relaxation Station ran out and the interns forgot to fill it."

"That's why I'm here, too." He kept grinning. "My printer ran out of paper."

"Don't you have a secretary who'll take care of that for you?"

"We call them *special assistants* here, Alice." He took a step forward. "*Secretary* carries sexist and misogynistic undertones."

"How . . . progressive of you."

"And besides," he said, "I can do things myself."

"Oh, can you?"

Oh, can you? It was the sort of line she'd normally cringe at. The sort of coy flirtation that made her hate girls she saw in bars. But here, under the fluorescent lights of the supply closet, she told her better self to shut up; she just went with it. Moaned at all the right times as he kissed her neck; gasped theatrically as he slid a hand up her skirt. Closed her eyes and leaned her head back against a half-furled THINK BRIGHTER poster when he buried his head between her thighs. And when it was over, and she was wiping herself off with Kleenex from a box she'd just opened, she realized, with a sort of lightness, that for the first time in six years she felt good about what had happened. Better than good, even. Happy.

Though maybe not entirely. There is, after all, the issue of the ring, which she spotted the first day she saw him in the sales meeting—a thin gold band, strapped around the fourth finger on his left hand. And there's what he said last week when they walked down Wilshire to get coffee after her team's morning meet-up. The quiet implication that things weren't great at home. She feels badly about that—though, if she's being honest with herself, probably not as badly as she should, particularly because alongside that guilt is a sense of thrilling excitement. Still, she knows she's crossed a line in the sand of Womanhood—a boundary that has been delineated by feminism and sorority and, God, probably a bunch of spear-wielding, breast-heaving Amazonians. She's turned her back on her sex, has somehow thrown a bone (ha ha) to the very patriarchy that she half-drunkenly bitches about every Friday night. She should be atoning somehow, she thinks. Call his wife (*Marissa*), come clean, and swear off men. Really, though, every time it happens all she wants is for it to happen again.

"You ready?"

They've finished the wine. Jonathan has finished talking. He's paid the bill. All without her noticing.

Alice smiles. "Yup."

Jonathan hates Wilshire—even though Think Big has its offices there, he calls the boulevard soulless and corporate—so he takes South Wilton to Beverley Boulevard, then heads west, toward Westwood and Alice's apartment. It's after ten, so there isn't much traffic, and as Jonathan smoothly works through the Alfa Romeo's gears the car gains speed and begins to purr. Alice rests her head against the window as they drive through Fairfax, and as they pass the cross streets she counts them and says their names silently to herself: Poinsettia. Martel. Crescent Heights. Each one stretches out toward the hills, where the glinting light of mansions replaces the need for stars.

"You want to talk about it some more?" Jonathan says.

"What?"

"Your brother not calling your mom. Your half sister's wedding."

They've crossed into West Hollywood. On Robertson, a line of men snakes around the entrance to a bar. Above them, clouds of cigarette smoke unfurl themselves like balls of string.

"There's not much to talk about. Paul doesn't want to talk to Mom, and he thinks Eloise is a spoiled bitch."

In front of them, a stoplight turns yellow and Jonathan speeds up.

"And do you?"

"Do I what?"

"Think she's a spoiled bitch?"

"Of course," Alice says. "That's what she is."

She reaches for the radio and tunes it to a Top 40 station. A song that she's never heard is playing, and she turns it up.

Alice turns in her seat and looks at him for a moment, at the way the dull glow from the streetlamps washes the wrinkles out of his forehead and smooths away the creases at the corners of his mouth. They stop at a red light, and she pulls one knee up to her chest.

"You want to come up for a drink?" she asks him.

"Huh?"

"When we get back to my place," she says, hugging her knee closer. "Want to come up for a drink?"

He scratches his widow's peak and turns back toward the road.

"Oof," he says. "I wish I could. God, I wish I could. I can't, though. It's already late. And Marissa . . . if she has to put the kids to bed by herself again . . ."

"Right." Alice puts both feet squarely on the floorboard in front of her. She reaches forward to change the radio station. "No, I know. You're right. It's late."

Jonathan reaches over and squeezes the back of her neck.

"Next time," he says.

The light turns green.

Donna

May 3

"Ma'am? Can I help you?"

Donna looks at the crook of her left arm, where she's slung five or six dresses. "Oh, thank you, but I'm sure I'll manage," she says.

The salesgirl smiles. KIM, her name tag reads. She's dressed all in black—everyone in the department store is dressed all in black, Donna's noticed—and she can't be older than nineteen or twenty. She wears heavy eye shadow and she's straightened her dark hair so it falls in solid curtains on either side of her face. A piano rendition of John Lennon's "Imagine" twinkles throughout the store. The air's fragrant with synthetic rosewater and sandalwood.

"At least let me start a dressing room for you?"

Kim's smile widens, and she reaches for the nest of dresses, all tangled up in their individual hangers.

"I . . . uh, I . . ." Donna stammers.

Kim works on commission; there's no stopping her.

"That would be nice," she says. "Thank you."

"Let me show you where I'll be setting you up."

Donna follows her, watching her thin waist sway in her black pants as they slither past racks of expensive blouses and khaki trousers. Near a table stacked with neat piles of V-neck sweaters, she catches her reflection in the mirror. She's all hips. And not good hips. Not Kim hips. But *hip* hips, the kind that can't be controlled with a pair of stretchy black pants. She can't remember when that happened—when she suddenly exploded horizontally. Hair has escaped from behind her ear and now hangs in front of her eyes: a mess of brown and dyed russet and scraggly gray roots. She'll need to schedule a coloring appointment before she leaves for London. From the looks of it, she'll have to schedule a lot of appointments before she leaves for London.

"Here we are," Kim says, unlocking the door to a small dressing room with a bench and a full-length mirror. A handful of clothing pins dot the carpet like pine needles. Kim crouches down to gather them up, and as she does so, the hem of her shirt lifts an inch, revealing the elastic band of her thong and a small tattoo. A rose in half bloom. Donna looks away, casting her eyes down to her cell phone—her new cell phone—which she's got cradled like a relic in her right hand.

"Expecting a call?" Kim asks. She slips the pins into her pocket.

"Yes." Donna blushes. "Or maybe."

She had been so proud of herself. Scheming up the idea to get an out-of-state cell phone number. But Paul still hasn't answered, nor has he been curious enough to call her back. And then there was the thing the salesman at the AT&T store had said. He'd asked her why she wanted a new phone, and she'd just come out with it: explained Paul, and his silence, and how she needed to con her own child into picking up when she called.

"Why don't you just e-mail him or something?" the salesman had asked.

"I've tried. He just ignores me."

He rubbed the back of his neck, then fingered a zit at the corner of his mouth. "Man," he said. "If I tried ignoring my mom for even two *days*, she'd go nuts and strangle me."

Donna nodded. "Yes, that's an option I've also considered."

With a few chords the medley shifts, and "Imagine" blooms into "Bridge over Troubled Water."

"You've picked out some gorgeous pieces," Kim says. She hangs the dresses on a hook next to the mirror.

"Have I?"

"Absolutely. That purple scoop-neck is one of my favorites."

Donna knows that Kim's paid to be sincere—she's not fooling anyone—but still, she'll take it. She can't remember the last time she was prepared to spend this much money on a dress. Paris, maybe. Or possibly during the first few years she and Eloise were back in Chicago. But that was over three decades ago now—what if her tastes haven't kept apace with trends? She's tried to choose dresses that might impress Eloise, dresses she thinks of as *chic* and *sophisticated*. A champagne A-line. A navy tunic. But those garments were designed for younger women, weren't they? Women whose bodies haven't started to sag and settle and surrender to gravity. Earlier, at the Nordstrom on the opposite end of the mall, she'd tried on a violet shift and had just about wept when she turned to inspect herself in the mirror: she looked like a sausage, dipped in cheap nail polish and stuffed into a casing fit to burst. She saw herself escorting Eloise down the aisle (because God knows Henrique won't be there to do it), not walking, but *waddling* alongside her daughter as her statuesque in-laws tried their best not to gawk at her ass.

So, *yes*, Donna thinks. Kim can lie through her bleached teeth as much as she'd like. She's just happy to have someone who's complicit in this Decision of the Dress.

"Are we looking for something for a special occasion?" Kim winks. "Or are we just treating ourselves?"

Donna fixes the strap of her purse so it rides higher on her shoulder. "Actually, my eldest daughter's getting married. In England."

"How exciting!" Kim claps. "In London?"

"In Dorset. In the southwest. But I'll be staying with her in London for a week or two before."

"I've always wanted to go to England." The last dress—a cream-colored wrap—won't fit on the hook, so Kim drapes it across the bench. "The closest I've ever been is Toronto."

"Hm." Donna nods. "I've actually got a picture of her." She rummages around for her pocketbook. "Would you like to see it?"

"Of course."

Donna hands Kim the wallet-size photo that she keeps in her purse. The edges of it are brown and worn.

"Gorgeous," Kim says. "Though, she's . . . young?"

She takes the photo back. "Oh, she's just a little girl there." She looks down at it. Eloise stands on the Champ de Mars; the Eiffel Tower poised in the background looks to be the size of a cheap souvenir. Three and a half years old. She's sporting her beloved tiny pink backpack and a pair of Lacoste sneakers (Donna's still got those things, she thinks, stashed away in the attic somewhere), and her hair's so light, so blond, that you can hardly tell it's there at all. It's April: the sky is a tepid blue that threatens to revert back to gray; clouds hang like lazy brushstrokes.

Donna runs her finger along the picture's edge, feeling the stock of the photo paper. Henrique, her husband, had been supposed to meet them that day, but hadn't.

"Paris as a little girl, and now living in London." Kim rolls the clothing pins in the palm of her hand. "Quite a life."

"We lived there. In Paris. That's where I met and married her father." Donna knows she sounds boastful, but she can't stop. "Eloise—sorry, my daughter—she was born there."

"Born in Paris!"

"We had a lovely home. Well, actually, *many* lovely homes." She grins. "But the one in Paris was the loveliest. Right in the heart of the Sixteenth.

An old nineteenth-century revival with a *chambre de bonne* that we used as Eloise's playroom."

Kim's still smiling: she has no clue what any of this means, but it's important to Donna that she knows it. It's terrible, this need to gush over her past—a past that was hardly ever hers in the first place. It flies in the face of the Midwestern humility to which she's always subscribed. Still, though, she can't stop herself once she's started. It's as if she's suddenly infected by this awful snobbery, a need to list and catalog the privileges she once enjoyed before her unceremonious return to Illinois, and the PTA meetings that followed. Before Alice fled to a far-off city and a disaster that won't leave her; before Paul left for a man and a life and years of cruel silence. Before the word *widow* became a part of her daily vocabulary.

"Two blocks from the Palais de Tokyo, and an *exquisite* view of the Arc from the master bedroom, if you can believe it. A formal dining room with all the original windows and the *perfect* amount of chinoiserie. Really, a complete dream."

Kim looks over her shoulder.

Donna hears herself; she stops.

"In any event, that was a long time ago." She slips the picture back into her pocketbook. "But that's her. That's my Eloise."

"Well, you and her father must be thrilled."

"I . . . well." Donna swallows and feels her throat bulge. "Her father's no longer with us."

"Oh, God. I am so sorry." Kim brings a hand to her mouth and Donna notices her fingernails: acrylic, French-tipped. "Did he . . . did he pass on?"

"You mean did he die? Yes. He did."

This is a lie, and one she's grown accustomed to telling: Henrique is still very much alive. But the temptation to fantasize, to imagine the thousands of bloody and gruesome ways that her ex-husband could have met his end—well, that's simply too seductive to ignore. She wonders how Kim is conceiving of it: if she's settled on something pedestrian like a heart attack, or if she's let her mind wander into darker territories. Donna won't give her an explanation—she never does. She prefers instead that the strangers she lies to imagine and reimagine Henrique's death on their lunch breaks, their drives home. She comforts herself knowing that, at least for the next few hours, Kim will be killing Henrique in her mind. A thousand tiny deaths.

It's easier, just claiming he died. It saves her from the torture of having to explain what Biarritz, and seafood paella, and the Simons' Spanish au pair (*Maria-Elena* was the bitch's name) have to do with her failed marriage. (The answer, Kim, is *everything*.) The lie, like most lies, is a defense. It saves her from the horror of admitting she's a cliché.

Kim knocks on the dressing room door.

"How's everything going in there?"

Donna's just slipped on the purple tunic and she stares at herself in the mirror. She turns left, right, examines her uneven profiles.

"Going well!" she shouts.

The thin fabric scrapes at the extra skin just below her armpits.

"Can I get any other sizes for you?"

What is Kim implying?

"No, not just yet, dear." Donna does her best to mask her annoyance. "Still working through the ones I have."

Kim says something in return, but Donna can't hear it. She's too busy wiggling her way out of the purple disaster, letting the brittle cloth gather on the floor around her ankles. She faces the mirror and grabs a handful of pale flesh on either side of her waist. She squeezes. Fat globs together in her fists, and blue veins threaten to burst. Errant hairs sprout from freckles. She prods at one of her breasts, lifting it up, letting it fall and slap against her upper ribs.

She could blame her second husband. She could say that things turned south when she married Bill, two years after she and Eloise packed up their lives in Paris and moved back to Chicago. (Henrique had given Donna no indication that Maria-Elena was going anywhere, and she wasn't about to accept the . . . er . . . *modern* arrangement that he had proposed to her. France had opened her eyes, but she was still from Indiana, a Hoosier at heart.) Before too long Alice was born, and then, two years later, Paul. Soon, Donna forgot what it was like to eat a meal sitting down. She tried to hold on to vestiges of her old life—despite Bill's grumbling, she declared Tuesdays to be coq au vin night; she spoke to Alice and Paul in a mash-up of English and French. At night, she read French novels, and watched French movies, and listened to the news on Radio France. But constantly reminding herself of the person she used to be was exhausting. Besides, the reality of her new life was too flagrant to ignore. Instead of being chauffeured around in black cars driven by quiet, angular men in wool hats, she drove the car that Bill bought her, a used Ford station wagon—the only thing he could afford on his accountant's salary. If Henrique, with his prominent law career and his opinionated aristocratic friends, had offered her a chance to transcend her suburban American upbringing, then Bill had yanked her back to her roots. He had reminded her that she was, and always would be, middle class. There were no more galas, no more Augusts in Provence, no more last-minute dinners at Le Meurice. Now there was Sunday football, and big-box retailers, and celebratory dinners at the Cheesecake Factory in Oak Brook.

"He's a good man. Salt of the earth," her own mother had told her when she called with the news of Bill's proposal. "Don't turn your nose up at him."

"I didn't say that I was going to."

"Because from where I'm sitting, these sorts of offers aren't going to come along every day. Not when you're pushing thirty-two and you've already got a kid hanging off you." She didn't hesitate to add: "Most men are scared of kids."

"Thanks, Mom."

"Well, what's the other option, honey? Go back to Paris, find another job teaching English, and marry some other rich frog who's got a thing for Spanish floozies?"

"I think you've made your point."

"Just say *yes,* Donna. For Christ's sake, say *yes.*"

She did.

Donna cocks her head to the left. She pokes her other breast.

She could blame Bill.

She shakes her head: No. She couldn't. After all, she'd loved him. Maybe not with the same naïve passion with which she'd fallen for Henrique, but she *had* loved him, in her way. He hadn't been perfect. He'd made his mistakes, and unforgiveable ones, at that. But turning Donna into . . . God, into *this thing* that she's staring at in the mirror hadn't been one of them. And anyway, hadn't she learned to treasure the life he gave her? While the initial shock of returning to the world she'd fled was disappointing, disorienting, the truth was that there was a homey comfort in falling back into old routines. While the tedium of life in St. Charles certainly dragged on her, she also felt strangely cleansed by rediscovering the pureness of the suburbs and the simplicity of life with Bill.

Besides, Bill's dead. And not fake dead, but actual dead, which makes the whole business of blaming him for turning her into a Midwestern housewife feel a little tacky.

She sneaks out of the store before Kim comes to check on her again. She considers leaving the dresses (all of them tried on; all of them discarded) on the floor in their little humiliated heaps—it would make for a faster getaway—but her guilt gets the better of her, and she hangs each of them up, flattening out wrinkles, picking away bits of lint. She's hurrying past the food court when her phone begins to buzz. Her heart skips a beat, and she quickly rehearses what she's planned on saying when Paul calls: excitement, without being saccharine; joy, without being scripted. But when she finds the phone, its screen is dark. No missed calls. No long-lost sons.

And yet: more buzzing. She reaches farther into her purse, past half a packet of Kleenex and a box of Altoids, and finds her other phone, her real, guilt-free phone. A text blinks on the screen. Her neighbor Janice, from across the street. *House Hunters International and wine 2nite?*

Donna squints as she hunt-and-pecks *y-e-s* and presses send.

In the mall's garage, she finds her car and digs through the center console for her parking ticket and the joint she rolled earlier this morning. She lights it and reclines in her seat. Three rows to her left, a car door slams and footsteps echo. Donna inhales and lets the pot swirl in her lungs. She's new to smoking—it's a habit that she's made a very conscious effort to cultivate over the past three years, ever since Bill died and, in her grief, she reached the conclusion that she needed to start having a little more fun. She coughs. She's still getting the hang of it, the shock of hot air and smoke searing her throat. She likes the repetitive action, though—joint-to-mouth, joint-to-mouth, joint-to-mouth—and how the weed makes her feel, slowing things down until each blink seems as long as an afternoon nap.

She fishes beneath the passenger seat for her copy of Carole King's *Tapestry* and slides the disc into the car's stereo. She flips forward three songs, to "It's Too Late," slides deeper into her seat, and laughs.

"Jesus, what took you so long?"

Janice has come out to the driveway to meet Donna wearing an old Michigan State shirt. She's barefoot and holding two sweating glasses, filled nearly to their brims with vodka martinis. Two weeks ago she cut her hair short, in the same boyish fashion that more and more women Donna's age seem to be favoring, and now, in the humidity, it flares out clownishly over her ears.

"I took the scenic route." Donna closes the door and locks the car.

"There are no scenic routes in Illinois. In the meantime, you've left me no choice but to drink alone."

"I'm a terrible friend."

"Mmm." Janice sips from her glass, and a few drops of booze splatter on her khaki capris. She waves across the street, to Sylvia Watson, who's watering her azaleas. "Anyway, then, let's see it."

"See what?"

"The *dress,* you drip."

Janice hands Donna her martini.

"Oh." She drinks, and winces. "I couldn't find one."

"You spent all day at Oakbrook Center, and you couldn't find a single dress."

"Oh, I found some, sure, but they all looked so *god*awful on me. Like I was a piece of overripe fruit." She takes another sip; this one goes down easier. "I should probably just try Ann Taylor or something."

"Never admit that kind of defeat."

"That's easier for you to say. You've still got the hips of a nineteen-year-old."

"Oh, boo-hoo. What's wrong with your eyes, anyway?"

"Whaddya mean?"

"They're all red. Were you crying? Christ, were the dresses *that* bad?"

Donna smoked over an hour ago, but suddenly she feels a dull burst of lingering paranoia.

"Pollen," she says. "So much pollen in the air today. Happens to me every spring. All those goddamned flowers."

Janice takes half her drink down in a single gulp. "Speaking of which, what do you say we take this inside? I can see Sylvia just itching to come say hello, and I swear to God if I have to hear another word about that sick dog of hers, I'll keel over and die."

"I thought Poppy died two weeks ago?"

"As if we could be that lucky. Her last round of doggy chemo bought her another month or two." She finishes her martini. "The world's not a fair place."

"You're awful."

"That's probably true. Now, come on."

In the living room, Janice flops down on a beige sofa. Her feet dangle inches from a small square side table, on top of which sits a blue lamp, along with a framed picture of Janice, her husband, Gary, and their daughter, Amy. Donna picks up the photo to inspect it closer. They're on a beach somewhere along Lake Michigan, and they're wearing jeans and matching black polo shirts. All three of them have been professionally posed within an inch of their lives, heads tilted just so, faces stretched and pained, the unnatural smiles drooping. Donna wonders how much the photographer had charged. Whatever it was, Janice overpaid.

"What a lovely picture," she says.

"Oh, that?" Janice doesn't bother looking up. She wiggles her big toes. "We took it last summer, when Amy was home from Boulder. Last week I finally got around to getting the damned thing framed."

"Hm." Donna sets the picture down. She walks around a squat coffee table loaded with the sort of hardcover, glossy-paged books that everyone's expected to have, but no one's expected to read: a visual history of modern American art, Nate Berkus's *The Things That Matter*, Barbra Streisand's *My Passion for Design*. She's about to sink down into an overstuffed leather chair when Janice says:

"Oh, hey, before you get around to making yourself comfortable, would you mind?" She taps her ring against her glass.

"I've hardly made a dent in mine yet."

"Well, whose fault is that?"

"Oh, give it here."

Donna slips out of her shoes and pads into the kitchen, where she finds the martini shaker in the sink. She rinses it out, and then fills it with ice from the automatic dispenser on the freezer door. The whole room smells like orange juice and bologna, and Donna wonders what Janice could have possibly made for lunch.

"Whatever happened with the Reynoldses' tree? You never told me." She unscrews the cap from the vodka bottle and lets the viscous booze slop into the shaker.

"You mean *my* tree."

"Where the hell is your vermouth?"

"Oh, I ran out on the last round. If you're feeling ambitious, squeeze a little lemon in mine. If you're not, plain ol' vodka's fine."

Donna drains the drink into Janice's glass and returns to the living room.

"Your tree, their tree. Whatever. What happened with all that?"

"Give me that." She snatches the glass away from Donna. "Incidentally, it does matter whose tree it is. It matters very much." She drinks and stares up at the ceiling. "And, for the record, it's ours. The most substantial part of the root structure is technically on our property."

Donna sinks into her chair and looks out the window. Next door, in the Reynoldses' front lawn, the sycamore's leaves obscure the twilight.

"And they still won't agree to cut the damned thing down?"

"No! Even though the roots are practically tearing up our entire driveway."

"Did you . . ."

"Tie floss around it like you said?"

"Yes."

Janice props herself up on her elbow and sets her drink on the floor. "I did. Crawled out there wearing all black in the middle of the night like some goddamned spy, and you won't believe what happened."

"Tell me."

"The next day, I was standing at that window right there with a pair of binoculars. I wanted to see if the bark on either side of the floss was starting to dry out and die, like you'd said it would. Anyway, I couldn't see it, the floss. So, that night, I dressed up all in black again and went out there to check if it was still there, and the damned thing was gone."

"*No.*"

"Swear to God. This morning I saw some crows picking around the trunk. I'm guessing one of them pecked it off or something. Just as easy as that. How's that for a 'fuck you.'"

Donna laughs, though privately she's relieved. She'd given Janice the idea of using floss to kill the Reynoldses' tree two weeks ago, after she'd seen an episode of *Judge Judy* in which the defendant was accused of using a similar method of arboreal sabotage. It had been an evening almost identical to this one—Janice sprawled on the couch; Donna propped in her chair; both of them waiting for *House Hunters International* to begin so they could ignore it and continue to drink. And like now, they had been gossiping in that way that's particular to two people who've lived across the street from each other for three decades, and who've built the foundation of their friendship on dissecting the lives of those around them.

A phone in the kitchen rings, and Janice sighs.

"Just when I was getting comfortable."

She hauls herself off the couch, and Donna is left in the room alone. On the muted television a couple frets over choosing between three apartments in Barcelona. Donna's been to Barcelona. Many times, as it happens. So many times, in fact, that she grew bored with the place. She had told Henrique that she'd sooner die than ever have to go back there again. "Nothing but sweaty tourists, architecture that's trying too hard, and a lousy church that looks like a sand castle. I prefer Lisbon any day, if you insist on heading that far south."

Donna smiles: those had been her exact words.

"Well, Gary's drunk." Janice wobbles back into the room, holding a new cocktail.

"Oh?"

"Played nine holes this morning and has been throwing them back at the clubhouse ever since, evidently."

"Oh, my."

"He's too bombed to drive. Was begging me for a ride home."

Janice reclaims her spot on the couch. In Barcelona, the couple's dream apartment, a two-bedroom in Les Corts, hangs in the balance. *House Hunters International* fades to commercial.

"What'd you tell him?"

"What'd I tell him? I told that son of a bitch to get a cab."

Donna laughs. Janice and Gary have one of the most functional, healthy marriages she's ever encountered, but she appreciates the effort Janice puts into making things seem otherwise. She's always thought it to be the polite thing to do.

"And what'd he say?"

"That he didn't have any cash."

"Oh, *no*."

"I told him he should've thought of that before he bought his last scotch."

Donna laughs—harder, this time—and in doing so spills what's left of her drink onto Janice's white carpet.

"Shit. Here, lemme get—"

"Oh, forget it, would you?" Janice says. "We're replacing the carpet with hardwood floors in a month, anyway. And in the meantime, vodka hardly stains."

Donna sits down again. She kicks her feet up onto the coffee table and lets her shoulders slouch. The commercials end, and she clicks her wineglass against her teeth.

"You're so good with him," she says. "Gary, I mean. You're so good with him. I'm terrible at men."

Janice turns over on her stomach. Her capris bunch up around her knees. "You're only saying that because one husband left you for some Spanish slut, and the other one died."

Donna knows that Janice is trying to make her laugh, but still something stirs in her gut.

"And Paul," she says. "Don't forget Paul."

Outside, the streetlamps buzz. The sycamore—alive, rooted, destructive—sways.

"He still hasn't called you back?"

Donna shakes her head. "Not a word."

"What a drama queen." Janice sits up. "Or maybe you're the drama queen. You still haven't told me what this is all about."

"It's nothing," Donna says. Though, is it? No, it's not. It's something. She remembers how the AT&T salesman's forehead had creased as he scrunched up his face and said, *Two years is a long time*. "And I don't want to bore you."

Janice considers this as she quietly watches a yogurt commercial.

Then, she says, "Give me your phone."

"Huh?"

"I *said*, give me your phone."

Janice leans forward and braces herself on the coffee table. With her index finger, she hooks Donna's purse and drags it over to her.

"Where the hell is it?"

Donna says, "The outside pocket. What are you doing, anyway?"

"*I'm* going to call that fucker," Janice says.

Paul

His phone buzzes against his thigh. Cradling it in the palm of his hand, he looks at the Indiana number flashing across the screen, then returns it to his pocket.

"My God," Paul says, leaning into Mark. The bar isn't crowded, but it's pretending that it is; Paul can hardly hear himself above the music, some pop song he knows from the radio but that the DJ, a third-rate drag queen named Tina Burner, has remixed within an inch of recognition. "She's calling again."

"WHAT?!"

Paul pulls Mark closer to him and presses his lips up against his ear. "MY MOTHER! SHE'S CALLING AGAIN!"

Mark nods, but he keeps his eyes fixed on the bar, where Preston, the taller half of the couple they've come to Maryann's with, is trying to corral the bartender and order a round of drinks. There are only four other people lined up alongside him, but the bartender—a guy with muscles that look like they're pumped full of air, and who's wearing a white T-shirt with pit stains and a slogan—KEEP ON LOOKIN'—is busy pouring a round of shots for a blond kid in a tank top who looks about half Paul's age.

But then again, he thinks, they all do. A bunch of grad students and waiters and God-knows-what-elses who haven't discovered their first wrinkle, their first gray chest hair; who haven't started worrying about things like colon cancer and still think cocaine is fun; who haven't been burdened with the rationality of experience; who don't need to be up at six forty-five so they can catch the eight o'clock SEPTA to Bala Cynwyd and—Christ. Who was it that said, "Old age is a shipwreck"? Charles de Gaulle? It was either him or Debra Winger—Paul can't remember. Whoever said it had a point, though hardly as it applies to gay men, he thinks as he watches the bartender pour a steady stream of tequila down the twink's fleshy throat. Old age for gay men is hardly as repairable as a shipwreck. When a boat crashes into an iceberg, say, and sinks to the bottom of the Northern Atlantic, there are still gems that can be recovered: artifacts and memories and hidden bits of history. With gay men, on the other hand, some new analogy is needed: a nuclear winter, maybe, or global warming. Something irreversible that has layers of denial and repression. It's why people Paul's age still listen to pop music and black out on Saturday nights. It's why he and Mark are here, on a Tuesday, waiting for Preston to hurry up with the drinks so they can stop chewing ice and more successfully forget about how they'll feel tomorrow morning. It's why . . .

"WHO DID YOU SAY IS CALLING?!"

Paul glances over to his left, where Crosby, Preston's boyfriend (no, fiancé—he can never remember that. They got engaged two months ago) is looking up at him.

"WHO'S CALLING?" Crosby says again.

Preston. Crosby. Think of that wedding invitation. For fuck's sake, it's like they made up their own names.

"MY MOTHER!"

At the bar, Preston flips his blond hair out of his eyes. Above him, a small television screen plays a music video that doesn't correspond to the song that thumps on the speakers: a seventies disco diva, emerging from a beaded curtain, trailed by a cloud of smoke.

Paul tries not to think about how long it's been since the floor received a proper mopping.

"WHY DON'T YOU PICK UP!?"

Paul opens his mouth to respond, but Mark cuts in.

"It's a long story," he says. "Aha, just when I thought I'd die of thirst."

Preston wedges his way up to the high, circular table they've gathered around. Between his two massive hands, he balances four glasses. "Right, okay," he says, distributing them. "A bourbon on the rocks for Paul. Mark takes the Guinness. I've got the IPA. And a vodka-soda for my babe." He leans over and kisses Crosby on the cheek. "In any event, gents, I'm sorry that took so long. Evan was predisposed, pouring a round of regret for some teenybopper with nary a pube to be found, no doubt. Had to practically lasso him to get his attention."

The bar is pure back-room Berlin: black walls and black floors and waist-high black boxes that, at least on weekends, play stage to go-go boys in tighty-whities, their cocks bouncing and flopping to Whitney Houston. For now, though, they're empty save the drunk twink and his band of merry boys; the only thing making use of the dance floor is a pair of colored spotlights, playing a game of erratic, loopy tag. Posters and fliers plaster the walls of the square room, advertising strip-bingo nights and eighties theme events and a biweekly dance party hosted by the statuesque Catherine de Veuve—a blond New York queen who's 80 percent legs and 20 percent hair and who's the reason why Miss Burner has been relegated to Tuesdays.

"I'll tell you one thing: Evan could pour me a round of whatever he wants, whenever he wants, and I'd be there to drink it up," Crosby says.

"Christ, Crosby," Mark says. "There's no accounting for taste."

"Look at his arms. Like you'd kick that out of bed."

"He may have arms . . ." Mark slugs from his Guinness. "Unfortunately, though, there's no such thing as a gym for your face."

"Oh, for fuck's sake." Preston slips his long arms around both of them. "You're both being absolutely terrible. Under normal circumstances, I'd enjoy it. Would revel in it, really. It's Tuesday, though. And Tuesday's hardly a time for reveling."

They met the couple a year and a half ago now, about six months after they moved from New York to Philadelphia. A fellow Ph.D. candidate of Mark's at Columbia had suggested that he look Preston up once he arrived at Penn, where Preston had recently won a tenure-track position teaching Georgian literature in the English department (his thesis—an exploration of the use of eating utensils in Jane Austen's earlier work—remained a constant source of anxiety and wonder for Paul; he could scarcely pick up a fork anymore without thinking of the Bennet sisters). Within a week of arriving at Penn that August, a dinner had been arranged. Paul's first impression was that they were sort of an odd couple: Preston, with his lanky, ropy build, his boyish face, his inexplicable Etonian affectations; Crosby, with his short, thick frame, perpetual tan, and tendency toward business-casual attire. Preston had selected the restaurant—a small Italian place on Chestnut that couldn't have had more than ten tables. ("Don't be fooled by the red-and-white tablecloths," he'd said to Paul when they walked in. "The food's heavenly. Order the linguine with clam sauce and then look me in the eye and tell me that you wouldn't *murder an infant* for a second serving of it." Paul did as he was told, and found that Preston had been right: the food was delicious.) Over the course of one, and then two, and finally three hours, the men had gotten to know one another: Preston and Mark explaining their research; Crosby discussing his plans for when he finished his M.B.A. at Wharton; Paul trying to detail the nature of his work at the clinic without coming across as pathological himself. Fifteen minutes short of midnight, they finally paid the bill and stumbled home, their mouths tasting like cotton and their minds whirling through a Chianti fog.

"Speaking of reveling," Mark says, "I'm liable to be deaf by the end of the night if this music keeps up. Anyone mind if we take this all downstairs?"

Preston performs an urbane bow; Crosby lightly elbows Paul in the ribs and rolls his eyes, and Paul smiles. On the other end of a near-vacant dance floor, Tina Burner finds her footing again and the beat, once irregular and vapid, becomes fuller, louder. Mark catches Paul's eye and mouths *let's go.*

It's tamer at street level—more suburban wine bar than East German disco—though the bass from upstairs still manages to disturb the peace whenever someone opens the door and stumbles down the staircase connecting the two floors. There's an empty red couch beneath a framed portrait of a trio of bronzed, shirtless surfers, and they make their way over to it.

"So, wait," Crosby says, "*why* does your mom keep calling you?"

Paul sinks deep into the velvet cushions. He fingers a crusty stain next to his left thigh. "To tell me that my half sister Eloise is getting married."

"Well! That's great!" Preston clinks his glass against Paul's. Paul looks at the naked ice cubes and shriveled lime at the bottom of his cup and regrets drinking his bourbon too quickly.

"Eh," he says.

Crosby angles himself on the sofa so he can face Paul. "What do you mean *eh*? I love weddings. I *kill* at weddings."

"It's true," Preston says. "He loves them. Dances with anyone. Grandmothers, bridesmaids, groomsmen. One time I thought the mother of the bride was going to send out an amber alert when he took up with a flower girl during the electric slide. Would've caused a terrible scene, really." Crosby rolls his eyes again, and Preston grins. "In any event, why the ambivalence, Paul?"

"To be honest, it's more of a matter of—"

But he doesn't finish, because Mark cuts him off. He stands, drink in hand, and says: "Eloise's father was Paul's mom's first husband. Some bigshot French guy that she met in Paris. Obviously it didn't work out—there's a story there, but for expediency's sake, let's keep it at that: it didn't work out. As evidenced by the fact that Paul is sitting here with us, and he was sired by a different fellow: Donna's *second* husband, a certain Mr. Bill Wyckoff." Here, he takes a breath. "Rest in peace, of course."

Preston finishes his vodka. "Ashes to ashes, my friend."

Mark continues: "In any event, Paul thinks that his mother always treated Eloise a little differently. Showering her with attention, presents, and all that, because she was—how did you describe this to me, Paul? Oh, right—she was *the last tie to a past that his mother was desperately trying to hold on to.* Sorry if I paraphrased that, but really, you get the gist. Am I missing anything?" He pops a piece of ice into his mouth. "Oh, right, *right,* there's also the issue of Alice, Paul's older sister—or *full sister,* I should say, as they both claim Bill, Paul's father, as their creator. She's got issues with Eloise, too, though I suspect they're different than Paul's, and—from what I know of her, which is actually quite a lot—I doubt she'd ever come out and admit them." He crunches down on the cube. "Does that cover it?"

Preston stands and begins to applaud; Crosby says something trite like *fucking family.*

Paul swallows hard and looks down, in case he starts to blush. Mark started doing this—cutting him off, telling his stories, stealing his punch lines—ever since he got the job at Penn and they moved to Philadelphia. Or—no, Paul thinks, recalibrating. That's not entirely true. For the first six months they lived here, things were as wonderful (at least relatively) as they had been in New York. Still unsure of his own future, Mark seemed to appreciate Paul's neuroses, his constant fretting—he even went so far as to tell Paul, multiple times a week, how he thought it was *healthy* that they could voice all their insecurities to each other without fear of judgment, or some irrevocable shift in the power dynamics of their relationship. Mark was initially having trouble finding his footing at the university, and Paul's presence and general disposition when he came home from work helped to create this scrappy *we're in it together* vibe that kept him sane.

But then there was a shift. A paper Mark wrote got published in *The American Journal of Personality and Social Psychology* and ended up winning some award, the name of which Paul can't remember. It was big, though—it must have been—because within a year whispers started circulating around the department that Mark might be considered for early tenure. The rumors were premature, of course—he'd hardly been there three semesters—but the very specter of the possibility did something to Mark, changed him. At home, Paul felt the tenuous balance between them slipping: Mark started to correct him more than he ever had before; his voice took on a patronizing uptick.

More and more, Paul has become obsessed with the idea that he embarrasses Mark.

Still staring down, he hears Mark say, "Sorry, babe."

Mark leans over and kisses his cheek. "You've just got a tendency to drag that story out a bit, so I figured I'd help with the CliffsNotes."

An hour later, and the crowd's picked up a bit. It's nothing like a Friday or a Saturday night, but at least there are enough people milling around that Paul no longer has to worry about Preston speaking too loudly; other voices are drowning him out. He sucks down the dregs of his third whiskey and winces as it stings his throat. He's still smarting from Mark's performance, not so much because of the way he characterized his relationship with Eloise—that was all spot on—but rather because of how wantonly he glossed over the issue of his father's death. Mark knows how devastating that was for Paul, not only the death itself, but how his mother had reacted to it; how, once Bill was finally buried, she took every effort to erase any sign that he'd ever existed; how, when Paul accused her of rewriting history, she'd said those things, *those terrible things*, that characterized her marriage to Bill—and thus, by extension, Paul and Alice's existence—as some lowbrow mistake. How she'd given him no choice but to ignore her, even here, even now, as she calls him repeatedly from a fake Indiana number on a random Tuesday night.

Thank God for bourbon, though, he thinks; his irritation and hurt toward Mark's callousness are becoming foggier, to the point where he's quickly forgetting their nexus. He smiles to himself, drunkenly, stupidly.

Mark also probably had a *little* bit of a point, he thinks: Paul *occasionally* has a tendency to draw stories out. Not without reason, he'd argue. But he would admit the tendency is there.

He feels Mark's hand grip his thigh. "What're you grinning over?"

"Just thinking about the whiskey you're about to get me."

Mark squeezes his knee. Paul spills the two ice cubes that are left in his glass. They both laugh.

"Is that so? By my count it's your turn to buy a round."

Paul lets his chin hang down to his chest, and he frowns.

"Oh, all right, but only because you're cute when you're upset," Mark says. "Actually, let's wait a sec. I want to enjoy the show."

Paul glances over at the bar, where Mark is looking, and sees Crosby and Preston talking to a brunet twenty-something in a leather jacket. He's empirically cute—his face is symmetrical and he's got nice hair—and well dressed in that way where he can probably make cheap clothes look expensive, and they've got him sandwiched between the two of them, laughing.

"Oh, come on," Paul says. "We know how this plays out. Just get me my whiskey."

Mark leans forward. "Hold on, this is where it gets good. Preston's going to go to the bathroom, and Crosby's going to go in for the kill."

"You make it sound like a fucking nature documentary."

Still, he watches, though he hardly needs to; Preston and Crosby have their act down to a fine science, and Paul's seen it in action enough times to know what comes next. As Mark predicted: Preston excuses himself and slinks away from the bar, letting his hand lightly brush the kid's shoulder as he heads to the bathroom. Once he's gone, Crosby edges an inch closer, repositioning himself so he's facing the kid head-on. He runs a hand through his own hair, which is just long enough, and just floppy enough, to make running a hand through it acceptable, and then he lets that same hand fall to the kid's waist, where it rests casually on his hip. The kid looks startled at first—he flinches—but Crosby keeps right on going, as if his hand has been there for the past hour, as if he's got some basic right to be touching him. He flexes his biceps intermittently, like he's got some weird twitch—still, weird or not, when he does this, Paul finds him suddenly more attractive, in the same way he's turned on by undergrads on spring break in Daytona Beach who've got bad tattoos, or the gay-for-pay porn actors on the amateur sites he pays to watch when Mark's away (and not away). Crosby pulls the kid's head closer so he can whisper something. The kid laughs and turns to see if anyone else heard what he just heard, and Paul, at least for a moment, quietly seethes over the fact that Crosby has never whispered in his ear, and he likely never will, so Paul will have to go on guessing as to what it is that he actually says.

Mark taps Paul's knee. "Here comes Preston. Lock and load."

He's already got his jacket on, and he stands for a moment by the bathrooms, eyeing Crosby with an air of paternal pride—a father beaming at a son who just shot a three-pointer to win a high school basketball game. The bar's air-conditioning whirls to life, and Paul feels a goose-bump chill raise the hairs on his arms.

Preston swoons toward them.

He says, "Well, I think it's about time the missus and I call it a night. Early classes tomorrow and all."

"Oh yeah? How early?" Mark winks.

"Dreadfully early, I'm afraid." Preston smiles wryly. "Breakfast-time early. *Pre*-breakfast-time early, even. You know how these young 'uns can get."

"Eager beavers, they are."

"You're telling me."

"And all for lessons on the significance of a teaspoon in *The Mill on the Floss*."

"Yes," Preston says, as Crosby and the kid materialize beside him. "Well. Among other things. Mark"—he sticks out a hand—"see you on campus tomorrow. And Paul"—he plants one on his cheek—"call your mother back."

Once they've left, Paul asks, "Do you think that they ever go home with just the two of them? Like, on their wedding night, do you think they'll come to Maryann's after the reception to find some twink to sleep with?"

Mark collapses into the sofa, the cushions swallowing his head, his neck, and he grins. "We-ell, whatever works, right?"

"We-*ell, somebody's* changed his tune."

"What's that supposed to mean?"

Paul settles into the devastating realization that he's not going to be getting his whiskey anytime soon. "I just mean that when you first saw them skip off with someone at that house party in Rehoboth, your opinions were a little more . . ."

"Homo-normative?"

"I guess that's one word for it. I was going to say *traditional*."

Mark shrugs. A black leather ottoman sits in front of him, and he tosses his legs atop it.

"I've changed my mind," he says. "People change their minds."

The air-conditioning dies, and other noises emerge from the silence in which they've been hiding: beers fizzing, bottles opening, Tina Burner muscling her way through the last hour of her set.

Mark continues, his voice acquiring a lilting, pedagogical edge: "Just last month I was reading this article—or, essay, I guess; it wasn't like some peer-reviewed thing—that Alcott Cotwald published in *Brain World*—"

"I thought you said that magazine's a joke."

"I *did*. But when—"

"When *Alcott's* publishing in it . . ."

Mark finishes what's left of his Guinness and licks the bubbles from his lips.

"He's a brilliant behavioral economist."

"You like him because he's hot and has a British accent."

"I've never even met the man. We were in Asheville when he came to Wharton to lecture."

"You've shown me his pictures. Were you ever going to get me my whiskey?"

"Can you just let me finish?"

Paul doesn't answer; he stares at the bar, where half-filled bottles of vodka and rum and tequila stare at their own imperfect reflections in the mirrored backsplash.

"O-*kay*," Mark says. "Anyway. Alcott looked at the risk-reward analysis of remaining faithful in monogamous relationships. Which, I mean, that's nothing new from a research standpoint. Graduate students have been writing subpar dissertations about that shit for years. I should know—I've had to sit on enough of those fucking committees. But what Alcott did that was different is that he looked *specifically* at couples that have some sort of understanding or arrangement when it comes to monogamy. So, he basically took all those pop-psych, 'sex-positive,' narcissistic Dan Savage ramblings and gave them some academic backing. Which, obviously, Savage has just *creamed* himself over, but that's beside the point."

Someone knocks over a Rolling Rock. The bottle rolls along the bar, gushing its foamy insides; the bartender snatches it and rights it. With an ash-colored rag he goes about sopping up the thin amber puddles.

"Another smart thing he did was that he looked at all kinds of couples: gay, lesbian, straight, bisexual, trans, questioning, queer, non-gender-identifying—fuck, am I forgetting anyone? He even took an historical account of other ethnic and cultural groups that've had a history with . . . er . . . different variations on monogamy."

Bulldozers rearrange debris inside Paul's head—not removing it, just piling it into bigger and less organized lumps—laying the foundation for tomorrow's hangover.

"Yeah?" he says.

"The Comanches, the Greeks, even the Samis. All of them practiced versions of monogamy that allowed for some . . . practicalities."

"Or some fucking around."

"But how is it 'fucking around'—which, by the way, I think is a pretty vulgar description of it—if there's an agreement that states otherwise? 'The empty moral obligations of postwar Christian society have led to a construction of monogamy that discounts very concrete sexual realities. Even more troubling, though, is how readily we reject those realities as negatives when perhaps the real cost of the new monogamy is the death of wholly human desires.' "

"That doesn't sound like your prose," Paul says. "You hate the word *society*."

"It's a quote from Alcott's essay."

The bulldozers continue their industrious dozing. Paul scratches at the plots of stubble on his cheeks.

"So what are you saying, exactly?"

"I don't know." Mark shrugs. "Maybe that Preston and Crosby and all our friends who are like them are on to something? Maybe they've got, like, a more evolved view of relationships than this puritanical one-person-for-the-rest-of-your-fucking-life routine. I mean, you figure that they both want to be with each other, and they realize that this . . . this *other* thing is just sex. Or, no, that's discounting it. It's not *just* sex, it's actually a very real desire that they're acting on within the confines of a set of rules that they've established, instead of society—"

"*Society.*"

Mark plows on: "And honestly, I imagine the costs of that decision are far less than the costs of, say, your standard, Middle American, heteronormative, monogamous marriage, where these feelings are repressed, and someone ends up 'cheating' or 'straying,' because, really, you can only repress something that's inherently human for so long. And then the 'affair'—God, what a terribly *vague* term that is—ends up defining the rest of the marriage, if, in fact, the marriage manages to last at all."

Paul doesn't want to ask. He feels like he's standing ten feet away from the mouth of a deep chasm, and he hates heights. "So you're saying this is something you might want one day. This Alcottian view of monogamy."

"I think so. Yeah, I do. It just seems to make sense to me." Mark reaches over and wraps his hand around Paul's inner thigh. He kisses his neck, sweetly, and swipes his empty cup. "*Now* I'll get you that whiskey."

Paul takes the glass back from him and sets it on the floor next to the couch. "You know, actually, it's late. Let's just go home."

Mark kisses him again, this time on Paul's cheek. His lips feel dry. "You sure?"

"Yeah, I can already tell that I'm going to feel like shit tomorrow."

Mark smiles and helps Paul up off the couch. "Such an adult these days."

A layer of fog floats over the Delaware, pooling along the hulls of container ships. In Center City, the thousand lights on the Comcast Building, the Circa Center, and One Liberty Place form bright smoky clouds that stamp out the dark patches of the skyline. They walk west up Pine Street, and as they cross Broad, Paul glances north, toward City Hall, where arches are tiered upon arches: a wedding cake of a monument.

At the intersection of Pine and Eighteenth, his toe gets caught between a slab of asphalt and an upended cobblestone, and he stumbles.

"Nice save," Mark says. "You all right?"

"I'm fine." He steadies himself. "I'm fine."

Paul rubs his eyes and gazes skyward. Somewhere, an airplane thunders and yawns; a pigeon that was picking its way across the clinic's parking lot floats upward and settles on a power line. On Route 7, a car honks, and Paul feels it poke holes in his brainstem. He forces himself to blink. He runs his tongue across his teeth; his mouth is dry, filled with the dust of last night, and each time he yawns he thinks he tastes bourbon. He's forgotten what it's like not to worry about hangovers.

"Do I have to get in now?"

"What?" He looks at Wendy, who has her trembling arms wrapped around a trash can. The loose skin around her triceps flattens out against the tin like a pair of fleshy wings.

"Jesus, Paul, could you pay attention?" Her nostrils flare. She breathes deeply. "I asked if I had to get in again."

Paul clears his throat and swallows. "Oh, right," he says. "Yes, I'm afraid you do."

Wendy's head hangs. "I knew it."

Paul tries to regain his footing. "It's part of the treatment regimen. If at any point you——"

"Save it." Wendy lifts up a hand, but she doesn't look at Paul. "I'll do it."

Paul adjusts his belt and starts to roll up the sleeves of his shirt. "You need some help getting in there?"

"I've got it," Wendy says, shooing him away. "Wouldn't want you to break a sweat." She looks down at her khaki pants and white Keds. "Can I keep my pants rolled down?"

"We'd prefer it if you rolled them up."

"Of course you would."

Wendy kneels and forms high cuffs with each hem. Blue veins draw maps across her ankles.

Paul looks up again and tries to determine how the clouds shift.

"All right," Wendy says. "All *right*."

She grips the rim of the bin and braces herself, tightening her hold until her knuckles fade to white. (Paul wants to point out what an improvement this fact alone is—two weeks ago, the thought of holding a trash can as if it were a lifesaver would've sent her into a tailspin!—but he resists; she needs her focus.) Lifting one foot and then the other, Wendy lowers herself into the abyss.

"An eleven," she says.

"An eleven?"

"I know you're going to ask what my anxiety level is, so I thought I'd tell you. It's an eleven. Write that down. *Eleven*." She raises her arm and hides her face in the crook of her elbow. "Christ, the *smell*."

She's right—it's bad today. Paul woke up late this morning, and Mark took forever in the shower. He missed the eight o'clock SEPTA and had to catch the eight fifteen, which ran local—*hyperlocal, even*—stopping not just at the less-trafficked stops, but at stops Paul didn't even know *existed*. All of this added up to Paul being robbed of his standard half hour to Dumpster-dive when he got to work this morning. Instead of searching for junk in his preferred roster of places (the Bala Cynwyd SEPTA station; the parking lot of a Fresh Grocer a half mile away; the women's restroom at the clinic), he barely had enough time to grab two bags full of shit from the Dumpster outside the Macaroni Grill next door. So: it's all half-curdled alfredo sauce for Wendy today, Paul figures. And, by the smell of it, a few loaves of stale focaccia. Some raw chicken breasts in an unpleasant state of decay.

Paul nods at Wendy and suppresses a gag.

"Still an eleven?" he asks.

Her face is still hidden by her arm. Still, she manages to say: "A fucking *twelve*."

He scribbles the figure down on his clipboard, even though he knows Goulding will yell at him later for it. ("Our scale goes to ten. Accepting a score of *twelve* allows them to hyperbolize their anxiety, which is exactly what we're trying to prevent.") Across the lawn he sees Goulding in his office, seated behind his desk. His fingers are pressed together so his hands form a sharp triangle, and he nods as the man and woman sitting across from him speak. Or, more accurately, as the woman speaks: the man's not saying anything, so far as Paul can tell; he's slouching, in his own world, as he stares at the giant globe Goulding keeps in the corner of his office. One of those ancient ones where all the countries are in sepia tones and the ocean's the color of parchment paper and Zimbabwe's still labeled Rhodesia. A new victim, Paul thinks. The man.

He watches the woman sit down again and reach for her purse. As if Goulding can feel Paul's gaze, he turns in his chair and locks eyes with him. Paul blinks first, and looks down.

"Paul, are you listening to me?"

Wendy still stands in the trash can. She looks taller than normal; her hipbones are an inch higher than the rim's bin.

"Wendy," Paul says, "get down off your tiptoes, please."

"Why should I? You're not even listening to what I'm saying to you."

He says, "That's not true. Of course I am."

She lowers herself back to her heels, slowly. "Yeah? Then what'd I just ask you?"

Paul sighs. The clouds have stretched themselves out into thin, barely there scrims. He squints and wonders how long he can get away without answering.

"Well?"

Not very, as it turns out.

He says, "You're right. I'm sorry. I wasn't really listening."

Wendy shifts her feet, and Paul hears something squishy and wet: the sound of toes sinking into pasta and soggy calamari.

"What's with you today?" she asks.

"I don't know. I'm hungover." Paul sits cross-legged in the grass. He tilts his head back so he can look up at Wendy, and with his right hand he shields his eyes from the sun. "Wendy, how long have you and Hank been married?"

"Have *Hank and I* been married?"

"Yeah. How long?"

She glances down at her ankles, at the filth that Paul imagines is swarming around them, and she scrunches up her nose like she's just smelled something obscene. "Thirty-seven years," she says. "It'll be thirty-eight in July. Can I get out of here, please?"

"No, not yet." Paul checks his watch: another fifteen minutes. "Can I ask you a question?"

"It's not like I'm going anywhere, am I?" Her bravado is thin; her voice cracks with nerves. "Well, then, let's have it."

"Right, okay." Paul pulls up a tuft of grass. He sifts through the blades until he finds the longest, thickest one, which he uses to tie a few loose bows. "What do you think you'd say if Hank . . . God, I really don't know how to ask this."

And this is the truth. At Maryann's, questions like Paul's are so commonplace as to seem banal. But here, as he considers Wendy's pearls and her frayed white cable-knit; as he looks beyond her, past the manicured grass of the clinic's lawn to the Macaroni Grill and the other little suburban temples that dot the background, he wonders if it's possible to say what he wants to say without coming across as some deviant sex pest.

"Just *ask*!" Wendy suddenly shouts, and Paul flinches.

"Okay, *o*-kay," he says, and drops the blade of grass—now just a frayed mess of angry green knots. "What would you do if Hank came to you and . . . and proposed that, maybe, just as some sort of, like, *experiment* or something, you guys try to have a . . . like, a *guest star* in the bedroom once in a while? Not anyone with a recurring role—that's not what I mean. Not like when Lisa Kudrow played Phoebe's twin once in a while on *Friends*. That's not what I'm talking about. More like when—"

"Paul."

"Yes?"

"I'm standing in garbage. I am *literally standing in garbage*."

"Okay? I mean, yes, of course, I know you are, and I'm very proud that you are, and—"

Wendy shakes her head, slowly. Her white Carol Brady cut doesn't move an inch. "I'm *literally standing in garbage* and you're *speaking in metaphor*."

Paul scratches behind his ear. He shifts how he's sitting, uncrossing his legs and then crossing them again. His ass is wet; the seat of his pants sticks to his skin.

"I guess I see what you're saying," he mumbles. A spot of brightness burns on the back of his neck, and he feels his cheeks flush red. He says: "What would you do if Hank told you he wanted to start having threesomes?"

"No one would want to have a threesome with Hank and me. My tits— which, incidentally, were *nowhere* to be found when I actually could've used them—sag around my ankles, and Hank's got liver spots on his pecker. Anyone who saw us naked would run in terror."

A solid point, Paul concedes. This whole time he'd been wondering *what* would happen if he and Mark woke up with some John Doe sandwiched between them, but he'd never considered the fact that John Doe might not even *want* to be sandwiched between them to begin with.

"But let's just pretend for a second that they did," he says. "Let's pretend that you've got a horde of men lining up—"

"Are they good looking?"

"Sure. Yes. They're good looking."

"How good looking?"

"Very good looking. Now let me finish. Let's say you've got a horde of *very good-looking men* lining up to have sex with you. Would you . . . I don't know, would you want to sleep with a few of them? Under the pretext, of course, that it was sex and absolutely nothing more, and that it in no way was going to threaten your emotional relationship with Hank. I mean, would you . . . ask him for permission to, you know, do it?"

Wendy thinks. For once her face is flushed free of the clicking jaw and twitching eyes and other anxious tics that have controlled her features since climbing into the can. A small success, Paul thinks.

"Of course I would," Wendy says. "And anyone who says that she wouldn't is trying to sell you something."

Another plane arcs across the sky, and its contrail bleeds into the last remnants of the clouds.

Paul asks, "Now, what if the tables were turned? What if Hank had a line of gorgeous women wanting to sleep with him, and he came and asked *you* for a get-out-of-jail-free card?"

Wendy swats at a fly that's circling her nose; she grips both sides of the trash can to steady herself.

"Who says that he hasn't?" she says.

She looks uncomfortable, Paul thinks, and it's got nothing to do with the trash can.

He asks, "What'd you do?"

"I slapped him," she says. "And then I told him he was lucky I hadn't kicked him in the balls, and that if he asked me again, he'd better start looking for a divorce attorney."

"You sound like you regret that."

"Maybe I do? I don't know. I'm a jealous bitch, Paul. I really am. But then I think to myself, a lot of women would have done the same thing, right? More than that—a lot of *people* would have done the same thing." She clicks her jaw and says, "So, what, Mark's asking you to spice things up?"

"I never said that."

"You're an awful liar."

She peers down into the trash can and says: "Relationships are awful. They'll kill you, right up to the point where they start saving your life."

Paul reaches for another tuft of grass. He scours his brain for some winning response—a gem of wisdom that will complicate and trump Wendy's—but nothing comes to mind. Instead, the alarm on his phone starts singing: a digitized Bach cantata that Mark downloaded for him, and that he hardly ever recognizes.

"Twenty minutes is up," he says, looking away from his watch and standing up. Blood rushes to his head. A wave of dizziness washes over him. "You're done for the day."

Wendy's shoulders fall away from her ears, and her chest deflates, like some balloon that's been lodged just above her heart has finally burst.

"Give me a hand getting out of here, would you?"

She wipes both palms against her khakis, then reaches a hand out for Paul. He takes it, wrapping his fingers around hers to help her balance, and she carefully steps out of the trash can and onto the grass. They both stare down at her feet. Oil-soaked basil coats three of her toes, and her ankles are caked in what looks like vodka sauce. Three worms of spaghetti orbit her left calf.

Wendy stares down at the mess and paws her soles against the grass. Paul moves a wiry strand of hair away from her eyes, then leans over and quickly kisses her cheek.

"What was that for?" she asks. She's still hoofing her feet against the ground, trying to wipe them clean.

"I don't know," Paul says.

Behind him, Paul hears the smooth swoosh of the clinic's electronic door sliding open. Then, a voice Paul recognizes calls his name. He cringes as he hears it beckon him inside.

Goulding flips through an anemic file folder, reading and then rereading the three pages it contains. Paul watches him from across the desk. He's sitting in the same chair that, minutes ago, was occupied by the woman with the flailing arms—the wife of the clinic's latest victim—and he's pretty certain he can smell traces of her perfume: something citrusy and cloying. It's either that or the overpriced candle that's flickering on the credenza behind Goulding's desk. Paul clears his throat, but the doctor doesn't look up from the folder, so he takes a moment to gaze around the office. He's been in here a hundred times before, but he still can't get over how industriously the place has been littered with utter *crap*. Expensive crap, but still crap. An antique sword uncovered from some Ottoman treasure trove extends across the top of a bookshelf. In the corner, by the office's door, a small wooden bear hugs the base of a Black Forest hall stand. Propped on top of a Louis Vuitton steamer trunk in the center of the room sits a glass Tommaso Barbi chessboard with one of the queens missing. They were all gifts, Goulding told Paul the first time he was in here, but Paul's never believed him. Because, really, who in his right mind would spend over two grand on a terra-cotta dog the size of a go-kart, only to give it to a shrink?

There's art, too, but these selections Goulding takes credit for. The biggest piece hangs directly behind his desk: a Robert Gober drawing of two nude bodies in a languid, tangled embrace; his cock flaccid in a tuft of fine hair; a single nipple of hers sticking out like a speed bump from a shallow pothole. They're all like this—images of the hypersexualized and risqué. A collection of early penis sketches from Warhol's *Sex Parts* series, for example. The first time Paul saw the collection, his eyes shifting uncomfortably from torso to hip to ass, he asked the doctor if he had an interest in contemporary art, or possibly the human form. Goulding told him neither. "It's a good way to get people to let their guard down," he said. "Sex makes people squirm."

Across the desk, the doctor closes the folder and presses his fingertips together.

"I'm going to transfer you off the Wendy Kingsland case," he says.

Paul was expecting this; still, he feels the blood drain from his face.

"I . . . I feel like we've been making some real headway, though," he says. "Today she stood in the can for a full twenty minutes."

"Was that before or after you kissed her?"

Goulding winks, which makes Paul feel at once more at ease and infinitely more uncomfortable.

"I was proud of her." He takes a half-assed stab at recovery. "I guess I got overly excited."

"And thankful, too, I imagine!" Goulding smiles. His veneers dazzle. "After all that *relationship* advice she gave you."

Paul's jaw goes slack, and he stares at the doctor in disbelief. He tries to protest, but is only able to manage a deflated *huh*.

Goulding unclasps his hands and raises his palms. He shrugs. "It's my clinic, Paul," he says, as if ownership alone is a sufficient enough explanation for this level of Orwellian fuckery. "I know things."

Out on the lawn, someone picks up Wendy's garbage can and lugs it back toward the clinic's storage shed. A member of the custodial crew crouches on her hands and knees to untangle fettuccini from flattened blades of grass.

Along the convex face of a copper paperweight, Paul sees his own distorted reflection. And then, looming in the background behind him, the bookshelf. The ottoman saber. Rows upon rows of Goulding's books, their spines forming bands of white, red, and black. A hundred copies of the same analytic trilogy: *Murdering Your Compulsion, Killing Your Obsession, Torturing Your Way to a Peaceful Mind.*

"I guess my point, Paul, is: Do you want to help people? Do you *still* want to help people?"

"Of course."

"*Or*, do you want to be *helped*?"

Paul looks down: this is a fine distinction.

"That's what I thought," Goulding says, before Paul can answer. "So, tomorrow you'll be starting on a new case. A rather interesting one, I'd say. I'll be supervising, at least until we're . . . back on the same page again. But we could really use a man with your . . . *physical* capabilities." He slides the folder that he's been reading across the table. Paul opens it and sees a picture of the man he saw sitting in Goulding's office earlier that afternoon.

Goulding adds, "And I want to make it perfectly clear: this isn't a demotion. I in no way want you thinking about that. In fact, my worst fear with all this is that tonight you'll find yourself sitting across the table from . . . Mark? Is that your *partner's* name? . . . and you'll be complaining about what an *unfair* guy I am." Goulding chuckles. He buttons and then unbuttons his blazer. "So: no talk of demotion. Rather, let's both look at this as a *learning* experience where you can really start to challenge yourself."

The air-conditioning kicks on—a subtle industrial whirl—and Paul begins to read.

Rick Erwing. Terrified of driving. Is irrevocably convinced he'll hit someone, or *has* hit someone, without knowing it. Each morning he spends nearly four hours circling his block in his blue '98 Camry, looking for dead bodies. The pattern's so predictable, so punctual and exact, that the neighbors have reported scheduling their mornings around it.

Paul's phone buzzes in his pocket. He imagines his mother on the other end of the line, her lips pursing as she waits for him to answer, and he reaches down to silence it.

Alice

"Have you RSVPed yet?" she asks, and cradles the phone against her shoulder.

"I said I'm not going."

"Goddamn it, Paul."

"I already told you, Mark and I are doing something that weekend."

"I refuse to acknowledge that glamping with a bunch of fucking homos in the Poconos is an excuse to miss Eloise's wedding."

"Actually, our plans have changed," he says. "We're going to Six Flags in New Jersey now."

"The repulsiveness of your narcissism is actually impressive."

"So is your willingness to grovel at Eloise's feet."

She wants to scream. Instead, she just comes out with it: "She asked me to be a bridesmaid."

"*What* did you just say?"

"I got an e-mail from her this morning. She said that it would mean a lot to her. Invited me to the bachelorette party in London. The whole nine yards. Even told me I could bring a date."

"You're not actually thinking of *doing* it, are you?"

"I don't know. I have to go."

"What, got another date with a married dude?"

She never should have told Paul about Jonathan, she thinks. She knew it was a mistake as soon as she mentioned it to him, the way he pressed her for details like he was taking record of her sins.

"No, asshole." She lowers her voice. "I have my group."

"Oh."

Paul's quiet for a moment, and Alice relishes the silence and then the white noise that drowns it out. Office chairs squeaking, Xerox machines belching copies, her brother's rhythmic exhalations, sounding at once right next to her and also twenty-seven hundred miles away.

But then he says: "He's never going to leave her, you know."

"You're quoting lines from movies now." Alice pinches the bridge of her nose. A migraine threatens. Tiny fists practice right hooks against her temples. "And besides, I don't *want* him to leave her," she lies. "It would ruin the whole point of what we're doing in the first place."

"Sure, pal."

"Good-bye, Paul."

"I swear to God, Alice, if you agree to be a bridesmaid in that *fucking*—"

She hangs up and immediately turns to her computer. In a flurry, she signs into her personal e-mail and finds the note from Eloise; she doesn't bother rereading it, she just clicks *reply*. Flexing her fingers, she types furiously, punishing the keys: *Yes. Absolutely. Count me in. Xo. A.* Send.

Alice watches the e-mail vanish into the ether, then she leans back in her chair and breathes. She glances around the corner of her cube to see if she can spot Jonathan; he's on the phone. Beyond him, smog wraps around the shoulders of the Hollywood Hills. She fantasizes for an instant about what he'd look like dressed as Hugh Grant in *Four Weddings and a Funeral*. Shit, she thinks. She sent that e-mail too quickly. The way Eloise had reached out to her had been so precise and charming, filled with just enough anglicisms to remind Alice that she lived in London (*colour, theatre, aubergine*), while coming across as only mildly pretentious or phony. She'd even told her to bring a date, for Christ's sake. And how had Alice replied? With five words. Not even a complete fucking sentence; just a string of brutish fractals.

She opens a new window and begins to type. *Dearest Eloise,* she writes. *Please forgive me.* But then—no. God, no. That sounds like she fucking killed someone. Try again. She cracks her knuckles. *My apologies, dear sister.* "Dear sister." Too *Little House on the Prairie.* And also, Paul was right: she is their half sister. She's not good at this; she doesn't think in platitudes. *Eloise, look, I'm sorry. I was yelling at Paul, who was being very Paul.* She holds down the delete button again. Throwing Paul under the bus—now she's just being a traitor. She snaps both her fingers together and blinks, trying to will herself into inspiration. But then, reaching for the keyboard once again, she catches a glimpse of the time, bold and angular in the left-hand corner of the screen: *2:45.*

She's going to be late.

The Healing Women's Grieving Group meets on Tuesdays at three o'clock, in the basement of a community center near Robertson and Melrose. It sounds drabber than it is, Alice tells herself as she circles the parking lot at ten past three, searching for a space. Last year, the city renovated the center; men were hired to paint over the graffiti and update its utilities and install oceanic-themed steel cutouts along its façade: zigzaggy waves hiding the gutters on the roof, a dolphin leaping over the front door. It all combines to create a sort of early aughts, South Orange County aesthetic (all the lettering's done in stainless steel; there's an enthusiastic embrace of both teal and purple), but still, despite her taste, she finds it charming. She pulls her Camry into a spot in a far corner of the lot, next to a utility shed. And besides, she thinks as she grabs her purse and locks up, they have free food.

Weak coffee and these cheap butter cookies that she'd never be caught dead eating in public, but that here, in the community center, she devours by the handful. It's fine. I'm allowed. I'm *grieving*.

"Oh, gosh," she says. The door to the basement slams shut behind her, and she can hear its metallic echo bouncing up the staircase. The women in the group have already arranged themselves into a rough elliptical ("the healing circle"), and each of them turns to look at her. "I'm so sorry I'm late. There was . . . traffic. On Santa Monica."

The group's leader, a postmenopausal Diane Keaton–ish figure named Karen, smiles. "It's fine, Alice. We were just getting started." In one hand she holds a steaming cardboard cup; with her free hand, she points to an empty folding chair. "We've saved a place for you."

Alice mouths *thank you* and bows shallowly. She immediately regrets doing this—the whole *namaste* bowing thing. She always does, and yet she can't seem to stop. Whenever she wanders into somewhere vaguely metaphysical—a one-off yoga class, a high-end spa in Brentwood, grieving groups—she finds herself hinging over, bowing. It's a weird, uncontrollable affectation, and a phony one, at that. It's not that she actually believes bowing to be some transcendental sign of respect—she doesn't. Rather, it's more a matter of fear of getting found out, she figures. Like if she doesn't bow, these women will see her for the person she really is: someone who doesn't buy into the healing power of groups, or crystals, or kelp facials; someone who's here because her brother begged her to go; someone who suddenly wants a stiff whiskey-soda, light—*very light*—on the soda.

"Okay," Karen says, once Alice is seated. "Now, where were we?"

She's acting ridiculously, though, she thinks, glancing around her. It's not like any of these women are hiking into the Himalayas to discover their own inherent Zen anytime soon, either. They're professional, stylish, put-together. Save the dark circles beneath the eyes of the blonde sitting next to her, or the puffy cheeks of the new redhead across the circle, they look, for the most part, like her: educated and reasonable; healthy, save a few secret weekend vices; the unlucky targets of random tragedies.

The women collectively stare into their cardboard cups. Someone's phone, lost in the depths of a purse pocket, buzzes against a set of keys. Struggling with the silence, Karen ventures an answer to her own question.

"Right," she says. "The opening mantra."

Karen stands and takes the limp hands of the women on either side of her, and, after a bit of gentle prodding, the rest of the group follows suit, standing and forming a loose ring of ambivalence and sweaty palms.

Karen says, "Good. Now, let's begin." She breathes in and closes her eyes. "*This is whole and complete. That is whole and complete. This and that are whole and complete.*"

With each clause, another voice joins her . . .

"*From wholeness comes wholeness.*"

. . . until the room reverberates with a sort of morbid, spoken symphony. Alice mouths the last sentence of the mantra—*When a portion of wholeness is removed, that which remains continues to be whole*—but she can't bring herself to say the actual words.

"*Peace,*" Karen sighs. "*Peace, peace, peace.*"

Alice glances around her: heads are bowed, and eyes are still closed. There's one exception: the new redhead stares back at her. She raises an eyebrow and risks a smile. Alice grins back before Karen instructs the women to sit back down.

She retrieves a clipboard from beneath her chair and slips on a set of wireless frames, perching them on the end of her nose.

"Before we get started, I'd like to take a moment to make just a few announcements."

The folding chairs creak as a few of the women shift their weight. Footsteps thunder from upstairs, where the center's staff prepares for a birthday party. Alice tears at a cuticle.

"I'll start with the most . . . well, the saddest," Karen says. "I got a call from Valerie Gonzales this morning. Her husband, Richard, finally passed last night. Stomach cancer, I think most of you will remember. She seems to be doing about as well as one might expect, but she did say that she wants us all to know that . . ." Her eyes fall to the clipboard. "That . . . she really cherishes the support that we've been able to provide her through this . . . this difficult time, and that she hopes to be back in a few weeks or so." She adds: "The funeral's scheduled for this Friday, at St. James Episcopal on Wilshire."

There are murmurs of condolence. Alice nods solemnly. She wonders if any of the other women are secretly thinking the same thing that she is, or if she's alone in counting Karen's grim announcements as the most therapeutic part of the weekly meeting. It's not that she wishes ill on any of the women sitting around her—that's not it at all, is it? No. Of course it isn't. She *likes* Valerie Gonzales. Really likes her, actually. And yet, here Alice is, finding acute, Germanic comfort in the fact that Valerie's husband has just died. While her luck has been shit, for someone else it's been shittier.

She keeps nodding, and wonders if it's possible to feel spectacularly better and worse about herself at the same time.

"Okay, then." Karen flips to the next page on her clipboard. "Alice," she says.

A radio voice trickles down from upstairs. *L.A.'s number-one station for hits from the eighties, nineties, and today.*

"Yes?"

"It's your turn to share."

"Didn't I just share last week?"

"You last shared in February."

"And wasn't that last week?"

Alice strains to hear the first three chords of the Cure's "Boys Don't Cry."

Karen says gently, "Today's May seventeenth."

"Oh. I see."

"Alice." Karen leans forward. She crosses her knees and rests her elbows on her thighs. "If you want to conquer your grief, you've got to let it speak."

The song rattles on. Robert Smith wails.

"I just feel like whenever my grief speaks it bores people," Alice says.

Karen frowns. "I don't think that's true. We're here for you," she says. "We're here for each other."

The woman seated to the right of Alice—a bottle blonde called Beth—squeezes her knee. From the rest of the circle, she's offered nine variations of the same weak smile. The redhead arches an eyebrow.

Alice stands and flattens out the wrinkles from her jeans and blouse. She clears her throat. "All right. Okay."

Karen folds her hands across her lap, and Alice tries picturing her as Kay Adams, or Annie Hall, or Nina Banks from *Father of the Bride*. She imagines her wearing a white turtleneck, drinking a glass of merlot in the middle of some fabulous kitchen. Big bay windows. Countertops of reclaimed wood and white swirling marble. Basil growing on the windowsill. Bowls full of fruit that's actually meant to be eaten.

"I had a miscarriage," Alice says. "I was at the end of my second trimester, and I had a miscarriage."

She begins to sit down again, but Karen asks, "When?"

Alice wants to not hate this woman; she wants to trust her, to be guided by her, but right now all she can think of is throwing Karen clear off a high overpass onto the 405. She's just doing her job, Alice tries telling herself. Even though she knows the answers to her own goddamned questions, she's just doing her job. It's all part of the process: explore your grief until you're the one telling the story, instead of the story telling you. She had read the brochures, had spoken to former members; she had signed up for this.

"It'll be six years this September." Alice sighs.

Beth squeezes Alice's knee again, and when she slides her hand away, Alice wonders if she could ask her to keep it there a little bit longer.

She'd been living in Mexico City, she explains to the group. For a little over a year. Ever since she graduated from UCLA with a double major in

Cinema & Media Studies and Spanish. (She leaves out details that she deems unimportant: That she'd gone to UCLA because she hadn't gotten in to Stanford or Pomona. That she spent the first year and a half sulking about it, making friends selectively with other undergrads who had been relegated to their safety school, trying unsuccessfully to transfer to those two other institutions that didn't want anything to do with her. That it wasn't until she took a survey course in Latin American film, during the spring of her sophomore year, when things began to turn around. After watching Cuarón's *Sólo con tu pareja* in a darkened lecture hall, Los Angeles seemed to open up to her; the streets and palm-lined boulevards now unfurled themselves in ways that seemed beautiful and chaotic, as opposed to crowded and unorganized.)

"I was lucky," she says. "At school I joined the Latin American Film Society and met a rich kid from Mexico City. A *Chilango*. His uncle knew a woman who ran a small production company. Banditas, it was called. Their distribution arm was looking for an assistant. Someone who could eventually help them leverage the American market."

The women nod; they understand. This is Los Angeles.

She had taken to D.F. immediately. She got an apartment in La Condesa, a big alcove studio right off Calle de Durango, a five-minute walk from the Parque México. She liked the messy energy of the place, how it straddled a thin line between progress and disaster, how it couldn't decide what to do with, or how to treat, the European echoes that Cortés had left behind. She spent her weekends in the Bosque de Chapultepec, reading magazines in the shadow of the old castle, lying to the odd American tourists who approached her for directions, telling them in a halting English that she didn't speak their language. In the afternoons, if the weather was nice and if the smog wasn't stinging her eyes too badly, she'd buy a *torta* from a street vendor (she only got sick twice, and she never once was kidnapped, despite Paul's incessant predictions) and sit at the base of the Monumento a la Independencia, where she'd watch *quinceañera* parties pose for pictures along the flanks of long pink limousines. Fourteen-year-old boys wearing ill-fitting tuxes who reached into the girls' loud gowns, through folds of tulle and lace and silk, so they could grab a handful of flesh.

"And the job?" Karen asks.

"It was . . . it was wonderful," Alice says, as she always does, though she's starting to believe herself less and less. It was interesting, and sounded exotic to people when she spoke of it, and she liked that. She liked that Eloise called the job "worldly" and "sophisticated." She liked that she could join her mother and her half sister in the experience of living and working abroad; that she wouldn't be lumped in with her father's pool, whose sense of geography began in Wicker Park and ended in Sarasota, Florida. But the job *itself*? The *day-to-day* of it? It was . . . fine. The problem, she figures, is that she'd naïvely assumed that an intellectual interest (*passion* was the word she used most often when describing her attachment to Mexican cinema) would translate into some sort of fulfilling career. If anything, her stint with Banditas made her hate the movies she'd loved just months before. She learned too much about them, and about the artistic sacrifices that were made to get the pictures produced. "It's like I'm learning how the sausage gets made," she remembers having told her brother during one of their weekly phone calls. "And it's disgusting."

"Of course it's disgusting," Paul had replied. "It's Hollywood."

"Actually, it's Mexico City."

"You know what I mean."

She realizes now that her mistake had been trying to do something she loved for a living.

Karen twirls a jade necklace around her finger. "The boy? I mean, the man," she says, apologetically. "Where does he come into the picture?"

"Right," Alice says. "I'm rambling. I'm sorry."

Karen says, "You need to stop apologizing."

"Sorry."

The redhead smiles.

"A *Chilango*," Alice says. "Grew up in D.F., but went to school at Boston College. Not in the industry or anything. A consultant, actually. He worked in McKinsey's Mexico City office."

"His name?"

"I'd prefer not to say."

It was Alejandro. Ten months after Alice arrived from L.A. they met at a bar in La Roma—a small, angular place that served one type of *torta* and eighty different kinds of mescal. She'd gone there with two coworkers, and first saw him standing next to a cigarette machine. When she went to the bar to get another beer (she hated mescal; she thought it tasted like you were gargling a chimney), a bartender with skulls tattooed on his wrists started hassling her over a tip, and Alejandro swooped in to save her.

"Thanks," she said. He had dark hair and those sharp green eyes that reminded her of certain Italian actors who were always cast as members of the aristocracy. A young Marcello Mastroianni, maybe.

"You're American?" He gave the bartender the twenty pesos to get lost.

"*Sí*," she responded in Spanish. She was afraid he'd think she was helpless. Just another *gringa* tourist.

Behind her, someone lit a cigarette. She heard the first flick of a match, smelled the first waft of tobacco.

"Here on vacation?"

"*No.*" She ran a hand through her hair. "*Vivo aqui. En Condesa.*"

"We can speak in English, you know."

She grinned and took a sip of his mescal, resisting the urge to pull a face. He grinned back.

"Okay," she said. "*Si quieres.*"

"*Sí, lo quiero.* I need to practice."

He didn't, though. His English was perfect. He'd attended an American school in Lomas de Chapultepec before shipping off to Boston College, and after graduating he'd spent two years with McKinsey in New York before asking to be transferred to the company's Mexico City office.

"My mother was ill," he said.

"Is she okay now?"

"Healthy as can be." Behind them, someone dropped a *torta* to the floor and cursed. "To be honest, she wasn't really that sick. I was just tired of winters in the Northeast."

After an hour, Alice's coworkers found her and whispered that they were headed home, but encouraged her to stay.

"Oh, don't worry," she whispered back *en español*, "I am."

She was enjoying herself, and she could tell that Alejandro was, too. He kept finding ways to lean into her; he'd blame the people standing on the opposite side of him, but when Alice glanced over his shoulder, she'd see that there wasn't a single person within three feet of them. He convinced her to try three different kinds of mescal. The last one she actually liked, or at the very least tolerated, though she doubted it was the drink itself; by that point, she figured, she was drunk enough that her brain was filtering out the booze's smokiness, its ash. They talked about the things she missed from the States ("not going to bed nervous that I accidentally used tap water to brush my teeth"), and the things that surprised her about D.F. ("People have shockingly nice shoes. In L.A. all I ever wore were flip-flops"). They discussed the city's unsettling ethnic and phenotypic divisions; how once you crossed into the wealthy enclave of Polanco, people suddenly became taller, fairer, thinner, and more European looking than their European ancestors could ever have hoped to be. They shared how that particular neighborhood made them uncomfortable, hyperaware of their own privilege. After two more drinks, they sheepishly admitted that because it had the best restaurants, maybe Polanco wasn't so bad.

"You just have to know what you're getting yourself into, I guess," Alice said, sucking on the end of a cocktail straw. She was drunk enough that she wanted to throw a few pesos into the cigarette machine and buy a pack, but not so drunk that she was unworried about what Alejandro thought of smoking.

He said, "Right. I actually live there."

"I have a lot of friends who do, too." She set the straw down. "I live closer."

"Oh?"

"About a ten-minute walk."

She let him poke around her apartment while she emptied half a bottle of red wine into two water glasses. There wasn't much to look at, she realized for the first time: a full bed tucked away behind a set of French doors; a living area with a love seat and a matching set of Ikea side tables; a framed poster for *Sólo con tu pareja* that she'd found while digging through a stack of old movie memorabilia at a flea market in Coyoacán; a pile of scripts covered in Post-its.

"Who's this?"

He was holding a picture of her, Paul, and Eloise that she kept on one of the side tables. Her father had taken it the last time they had all been together, at Alice's graduation from UCLA. Half the time she forgot it was even there.

Alice circled around the couch to hand Alejandro his glass and look at the photo. She was still decked out in her cap and gown, and she clutched a bouquet of flowers to her chest. Paul's eyes were closed, and Eloise's hair looked perfect.

"That's my brother," she said, pointing at Paul with her free hand.

"You two look alike."

"You think?"

Alejandro squinted. "Sure, same color hair and all that." He had started to slur his *s*'s. "And who's that?"

"My half sister."

"I see."

She watched as his eyes traced Eloise; as he took in the way the sun shone through her light hair, the plunging neckline of her blue dress, her tan athletic shoulders. She was used to it—all the men who'd ever stopped long enough on the way to her bed to notice the picture did the same thing.

You look so happy, they'd say. And then: *Who's the guy? Are you twins?* And finally: *Who the hell is* this*?*

She drank as much merlot as she could manage in a single gulp, and set the glass down on the table.

"Come on," she said, and unfastened his belt.

Upstairs in the community center there are more footsteps, but these new ones are lighter, softer. Kids, Alice figures. Here for the party. She thinks she hears a balloon pop.

"We were together for about a year before I got pregnant. We weren't as careful as we should have been," she says, and leaves it at that.

"How did he react to the news?"

She's gripped by the urge to say that he'd been awful. That he'd given her some terrible, misogynistic ultimatum: get rid of it, or get out. Something that might paint her as more of a victim, more of a martyr. Something that would squeeze out whatever empathy was left trickling through these women's veins.

"He was wonderful. I was terrified, but he was wonderful. Honestly, my first instinct was to buy a ticket back to L.A. and call this doctor I used to see when I was in college and schedule a . . ." A balloon pops. This time she's sure of it. "But anyway, he told me that he'd support me, regardless of what I decided. It was like he was following a script or something. How to Be a Great Boyfriend When You Knock Up Your Girlfriend, as written by Joan Didion." This gets a few laughs—it always does. Alice shrugs. "So I decided to keep her. The baby, I mean. It was a girl. Or, I learned it was a girl. I figured if he could be this amazing when things were so shitty, then he'd be an even more amazing dad."

What else is there, she wonders. She's feeling like a leaky faucet today—all these subtleties just spilling out—she supposes she could tell them all the details she typically excludes. The stuff about how, while she squatted on her bathroom's cold ceramic floor, staring at her fifth positive pregnancy test, she felt an unsettling mix of panic and shame and triumph.

Panic for reasons that were obvious; shame because she'd graduated magna cum laude and she'd grown up in St. Charles and she could already hear her father's voice, should he ever find out; triumph when she considered her half sister. When she was nineteen, Eloise suddenly began suffering from agonizing cramps whenever she got her period. After three months of them, her mother insisted that she fly back from Yale to see her gynecologist. Ultrasounds were performed, and a cyst was found. There was more: evidently, the haywire cells had existed for longer than Eloise had felt the cramps, because they'd decimated her uterus. Her chances of ever having children, the doctors told her, were next to nothing.

And here Alice was, holding her knees in an empty bathtub, pregnant without even trying.

"How did your parents react?"

"To me getting pregnant without being married? They were happy."

That's at least mostly true, Alice thinks. Her father approached the news with his characteristic gruff pragmatism. He wanted to know when Alejandro was going to propose ("Not *if*, Alice. *When*"), and she did her best to convince him that his Victorian social norms had been long since uprooted, and that neither she nor Alejandro thought matrimony to be a prerequisite for parenthood. Her mother, meanwhile, was ecstatic. Donna had shouldered Eloise's infertility as if she were somehow the cause of it, as if it were a deficiency in herself. Alice changed all that, untangling Donna from a bizarre maternal guilt. Donna started calling more; instead of every two weeks, she'd check in every two days. And for once, Eloise ceased to be the marquee subject of their conversations. With a baby growing inside her, Alice was spared the sting of hearing about her half sister's latest promotion at the foundation, or the charming Englishman she'd just snagged, or the marathon she'd just run. She could talk about herself and have her mother listen without worrying that she was boring her.

Karen clears her throat, and Alice looks up. "And the . . ."

"The miscarriage. I know. I'm stalling," Alice says. "I was at a meeting with two foreign distributors, and I realized that I hadn't felt the baby kick at all that morning. And this struck me as strange because . . . God, she *loved* to kick. Afterward, I read a bunch of stuff online about how these mothers suddenly stopped feeling their baby's heartbeat, but . . . I don't know. I think it's like how some people say they can distinguish between their child's cries. Like how one wail means that she's hungry, and another one means she's tired. I think that's all a load of bullshit. I mean, I can barely feel my own heartbeat, and that's when I've got two fingers pressed up against my neck. How am I supposed to feel my unborn daughter's?"

One of the women looks at the ground, and Alice wonders if she's said something wrong. She continues. "I went to the doctor once the meeting ended, which now, I'll admit, seems a little . . . I don't know. Seems a little . . . like I skewed my priorities or something. Like I should have gone straight there when I felt something strange, or even when I suspected that I felt something strange, and if I'd done that—if I'd acted on that instinct—she would have lived."

"But—"

"Yes, I know what you're going to say, and I'll tell you what I tell you every time: fault isn't objective."

Karen doesn't respond.

"They couldn't take her out," Alice says. "They said there were complications that made surgery . . . unsafe. So they couldn't take her out. I had to wait until I delivered her on my own. That was the worst part. I'd heard about it happening before. Someone had a friend who had a friend who this happened to. Something like that. So, I knew that it happened, but still . . . this idea that your daughter is inside of you, and has been relying on you, but that you've suddenly somehow betrayed her . . . like, without any input from you, your own body has suddenly made an active and deliberate decision to murder the one thing you've created that has the potential to be worthwhile. And in case you want to forget, in case you want to have a few glasses of wine and remind yourself that you're capable of being happy, you can't. Because there the evidence is: decaying inside of you."

Alice wipes her eyes with the back of her hand.

"It's sort of crazy, isn't it? I keep calling her my daughter, like she was actually here or something, but she never even took her first breath, and I'm a *liberal*. It's like I'm completely fucked up about a life that's totally imaginary." She looks down. "I'm sorry, Karen. I'm completely *messed* up.

"Anyway, Ale . . . my boyfriend left. A month later. McKinsey offered him a position in Buenos Aires, and he took it. I want to blame him. I feel like it would make this all so much easier. If I could just say, 'What a shitty thing to do, leaving me alone like that.' I can't, though. I was a fucking monster. I wouldn't let him touch me. Not even when she'd finally been . . . I wouldn't let him touch me. Twice I told him it was his fault. Didn't provide any evidence, didn't cite any examples. Just yelled at him and said he was the reason our daughter was dead."

She considers what she's edited away: How, a week after it happened, she crashed her bike into the side of a taxi. The driver complained that she'd done it on purpose; she told the police that she'd had too much to drink, even though the *alcoholímetro* the cop was using suggested she'd hardly had a sip of beer. How getting out of bed each morning was becoming a more and more herculean effort. How she started showing up to work late and unfocused: three weeks before the baby's due date, she mistyped four figures into a spreadsheet, which—if her boss hadn't caught it—would've cost the company over a million dollars and Alice her job. How it was becoming harder and harder to get a bottle of wine to last more than a single night.

"Where is he now?"

"I don't know. From Buenos Aires I heard he went to Santiago. When I came back to L.A. at the end of that year I considered trying to track him down, but . . ."

"Yes?"

She tries to remember how many e-mails she sent, and how many bounced back. One every week, she figures, for almost a year. Fifty-two.

"But I just didn't."

She remembers how she forbade her brother from investigating Alejandro's whereabouts on Facebook or Google or anywhere else. Paul had just started at the University of Michigan, and he had taken his spring break to travel down and be with Alice. Donna and their father had come with him. Eloise had promised to fly over from London, but some big disaster at the charity ended up happening at the last minute, and she had to cancel her trip. In her stead she sent Alice a dozen irises, along with two new bulbs, planted deeply in glazed ceramic pots. *Even in the darkest times,* the accompanying card had read, *hope springs eternal.*

They were all sitting in Alice's living room when a man driving a beat-up VW van swung by with the delivery.

"What a lovely thing for your sister to say," Donna said. She was folding laundry on the couch. "How thoughtful."

Paul scoffed. "It's condescending, is what it is. Condescending and cliché."

Alice remembers watching their reflections float across her dark television screen as she counted the days until they'd all just leave.

"Alice?"

The women stare at her; Karen cocks her head to one side. Upstairs it sounds like a riot has erupted: a bunch of munchkin feet sprinting in every direction at once, voices clambering over one another to be heard.

"I'm done," she says.

Paul

The mannequin slams against the hood of the Nissan, leaving it with a watermelon-sized dent. Breaks squeal and tires smoke. From where he's standing, curbside, Paul can hear Rick Erwing's suicidal cries of disbelief as the poor son of a bitch white-knuckles the steering wheel. Paul looks down at the mannequin, whose arm is bent above its head at an impossible angle and whose mouth is frozen in a clownish, inanimate smile.

"You need to throw them harder than that," Goulding says. Paul can feel the doctor's breath on the back of his neck. He smells coffee, lurking behind a thin layer of Listerine. "I want their heads to roll. Literally. I want the mannequins to fall apart. I want Rick to *see them fall apart.*"

"My arm feels like it's about to fall out of its socket," Paul says, rubbing his right shoulder. Strewn at his feet lie an army of mismatched figures: nippleless women, castrated men, prepubescent children, Band-Aid-hued babies the size and shape of footballs. He thinks about how he'll have to spend the next hour hurling them at Erwing's car as he drives in circles around the parking lot, and his arm aches more.

"Think of all the good you're doing," Goulding says.

Inside the car Erwing bangs his head back against his seat. The clinical worker sitting next to him makes a note on her clipboard.

The doctor continues, "Before he came to us, this man could hardly pull out of his driveway without thinking that he'd run over someone. And I'm not talking about just some idle worry, Paul. Like how you or I might wonder throughout the day if we remembered to turn off the lights before we left the house. Rick was *consumed*. He'd have to stop every ten yards or so to check the tires for blood and little bits of brain. It would take him nearly two hours just to get around the block, and then once he'd done *that*, he'd be worried that he missed something, so he'd have to start the whole thing all over again, retracing his steps." Goulding wipes sweat from his glasses with the end of his tie. "That's crippling, Paul. That's no way to live."

Paul swats away a gnat. Philadelphia celebrates summer by exploding in bugs.

"And you think this is actually helping him?" he asks.

Goulding's mouth twitches, and Paul worries that he's insulted him. "I'm sure of it," he says. "Absolutely sure of it. The first two months he spent on the couch were helpful to get the lay of the land, so to speak. But if he's going to be free of this thing, this sort of immersion therapy is necessary."

With the polished toe of his loafer, Goulding nudges one of the mannequins. A bald, sexless eight-year-old. "Speaking of, let's give it another go, shall we?" He unholsters a walkie-talkie from his belt and Paul hears static, the sound of Velcro being torn apart. "All right, Marcia," Goulding says. "Let's try again."

Paul watches Rick Erwing shake his head and mouth a tirade of silent pleas. Marcia reaches her arm through the sunroof and confirms Goulding's instruction with a thumbs-up.

Goulding lifts the mannequin by its left ankle. "Use one of the kids this time."

"You know, my right shoulder is really starting—"

"Paul, I really need you to be a team player here."

The Nissan's ignition sputters to life. Heat waves dance across the empty parking lot.

"Sure," Paul says. "Of course."

The car swerves around a cone, and he thinks of the conversation he had with Mark last night, which was a reenactment of the same conversation they've been having for the past two months. They'd been in the kitchen. Mark was cutting leeks for a frittata, and Paul sat across the counter from him, his chin resting on his fist, his gaze locked on the spice rack on top of the fridge. On Mark's iPod Nina Simone crooned, and in his head Paul repeated the word *curry* enough times for it to lose its meaning.

Between the two of them, Mark's the more skilled and knowledgeable cook. It isn't that Paul is a total mess in the kitchen, it's just that with Mark around there doesn't seem to be any point in trying. He's always there to step in, to stop Paul from burning butter, to show him a better way of slicing onions. He navigates a stove with a sexiness that makes Paul feel content with, if not dully embarrassed by, his own incapability.

"What's wrong?" Mark asked him. "You've got a face like a wet weekend."

A pan with caramelized onions sat on the stove, and the kitchen grew claustrophobic with their smell.

"A what?"

" 'A face like a wet weekend.' A bad mood. It's a saying."

"Huh." He'd never heard Mark use the expression before. He let his eyes trail down from the spice rack to the fridge's white face, strewn with magnets that they'd collected over the nearly four years they've been together: a black-and-white shot of the Empire State Building at night; a Winston Churchill saying, now clichéd, given to Paul by one of his mentors from grad school; a magnetized save-the-date for Preston and Crosby's wedding.

He imagined the other expressions coiled up in Mark that he'd never heard him use. Pithy turns of phrase that might be sprung on him in the next hour, day, month, year. How, once he'd heard one of them, he'd spend the rest of the day wondering where Mark had learned it, and how it had managed to not become a character in their story until now.

The hardest part of a relationship isn't staying with the people we love—it's actually getting to know them.

"No," Paul replied. "I'm not in a bad mood. Or not really, I guess. Thoughtful, maybe. But not bad."

"Anything you want to talk about?" Mark scooped the leeks into a mixing bowl.

Paul considered this; he thought about the looming headaches that would unravel if he were to speak. He spoke.

"I just . . . are you sort of waiting for my green light with all of this, or something?"

Mark tossed a fistful of chopped peppers into the bowl. "What do you mean?"

"Just with this . . . open relationship idea. Am I the roadblock to that?"

"I never said I wanted an open relationship."

Outside a streetlamp flickered and succumbed to the night.

"Okay, fine. Monogamy with terms and conditions. Whatever you want to call it." Paul leaned forward and plucked a pepper from the bowl. "Are you waiting for my . . . like, my go-ahead with it?"

"I guess?" Mark pinched salt into the bowl. "Yeah, I guess that's probably true."

Paul looked down and drew circles on the counter. He said, "I don't even know what that would look like. If we did what you're suggesting, I mean."

Mark wiped his hands against his pants and reached behind him for the rosemary. "It would probably look very similar to how it looks now," he said. "Except that we'd be more open to situations that we might have otherwise been closed to. Hey." He reached across the table and tapped the top of Paul's head. "Are you stressed out about this? Because you shouldn't be. If it's something that you don't want, then—"

"This doesn't stress you out?"

"What do you mean?"

"I mean the prospect of all this. Of us sleeping with other people. It doesn't stress you out?"

"Not really."

"How—"

"Because I know you're not going to leave me." Mark shrugged. "And I'm not planning on leaving you. We'll set rules, and we'll follow the rules, and the relationship will probably be better because of it." He thrust a spoon into the bowl and began tossing the mixture in tight, quick loops.

The Nina Simone track ended in a fizzle of violin. A bit of pepper lodged itself between two of Paul's molars.

"You sound so sure about all this," he said.

Mark shrugged for the second time. "I am."

And this is the part of Mark that astounds Paul, because if Paul is sure of nothing, if his life amounts to a sort of walkabout through a vistaless ambivalence, then Mark is sure of everything. The best way to cut an onion, the direction the economy is headed, the healthiest means to confront the boredom of monogamy. It doesn't matter if any of those beliefs is ever proven wrong. His sureness can't be rattled. He'd just acrobatically throw his stock into being sure about something else. And he'd do it all with a blithe confidence that at once scares Paul and makes him dreadfully envious.

The Nissan slows and speeds up again. Sweat pools above Paul's lips. He grips his mannequin child tighter.

"Okay," Goulding says. "Get reaaaaaaady . . ."

Birds chirp on a telephone wire high overhead, indifferent to the insanity unfolding at their feet. Erwing steers the car around the lot's last corner, and its tires groan. Paul swallows. He tastes starchy memories of the dumplings he had for lunch.

"THROW IT!" Goulding shouts.

Paul hurls the child as hard as he can, and his right arm protests with a white-hot pain. There's the clamor of plastic against steel against asphalt, the familiar burnt-rubber screech of four bald tires. He looks up expecting to find the mannequin reduced to a pile of out-of-whack limbs, but instead sees it sitting upright, calmly, like it's just sat down to take a rest. His shoulders slump.

"Goddamn it, Paul!"

The birds flutter away, annoyed. The Nissan rolls to a stop.

"I—I thought it was harder?"

"You *thought*!?"

A slow rage boils near the bottom of Paul's throat. He swallows it down.

"Sorry," he says. "Next time will be harder."

Goulding squeezes the bridge of his nose, and Paul counts as he takes seven deep breaths.

"All right." He cleans away more sweat from his glasses. "Everything's all right. We'll just . . . try it again. And Paul, this time, *please*—"

Paul says, "I know. I got it."

Mark cut off a thin slice of frittata and reached it across the counter. "Here, try this. Tell me what it needs."

Paul bit down—it was delicious. Hearty and filling. It needed nothing. Mark's cooking rarely did.

"Salt. Just a little more," Paul said. "Don't you think it's just asking for trouble, though?"

"What's asking for trouble?"

"I don't know, this whole *other people* business. The whole thing feels like opening Pandora's box. Who's to say that one of us won't fall in love with someone else?"

"But isn't that always a risk?"

"Sure, but why compound it by actively recruiting that someone else, and then asking them to get naked?"

A car honked outside.

"Are you worried that I'm going to leave you?" Mark asked.

"No," Paul answered. "I'm honestly not."

He is though, of course. Not unreasonably so. At least *he* doesn't think unreasonably so. Wasn't anyone who was or had ever been in love terrified, at least to some tiny degree, of love deciding to take its business elsewhere? And wasn't that partly the thrill of it all? Knowing that you were sharing something vulnerable that required your protection? So, okay, yes—he's worried that Mark will leave him. But somehow admitting that would feel like losing.

There are also the more complicated concerns: the pins and needles of Mark's own unhappiness. These are the actual reasons (as opposed to half-assed academic ones) behind why he finds Alcott Cotwald's theories so compelling. There are the ways in which Paul isn't satisfying him, and the ways in which he never actually could. There are the worries that Paul mulls over during long showers, the questions that he doesn't ask because the last thing he wants are answers.

"We'd have rules," Mark reiterated. "There would be boundaries. Things that we were both comfortable with."

"Like what?"

Mark dashed salt onto the frittata.

"I don't know, we'd have to talk about it, I suppose."

"Well, can you give me an example?"

He rested both of his elbows on the counter. "Like, you'd always be safe. Condoms would be a must. And . . . what else. Oh, here's one—if there's a chance that someone might become something *else*, then it's probably not a good idea."

"I don't understand."

"Sure you do."

Paul thought. "You mean if there's a chance that, like, a guest star might become a series regular who, a year in, snags his own prime-time spin-off."

Mark cracked open a bottle of beer.

"I've never thought about it in such sitcom-ish language before, but sure."

"And the chance that, *despite our best efforts,* that will always remain a possibility doesn't scare you."

Mark blinked. "No."

And maybe he was right, Paul thought. Maybe it was as simple as Mark was making it out to be: fuck around, get their rocks off, congratulate each other with high-fives, and then kiss and say their I-love-yous before they shut off the lamps each night. It sounded so easy when Mark painted it as a hypothetical. But therein lay the problem, Paul realized: *he couldn't exist in hypotheticals.* He never could. Not as a kid, and certainly not now. Mark did it masterfully; he constructed a future within a vacuum, something smooth and motionless, like a slab of ancient obsidian. Paul's future, meanwhile, bore a tangle of implications. A litany of *how abouts* and *yeah, but what ifs.* And each time he addressed one of those imagined scenarios—each time he took a sword to its head—three more terrible possibilities would appear in its place.

"Hey, I love you, okay?"

Mark said that to him this morning, before he set off on the ten-block walk west toward Penn's campus.

Paul was standing in the kitchen, eating a slice of reheated frittata, and Mark hugged him from behind.

"I love you, and I'm not going anywhere."

"Love you, too," Paul said. "This thing's delicious." He'd been staring out the window, watching a squirrel navigate a space between two rain gutters.

"I'm glad you like it."

Mark kissed his cheek. He smelled like patchouli and mint.

"You feeling okay about last night?"

103

Paul nodded.

"Good." Mark mussed his hair. "I'm going to be late, but have a great day. And don't think about all this too much, okay?"

"Okay."

"You promise?"

Now Paul's mouth was full, but he managed a *yup*.

It was a lie, obviously. Paul knew it was a lie, and Mark must have, as well; there's no way that Paul wasn't—isn't—going to spend some part of every moment of today considering and reconsidering the conversation he and Mark had last night. He's obsessive; he obsesses. It's what he does; it's how he survives. It's a trait that he's always had a keen sense of, but that he's just now getting around to self-diagnosing.

The unshackling of denial for a set of new chains is liberating.

Goulding launches his clipboard toward a lamppost. It's an impressive throw—perfectly aimed, and with startling velocity—a particle-board Frisbee, which collides with the post and shatters into five jagged pieces.

"*PAUL!*"

The Nissan's stopped at an angle, and the driver's-side door swings on its hinges. Erwing's on all fours, dry heaving onto the pavement. Next to him lies a female mannequin—this one full-grown and voluptuous, with hips and tits that remind Paul of the dolls he and his sisters used to play with. Her blond hair is a rat's nest of knots, but otherwise her plastic form is intact.

"For *fuck's sake, Paul!*" Goulding yells. On the opposite side of Route 7, two mothers in athletic shoes stop pushing their strollers for long enough to gawk. "What kind of pansy-ass throw was *that*?! I've seen *eight-year-old girls* who can throw a softball twice as hard!"

Marcia kneels down beside Erwing, asking a series of post-round questions.

Paul clenches his teeth until his jaw flexes. Enamel grinds against enamel. He marches forward, takes hold of the mannequin's stiff wrist, and drags her back to the pile of bruised, naked bodies between him and Goulding.

"You've got one more shot at this," the doctor says. He's collected the scraps of his clipboard, and he uses one of them to point at Paul. "You hear me? One. More. Shot. You screw it up this time, and it's answering phones and taking lunch orders for the next year."

The Nissan's door slams shut. Paul reaches for a shoebox-sized baby with blue, lidless eyes. He rolls his shoulder in its socket, loosening the screaming muscle.

He grips the baby's neck and thinks back to the doctor's question from last month: whether Paul wants to help, or whether he wants to *be* helped. It was a glib, condescending thing to ask—but then, glib and condescending don't necessarily render a question untrue or inaccurate. Sure, Paul isn't slipping on a pair of gloves each time he has to shake someone's hand, but is he really that far off? His obsessions don't manifest themselves physically, but they certainly lay other species of snares and traps in hidden corners of his mind. They lasso him and hogtie him and yank him away from logic and rational thinking. They spin him into vortexes where one thought grapples with another, which grapples with another, which grapples with another, until it's three o'clock in the morning and all he can think about is all the problems he's still left unexamined.

What's your anxiety level? he asks himself. Off the fucking charts.

"Remember, Paul," Goulding's voice growls two feet behind him. "You fuck this up *one more time . . .*"

The Nissan's halfway around the parking lot. Goulding breathes audibly, his nostrils flaring. Paul plants his heels and begins to sweat.

"Throw when I tell you to this time," the doctor says. "Let's try to minimize the chances of this being yet another failure."

He thinks of Wendy standing in the trash can, her ankles sinking into wet webs of spaghetti and linguini. He thinks of her fleshy arms trembling as he cajoled her into hugging the thing she detests the most. Or, better yet, he thinks of Rick Erwing. He thinks of how his fingers must ache from gripping the steering wheel so hard; he thinks of the synthetic pine smell leaching out from the felt tree that dangles from the rearview mirror. He thinks of limbs bouncing off the windshield, of heads lodged between tires.

The doctor says, "All right, fairy, let's see what you've got."

He thinks of his own awful thoughts, launched like naked plastic bodies assaulting his consciousness.

"NOW!"

Paul spins and throws the baby as hard as he can, squarely and exquisitely at Goulding's face.

Donna

The joint's end burns uneven and ragged, like loose cloth hanging from a Molotov cocktail. Donna squints at the embers, willing them into focus as she slowly rotates it in a lazy circle. For the past hour and a half she's been mindlessly reading an old copy of *Architectural Digest*, and now ash and charred weed scatter across the foyers and bedrooms printed on the magazine's pages. She blinks once, twice, savoring the cosmic and heartbreaking way the earth pauses each time she closes her eyes. An ember lands between her first two fingers, and she watches it burn a speck of skin for a few seconds before the pain registers. How many house fires start with a scene like this, she wonders. A divorcée-cum-widow, wearing a ratty pair of jeans and one of her daughter's old sweatshirts, sitting cross-legged on the living room floor, toking on pot. *Toking*. Do people say that anymore? She hopes they do—it's too ridiculous a word to retire.

"I'm toking on a blunt," she says aloud, and laughs. *Toking*. How delicious.

She cranes her neck around to look at the empty couch behind her. Since she took her first hit off the joint she's had the very real sense that someone's been sitting there, listening to her and her thoughts. So much so that when she says something clever—something like "I'm toking a blunt"—she instantly turns to see if her faceless guest is enjoying her wit as much as she is. But then—no. She's alone. Just her, and her magazines, and her glass of Shiraz, and her joint. Her joint on which she's toking.

She laughs again, and takes another hit. The smoke curls around her insides and she feels that marvelous burn in her lungs and, finally, she exhales a shape-shifting cloud. But something strange happens as her lungs empty: deep within the kangaroo-ish pocket of Alice's old sweatshirt, she feels a faint vibration. At first Donna's sure she's hallucinating; her faceless friend from the couch, the one who's wily enough to disappear every time she turns around, is pulling a fast one on her. But then, she feels it again: a vibration just above her hipbone. With the hand that's not holding the joint, she digs into the pocket until her fingers graze something solid: her new cell phone. She holds it tightly, and a lazy eternity passes, but then, *then*—yes, she's sure of it—it buzzes *again*.

"*Fuck.*"

She yanks it out into the open air and sees Paul's number blinking on its screen.

November 22, 2012

Swinging the oven door open, Donna leans over to peer inside. Heat sears her cheeks; she blinks away the dryness. Using a small brush, she starts basting the turkey, painting strips of melted butter onto its puckered skin. Fat oozes and spits in the pan, and she makes a face. She hates turkey. Stuffing it, cooking it, eating it. Washing down its dusty aftertaste with gulps of sauvignon blanc. If she had her way, she'd serve a filet mignon for Thanksgiving. Pair it with some asparagus in a hollandaise sauce, instead of the mishmash of croutons and apples and giblets that passes as stuffing in America. But then—her son had been insistent. It was the first holiday they were celebrating since Bill's death, and so help them God, they were going to have turkey. "He loved it," Paul had said the week earlier, when he called from New York to give Donna his flight information. "The dark meat especially."

Donna tries to remember if this is true, and she can't. It seems to her like one of those memories that she's become all too familiar with during the past several months—an inflated recollection exaggerated after the fact to give a life more character than it may have actually had. Still, she hadn't wanted to upset Paul, particularly now, when he seems especially prone to getting upset. So, on the way home from the airport, they'd gone to the store. Had picked out a bird. And then, while Paul squirreled himself away in his old room upstairs, she'd buried herself in every cookbook she owned, trying to find the most painless way to prepare the damned thing.

"Alice?"

Her daughter's lying down in the living room; Donna's head is still in the oven. It's questionable whether Alice heard her. Donna takes in a breath of oil and brine, and calls out again:

"ALICE!?"

"You can stop yelling. I'm right here."

She stands in the kitchen doorway, holding a glass of red wine with two hands. It's the same glass that appeared a week ago, when Alice first arrived from Los Angeles, and which has remained attached to her (almost anatomically, Donna thinks, the glass melding into skin) as it refills itself with a sort of quiet and autonomous frequency. She wears slippers and black mesh shorts and an old high school track shirt, and draped over the whole mess is the long gray knit cardigan that Donna had bought her for her seventeenth birthday. The same sweater that Alice had proclaimed to *loathe* before shoving it to the back of her closet.

Alice takes a sip of wine and swaddles herself in the cardigan, pulling it across her shoulders like it's woolen chain mail.

Donna wipes her hands against her apron. "I didn't know if you could hear me."

"Well, I could."

Donna smiles. She reminds herself again that this is nice. That even though Eloise is spending the holidays in London with Ollie's family, having at least two of her children home is nice. A blessing, particularly now that she spends so many days in this rambling, falling-apart house, alone. Yes, all right, Paul has warned her that he'll have to spend much of his time in his room, working on his thesis. And maybe Alice isn't *really* Alice—the drugs the doctors prescribed her after she returned from Mexico City have whittled away her personality in ways that Donna is still trying to understand, sharpening some corners while dulling others. Still, though: *nice*. The warming sound of footsteps as someone other than she moves around upstairs. Coming into the kitchen in the morning to discover, happily, that Paul or Alice has made coffee. For these peculiar comforts, she's happy to entertain the strange ghosts of her children's other lives.

Donna hears Paul open and close a door.

She says, "I can't tell if this thing's done. Does it look done to you?"

Alice steps forward, though she's still halfway across the kitchen from the oven. "Yeah. Sure."

"*Alice.*"

"*Mom.* I've never made a turkey, all right?" She slept until eleven, but she still sounds exhausted. "What's the meat thermometer say?"

"It says it's done, but I don't know." Donna glances back at the bird. "Don't you think it looks a little . . . *pale* still?"

Alice shrugs. She leans against the counter and takes another sip of wine.

Donna closes the oven door. She figures another fifteen minutes can't hurt. The last thing she needs is one of them ending up in the hospital with worms.

She says, "Alice?"

"Yes?"

"Should you really be . . . I mean, is it a good idea to be drinking on the . . ."

"The crazy-person pills I'm taking?"

Donna reaches back to untie the apron.

"You're always so *hard* on yourself."

Alice leans across the counter for an open bottle of pinot noir, and Donna watches as she drains what's left of it into her glass.

"They only say that because alcohol is a depressant, and the fuck-ups who typically take pills like Klonopin are depressed." She throws the empty bottle into the recycling bin below the sink. "Thankfully, while I may be your typical fuck-up, I am not, categorically, depressed."

"All I'm saying is that maybe it would be a good idea to slow down. It's hardly noon."

"Mom. *Donna.*"

Donna winces. "Yes, dear?"

"I'm an adult."

"I know that, sweetheart."

"I can make adult decisions."

"Of course you can."

"So *please* stop—"

The angry thuds of Paul galloping down the stairs interrupt her. He slides into the kitchen wearing only his socks and a pair of pajama bottoms. He needs to eat more, Donna thinks, glancing at his ribs. He needs a haircut, and he needs to eat more.

"Mom?" he says.

"What can I get you, sweetheart?"

"What'd you do with Dad's chair?"

"Which chair?"

"Don't play dumb."

Donna drapes her apron over the back of a chair. She notices a small puddle of water on the countertop next to the sink, and to avoid having to look at her son, she begins wiping it up.

"I'm sorry, honey, I don't know what chair you're talking about."

"Then come here," Paul says, and pushes open the door that leads out of the kitchen. Reluctantly, she follows him into the living room and finds him standing in the empty spot where Bill's old leather armchair had sat for thirty years, its existence now reduced to a darkened square of carpet.

"Here," Paul says, pointing at the ground. "Dad's chair used to be *here.* I . . . I came down here because I wanted to sit in it while I read, but now it's gone. So I'm asking you: *What did you do with it?"*

She looks at him squarely and says, "I got rid of it."

"I was going to take that chair to New York with me, Mom."

"I'll get you another chair."

"That's not the point!" He grabs the back of his head and looks around the room. Donna stares at the ceiling. "Wait," he says. "*Wait.* Where are all the pictures of Dad?" He rushes over to the bookcase, where Donna's rearranged pictures of Paul, and Alice, and Eloise. "There were like *ten* pictures that had Dad in them in this room. What happened to them?"

What was she supposed to say to him? Without hearing some approximation of the truth—the very thing she'd so consciously kept from him— how would he ever understand her choice to rid the house of Bill and the conflicting memories she had of him? How could he empathize with that peculiar feeling she experienced six months ago, when the rawness of her grief gave way to logic and rationality?

All she says is "I got rid of them, too."

February 10, 2012

Janice reaches forward from the second pew and hands Donna a balled-up Kleenex.

"You've got some mascara on your cheeks, hon," she whispers.

"What? Oh, geez."

Donna dabs at her eyes, even though she knows it's useless; she'll start sobbing again just as soon as the service begins, which will be any minute now. Next to her, Eloise wraps and unwraps her own tissue around her middle finger. Her cheeks are flushed and damp, though still, even under the weight of her grief, she maintains a dignified posture, her shoulders pulled back and her spine elongated. Donna watches her daughter as she stares at a spot on the stairs leading up to the altar, where a blown-up, framed picture of Bill stands between two vases stuffed with lilies. She had a hard time deciding on it. Initially, she wanted to find a photo of him right before he died—or, at least, right before the cancer hit. Something that caught how people most recently remembered him. It seemed crass to throw up some glamour shot of her husband from thirty years ago, she thought; some athletic portrait where he appeared farthest from what he lately was, which was broken and in the early stages of decay. But finding evidence of the most recent Bill proved to be harder than she expected; over the past few years, they'd had little occasion to take pictures. Their children were all grown, all living independent, separate existences in different states and foreign countries. And their own lives—Donna's and Bill's—hardly required documentation; their weekends were most often spent trying to conceive of ways of acknowledging each other's company while staying in separate rooms. The pictures they did have were awkward or blurry—snapshots that were taken reluctantly, with the knowledge that this would be one more thing they'd have to find a place for, one more object they'd have to file away.

And so she'd gone against her initial intuition. She chose a picture of him from thirty-some-odd years ago, when he still had a full head of chestnut hair, and his face wasn't bloated or creased. He must have been thirty-four, she figured. Maybe thirty-five? He was wearing waders and a canvas vest covered in fishhooks. A craggy, dust-colored peak loomed in the background. It was their honeymoon. A camping trip to somewhere in Yellowstone. It had been his idea. She hadn't been camping since an ill-fated Girl Scout trip in junior high school, and privately she wasn't too keen on giving the whole thing another go. Still, though, she'd agreed. She reasoned that Bill was a new start—not just for her, but for Eloise—and camping was just about the furthest thing away from Henrique.

There were bugs, she remembers. Bugs, and strange phantom sounds that kept her up at night. Wind brushing the loose fabric of the tent. The sense of a million eyes watching her when she crept out to pee. She hardly slept. She wishes she'd chosen another picture.

The priest speaks about Bill fighting admirably against the sickness that took him, about him being in God's hands now, and about faith being a bedrock. His voice is too lulling. Donna worries that the hundred or so people who've gathered to pay their respects to her husband might drift off and fall asleep. She tries to remember the last time she and Bill were in this church. A decade ago, probably. Could easily be more. She wonders how the priest cobbles together his eulogies in situations like this: if he has a stash of ecclesiastical Mad Libs for those occurrences when he has to preside over the death of a total stranger.

She thinks of her children. She wants to drill inside their heads, to split them open and excavate their thoughts. She wants to know what they are feeling, and what forms those feelings take. Are they enduring the same bowel-loosening cocktail of heartbreak, memory, grief, and, above all, regret? Do they, too, feel daunted by the years of obscure and shapeless loneliness that now lie before them? And amid all that, do they find themselves clinging to the unexpected and sickening bits of pleasure that come from having a dead father? All that wonderful sympathy and attention?

Eloise reaches over to hold Alice's hand: Alice, whose eyes are enviously dull, Donna thinks, like she's watching a rerun on mute. Over a sullen breakfast that morning, Paul accused her of taking more Klonopin than what her doctors in Mexico City had prescribed.

"I saw you this morning in the bathroom," he yelled, throwing two cold eggs and a piece of toast into the trash compactor. "It's like you *want* to look like some dead, lifeless fish at your own dad's service."

"It's a funeral, Paul," Alice had said. "What were you hoping I'd do, the fucking Macarena?"

Donna had tried half heartedly to prevent a fight from erupting, and when Eloise stepped in to play peacemaker, she'd slipped upstairs to the bathroom that Paul and Alice shared. She rummaged through the amber vials in her daughter's toiletries bag until she found one labeled *Clonazepam (generic for Klonopin)*, and, unscrewing the childproof top, she shook three of the tiny yellow pills onto her palm. Paul and Alice continued fighting directly below her—their voices pressed up against her feet—as she neatly lined the Klonopin up along the center of her tongue. In a moment she felt the tablets melting, mixing with her saliva. They tasted sweet, which surprised her, not at all chalky and medicinal, like aspirin, but more like cheap drugstore candy. But then something gripped her. Responsibility, she figured. Or, perhaps more accurately: guilt. She spit the pills into the toilet bowl and watched as they danced toward the bottom, staining the water gold.

"And now it's my understanding that we've got some folks who'd like to say a few words about Bill."

Feedback whines over the speakers.

The priest adjusts the microphone pinned to his robe.

"And so first I'd like to introduce Bill's son, Paul Wesley Wyckoff."

Contained and apprehensive applause ripples through the church. At the far end of the pew, Paul stands up and quickly brushes the wrinkles from his suit. In his right hand he clutches a set of papers—a speech—folded in half.

"Hello," he says, once he reaches the podium. "I, uh. Excuse me." He unfolds the speech. His voice cracks.

Donna wishes she'd taken Alice's pills when she had the chance. Because now her spine sweats and bile churns at the base of her throat. She swallows hard, and worries that she might vomit.

April 5, 2008

Donna hangs up the phone.

"Well, there you have it," she calls into the kitchen. When Paul called, he asked if both his parents could be on the phone. Donna took the old one in the living room, and Bill cradled the cordless next to the stove.

She looks at the vase of hydrangeas sitting on the coffee table and waits for her husband to say something.

When he doesn't, she says: "At least now we can stop pretending to be interested whenever he talks about some girl he's just met."

Looking at her nails, she frowns: they're a mess. A bunch of chipped paint and shreds of ragged cuticle skin. She'll drive to the Charlestowne Mall tomorrow and get a manicure.

Bill appears in the doorway that leads from the living room to the kitchen. He's poured two glasses of red wine, big ones, and she can tell he's already had one without her. He frowns at something imperceptible; he moves with drunk determination.

"I can't believe it," he says.

"What, that Paul's gay?" Donna reaches forward and readjusts the vase; the hydrangeas were off-center. "Oh please, Bill. He collected My Little Ponies as a kid. His favorite movie was *Sister Act*."

Bill collapses into his armchair—an old leather mound with a torn back that Donna's been waging a war of attrition against since they got married.

"Maybe he'll grow out of it," he says.

"I can't tell if you're kidding or not."

He swallows half his glass of wine and sets it on a side table, next to a copy of the second volume of Robert Caro's biography of Lyndon Johnson.

"He needs to grow out of it," he says this time.

Donna balks. "I'm sorry, what is this? Nineteen fifty-seven? Is Eisenhower still president? Our son's gay, Bill. People are gay. THERE ARE GAYS AMONG US. You were fine when Dick and Judy Parsons's daughter came out as a lesbian, why—"

"That wasn't our own kid. And lower your voice."

"What, you're afraid that the neighbors might hear us?" She stares at her glass of wine, but she doesn't touch it; she's too infuriated to drink. "We've *talked* about this. When he was sixteen and we thought there might be a chance, we talked about what we'd do if he ever came out."

Bill shakes his head. "That was all just speculation. It wasn't real. This— this is real."

"He was hoarding copies of *International Male* catalogs beneath his bed!"

"You were snooping."

Donna wants to scream. Instead, she grabs the nearest throw pillow and presses it against her face, breathing into the frayed silk. That tone that she so hates has begun to creep into his voice; a cadence and tenor that reminds her of the way her own father kept her mother in check. *You and the kids can play like you're in charge*—that's what she knows he's actually saying. *But at the end of the day, I pay the bills.*

Bill clears his throat.

"He needs to figure this out before he comes home again."

Donna lowers the pillow.

"Figure what out? This is nuts."

"He needs to get over this 'I'm gay' crap. Until that happens, he's not welcome here."

She doesn't know whether to laugh or throw the vase at him, hydrangeas and all. Studying his face, she waits for him to take it back, to soften the blow, to realize his own sudden absurdity.

And when he doesn't, she simply says: "No."

"Excuse me?"

"I said *no*, Bill. No. He's our son. He can come home whenever he damned well pleases."

"Donna, I pay the mortgage here. I pay—"

"Oh, you pay, you pay, you *pay*. And what, you think that puts you in charge?"

He starts to say something, but she has no interest in hearing it.

"I see you sitting there, in that *god*awful chair, thinking that you're somehow brave for . . . for I don't know what, to be honest. For sticking to your guns? For suddenly deciding to have a belief about something? Well, you're not, Bill. And I don't have a problem telling you that. You're acting gutless, and that's the truth. You're acting like a goddamned coward."

He finishes his wine and crosses one leg over the other. She wonders how long that stupid biography of Johnson has been sitting there. She wonders if he'll ever get around to reading it.

"And what, you think you're being some liberal hero? Allowing our son to choose this life for himself?"

"No one's choosing anything. And no, I'm not a hero, Bill. You accept your son for who he is and where he's at not because you're heroic, but because you love him."

She stands up and reaches for her glass of wine.

"I haven't changed my mind," he says. "He gets this taken care of, or he doesn't come home."

Donna drinks, swallows, and runs her tongue across her teeth.

She says, "Yeah? Then how about this: Unless you wake the fuck up from this bigoted, Neanderthal dream of yours, I'm leaving you. You got that? I'm out of here, and I'll tell the kids exactly why I left."

She finishes her wine and watches the color slowly drain from his face.

February 10, 2012

Paul sobs through the last paragraph of his eulogy, and so does everyone else. As Donna watches them, she begins to cry herself, though for reasons only she can understand. She hadn't left Bill, though perhaps she should have. The truth is that he loved her more than she loved him—that had always been the case, and it always would be—and she used that terrible fact to her advantage when she blackmailed him two years ago. *You wouldn't leave me,* he'd said, testing her when she threatened. *Oh, yes,* she'd responded, *I would.* They'd both known that she'd meant it, too. Because like all relationships, theirs was one in which one party had settled; in which, in the event of some dissolution, one party would leave with less heartache, less anguish, less personal unraveling. And that party, of course, was her. She'd thrown her ace on the table, and now Bill faced the awful reality of loss.

What did she want him to do, he asked. How could he get her to stay?

"Don't ever mention this conversation" is what she'd said. "You act happy when you see him. You love him like you've always loved him. I don't care if you have to pretend. You do what you need to do."

He agreed. It was a bitter resignation, but she didn't care; she knew that the unbalanced nature of their love would compel Bill to keep his word, no matter how spiteful he became, and that was all the assurance Donna needed. Paul was a fragile and sentimental boy who had grown into a slightly less fragile and sentimental man, someone who lived in romantic superlatives, that the truth could so readily destroy. Still, watching him now as he descends the shallow stairs from the pulpit, his shoulders folding in on themselves, Donna wonders if she did the right thing.

They had been close, after all. While Paul had gravitated toward Donna when he was a boy, when he reached adolescence he withdrew from her and began spending more time with Bill. At first she was hurt—in so many ways she'd come to view Paul as special, a more exact mirror of her than Alice had ever been—but in time she quietly accepted the shift in alliances. She understood that Paul craved a masculine energy, something that could reaffirm the parts of himself that he'd suddenly begun to doubt. And so, she let him go.

Alice stands as Paul returns to the pew. She holds him as he cries, his body convulsing.

As for Donna, she's only told one person of that awful agreement she and Bill had made: Eloise. It happened two nights before her husband died, when the doctors informed her his death was imminent and her children, at her urging, flew back to Chicago. Paul and Alice had left the hospital for the evening, but Eloise remained at Bill's bedside with Donna, where they both watched him sleep, his skin already gray and cold. Listening to the incessant chirping of the machines that were tracking Bill's death, Donna wrestled with what to say to her daughter. She knew she had to tell someone. For the past four years, she had felt the secret slowly eating at her. It existed on the fringes of whatever wan happiness she felt, threatening always to flood in; she'd be in the garden, enjoying herself, when she'd suddenly remember the deception that belied that brief moment of peace. Briefly, she'd considered telling Alice, but that thought quickly faded. She knew the fierce loyalty that Alice felt toward Paul, as well as her father; the news would thrust her into an impossible position. For better or worse, though, Eloise floated along the peripheries of those relationships. No matter how hard she tried to crack Paul and Alice, they wouldn't let her in. Instead, they were content to relegate her to a pedestal—but a pedestal built of spite and malice. Watching her eldest daughter try to find equal footing with her half siblings used to break Donna's heart—and in many ways it still did. Now, though, as Bill took his last shallow breaths, she realized this distance had its advantages.

Swallowing the dregs of the coffee she'd spent the last four hours drinking, Donna told her. She just came right out with it.

Eloise listened, and when Donna was finished, she nodded. "I suspected as much."

"You did?"

"The last few times we were all together he treated Paul like an absolute stranger."

They were quiet for a moment, and Donna remembered last Christmas, when she screamed at Bill for being so cold to his son. She'd spent the holiday terrified that Paul was going to ask her if something was wrong, if he'd done something to upset his father, and she'd have no choice but to come clean. He didn't, though, and Donna was once again thankful for how convincing denial could be.

"Please don't say anything to Paul," she asked Eloise. "Or Alice."

Her daughter took her hand. "I'd never do that, Mom."

November 22, 2012

It'd been a gradual scrubbing away of Bill, not a full-blown yard sale. That's what she wants to tell Paul, but she knows it won't matter. The process won't interest him so much as the end result: his father has vanished. For the past thirty minutes she's been following him through the house, enduring his lashings as he's embarked on a full cataloging of all his father's possessions that are now missing: golf clubs, clothes, a fly-fishing rod. In short: everything.

"Oh my God," he says, burying his face in his hands, "this is fucked. This is so fucked."

She looks to her daughter for some kind of support, but all Alice does is finish her glass of wine. Donna crosses to the sink, where two pounds of boiled potatoes steam in a colander. After fetching a pot and a carton of cream, she starts mashing them. Anything to distract herself, she thinks, anything to keep her from looking at Paul.

"You did this because you hated him," he says. His ribs heave and expand with each breath.

She doesn't say anything. Instead, she runs cool water over a bunch of carrots and watches it splash against the counter, making a mess. She wonders if her son can tell that her pulse has quickened, if he can hear it thumping against her temples. She wants, desperately, to tell him the truth. She wants to explain how, once the pain of Bill's death had subsided, the only thing she could focus on was getting rid of him and the terrible lies he left in his wake. She wants to explain that her reason was him, was Paul; that after surviving her second disaster of a marriage, all that she had left was what actually mattered: her children. And she almost does—she almost tells him all this. After pummeling the mashed potatoes to a milky consistency, she almost lays everything bare, and saves herself the horror of falling on her sword. Her mouth opens, and she has it all there, stored in the base of her lungs. But then, suddenly, she stops. She doesn't. Her own devastation has been enough for one lifetime, she figures; there's only so much disappointment one family can be expected to take.

She says, instead, "Your father wasn't the man I thought he was, and we needed a change."

A half-finished glass of water sits next to the stove, and Paul hurls it against the wall.

Alice stands up, steadies herself, and leaves the room.

"Bullshit," Paul says. "You're embarrassed by him. *That's* why you did it."

Donna stirs an extra tablespoon of butter into the potatoes and watches it melt.

"You always thought you downgraded when you married Dad," Paul says. "Just because he wasn't some rich French asshole."

Reaching for a knife to chop the carrots, she cuts her finger.

"You're right," she says, and closes her eyes.

"I knew it. You married Dad so you'd have someone to pay the bills, and now that he's gone you can go back to pretending you're special. Well, guess what, Mom, Dad was special to *me*. And now you're . . . what? You're trying to erase him from our goddamned lives."

She wraps a paper towel around the cut.

"He should be erased. I was young and desperate. It was a mistake to marry him, and an even bigger mistake to waste thirty years of my life with him."

Her finger throbs, and she feels her anger pulse with it. Finally, she bursts. She stares at Paul and says, "There, are you happy now?"

Ten minutes later, her son is gone.

June 10: Present

She presses the phone to her ear. "Paul?"

Her throat still burns from the pot, and she coughs.

She says, "Is that you?"

"Who the hell else would it be?"

Her mind gets wrapped up in the question; she's thinking through a screen.

"How are you, sweetheart?"

"I just assaulted my boss and lost my job."

"That sounds lovely."

She realizes immediately that was the wrong response, and she should probably correct herself, but she doesn't—she's just so happy to hear his voice again.

"If you're going to be a bitch, I'll just hang up."

Donna stands up and knocks her knee against the coffee table. Pain radiates up her thigh.

"Ow, *shit,*" she says. "No, honey, wait. Please don't hang up. I'm so sorry about your job. It's just . . ." She searches for the words. They're there somewhere, she knows, hiding behind a wall of smoke. "It's just so good to talk again."

"I know why you've been calling." He's curt, unfriendly, transactional. It's not good to hear him again, she decides. He's acting like an asshole.

"You do?"

"Eloise's wedding."

She reaches down and rubs her knee. "Well, that's one reason. But also it's been two and a half years since—"

"I'll go, all right? So you can stop calling from random Indiana numbers to beg me. Because I'm fucking going."

PART TWO

Everybody has a heart.
Except some people.
—BETTE DAVIS,
All About Eve

Mark

Paul's a wreck. Mark looks on from the kitchen as, in the living room, Paul slides farther down on the couch and rubs his face, panicked. He taps his forehead before kicking his feet up, the muddy heels of his loafers slamming down on the coffee table. Or, specifically, on top of the first edition of Irving Penn's *Moments Preserved* that Mark had unexpectedly (and ecstatically) stumbled upon last year at Cappelens Forslag in Oslo. He'd bought that book with the money he was given when he won the Gunnar Myrdal award for the paper that put him on the map at Penn: a study of risk distribution and reindeer herding among Swedish Sami populations, with a particular focus on the two winter cycles of that peoples' eight-season calendar: Tjakttjadálvvie and Dálvvie (the Season of the Journey and the Season of Caring, respectively). In fact, now that he's remembering, he paid nearly a thousand dollars for that book (which was roughly half the price of the coffee table, which he'd also bought), and now he watches as dirt and grime and guilt and whatever else Paul's tracked home from Main Line Philadelphia smears across its glossy jacket.

He opens his mouth to say something, but he stops himself. *Generations of observation and experience have taught the Sami that the risks of startling a reindeer when it's confused or straying from the herd far outweigh the rewards of correction; a startled reindeer will often stumble or fall while fleeing along high, steep slopes, resulting in death or injury.*

"There was blood everywhere," Paul says. "Like, *everywhere*. I guess I hit him pretty square-on, because I swear he was bleeding out of his eyes."

Mark says, "Can I get you anything?"

"A whiskey, I guess."

He wrestles two ice cubes from a tray and pours some Knob Creek into a tumbler. Typically he'd keep it to two fingers—Paul gets irritating and needy when he's drunk—but given tonight's circumstances, he fills the glass a little more than halfway.

"Here you go."

"Thanks." Paul takes a long sip and sinks farther into the couch. "I had to pinch his nose and help him hold his head back while we waited for the ambulance."

"I still don't see why an ambulance was necessary."

"Too many people at the clinic are terrified of blood. Germs, you know? Didn't stop them from pressing their faces against the window and gawking as Goulding ripped me a new one, though." Another long sip. "In any event, it was humiliating."

"And then you got fired."

Paul stares down into his glass. He swirls the ice. "And then I got fired. The man's blood was *literally on my hands,* and he fired me." Paul's voice softens. "At least he's not going to press charges. He said he wanted to be the bigger man."

Mark frowns and works through a series of mental calculations. Paul's pay at the clinic was middling. Peanuts, really. Particularly when Mark compared it to the ludicrous raise he demanded from the university, and received, once he'd snagged the Myrdal award. If anything, what Paul brought back from the clinic afforded them cash for booze, and pretty shitty booze, at that. But there were other risks at play. The biweekly paycheck provided Paul with a sense of worth, however small, which was crucial to his own delicate process of self-actualization. A process that Mark has been gently guiding for the duration of their relationship.

He frowns harder: he wonders if a pint-sized mannequin has derailed his efforts. He needs to work on Paul's temper.

"You're disappointed in me," Paul says.

"What? That's crazy." Mark wraps an arm around him. "Goulding was an asshole." He pulls Paul closer. "If this hadn't happened, I was planning on telling you to quit, anyway."

"Yeah?"

"Yeah. That place was a madhouse."

He strokes Paul's shoulder until he feels it relax, and then he stops.

He loosens his tie.

"And look at it this way—now you won't have to beg for time to go to the wedding."

Paul drains the rest of the whiskey. He says, "I know that you think I should go, and I already told you that I'm going to. You win, okay? Christ, I called Donna this afternoon for the first time in two and a half years to tell her as much."

Mark feels the tug of victory, but he resists a smile. *A reindeer wanders away from the herd toward a craggy precipice. The Sami approach it gently, calmly. A dead buck means three less calves come spring.*

He rubs Paul's leg. "I'm sorry, kid. I shouldn't have brought it up. I know you're stressed."

"It's fine. And it was nice of you to offer to come along with me, though I wouldn't wish this wedding on my worst enemy." Paul buries his face in his hands, and Mark prays that he doesn't start crying, though he knows that awkward moment is inevitable.

"God, I'm such a mess."

Tears rage against the floodgates, threatening to burst them open. Mark grabs Paul's head and buries it against his chest. He looks past the errant wisps of blond hair toward the framed Munch print that hangs on the opposite wall. He wonders if it's crooked.

"Hey," he says. "*Hey*. Knock that off, all right? You're not a mess. At all."

Paul's tears form damp patches on Mark's shirt, and his nose runs against his tie. Mark does his best to ignore his irritation over an unscheduled trip to the dry cleaner. The painting's definitely crooked.

"And you're doing the right thing. Going to Eloise's wedding. That's the right thing to do, and I'm happy to do it with you." He adds, "In fact, I'll start looking into tickets tomorrow."

Mark scrolls through the new messages in his inbox: Facilities will be closing early for the Fourth of July holiday. Non-tenure-track faculty members are demanding representation in university governance. Next week a visiting economist from Princeton will be giving a lecture on "inequality and stagnation" titled "The Greater Depression." Amanda Lyons, one of the students in Mark's summer-term Behavioral Economics survey course, wants to meet with him at eleven thirty about an essay that's due next Wednesday. He checks the clock next to his computer: eleven ten. He fires off a reply saying that he's happy to meet and banks on the hope that she won't check her e-mail in the next twenty minutes.

He scrolls through the inbox a second time to make sure he hasn't missed anything, and his frustration develops a dull, blunted edge. Not a single word from London.

Mark drums his fingers on the arm of his chair, then pushes back from the desk to admire his office. The books are what he looks at first: all hardcover first editions, alphabetized by author, and divided evenly among the room's three teak cases. In the space between them hang his diplomas—

the first recording his bachelor's in philosophy from Amherst; the second his Ph.D. from Columbia. They are displayed in matching Pottery Barn frames that cost $69.99 each. He knows this because, when Paul presented the framed diplomas to him as a sort of congratulatory gift for his appointment at Penn, he googled the price. Back then he'd done so because he was sensitive to how much money Paul had spent on him; he knew that Paul had moved to Philadelphia because of him, and he'd feel awful if his boyfriend had gone broke over a set of frames on his account. Mark was heartened by the gift. He'd still felt like an unqualified impostor in academe—and the little conscious gestures that Paul made to acknowledge his worth helped him feel like he belonged. Like he deserved to be there.

Now he thinks they look tacky, hanging there. The sort of self-conscious accoutrement you'd expect to find in a dentist's office, right next to a smiling, plush-toy tooth. He knows he can't take them down. Not yet, at least. Now that Paul's unemployed, he's liable to swing by at any moment, and if he were to see the diplomas off the wall—stacked in a corner, say—he'd be crestfallen. He'd get all wounded and teary eyed, like one of Mark's students whom he's just smacked with a D. So, he'll keep them up. For another year he'll let them hang there, gathering dust. Then, once Paul has forgotten about them—once some other minimal crisis has taken hold of his thoughts—Mark will quietly replace them with something else. A Gustaf Fjaestad print, maybe. Or a smartly framed Öyvind Fahlström. Lately, he's been really into Fahlström.

He walks over to a credenza (cherry, midcentury modern—these things matter) on the far side of the room and flips through a set of hanging file folders. They're color-coded and labeled with obvious, one-word titles: GRADES, COMMITTEES, PAUL. He's not looking for anything in particular so much as he's appreciating the organizational system that he's created. The clean, sharp edges of papers clipped together. The absence of Post-it notes and frantically written to-do lists. Meandering through the department's halls, he'll often find himself becoming mildly disgusted as he pays visits to his messier colleagues. The towering stacks of loose-leaf paper, threatening to topple over if anyone should dare open a window. Books left open on desks, their pages gaping like the ribs of some pathetic dismembered corpse. On two separate occasions, a sleeping bag, stuffed behind a plant with brown and brittle leaves. It's like they're trying to patch together nests, Mark thinks. A shitty tangle of twigs and trash. He'd seen something similar last February, on the fire escape outside the bedroom he shares with Paul. A pair of starlings had built it over the course of four industrious days. On the fifth day, Mark knocked it down. The squawking had turned unbearable.

Light spills onto the grass in front of College Hall, where two girls and a shirtless boy lounge with their arms propped up on the feet of a Benjamin Franklin statue. Typically, on a day like today, the lawn would be rammed with undergrads, and Mark would be driven to near paralysis over the options of chests to admire, of abdominal muscles to count. But it's July. The middle of summer term. The only students on campus are slackers with beer guts who failed a class last fall, or pasty strivers who've never set foot in a gym. Maybe the rare refugee who can't bear the thought of four months back in the suburbs. Point being: the options are not what they should be.

A knock startles him.

"Professor Gordon?"

Amanda Lyons doesn't wait for Mark to open the door—she knocks and comes right in. They all do.

Mark checks his watch: eleven thirty.

"You said you were available to meet now?"

She holds her iPhone up—evidence to justify her presence—and Mark sees the e-mail that he sent twenty minutes ago.

"Of course." He smiles and motions to a chair on the other side of his desk. "Take a seat."

Amanda blushes and lets her bag drop to the floor. She's dressed like she's ready for an afternoon date: frayed jean shorts that accentuate her tan legs, a spaghetti-strap tank top, a cream-colored cardigan that she's currently wriggling out of. Her face is caked with makeup. Many of his female students doll themselves up in similar fashion when they come to see him, and Mark appreciates the effort, the subtle acknowledgment that they're willing to pursue other arrangements to help their GPAs. It's misguided, of course, but Mark encourages it nonetheless. He likes the flaming chili pepper that appears next to his name whenever he checks ratemyprofessor.com.

"Right, then," Mark says. He leans back in his chair and presses the tips of his fingers together pedagogically. "What can I do you for?"

"I . . . I . . . " Amanda stutters and grins, realizing what Mark has just said. Then, composing herself, she mutters: "I don't think I'm doing this paper right. The one on altruism and fairness." She leans over to fish the draft out of her backpack. Brown hair falls in her face.

"Well, let's take a look." He stands, crosses to her side of the desk, and sits on its corner. He picks up a shard of reindeer antler that he found during his last trip to Lapland and strokes a smooth patch of bone. He says, "And remember, all I'm looking for here are your thoughts. Your response to the Knox and Wright texts. How are they speaking to each other? How are they complicating each other? There's no 'right' way to do this, per se."

He smiles again, pleased this time with the vagueness of academia. Stake-free crises couched in a lovely, untranslatable jargon.

"Right, no," Amanda says. She hands him the draft. A pink staple binds the pages together. "I know all that. I guess I'm worried that my ideas aren't, like, *flowing*? Like they aren't making sense or something?"

Mark scans the pages, his eyes stumbling past the reductive, empty sentences that he's come to expect from eighteen-year-old minds: *society shapes our identities; every individual is unique.* Couched between these half-assed attempts at thinking are a series of vulgar summaries of the readings Mark assigned last week.

Amanda scrolls through her phone. She double-taps a picture. She sends a text.

"You're doing good work," Mark says, and sits in the chair directly next to her.

Amanda looks up. "I am?"

"Sure you are." He flips to the second page. "I guess what I'm looking for now is more of your thinking, though. Here, for instance. You say that *everyone's good on the inside,* and that's why we're altruistic."

"Right?" She tucks her hair behind her ear, and tilts her head, showing Mark her neck.

"How true is that?"

"What do you mean?"

"Well, for starters, what's the 'inside'?"

"Huh?"

"Are you talking about the soul?"

"I . . . yeah. I guess that's what I mean."

Amanda's phone buzzes in her purse.

"So you're presupposing that a soul exists."

"You don't think that it does?"

Mark smiles. "What I think doesn't matter." He folds his arms across his chest. "When was the last time you did something nice for someone?"

She says, "Last week, I guess?"

Mark leans forward. "What'd you do?"

"Uh, my friend Lindsay was having this *massive* bed delivered to our sorority house, but she's doing some internship at a blog in New York this summer so she wasn't there to sign for it."

Mark crosses his legs. "So you were there to sign for her."

"Yeah," Amanda says.

"That was nice of you."

She adds, "It was on a Friday afternoon. They gave me, like, a four-hour window, and they were still an hour late."

Mark says, "You gotta hate that."

"I was happy to help, I guess." Amanda shrugs.

"But that's an interesting point," Mark says. "Were you happy to help? Or I guess the more vital question is: *Why* did you help?"

"Because it was the good thing to do?" she ventures. "Because she'd probably do it for me?"

"Tell me a little bit about Lindsay."

"She's the president of my sorority. Her dad's some big producer in L.A. She's from Malibu. Um . . ."

"Sounds like she's a good person to know."

"What do you mean?"

"Do you want her to like you?" Mark reaches again for the reindeer antler. "Do you think she likes you more for wasting four hours of *your* Friday to wait for her bed so she could cavort around New York City? Is that, maybe, why you agreed to do it?" Amanda shifts uncomfortably in her seat. "As opposed to, say, out of some theoretical, intrinsic, altruistic 'goodness'?" He turns the antler over in his hand. He remembers where he found it: in a bed of arctic cotton weed a mile east of Abisko. "Which begs the more fundamental question of when we think we're being *good*, are we really just desperately yearning to be *liked*?"

"Uh." Amanda looks down. Her cheeks glow red.

Mark's computer chimes: a new e-mail has arrived.

"Anyway." He stands, smiles, and shepherds Amanda toward the door. "Something to think about as you revise, at the very least."

The trio that was lounging in Franklin's shadow has scattered. Across the lawn Van Pelt Library is ablaze in midmorning glow; the tall windows that line its first floor are slabs of blinding white. Mark slides in front of the computer and clicks on the new message.

From: Alcott Cotwald <acotwald@lse.ac.uk>
To: Mark Gordon <gordonmark14@faculty.upenn.edu>
Date: June 20
Subject: Re: Incoming

Mark,
Agreed re: missing each other in Philadelphia. Positively sinful.
Thrilled, though, to hear that we'll finally be meeting face-to-face on this side of the pond. Well done on convincing Paul

to make the trek, and to spend the week "doing work" in London prior. Am unsure what said work will entail, though I'm sure I'll manage to come up with something (wink). Must admit, though, a wedding in Dorset sounds ghastly. Nothing but sheep and assaulting accents, I fear. But duties must be done, pensions paid, etc. Suppose that's love. Meantime, no more talk of hotels. You two shall stay here, in my flat on Bermondsey Street. It's not large, so we must think of ways to get creative with space. Oh well. Shall send you to the rural banality of the Jurassic Coast with fond memories of the city (double wink).

More forthcoming.
Alcott

"Hey. Kid." Mark shakes Paul's shoulder, but he just mumbles something and repositions himself in his seat. Turns his head. Pushes his left cheek against the British Airways insignia on the headrest. Mark shakes him harder.

"Paul. We're almost there."

He jolts and rubs his eyes.

"Huh?"

"The captain just announced that we've started our initial descent." Mark reaches into the seat-back pocket in front of him. He hands Paul a plastic-wrapped toothbrush and a small tube of Crest. "Go brush your teeth."

Paul rubs his eyes again. He unbuckles his seat belt and stumbles toward the bathroom. Mark lifts the window shade halfway and morning light spills into their row. Five miles below them, the English countryside rearranges itself geometrically. Squares and hexagons and other angular shapes are stamped out like grassy emeralds. He sips his coffee and digs a fingernail into the Styrofoam cup. He doesn't know why he told the flight attendant he wanted some. He rarely drinks the stuff. Boredom was the reason, he figures. Too much time vacillating between reading theoretical texts under a less-than-luminary light and watching Paul dream.

He's not tired, even though he didn't sleep. Not a single wink over the past six hours. But then, that's not necessarily surprising—he never sleeps on red-eyes. There are too many observations that require his attention, too many minor phenomena to study. The ways in which his fellow passengers attract and repel one another. How they share each other's space only to create individual burrows in their seats. Piles of blue felt blankets and paper-wrapped pillows. Avoidance turned into a communal effort. *Although they typically live in colonies, the arctic lemmings are predominantly solitary animals. They breed and feed alone—facts that prove problematic, given their tendency toward rash and individualistic decision-making.*

They land and clear customs and, once they're in a cab and on the way to Alcott's flat, Mark begins to wonder whether they should stop somewhere along the way so Paul can pull himself together a little bit more. He had him use the bathroom at Heathrow so he could wash his face and comb his hair, but dark circles still shadow his eyes, and his cheeks are red and creased, like he's had his face pressed against a grill for the past eight hours. Mark leans over and kisses his cheek: he could use a shave. And a clean shirt.

Traffic on the M4 is light, and the cab makes good time. Mark crosses his legs and Paul leans his head against the window. On each side of them the sloped roofs of West London align themselves in imperfect rows. Brick chimneys belch smoke. A council flat, a dusty cathedral, an old television antenna obscure the city's skyline.

Paul asks, "So what is it that you're going to be doing again?"

The cab swerves around a Fiat. Mark clears his throat.

"Alcott's running a clinic," he says. "Looking at the way capuchin monkeys approach risk and group problem solving in captivity. He's already gathered all the raw data. He just needs someone to help analyze it." He adds, "He said he'd give me a coauthor credit when he publishes."

"Where'd he observe them?"

"The monkeys?"

"Yeah." Paul yawns.

They hit traffic—a small, contained pocket of it—and the cab pulls up next to the sort of miniature white van that Mark associates with European florists.

"The London Zoological Society," he says.

"That's it?"

"I think so."

"Hardly seems accurate."

Paul runs a hand through his hair, and it stands straight up on its ends. He looks young—a freshman the morning after his first college party. Mark weighs potential opportunities: this could be a good or a bad thing, depending on Alcott's tastes.

He says, "Why's that?"

"Who's to say all monkeys are the same? Who's to say French monkeys don't do things differently than British ones?"

Paul tries to suppress a grin. He's unsuccessful. The cab jolts over a pothole, and he smiles.

Mark pinches his thigh, and the smile erupts into a laugh.

The traffic begins to open up, and cars unpeel themselves from one another. The cabdriver tunes the radio to the news and cranks up the volume. Gear up for another hot day in London.

"What night are we having dinner with your mother and sister?"

"I don't even want to think about it." Paul sighs and puffs his cheeks. Mark catches the driver eyeing them in the rearview mirror.

"I think you're going to be pleasantly surprised."

"I think the chances of that are very, very low."

"But what night . . ."

Paul says, "Tuesday. Of next week. Donna gets in the night before. And then on Friday Alice has to go to that godawful bachelorette party."

Mark reaches into his bag for a bottle of water.

"You're not even a little bit upset that you weren't invited?"

The blocks closer to the city's center are fuller, cleaner, better cared for, shedding the anemic sparseness of the exurbs.

"Why would I ever be invited?" Paul says. "I'm not a bachelorette."

"Of course you aren't." Mark laughs. "I just figured that, perhaps, she'd want to—"

"That would be so Eloise, though, wouldn't it?" Paul interrupts Mark, which Mark considers pointing out, but doesn't; he likes to let Paul believe that he controls some of their conversations. "Inviting her gay half brother to her bachelorette party? She's absolutely the sort of person who'd do that. Like, one of those women who thinks it's cute and novel, as opposed to *totally homophobic and demeaning,* to invite you over for a 'girls' night.' It's like, *no, bitch, that's not how it works.* Just because we both like cock doesn't mean you get to treat me like some paper doll with a dick." Paul snatches the water from Mark, takes a swig, and continues, "Frankly, though, I'm sort of shocked that she didn't ask me to be in the bridal party. Never mind the fact that we've hardly spoken in two years. I guarantee you that she'd be willing to look past that minor detail in order to get some bougie diversity points for having some faggot—or, *this* faggot, specifically—up there holding an overpriced bouquet."

Mark smiles. He lives for moments like this one. Moments when Paul loses himself on one of his rants. He finds them adorable, particularly when they're directed at him. He can't quite articulate why. He likens it to how he feels when he successfully convinces Paul to wear his unwashed shin-guards from college soccer when they have sex, or when he thinks of what it might be like to watch other men fuck him: it turns him on.

He uncrosses his legs and catches Paul's eye. He winks and glances down at his crotch, where his half-hard cock is pressing against his jeans.

"Knock it off," Paul says, and looks out the window. Quickly, he turns back to Mark. "You're sure this is all right with Alcott? Us crashing at his place for a week and a half?"

"He's got a spare room. He's excited to finally see us."

"But, I mean, a week and a half. That's a long time. You're sure?"

Mark nods and adjusts his jeans.

Men in London wear better pants, Mark thinks. He's watching a pair of twenty-something finance types order coffee from a kiosk stationed at the entrance of Somerset House. They've both got their hands shoved in their pockets, and the blue and gray fabric of their trousers stretches tightly over their thighs. He stares for a moment or two longer, and then qualifies his initial observation: Maybe it's not the pants so much as what the pants do to their asses. It's got something to do with how the wool accentuates their natural athleticism, he figures. At least based on what he's seen during the past hour, a pair of everyday British slacks has the potential to turn a Londoner's butt into something Mark can imagine eating for days. American men could never pull these pants off—this fact he's sure of. Their legs are too bulky, too hyperinflated with clownish musculature. He thinks of Crosby, back in Philadelphia, wearing a pair of Paul Smith slacks: a pair of hot dogs shoved into two empty Pixy Stix.

The two men finish their coffees and exit onto the Strand, where they're consumed by the ebb and flow of midweek London. Mark frowns. He misses them, instantly.

"And you said what again?" he hears Alcott say to Paul, his voice lilting.

"I, uh, I didn't say anything, really," Paul stammers. "I just . . . I threw the baby mannequin at him."

Alcott howls. "And it hit him in the bloody *face*."

"Yeah . . . that's right."

"That's brilliant."

Mark turns from them and rolls his eyes. He's pleased that Alcott's enjoying Paul—that's a good sign—but privately he fears how many times he'll have to endure the melodrama of How Paul Lost His Job. He wonders how other people do it, how they're able to suffer through their lovers' retelling the same tired stories without reaching for a noose.

From the little table where they're sitting drinking lukewarm bottles of Perrier, he lets his gaze wander across the vast court of Somerset House. Children splash in the twenty or so tiny geysers of the fountain at the center of the square. Above them loom ancient stone bricks, ashy columns, and, finally, the House's green copper dome. Along the outskirts of the fountain tourists wander around, taking pictures with their phones—of the dome, of the children, of the gray sky, of handwritten signs hawking juice and wine and coffee and beer. They're fat, mostly. Fat and pink, their feet crammed into shoes with sturdy soles and cushioned supports. It had been Paul's idea to come here. This morning, over breakfast, when they were tossing around options of how they might spend the day, Alcott suggested that they visit an out-of-the-way pub he knew somewhere in East London. Paul, though, had practically begged for them to visit Somerset House instead. He said that he'd been there once before, nearly a decade ago when he came to London with his mother to visit Eloise, and that he remembered Somerset being "gorgeous" and "heartbreaking," but that, looking back, he suspected he had been too hungover from the night prior to properly appreciate it.

Mark had scoffed at the notion, and had felt a stinging parental chagrin over Paul's lack of taste. "For Christ's sake," he'd said. "Somerset House. Why don't we just take a ride on the London Eye while we're at it."

Paul excused himself and said that he was going for a walk; Mark finished his bowl of muesli and asked Alcott for a fresh towel so he could shower.

And then what had happened? Alcott had entered the bathroom, right as Mark was beginning to work conditioner through his hair. Over the steady splash of water-against-skin-against-tile, he'd heard the door creak open, and then the confident baritone of Alcott's voice: "Mind if I brush my teeth while you're in there?" Remembering the scene for the hundredth time, Mark chuckles: It had been a polite and marvelous question, but a silly one, too. Because of *course* Mark didn't mind. Earlier he'd practically extended Alcott a formal invitation to join him: disrobing down to his boxer shorts, then passing through the kitchen to linger while Alcott tidied up, absently stroking the line that ran from his chest to his belly button (should he have trimmed the hair on his stomach?) as he drank a glass of water. Still, despite his sureness, Mark was gripped with uncertainty as he waited for Alcott to make his move. And as each second passed, as the bubbles found new ways to coat his slick skin, this uncertainty grew in unfathomable ways. Grew so much, in fact, that when he did indeed hear the door open, when his predictions were confirmed, he experienced a rush of ecstasy at the sheer prospect that he had been so right—a sensation that manifested itself as an electric tingle, buzzing at the end of his prick.

"Sure," Mark had called out from the shower. "Come on in."

He listened while Alcott turned on the sink, and while he brushed his teeth. And when he reached to open the shower's curtain, Mark was there, rinsed of soap and half hard, ready to face him.

"So I was thinking," Alcott started. A smudge of toothpaste marred his lower lip. Mark would have to lick it off for him.

"Yes?"

Alcott's eyes fell to Mark's stomach, and then to his cock—which, God be good, was still half hard, maintaining the girth that it lacked in its bored and flaccid state. Mark willed more blood to rush to his groin—he wanted Alcott to watch it grow—but for some confounding reason, his body refused to cooperate. His dick just stood there, dangling at half-mast.

"We should go to Somerset House."

"Excuse me?"

Alcott reached up and wiped the toothpaste from his mouth. "It's not that bad, Mark. It's not like Paul's asked to go to Buckingham Palace. If he wants to go to Somerset House, we should go. We have all the time in the world to get drunk in pubs."

Mark felt himself shrinking. He wanted to close the curtain.

"Fine," he said. "Somerset House, though I refuse to pretend to be pleased about it."

"Good man." Alcott smiled. Then, he said, "Oops. Looks like you missed a spot." A cluster of soap suds still clung to Mark's left thigh, and with a single finger, Alcott reached forward and flicked it off before shutting the curtain and exiting the room.

And thank God for that, Mark thinks now. Brushing soap from his leg was hardly the orgasmic equivalent of a highly skilled hand job (his assumption was that Alcott was highly skilled), but in terms of significance, of implications, it bore the same weight. What would Mark have done if Alcott had simply closed the curtain? If he had simply defended Paul's awful suggestion, and then left? Mark doesn't want to think about it, mostly because it's a ludicrous impossibility. As if he's capable of so woefully misjudging Alcott's intentions—or, even less plausibly, his own.

Paul continues to revel in his own misfortune, and Alcott continues to indulge him. Mark finishes his Perrier and smacks his lips. Four steps in front of him, a tourist wearing a plastic backpack takes a selfie with a gold iPhone. *Ah, Somerset House.* Why does he hate it so much? He supposes it's for the same reason that he hates places like New York, or Paris, or Venice, or Rome. Places that were once interesting and authentic, but have since forged some pact with Global Tourism to become picturesque caricatures of themselves. Well-lit dollhouses meant to be admired by the Other, instead of occupied by the native. Where else is there to escape to? Berlin, maybe, but that won't last long; he's read too many *New York Times* travel section pieces on the place to believe it has a chance of escape. Scandinavia's headed for the same vulgar fate, too, he fears. All those Danish and Swedish television shows getting new, American treatments. A girl's bloated body is found in a misty lake, except this one's outside Portland, instead of on the outskirts of Copenhagen. It's only a matter of time before hordes of fat Indianans in search of chunky sweaters do a bit of googling and start booking tickets to Denmark.

"That, Paul, is quite a story." Alcott wipes a few tears from his eyes. Was Paul's account of his catastrophe at the clinic really that funny? Had Mark missed something crucial in the initial telling of it? Or, is it possible that Alcott finds Paul genuinely and sincerely charming? Mark stops himself: he's above jealousy. It's a pedestrian emotion, one reserved entirely for the naïve and the insecure.

"Isn't it?" he says. "I get a kick every time Paul tells it."

"And I can see why!" Alcott stands. "If you'll excuse me for a moment, I've got to run to the loo. But once I'm back, why don't we stroll around a bit? We've still got a few hours before I've got to take leave for that dreadful faculty meeting." He appraises the buildings on each side of him. "It's been ages since I've been to Somerset House. I'd forgotten just how gorgeous the old pile of bricks is."

Mark says, "I think that's a lovely idea."

Alcott trots over to a visitor's center, and once he's out of earshot, Mark shifts his chair so he can face Paul.

"Great guy, isn't he?"

"He is. Very accommodating."

"And that accent." Mark leans back, and the front two legs of his chair lift from the ground. "Christ, have you ever heard such a sexy voice?"

Paul's peeling the label from his bottle of Perrier. He rolls the paper into a tight cylinder and drops it into the bottle.

He says, "Look, I know what you're doing, all right?"

Mark lets the chair's front legs drop back to the ground. "What do you mean?"

"Oh, come on, Mark."

"Seriously, I have no idea what you're talking about."

"A little subtlety never killed anyone," Paul says. He stands and gathers the three empty bottles. "That's all I'm saying."

Alice

The customs agent flips through Alice's passport, first assessing her biographical information and then glancing at her photo. Alice wants to point out that she was ten pounds heavier when the picture was taken, and that she was going through an unfortunate flirtation with bangs, but she keeps her mouth shut. This woman's seen worse, she tells herself, turning to glance at the line of haggard travelers behind her. She sees worse every day.

The agent examines the rest of the passport, and Alice thinks of her paltry collection of stamps: evidence of travel in exotic places like Canada, and Mexico, and the Bahamas. She clears her throat.

"It's a new passport. My old one was practically overflowing with stamps," she lies. "Qatar was my favorite."

The agent tucks a loose curl of red hair back into her cap.

"Business or pleasure?" she says.

"Pardon?"

"Are you here for *business* or *pleasure?*"

Alice considers the question. She rolls her left shoulder back and feels the joint pop in its socket. Behind her she hears the tired, gray discontent of people who've spent twelve hours on a plane to wait in a line, a sound that she finds not entirely different than a hospital ward. The same squeaking shoes, the same cavernous halls.

"Well?"

"I'm here for a wedding," Alice manages.

"So, pleasure."

"I—"

But the agent's through with listening. She stamps Alice's immigration form and her passport, and motions for her to clear the line. Walking down a sterile corridor, she joins a growing trickle of other groggy, red-eyed travelers. This is the part of traveling she hates the most, she thinks, as she adjusts her purse. Not the crowds, exactly, but the stark realization that she's just like everyone else. She passes a single mother wrangling a pair of screaming toddlers in matching Lacoste polos, and she considers nipping off to the bathroom for a Klonopin before remembering, with crushing devastation, that she'd stupidly packed the pills in her checked bag. On the opposite side of two glass doors she emerges into Heathrow's international baggage claim, a labyrinthine mess of luggage and indecision against which Alice closes her eyes for a few stabilizing moments. She hears the dull thud of traveling bags and roller suitcases being belched onto conveyer belts; of achingly polite British women announcing flights arriving, flights boarding, flights departing; of people haggling for space in nonexistent lines; of a hundred different voices speaking a hundred different tongues, all homogenized by irritation and annoyance—those wonderful global neutralizers that, like smiles, transcend the binds of language. And then, within it all, her name:

"Alice!"

She opens her eyes and sees the young man who sat next to her on the plane waving. They'd talked briefly—he had woken her up when the flight attendant passed through the cabin with cups of lukewarm coffee—though she can't remember his name for the life of her. He's some sort of consultant—that she knows—and he travels often, he'd mentioned that during their short conversation, but God, what was his name? It sounded like a consultant's name, she remembers. Something inoffensive and milquetoast and easy to pronounce. Daniel? David? Or, no: Dennis. It was Dennis.

He maneuvers around a man unfolding a stroller and makes his way to her.

"I was getting worried they'd detained you back at immigration," he says. His voice has a friendly, Midwestern lilt.

She smiles, wanly.

"I, uh, I guess I got stuck in the back of the line."

Cracking his knuckles, he reaches into his back pocket for a piece of gum. He offers one to Alice, but she declines.

"Really? I've always got the worst taste in my mouth after those long flights. Anyway, the trick to immigration is not to hit the bathroom between the tarmac and customs. People always want to stop in, wash their face, brush their teeth. All that kind of stuff, particularly on these red-eyes. You've gotta just plow through, though. Otherwise you get caught waiting for an hour just to have your stupid passport stamped."

Alice nods and raises her eyebrows.

"Platinum status on Delta, remember?" He winks at her. "I've got all kinds of secrets."

How old is he? Alice thinks. When they were in the air she pegged him as mid-thirties—but that was under the weird, blue glow of airplane lighting, where everyone, with the exception of the very young and the very old, bears the same tired pallor of middle age. Now, on the ground, she's sure he can't be older than twenty-three. His clothes—a pair of gray work slacks and a blue button-down with a faint sheen—look vaguely expensive, and nice, but nice for a fifty-something white guy who'll never climb above middle management. Alice guesses that his dad bought him the outfit—a sort of go-get-'em-son present for Dennis's first job after finishing undergrad. From his shoulder hangs one of those tech-y messenger bags that consulting firms always give to their employees so they'll appear hip or edgy when they're competing with Google, or Facebook, to recruit new talent from business schools. Alejandro used to bitch about his all the time, Alice remembers, but that didn't keep him from lugging it to every corner of Mexico City.

The same black roller suitcase, marked by a silver ribbon tied clumsily around its handle, begins another lonely rotation along the conveyer belt. Alice wonders how many times she's seen it. Three, she thinks. Maybe four.

"I forgot how annoying it is to wait at baggage claim," he says. "Normally I'm only at a project site Monday through Thursday, so I just need a carry-on." Next to him, a woman's suitcase topples over. Alice reaches down to help right it, and Dennis keeps talking. "But this time I'm going to be here for two weeks. Because it's an international project. Man, the points that I'm going to get from this thing."

Alice grins again and grants Dennis a small laugh. He's got a gash of razor burn just beneath his chin, and he's smiling more than any adult should. Maybe he's cuter than she initially thought he was. Maybe the airport has lowered her standards of cuteness to a thrilling level of mediocrity. Either way, he's noticed her staring. She reaches down to adjust her shoe and, in doing so, balances herself on his shoulder, kneading his muscles slowly with her fingertips as she stands up straight again.

She feels compelled to say something.

"Where are you staying?" she asks.

"The W. Leicester Square."

This makes sense, Alice thinks. She'd originally predicted the Westin, or maybe a Sheraton. But the W: this makes sense.

An electric siren whirs, and new bags join the black roller suitcase with the silver ribbon. They tumble forward on to one another at awkward angles. Passengers jostle for a spot along the belt. Alice watches as, within seconds, a hundred little traffic jams erupt.

"How about you?" Dennis says.

"Claridge's." Alice clears her throat. "In Mayfair."

"Whooooooa." Dennis winks again. "Fan*cy*."

Alice smiles again, this time genuinely. *Claridge's*. It is fancy, isn't it? She pictures the website where she'd booked her room: rotating pictures of the hotel's grand brick façade, a line of Maseratis and Bentleys and Rolls-Royces guarding the entrance. Tiled interiors spotted with fresh flowers, leather armchairs, and portraits of British Ladies with tight faces and round asses. The room costs upward of six hundred pounds a night, which she can't afford, particularly given that she's staying for the full week before trekking down to Dorset. She suspects, in fact, that once she pays the final bill, her debt, which has already settled solidly around twenty thousand, will teeter over toward twenty-six thousand dollars. She feels a sudden tug of anxiety, but she calms down by focusing on Dennis, and by telling and retelling herself that the debt's worth it; that if Claridge's won't impress Eloise, then nothing will.

When her sister had first invited her to be in the bridal party, Eloise insisted that Alice bunk at her flat in London for the week preceding the wedding.

"It'll be fun," Eloise had crooned. "We'll get ready for my hen do together and go to yoga in the mornings. It'll be like when we were kids."

Alice had politely declined, and reminded Eloise that they had never done yoga together. Not even once. A week later, she phoned her back to tell her where she'd be staying.

"*Claridge's!*" Eloise had exclaimed. She relished the shock and undertones of envy in her sister's voice. "How . . . my God, how lovely!"

"You'll have to come over one afternoon for tea," Alice said. She was still clicking through images of the hotel on her computer screen. She wondered how the doormen and porters would be dressed during the summer. She hoped they'd still wear their wool coats.

"If you'll have me!" Eloise laughed. "I haven't been to tea at Claridge's in years."

Alice promised her sister that of course she'd have her—that it would be her treat—and then hung up, feeling warm and satisfied.

Dennis threads his way through the crowd and returns with a bulky gray duffel bag.

"You see yours?" he asks.

She does: on the far side of the conveyer belt, a black, expandable upright, buried beneath a purple backpack.

"There it is."

"Which one?" Dennis says. "Let me—"

"I can get it." She touches his wrist, stopping him. "I'll just wait for it to come back around."

Dennis nods. "Claridge's. *Nice*."

Alice tucks her hair behind her ears. The suitcase disappears around a corner. She says, "Want to come see it?"

The porter closes the trunk, and Alice watches as the cab lurches away from the curb. On the opposite side of Brook Street, an early-morning street sweeper churns up dust, chewing gum wrappers, and other detritus of the city. There's a breeze—easy gusts that slice through the July heat. Above her, Alice hears the flags on the hotel's awning whipping in the wind.

She turns to Dennis, who hasn't stopped grinning since they escaped baggage claim at Heathrow.

"Uh, just wait here, I guess," she says.

"What, on the street?"

"I guess that's probably unnecessary."

He takes a step toward her and lightly touches her arm. His bag balances on his left shoulder. It sways, and Alice worries that it might fall.

"Why don't I get us a table in the Foyer? You can check in, and then we can have some breakfast. In fact, I'll even expense it." Flashing his corporate AmEx, he winks, and it's awkward, painful. Still, Alice finds the whole mess charming. Or maybe it's not the wink that's charming, exactly, but rather Dennis's flagrant desire to *be* charming that hooks her—like watching a puppy who can't quite climb a set of stairs try, and try, and try, anyway. Whatever the reason is, she grins. She agrees to his plan.

But like so many of her resolutions, this confidence is short-lived. Once she's inside the hotel lobby, once she's got her neck craned back so she can gaze up at the gilded chandelier dangling above the sleek marble floor, she asks herself, in so many words, what the fuck she's doing. What, precisely, does she expect to happen? What outcome is she trying to coerce into being? At the airport, she liked the way Dennis was so taken, so thoroughly impressed by her staying here, at Claridge's. She'd impulsively reasoned that it would be fun to bring him here, to bask in his idolization of her as she threw down her credit card and checked in to one of the poshest hotels in a city of posh hotels. But now that he's here, she doesn't know what to do with him. Instead of Dennis bumbling around like an idiot, it's Alice who feels out of place. Christ, is she planning on fucking him? She'd be lying if she said the thought hadn't crossed her mind. In fact, twenty minutes ago, as they sat knee-to-knee in the back of the cab, she'd considered sleeping with Dennis a real and viable possibility. The sex wouldn't be good; once she got him naked and exposed, his confidence would sink and she'd be left to direct him, rearranging his soft limbs into a series of positions that both prevented him from coming too soon and allowed her to maximize whatever minimal pleasure she was able to mine from the encounter. The alternative, though—sending Dennis away so he can jerk off to whatever porn he has stashed on his iPhone once he reaches his hotel—is too dismal for Alice to consider. And besides, she's lonely. She can say that, right? Yes. She's self-aware. She's in touch with her emotions. She attends a support group with semi-impressive frequency. She can say that: *she's lonely.*

A week before she left for London, she'd asked Jonathan to dinner, which was a first—he was the one who, up until now, had done the asking. Still, on a Wednesday afternoon, she'd put on some lipstick, gathered herself, and marched into his office. There was a Mexican place she loved in Venice, two blocks north of Abbot-Kinney. The décor was a little kitschy, but the chef served a mean *tacos al pastor*. A hidden gem, she told him. One of her favorite places in West L.A. And you know what? It would be her treat. (She left out the fact that it was the only place she could afford.)

And it was there, over greasy tacos and Mexican Cokes, that she'd floated the suggestion that, maybe, he'd like to be her date to Eloise's wedding. The idea itself was one that she'd been wrestling with for the past three weeks. At first glance, she admitted it seemed preposterous: a married man flying halfway around the world to attend a wedding with the woman he was fucking on the side. But then surely in the grand history of affairs much crazier arrangements had been made. And besides, the last three times they'd been together, Jonathan had stressed, and then stressed again, how suffocating and beleaguered his marriage with Marissa had become. For fuck's sake, he'd said—verbatim—that sometimes he thought it would just be *easier to call it quits*. So—no, Alice had finally decided. Her invitation to Eloise's wedding wasn't out of line. It was, in fact, perfectly logical.

She waited until his mouth was filled with pork and pineapple before she came out with it and asked.

"It'll be fun," she said, watching him chew. "Well, I don't know if that's totally true, ha ha. Really, I just don't know how I'll get through it without you, I guess."

He swallowed and wiped his mouth with a paper napkin.

"Wow," he said.

She'd doused her tacos with too much Sriracha sauce. She was starting to sweat. "I'm sorry. Too much, too soon."

"No! That's not what I meant by *wow*." He picked up a lone piece of pineapple from Alice's plastic basket and popped it in his mouth, before leaning across the table to kiss her—he didn't need to worry about getting caught out in public; Marissa didn't come to Venice. "I think it would be a blast!"

"But . . ."

"No 'but,' " he said. "It would be great to get away with you. I've been actually trying to devise a way to do it myself. You just beat me to the punch."

There was a *but,* though, and it came out once they finished their second round of tacos. The more Jonathan thought about it, he explained, the more he couldn't help but think that—maybe—they should hold off. On traveling together, that is. What if he were to run into someone he knew ("It's a terrible thing being the head of the company, Al—Big Data, Big Social Circle!")? What if pictures were posted online? Yes, he repeated, this time with more reluctance, they should really wait before they take a trip together. At least until he'd taken some action on the Marissa situation ("which won't be long now—you should have *seen* the way she acted the other night at dinner. The kids are terrified of her. I think, generally, she's just an unhappy person"). That seemed only fair, didn't it? He was having an affair, but he was still a good person, for Christ's sake. He'd call Alice as often as he could, of course, and they could Skype whenever he was in the office. She understood, didn't she?

Alice picked a wilted piece of cabbage out of her taco. "Of course I do."

Now, standing in Claridge's, she feels a wave of nausea when she thinks of him—or, more specifically, when she thinks of how she might soon, in a matter of minutes, be fucking someone else. She tries telling herself that she knows how all this plays out: Jonathan never leaves his wife, and Alice is left alone. She's seen too many TBS Saturday afternoon rom-coms and has known too many Other Women to think that it ends any differently. Still, there's this awful voice in her head that keeps suggesting that there might be a chance, that she's got reason—however illogical—to hold on to hope. In the meantime, though, she figures she's entitled to this; if Jonathan's still working things out with Marissa, then Alice is allowed to work things out with Dennis. She's entitled to fuck a twenty-three-year-old idiot in a hotel room that's causing her to spiral further into debt.

She blinks, and when she opens her eyes, the chandelier is still there, staring back at her with fifty bright eyes.

The Sleeping-with-Dennis Question will be a game-time decision, she decides. She'll let him expense their breakfast, because, well, why not, and then she'll just see what happens.

She checks in to Claridge's on Facebook and prepares herself for the worst.

"Miss?"

A woman a few years younger than Alice smiles at her. She wears a white silk blouse tucked into a pair of pressed black slacks. She's pretty, in an English way: fine blond hair, red cheeks. Possibly malnourished, though certainly not on account of having too little food. A name tag pinned over her right nipple reads *Anne*. Alice smiles back.

"May I help you with anything?"

"Oh, uh, I'm here to check in." She clears her throat. "I'm staying here for the next week or so."

She wonders how long she's been standing here, staring up into space.

Anne nods and presses her hands together at her waist. "Of course. How lovely. Right this way, then."

Alice follows her across the hotel's lobby and past a wide, curved staircase. On either side of the room, men in suits huddle around low glass tables and leather-backed chairs. She intentionally catches their eyes as she passes them, and she tries to imagine who they think she might be, what they might think of her. Listening to her footsteps echo in the airy space, she fantasizes what it will be like to bring Eloise here, of the look on her sister's face when Alice walks into the place like she owns it. She'll wait a few days. Four, maybe. Long enough for the staff to learn and remember her name. She wants the doorman to be able to call out to her when he sees her and Eloise approaching.

Anne stops in front of a low mahogany desk set beneath a pair of white columns. A young, mid-twenties man with red hair and thin, frameless glasses squints at a keyboard.

"This is James," she says. "He'd be happy to get you settled."

James looks up from the screen, stands, and fastens the top button of his blazer.

"Welcome to Claridge's, miss." He shakes her hand and motions to the chair across from him.

Alice sits. She sets her purse in her lap and glances over her shoulder to see if Dennis has found a seat in the Foyer. She wonders if he's managed to order them a pot of coffee. She needs to clear the cobwebs from her brain.

"Right, then," James says, repositioning his chair. "First things first. Can I have the name the reservation was made under?"

Alice gives the man her name. She fishes around her purse for her wallet and finds her Visa. "And here's a credit card, if you need one for, uh, incidentals or something."

James strikes a few keys, scrolls farther down the screen, and raises an eyebrow.

"Actually, I don't think we will be needing a credit card." He smiles. "Your stay with us, along with any subsequent charges that you might incur during your time at Claridge's, have been arranged for in advance."

The back of Alice's neck grows warm. She worries that there's been some kind of mistake.

"I'm sorry, but I—"

"Not only that, but it looks as though you've been upgraded to one of our Mivart suites."

For a hopeful, devastating moment she thinks of Jonathan, calling Claridge's from his gleaming glass office in L.A. But that fantasy fades as quickly as it materializes, and in the blank void of disappointment it leaves in its wake, the pieces come together, and things suddenly make sense.

"Would you mind telling me who covered the expenses and paid for the upgrade?" she asks—though, really, there's no need; she already knows the terrible answer.

"Surely," James says. He double-clicks the mouse and leans an inch closer to the screen. "Says here that the charges were made by a . . . a Miss

Eloise Lafarge." He looks up at Alice. "Quite the guardian angel you've got there."

She white-knuckles the handle on her purse to keep her hands from shaking, and when she opens her mouth to speak, she worries that she's only got the capacity to scream.

"She's my half sister," she manages.

"Well, lucky you." For a moment, James's voice sheds its practiced Mayfair accent and slips into a lilting Cockney. "The only thing my half sister's good for is polishing off a box of biscuits."

Alice turns around again, and this time she catches sight of Dennis, who has found a table near the entrance of the Foyer. Before him sit two steaming cups of coffee and a basket of assorted pastries, and Alice watches as he picks at crumbs from a blueberry muffin. She calculates her chances of making it to the elevator on the opposite end of the lobby unnoticed.

"Can you tell me how to get to my room, please?"

For a moment James looks confused by Alice's sudden change in mood, but soon professionalism takes over; he gives her a curt nod, provides her with clear directions to her suite (*seventh floor, take a left, room at the end of the hall. You'll see the plaque*) and asks how many keys she'd like.

"Two, I guess," Alice says. "Or, one. One's fine. Really, whatever's fastest."

Waiting for her in the suite's sitting room are a bottle of champagne in a pewter ice bucket and a plate of fresh, halved strawberries. She kneels down next to the coffee table and pushes the gift aside, leaving wide streaks of condensation along the glass surface. Then, Alice notices something else: a note from Eloise, typed on Claridge's thick, pulpy stationery, welcoming her to London and begging her to enjoy the booze and fruit. She rips the envelope in half and uses the card to cut the dust from two crushed Klonopins into a trio of fat yellow lines. With a rolled-up five-dollar bill she snorts the first of the lines and collapses back onto a sofa. Letting her head fall against the cushions, she tastes the drug's cloying sweetness as it worms its way through her sinuses and trickles down the back of her throat. The real effects—the sensation of walking on pillows of air, of being cloaked in a thick, invisible armor of ambivalence—won't come for another five minutes. And when they do, they won't hit her squarely, like cocaine, but will rather wash over her gradually, cleanly; chances are she'll hardly notice them at all until, suddenly, she won't be able to imagine living without them. Still, even as she waits for that blissful state of uncaring, she starts to feel better, somehow put back together. Her anger continues to lurk, but it's focused now, and more resolved.

Outside, she hears the faint whine of a siren. She listens to it echo down Brook Street and then dissolve into the rest of London. She worries that the Klonopin's taking longer than usual. Lurching back to the coffee table, she positions herself over the second line. There's no harm, she figures, in helping the drug along.

Wiping her nose, she reaches for the bottle of champagne. A Pol Roger Réserve Brut that would typically go for forty bucks. Given Claridge's extortionate markups, though, Alice guesses Eloise paid nearly five times that amount. But then, what was two hundred dollars to her sister? What was a Mivart suite to her sister? What was struggle, what was shame, what was empathy? She uncorks the bottle and fills her mouth with so much champagne that she worries her cheeks might burst. Then, in a moment of perfect clarity, she sprints to the toilet and spits it out. The water turns to a cheap, evanescent gold, which deepens to a brass as she empties the rest of the bottle.

In the living room, she polishes off the third and final line. Her rage now a fierce point of medicated light, she asks herself the same questions she's asked herself for years: How can her sister's compassion be so profoundly and selfishly misguided? Is she really the only person to realize that behind all Eloise's giving and caring is a subconscious, though thinly veiled, scheme to lord privilege over her siblings? It's a sort of false altruism, Alice considers, that's actually blind to the complications and nuances of other people. What infuriates her more, though, is how Eloise's goodness shields itself from reproach or criticism. After all, isn't she—Alice—presently lounging in some doped-up, drugged-out state in one of the nicest suites in London? Didn't she just squander a bottle of mediocre, overpriced champagne during what is surely only the beginning of an adolescent temper tantrum? And hasn't she been afforded the opportunity to do it all—to *keep* doing it all—on Eloise's dime? Never mind that Alice wanted to impress Eloise, to show her that she was just as capable of having nice things, and that Eloise brutally robbed her of that chance with her unwavering generosity. Never mind those facts. Because from the outside, if anyone's acting like a bitch here, it's her, it's Alice. What's worse, there's no way around it. No way to argue her way out of it. Nothing pisses her off more.

She stands up and begins pacing the sitting room, banging her knee against the wooden leg of an armchair in the process. She kicks it and feels pain radiate through her toes and ankle. The room feels overcrowded: every corner has a chair, or a love seat, or a settee. From where she stands next to the window, she can see her red face reflected in three separate mirrors. She hates it; she hates her sister for upgrading her. Suddenly, she craves the cool, sterile simplicity of a room at, say, the Marriott. The air-conditioning cranked up too high, the sheets an unnatural shade of white. Bad, mass-produced art on two of the four walls.

She remembers Dennis, and wonders if he's still sitting downstairs, waiting for her, watching her coffee get cold.

Her pulse drums at the base of her throat—she can feel it—and she considers crushing up another Klonopin, but she stops herself. Three might be overkill, even with her liberal standards. There's also the matter of logistics, she thinks: she's got two weeks ahead of her. Two weeks of hen dos, and dress fittings, and speeches, and Eloise's simpering magnanimity. And Alice would rather throw herself into the Thames with a hundred open wounds before enduring that shit show sober. No, she'll save the pills that she has left, let the supply that's already in her take its course. Besides, the rage and self-pity that she's feeling are drugs unto themselves. After all, there's a certain high that comes from knowing that no one could possibly understand what you're feeling. She imagines this is what Paul must feel like most of the time—and if that's the case, there's a chance that here, today, she understands her brother a little better than she did before. In fact, maybe Paul's had it right all along: while Alice has been tripping over herself to pretend everything's okay, maybe the better solution is to be perpetually pissed off.

The drugs are definitely not working as well as they should.

She walks to the other side of the room, where there's a small leather portfolio containing the menu for room service and the suite's minibar. Leaning against the wall (*there's* the Klonopin), she opens it. As expected, the prices are exorbitant. Ten pounds for a packet of peanuts. Fifteen for fifty milliliters of Beefeater gin. She flips a few pages further, to the mid-morning offerings. A standard English breakfast goes for thirty eight pounds. Christ, Alice thinks. Over fifty dollars for a pair of soggy scrambled eggs, a charred tomato, and an assortment of shriveled meats. Throw in a bowl of berries and a glass of orange juice, and she's basically looking at what she pays to rent her studio in Westwood.

She sets the menu down and chews on her thumbnail. She can't, she thinks. Or can she? No—no, she *can't*. This . . . it's too vindictive. *Paul* vindictive. She doesn't do things like this. She doesn't order twenty-pound pieces of toast just so her sister will have to pay for them. She doesn't consume as a means of revenge. Not even now, when she's been wronged in such a profound and inexcusable way and she's two Klonopin deep. There are still some standards she's got to maintain. And besides—*think of the calories.*

There's a chair next to the telephone, and she perches unsteadily on its left arm.

The operator at the restaurant answers on the first ring.

"Good morning, Miss. How may I be of service?"

Alice coughs. "I'd like five English breakfasts, please. All with scrambled eggs, all with white toast."

"Certainly. And will that be all?"

"Yes," she says. "Or, no. Five orange juices, five pain au raisins, and five orders of the Welsh Rabbit." She glances down at the menu. "Can you add bacon to the rabbit?"

"Of course. Though, that'll be an additional five—"

"Double the bacon, then."

"Certainly. Anything else?"

"No. Not now at least." She clicks her teeth, thinking. "You deliver room service all day?"

"Whenever you'd like."

"Wonderful," Alice says. "That's really, really wonderful."

"I'm pleased you think so." An awkward pause ensues. "You can expect your breakfast to arrive in the next half an hour. I assume you'd like multiple sets of cutlery?"

"I—" She can't possibly request a single fork, can she? No, she can't. There's something to be said for keeping up appearances. "Yes, please. Five sets."

She hangs up.

This is absurd, she thinks, both grinning and grimacing. Does she actually think a thousand-pound room service charge will register anything more than a blink from her sister? Eloise's father has clogged her trust fund with enough cash that Alice could probably *buy* the whole goddamned suite before Eloise suspected any suspicious activity. But it's the principle of the thing, Alice thinks as she opens the minibar and unscrews the cap from a twenty-pound airplane-sized bottle of Grey Goose. If Eloise wants to taunt Alice with generosity, then Alice has a right to show her where such loathsome and self-serving generosity leads.

She finishes the Grey Goose in a determined swallow and reaches for the Tanqueray.

It doesn't take her long to get drunk—thanks to the Klonopin, she's already feeling good and wasted once she's polished off the Tanqueray. Still, she's driven by a sense of duty, so she swallows half a bottle of

Kahlúa before deciding that she needs something to eat while she waits for her breakfast. Rummaging through the minibar, she finds a canister of almonds and, peeling away the can's tinfoil top, pops a handful into her mouth. They're salty, too salty, their rough skins coated with crystals, and despite all the alcohol she's just drunk, her mouth is already bone dry. She eats them anyway and muses over how she feels simultaneously full and empty; each nut feels at once like a drop in the bucket and a stone in her gut. The drugs, she figures, must be really kicking in.

Three-quarters of the way through the container she reminds herself that she needn't eat the whole thing to incur the full charge for it—she only needs to open the canister to rack up ten pounds. With a mixed sense of defeat and victory, she sets the almonds aside and unwraps three wheels of Brie. Using a wheat cracker, she breaks off a creamy glob from one of the wheels and scoops it into her mouth.

She leans back again, works the cheese over her gums and her teeth, and then swigs from a bottle of Perrier to rinse out her mouth. She tries to remember what she ordered from room service, but she's having a hard time thinking of it. Typically this is her favorite part of getting high, the moment where her short-term memory, the events of the past hour, seem to blur into an unrecognizable nothingness somewhere along the horizon of her mind. The Forgetting, is what she calls it. Forgetting what Paul was just bitching about, or the strange way Jonathan just looked at her, or—in this case—how she just squandered her sister's money. She tries to push the wall of short-term nothingness further; she wills it to consume her anger toward Eloise and her narcissistic altruism. It's not that she wants to forgive her sister, or that she wants to dispel her own rage—rather, she'd prefer to feel nothing at all.

But her efforts are useless. She swallows the mouthful of cheese and, looking at the mess she's made, is suddenly embarrassed and filled with a foggy, drunk sense of disappointment. Empty bottles are turned on their sides. Melted caramel glues torn candy wrappers to the glass table. She sinks further into the sofa and lets her shoulders slump. Crumbs form trails down the front of her shirt. Catching a glimpse of herself in the blackened television's reflection, she thinks: This isn't me. This can't be me. I don't know who it is, but it's not me.

Or maybe it is, and maybe that's the awful truth. Maybe instead of diluting her, the drugs actually coax her closer to a purer state. Her stomach clenches at the thought. Still, a question pesters her: Besides money, what does Eloise have that she, Alice, is lacking? She's as pretty as her sister, isn't she? Maybe not in some classic, Audrey Hepburn Waiting Outside of Tiffany's sort of way, but certainly in an early Rita Hayworth in a Bikini sort of way, and didn't men like that more, anyhow? And in terms of intelligence, it's not like Alice is lacking. She graduated a tenth of a grade point away from summa cum laude, and her thesis advisor had told her, with undeniable sincerity, that she had been a *very strong contender* for Phi Beta Kappa, even if she hadn't, ultimately, been selected. Granted, all of this occurred at UCLA, as opposed to Eloise's Yale, but still—didn't it count for something? Didn't it provide some justification for her confusion when she considered how her sister was blessed with an easy, gilded life, while she was reduced to taking her (married) boyfriend out for tacos? Isn't there some explanation for this gross inequality, other than the fact that Eloise had a rich dad and she had an accountant for a father?

No, there isn't. This is where her thoughts veer, where they invariably and inevitably dead-end. Just look at how her mother treats them both: Eloise like a prize, and Alice like an employee. No, there's nothing else but the wanton and slapdash workings of Fate.

There's a knock on the door, and then a polite announcement of *room service*. She throws the empty Perrier bottle to the ground and, once again disappointed in herself, she buries her face in her hands. Her forehead feels clammy, damp, and her eyes ache when she shuts them. The world lurches, and her gut shifts and repositions itself. Another knock, another call for *room service*, causes her to blink and look up.

"I'll be right there," she calls out.

And she will. She'll open the door, and invite the man in, and lift the warming covers from the army of silver trays, and eat eggs and ham and grapefruit until she makes herself sick. First, though, she reaches for her phone. Closing one eye to focus her blurry vision, she scrolls to her sister's mobile number, opens a new message, and types: *You're 2 kind. This room is gorgeous. I'm the luckiest sister alive* ☺.

Eloise

Seated in the breakfast nook of her flat in Chelsea, Eloise reads Alice's text message and sighs with relief. Smiling, she reaches for her demitasse—the white Royal Copenhagen one that Ollie had bought her last year when they'd taken a long weekend in Denmark—and breathes in the nutty espresso.

Ever since calling Claridge's to pay for and upgrade Alice's room, she'd been racked by nerves. Ollie had told her that she was worrying over nothing—who wouldn't be *thrilled* to discover that she was staying in one of the nicest suites in London, for free?—but Eloise knew not to rest so easily. She remembered her senior spring at Yale, when Alice had e-mailed her a photo of the dress she was planning on wearing to her high school junior prom. Eloise found it charming and admirable (*respectable* and *grown-up* were the words she'd used with her sister) that Alice had saved her earnings from the Blockbuster where she worked to buy herself a dress, but the gown itself was less than flattering. It wasn't a matter of Alice's taste so much as the quality of the dress itself; it looked . . . well . . . cheap. And so, the next weekend, when she and a few girlfriends took the train from New Haven to New York, she excused herself for a few hours to buy her sister a new dress—a gorgeous black A-line. She sent it via next-day Fed-Ex to St. Charles, along with flowers, a silver necklace, and a note, written on her personal stationery, that read *You Deserve This!*

Ten days later, she received a package from her sister. Inside (without a note) were the necklace and the dress, its twin spaghetti straps snipped in half.

But that was a long time ago, she tells herself now, licking a drop of espresso from her lips. Alice has grown up. *She* has grown up. It was just like Ollie had said last Wednesday: this wedding, in addition to all of the other things it's destined to be, will usher in some changes. It will be an opportunity to enter a new phase in her relationship with Alice—and, if he was willing, Paul.

Still awash with relief, still grinning and satisfied, she unfolds her laptop and clicks open her company e-mail. Yesterday, she had set a strict no-work rule for herself; she's taken these three weeks off to focus on her wedding, because God only knows how much more needs to be done, and how little time she has to do it. And yet, here she is, responding to questions and requests, and it's hardly nine o'clock. It's pointless to try to stay away, though, she tells herself; being indispensable means too much to her. That's always been her problem. She gets so wrapped up in being needed that she forgets to stop and actually consider what she needs for herself. Clicking send on a message, she recalls the fit that her brother had when she took the job.

"A nonprofit that helps children in developing nations by *fixing their deviated septums?*" he'd said over Christmas dinner. This was three years ago, when he was still speaking to her with semiregular frequency.

"That's right," she'd said, proudly. "It's called Mission: Breathe. I'll be helping to run their communications department."

"So you're doing public relations, is what you're saying. Public relations for deviated septums."

She remembers pushing the mashed potatoes to the side of her plate to make room for more salad.

"It's a terrible condition," she said. "In fact—"

"Do you know how many children under the age of five die of diarrhea every year?" Paul interrupted her.

"I—no. I don't."

"Seven hundred sixty *thousand*. How many children die from having deviated septums?"

"That's not the problem. They don't die from the deviated septums themselves, so much as—"

"Exactly."

He'd never explicitly apologized, but she forgave him, nonetheless. Paul was naïve and idealistic, which were two qualities that she adored in him, but which also often prevented him from understanding life's more nuanced complications. For instance, did Paul know that deviated septums are often the cause of childhood sleep apnea—a condition that, not *unlike* diarrhea, can also lead to death? Or, did Paul know that septoplasty isn't as easy a surgery as most people assume it is, and that, in the hands of an unskilled doctor practicing in a developing country, the procedure may put a child's life at risk? These are just a few of the myriad facts that Eloise has learned since helping to mold the public's perception of Mission: Breathe— facts that she's certain would change Paul's mind about the organization's worth, if he ever deigned to hear them.

She finishes her espresso and pulls her hair back into a bun. Three new e-mails have just arrived, all of them written in the same panic-stricken tone, a franticness that Eloise has come to expect from her colleagues whenever she's out of the office. ("What would they ever do without you?" Ollie often says to her. Eloise's reply is always the same—*oh, give it a rest*—but really, she had no idea. She expects the whole organization might burn to the ground.) She clicks the first message—this one from her assistant, a sweet but daft girl named Bee, from Essex—and begins to read. In two days, the *Daily Mail* will publish an online story about London's "top five most shallow charities," and Mission: Breathe has made the list. Evidently, some asshole reporter managed to get wind of the organization's financials and is now planning a story about how more cash is being spent to host lavish galas than to help poor children with deviated septums. Eloise shakes her head and frowns: accusations like this one make her fucking sick. After all, here she is trying to *help* people, and all this reporter could do was write about numbers.

She starts to respond to her assistant, but then, taking a deep breath, she stops herself and closes the window, opting instead to cue up her Out of Office.

On the other side of her laptop, next to a vase filled with the hydrangeas that Anka brought when she came to clean yesterday, sits the seating chart for the reception that she and Ollie have been working on. Next to it are the RSVPs that they've received, a collection of cards forming a neat, mother-of-pearl stack. Looking at the open places on the chart, she begins to sift through the names, cross-checking them with a spreadsheet of guests that she created nearly six months ago. She remembers when she first started hearing back from the people she and Ollie had invited. Using his letter opener, she sliced apart the envelopes one by one, tallying all the yeses. Once in a while she'd come across a no, and she'd do her best not to frown and to suppress her disappointment. Poppy and Hugo had a cousin's wedding in Sydney, and while Eloise *knew* how Poppy felt about a member of her clan hitching up with an antipodean, her aunt would no doubt *skewer* her if she missed the nuptials. And given that this was the aunt with the house in Lacoste that's empty for practically fifty-one weeks out of the year, and where Poppy and Hugo and Eloise and Ollie have spent the past four Bastille Days—well. Eloise understood, didn't she? Yes, she thought to herself, setting Poppy's card in a separate pile. She did. Life comes up; life happens. While they came few and far between, there were more regrets: Charlotte and Guy would be skiing in Las Leñas, and it's a trip that Charlotte had "stupidly" booked *ages* ago; Kristen, a classmate of Eloise's from Yale, had a memoir being released that week (after reading *Around the World in Eighty Days* in the wake of a messy breakup, she spent a year traveling the world, trying to find eligible men in foreign cities with untapped dating pools, like Accra and Vilnius. She's still single) and her publisher and agent were both insisting that she stay in New York (they were 90 percent certain she was a shoo-in for the *Today* show); an uncle of Ollie's named Cedric whom Eloise wasn't aware existed would have *adored* to come, and was flattered that the couple thought to invite him, but surely Ollie remembered how Cedric felt about traveling, and what atrocity transpired the last time he boarded a train? Nobody wants to see that again, Cedric assured them. *Nobody.*

As she tackled the pile, she found a steady rhythm for herself, a four-count beat: open, read, smile, log; open, read, smile, log. Soon, the routine became hypnotic, and then, finally, gleefully therapeutic: she considered how all those little envelopes (even the regrets, the tearful excuses) bore evidence of just how much she was loved and appreciated. She gazed at them, scattered across the breakfast table like two hundred warm hugs. Beyond them, her flat glowed with soft morning light, and London pulsed with the same refined excitement that first seduced her six years ago, when she moved here to get a master's in art history at UCL, and that continues to seduce her now, as she puts the final touches on the seating chart.

How could she not consider herself lucky, privileged? After all, hadn't that been the reason she decided to take the Mission: Breathe job in the first place? She'd been offered other jobs after grad school, positions that were more in line with the careers of her friends (a development role at the Tate Modern; VP of publicity at one of the big Haymarket firms), but still she'd chosen this, she'd chosen charity. She considered it her responsibility, a sort of noblesse oblige duty of hers to give back. And besides, the parties really *were* fabulous.

Thinking again of the *Daily Mail* reporter attempting to defame her efforts with claims of shallowness, she feels a sharp sting. Her blood starts boiling, and she hovers the computer's mouse over her e-mail, which she'd minimized at the bottom of the screen.

At the last instant, though, she yanks her hand away. To distract herself, she looks at the names of the two remaining guests who, nine days out from the wedding, she's yet to seat: Donna Wyckoff and Henrique Lafarge. Squinting, she rubs her temples; the riddle of what to do with her parents has been puzzling her ever since she received Henrique's RSVP (late) two weeks ago, his name scrawled out in fluid, Continental script. Since then, she's moved them around the seating chart in a dizzying game of hide-and-seek, trying to keep them apart while also contriving scenarios in which they might interact. It's been infuriating work, though—twice she's had to reseat an entire table of guests, and last week she was on the verge of revoking her father's invitation, just to make her own life a little easier.

Fearing that she's reached the end of her patience, she opts for the most obvious solution: she slams her computer shut and figures she'll deal with it later.

"Fuck it," she says, and downs the last dregs of her espresso.

At noon she takes the Tube to Canary Warf to meet Ollie for lunch at a bistro on Montgomery Square, a few blocks away from his office at Barclays London headquarters. She waits nearly thirty minutes before bringing up the issue of seating arrangements.

"What if I just sit them next to each other?" she says.

"As in side by side?"

"As in side by side."

"Huh." Ollie picks the onions out of his burger and discards them on his bread plate. He rolls up the sleeves of his shirt and loosens his tie.

"I mean, they're my parents. Is it that weird that they're going to be sitting next to each other?" Eloise looks around for their waiter, who told her five minutes ago that her salad was on the way. "Go ahead and eat," she says, though she knows he won't.

"Of course it's not weird." He reaches across the table for her hand. "It's just—I thought you said they didn't get along all that well."

"You're right," she says. "It's a horrible idea."

When she went on her first date with Ollie five years ago, Eloise was hardly speaking to her father herself. Henrique had taken up a third wife, a French soap star two years younger than Eloise, and she couldn't bear to face the child her father had become. But last year she received word that he'd left the soap star (or perhaps she left him—her father was rather vague on the issue, saying that *il etait près de se caser*). At first, she had a difficult time believing him: Henrique, ready to settle down? It was like asking Paul to get off his high horse. Yet, over the past twelve months, her faith in her father's proclaimed need for stability and maturity has grown. He canceled his annual boys' trip to Biarritz, which was a start, and from what Eloise could gather, more of his weekend nights were now spent reading at home, rather than buying bottles of champagne for women a third his age at some Parisian nightclub.

"Have you told your mum?" Ollie asks.

"To be honest . . ." Eloise pauses and stirs her iced tea with her straw. "I mean . . . To be honest, she's not totally aware that he's going to be there."

"Well, uh, don't you think that's the first order of business?"

"I'm going to tell her," Eloise says. "I just haven't found the right opportunity to."

The waiter refills her iced tea and apologizes again for her salad's delay. She smiles, but given how he's looking at her (terrified, like he's staring down the barrel of a gun), she worries that whatever she's doing is coming across as more of a sneer. Ollie, meanwhile, cracks a joke, a one-liner about the restaurant growing its own watercress that, in the hands of someone less charming, would come across as cliché at best and snooty at worst. The waiter laughs, though; any traces of Eloise-inspired terror fade, and he seems instantly at ease. Watching Ollie joke, she wonders what it's like to be so likable. She's always been liked, sure, but that's different; it's not the same thing. *Being likable* is an inherent state of being, while *being liked* takes work: a constant effort to suppress the parts of her that her siblings have called tone deaf or out of touch; a daily war she wages to keep her privilege in check. Sometimes, though, she just can't help it. Sometimes, her effort starts to show.

"I'm sure you'll figure it out," Ollie says, and looks down at his burger.

"I'll tell her that he's coming when I pick her up from the airport tomorrow," she says. "Honest to God, Ollie, eat. It's going to get cold."

He plucks a single French fry from his plate, pops it in his mouth, and smiles.

"Just—make sure you're managing your expectations," he says, once he's swallowed.

"What do you mean?"

He reaches for the ketchup and shakes a glob of it out onto his plate.

"You know, just, maybe don't expect *too* much to come from your mum and dad seeing each other again," he says, adding, "Because sitting them next to each other . . . that just sends a pretty specific message, is all."

"Oh, come *on*. Give me a little credit. I'm not trying to stage some kind of *Parent Trap* bullshit." She laughs and looks around the room again. "Honestly, at this point I might as well go home and make my own damn salad."

Is she, though? Trying to contrive some latent romance to bloom between Donna and Henrique? No, she tells herself. She's smarter than that; she's not that naïve. It's not that her mother doesn't love Henrique anymore—Eloise knows for a fact that she does; she's always mining Eloise for information about her father whenever they speak on the phone—but in the years since they divorced, too much animosity has been allowed to fester; too many walls have been built. And clearing away that rancorous mess is too Herculean a task for Eloise to consider. Still, though, would a minor reconciliation be too much to ask for? Not love, per se, but rather the subtle grace of an apology? Of forgiveness?

"Let's change the subject," she says.

Ollie wipes his mouth—he's finally given in and started on the burger—and nods.

"Have you spoken to your sister?" he asks.

"She texted me from the hotel. She said she liked the suite, thank God."

He sets down his burger. Mustard oozes out from beneath the bun. "No," he says. "I mean about the *job*."

Eloise smooths down her hair. "Not yet," she says. "I will when I see her."

The truth is, though, she still has no strategy for broaching the subject with Alice. On paper, the whole ordeal seemed easy enough: unprovoked, Ollie (because this is the type of man Ollie is) had arrived home two weeks ago and announced that he'd had a fantastic idea. An old classmate of his from Sherborne had just taken the reins of a film production company in London whose bread-and-butter were high-budget documentaries. ("Nature stuff, mostly," he'd said. "But also some big social justice pieces. The sort of stuff Morgan Freeman or Susan Sarandon would narrate.") This particular classmate, he went on to explain, had called on Ollie a few years back for a bit ("or, really, a quite substantial amount") of financial advising, and thus owed him a favor.

"What if that favor was hiring Alice to work in distribution?" He leapt up from the couch in the living room. "Brilliant, isn't it?"

Eloise stayed seated, and looked up at him. His blond hair was a bit tousled—it was the end of the day—which gave him a boyish look that was wonderfully at odds with his ropy rower's build. She thought the same thing she had when she first met him: this is someone who's been blessed to look perpetually twenty-three.

"I don't understand," she said.

"Come on. Think about it. How many times have you told me how much you suspect Alice hates her job?"

Eloise reached forward and straightened a stack of magazines on the coffee table.

"Yes," she said. "But—"

Ollie cut her off. "But what?! Think of it: You could save her from all that awful California sunshine! No melanoma for Alice!" Eloise tried not to laugh. "Finally, she'd get to have her big sister around to show her the ropes!"

Eloise smiled, even though she knew how naïve Ollie's suggestion was. When she'd called Claridge's with her credit card number, she'd been fearful—petrified, even—of Alice's reaction. And now—what? She was going to offer her a new job? Alice didn't take well to handouts, particularly when they came from her. Still, the idea of being helpful, of being *needed*—and not just by anyone, but by her own sister—was seductive in a way that Eloise couldn't ignore.

She asked, "And you're sure this classmate of yours—"

"Xavier Wolfson."

"Okay. Xavier Wolfson. You're sure he'd hire her?"

Ollie nodded. "Absolutely. Like I said—he owes me."

"Okay," Eloise conceded. "I'll mention it to her."

Eloise sets her mother's suitcase down next to the love seat in the guest room and flips on the light.

"Here we are," she says, stepping aside to let Donna enter.

"How lovely."

Eloise smiles. This morning she asked Anka to fit the bed with a fresh set of white cotton sheets, and to leave some hydrangeas in the vase on one of the two bedside tables. On the other one, she'd left her own, personal touch: an old picture she'd found of her and her mother outside the Palais de Tokyo, which she'd had matted and framed in a gorgeous ten-by-four-inch frame that she found last month at an antique store near Finsbury Park. She watches as Donna walks over to the window, past the picture, and opens the curtains, letting ashy light into the room. Her gaze falls down to the street, where it stays for a minute, tracking some unknown event, and Eloise finds herself wanting to know, desperately, what it is that has snatched her mother's attention so relentlessly. When she can't stand it any longer, she clears her throat, and Donna turns to her and smiles.

"The women in this city wear the nicest coats," she says, sitting on the edge of the bed and removing her shoes.

Should she mention the picture? It's just sitting there, unnoticed, a short arm's length away. Should she somehow point it out to her mother? Explain that she's had it framed for her, and that she intends to give it to her as a gift for traveling all this way? She draws in a breath to say something, but at the last moment she stops herself: something about drawing Donna's attention to the picture seems tacky, self-serving, like when Paul used to tell Eloise the price of the Christmas presents he'd bought her before she even had the chance to open them. No, she'll stay silent. She'll let Donna discover it on her own.

"Have you heard from your father yet?" her mother asks, suddenly.

"What do you mean?"

"Has he RSVPed? Is he coming?"

Eloise says, "I . . . I did," and reaches down to straighten out the corners of the bed. "I got it last week. He'll be there."

"A month late RSVPing," Donna says, bitterly. *"Quelle surprise."*

What is wrong with me? Eloise thinks, stopping just short of apologizing to her mother. Why do I feel so guilty? Surely her mother knew that Henrique would end up being at the wedding; he is, after all, her father. Still, Eloise feels like she's somehow failed her mother, like she's exposed her to an inevitable and obvious truth.

"The bathroom's en suite," she announces, loudly, to keep herself from fidgeting. "You'll find soap, shampoo, conditioner, a hair dryer—really, anything you might need, I think—in the bathroom. And if there's something that's not in there, just ask Anka, and she'll get it for you." She's babbling. She sounds like a concierge.

"Oh, I'm fine, sweetheart." Her mother lays back onto the bed, her legs still dangling over its edge. Eloise sits next to her and rubs her knee.

"You must be exhausted. Did you get any sleep?"

"Oh, you know me and red-eyes."

"Why don't you take a nap? We haven't got anything until meeting Alice and Paul this evening."

"And Mark," Donna says, sitting up.

"Mark?"

"Paul's boyfriend."

"Of course," Eloise feigns. "I don't know how I forgot about Mark." She stumbles through what she wants to say next, without appearing as though the only thing she cares about is her own wedding. "You two are speaking again, aren't you?"

"I've never been not-speaking to Mark."

Eloise says, "No. I meant Paul."

"Oh." Donna sighs. "Well, he called me about a month ago to tell me that he was coming, so I suppose that's a start?"

"It is!" Eloise feigns a smile: she's imagining her brother. She's imagining a scene. "Did you talk about . . . about Bill?"

"No," Donna says. "And we won't. He doesn't need to know about all that."

"I just think it's so unfair to you, *Maman*. You were doing him a favor. You were protecting him, for God's sake, and this is the thanks you get."

Donna smiles. She looks exhausted, Eloise thinks, and old. She reaches over and pushes a strand of hair out of Eloise's eyes. "Are jeans okay for tonight?"

"Black pants, maybe, if you've got them?"

Donna pulls her hand away. Her cheeks flush. "I, uh, I didn't know that I needed . . ."

Eloise gives her mother's knee a squeeze. Discreetly, she checks the clock on the room's east wall: no time for Harrods. "Jeans are fine."

"You're sure it's fine if I rest a bit?"

"*Maman. J'insiste.* I'll be out in the living room. If you need anything, just call for Anka."

"Or you?" Donna says.

Eloise nods. "Or me." She kisses her mother's forehead. "I'm so glad you're here, Mummy."

She swings by the kitchen and asks Anka to make her a *cortado*. In the living room she sits on the sofa and, on the coffee table in front of her, finds the copy of today's *Daily Mail*. Leaning forward, she flips to the hatchet job on "shallow charities" (*we've met teaspoons with more depth!*). She scans the two-page spread, past the scathing write-ups on the Kids Wish Network and the Victims of Alienating, Inconsiderate, and Narcissistic Parents Foundation (VAIN), until she locates a bloodred box topped with bold white letters that read MISSION: GREED. Reading through the article, she's momentarily put at ease. It's a lot of what she was expecting: a list of how many minor royals had been in attendance (seven) at the last gala; a few sentences balking at the cost of a table (fifty thousand pounds); some shallow puzzling over the necessity of the Eiffel Tower–shaped chocolate fountain, despite the evening's *very obvious* fin-de-siècle theme. A bit farther down, though, something does strike her: a disproportionate amount of page space dedicated to the cost of the centerpieces that graced the tables (a thousand pounds each). "Curious," the reporter, some hack called Rupert Gregory, writes, "that an organization dedicated to helping children sniff should squander eighty thousand pounds on gardenias and lisianthuses."

Her first thought is: the centerpieces really *were* lovely. Her second one is: fuck him. She wiggles her BlackBerry out of her jeans and opens a new message to Bee:

Just saw the DM *story,* she types. *Need you to draft response. Don't deny cost of flowers, but counter w/ number of surgeries funded in sub-Saharan Africa last year. Highlight places that people associate with starving, malnourishment, genocide, etc. Also—call Rachel O'Donnell, does gossip at* The Sun. *Tell her we've got a tip about possible Rupert Gregory drug problem. Anonymous source who's close to him. Ping me when you've done both.*

Thirty seconds later, her BlackBerry buzzes with a new e-mail from Bee. *Is that true about Rupert Gregory?*

Eloise rolls her eyes and types, *That's not the point.*

"But, Daniella, I called thirty minutes ago, and you said the table would be ready."

Eloise can barely hear herself speak: the Friday night regulars at Dean Street Townhouse have already settled in, their voices competing and blending together into a constant roar. She only ever comes here for lunch or cocktails—she'd forgotten how loud it could get during dinner. Maybe she should have made reservations somewhere else.

Daniella flips her hair and pouts.

"I'm so sorry, Miss Lafarge. I honestly thought the table would be ready by then. It's just that another large group is seated at the banquette you've requested, and they're just now enjoying their desserts."

Eloise feels her shoulders slump, and she corrects her posture. "Daniella, I'm in here literally three times a week for lunch."

"I know, and I really wish there was something else I could do."

A drunk Londoner in a suit passes between Eloise and the maître d's station, and she rears back so the beer sloshing over the rim of his pint glass won't splash down the front of her blouse.

"There's not another table or anything?" Eloise asks.

Daniella looks at her iPad. "Let me see," she says, clicking her jaw. "You're six, right?"

"That's right. I'd changed it at the last minute from seven. Ollie couldn't get out of work."

"Just give me a moment."

"Wonderful." Eloise is curt. "Let me know."

She backs away from Daniella's post and finds a bit of breathing room at the far end of the bar. Her family huddles together in a silent clump near the restaurant's front door, and she offers them a wave before looking down and puffing her cheeks. Why is she acting like this? What in God's name is her problem? She's never spoken to Daniella in such a tone before; among her friends, she prides herself on staying calm when restaurants fumble a reservation or a waiter screws up an order. But now—Christ, look at her: she's sweating like a maniac.

Nerves about her family, about how tonight will play out: that's the only explanation she can muster. But then, this is normal, she tells herself; the last time they were all together was three years ago, at her stepfather's funeral. Who wouldn't be anxious, particularly given the stakes? The main thing to remember is that she's entering the evening with high hopes for peace, and—come hell or high water—she's determined to hold on to them. Still, she can't shake how *awkward* and *totally unlike what she expected* the past forty-five minutes have been. For starters, Alice, who showed up first, greeted her like she was a complete and total stranger. Earlier, she had hoped to mention the potential new job opportunity before the rest of the family arrived, but that prospect faded quickly. Eloise doesn't know if it's jet lag, or the shock of not having seen each other in so long, or if her sister's drunk (she smelled, very faintly, of bourbon), or what, but the fact remains that the hug Alice gave her was one of the iciest that Eloise has ever received. And when she asked about the suite—*the suite that Eloise had so generously paid for*—all she'd been able to say was, "The what?"

"The suite," Eloise repeated herself. "At Claridge's. Where you're staying?"

Alice smiled, but almost as if her mouth wasn't attached to her face.

"Oh, it's super nice."

Super nice?

Eloise forged on: "Well, I'll have to come see it when I join you for tea."

Alice smiled again and nodded, as if she hardly remembered that she'd invited Eloise over in the first place.

Then there's Paul and her mother. She doesn't know what she anticipated happening on that front, though if she's being perfectly honest with herself, it was something more than what she witnessed. Some tears, maybe. A brief but heartfelt apology. At the very least, a goddamned hug. But what had her brother done? How had Paul signaled an end to the two-year cold war that had ravaged his relationship with their mother and drawn lines in the sand between his siblings? With a handshake.

He arrived, waited for her to come to him—for her to duck and dodge and wedge and wiggle through hordes of ale-soaked Londoners—and then he stuck out his hand. She'd taken it, of course, because that's who her mother was—a woman with class—but Jesus Christ: a handshake! Her single regret is that Ollie wasn't there to see it.

And Mark? Regardless of how ghastly her brother's behavior is at the moment, she still can't make heads or tails of what Paul sees in him. In fact, so far one of the few pleasurable moments that Eloise has experienced this evening was when Mark, implying that she wasn't capable of speeding along their reservation, scooted her aside and approached the maître d's stand himself. Daniella all but ignored him, and when she finally did speak to him, she simply thanked him for his patience—the hospitality industry equivalent of *please fuck off*.

"How'd that work out?" Eloise asked him when he came slinking back to the group.

"They must just be getting their legs underneath them. Seems like there are some kinks they've got to work out." He added, "We've been waiting for fifteen minutes."

"It's one of the most popular restaurants in London."

"Huh," he said. "Interesting."

He's loathsome. That's all there is to it, she thinks. She knows she shouldn't make such rash judgments, but with Mark, it's impossible; he's atrocious. After their tedious exchange about waiting for their table, he'd launched into an awful diatribe about the dining scene in London and how it paled in comparison to places like Copenhagen and Oslo. The whole speech smacked of the quality she despises the most: unearned snobbery. And he isn't even that good looking, Eloise thinks, allowing herself a moment of shallowness. Out of the two of them, Paul's definitely cuter. If anything, she supposes Mark carries himself with a bit more confidence, but for what reason she can't possibly guess. She's met doorknobs that she's found more interesting.

But then, she's also seen some *exquisite* doorknobs.

"How about a drink, sweetheart?"

Eloise blinks and smiles. She's been so distracted by her nerves that she hardly noticed her mother squeeze her way in next to her. Behind her, Paul, Alice, and Mark jostle for space.

"Just while we wait?" Donna says.

"I think that's a great idea. Here, let me——"

"No, no." Donna slaps Eloise's hand away from her purse. "You've been gracious enough. This one's on me."

"All right, all right." Eloise plays along. "Here, at least let me introduce you to the barman."

She waves over Charles, her favorite bartender at Dean Street, and leans over the bar to kiss his cheek.

"Charles, I want you to meet my mother."

He extends a hand and Donna takes it, lightly.

"Very nice to meet you," she says. "I think we'd like to order some drinks."

Charles nods. "What can I get you?"

"Bourbon!" Alice shouts, and Eloise nearly jumps. "Neat."

"Any particular kind?"

"Whatever you've got."

Charles lifts his chin to get a better look at her.

"Well, we've got quite a——"

"Then Maker's." Alice sounds exasperated; Eloise plays with the ends of her hair. "A double."

Donna smiles apologetically to Charles. "Okay, so one bourbon. Paul? Sweetheart? What would you like?"

"Vodka martini, dirty. Mark'll have the same."

Their mother nods, and turns back to the bar. "Right, then. My son and his—his friend will both have dirty vodka martinis. And for me, I'd like a French 75, and my daughter will have—"

Eloise leans forward. "Just a glass of the Picpoul de Pinet," she says. "Thanks."

Charles repeats the order and vanishes to prepare their drinks.

Paul, Eloise notices, is snickering.

"What?" Donna asks.

"Nothing. It's just—" Her brother runs a hand through his hair. "It's just, sometimes you're really unbelievable, Mom."

Donna looks to Alice for some sort of explanation, but she's gazing elsewhere, to an unfixed spot on the ceiling.

"I don't understand," Donna says. "What'd I do?"

"Mark's now *my friend*? I've lived with him for over three years now, Mom. What, are you afraid to tell people that he's my boyfriend? That he's my *lover*?"

"Partner," Mark corrects. "Your *partner*."

Eloise could kill him. She could kill both of them.

For a moment, Donna looks flustered, hurt, and Eloise worries that she might start crying in the middle of her favorite bar. But Donna regains her composure. She clears her throat and says, "Okay. Excuse me."

Charles is in the middle of filling a flute of champagne for Donna's French 75 when she waves him over. At first he looks befuddled—he sets the flute down and frowns—but when he reaches the bar, and Donna, he smiles.

"Something else, ma'am?"

"Actually, yes. There is. Do you see that man over there?"

She points at Paul, and he freezes. Eloise wonders if it's too late to

181

hide, or to throw herself in between Charles and her mother. To take the bullet and save herself the embarrassment of having to explain her brother later on.

"Well," Donna continues. "He's my son. He's the one who ordered the dirty martini, which I'm sure will be just delicious. In any event, if you remember correctly—and I'm sure you do; you seem like a real pro—I ordered a *second* dirty martini for a young man who I *stupidly* called 'his friend.' I want you to know, Charles, that this was a *terrible* mistake. Because the truth, which my son has just made sure to remind me of, is that the young man is actually his *boyfriend*."

Charles glances at Eloise; Eloise closes her eyes.

"They've been living together for years," she hears Donna say. "Isn't that wonderful? Charles? I asked, isn't it wonderful?"

"It's wonderful, ma'am."

"We're thrilled for Paul. Love is love, Charles. And we fully and unconditionally support his lifestyle—which, by the way, we wholeheartedly believe is *how he was born*, as opposed to some loosey-goosey *choice*."

"Are you finished?" Paul growls.

"I'm sorry, sweetheart. Was that the sort of explanation you were looking for?"

"I'll have your drinks in a moment, ma'am."

Someone taps Eloise's shoulder, and her eyes shoot open.

"What?" she hisses.

"We've got a table for you, Miss Lafarge." It's Daniella. Eloise, ashamed, feels her shoulders shrink. "If you all just want to follow me, I can have your drinks brought over to you."

"Of course. Thank you."

She gestures for Donna to follow the hostess. Alice goes next, and then Mark. As Paul turns to go, though, Eloise grabs hold of his wrist.

"Ow," he says.

"Was that entirely necessary?"

A couple moves past them, balancing six highball glasses between four hands. They look familiar—they're looking at her—and Eloise tries to place them. She can't, though, so instead she smiles.

"You're kidding, right?" Paul says.

"You could cut her a little slack once in a while, for Christ's sake."

"*Me? I'm* the one who needs to be cutting some slack?"

"Oh, give it a rest, Paul."

"You don't know, Eloise." His nostrils flare. "You have no idea the sort of relentless oppression that—"

She tightens her grip on his wrist and digs her nails into his skin. She can feel the faint pulse of his blood.

"No," she says. "No, you listen to me. I come to this restaurant *multiple times a week*, do you hear me? These are *my people*."

He starts to speak, but she clenches down harder.

"What's more, this is *my wedding*. I'm going to repeat that, so you fully understand it. *This is my wedding*. Do not fuck this up, Paul. Do you hear me? Do. Not. Fuck. This. Up."

She loosens her grip just enough for him to yank himself away. With his other hand, he rubs the wrist that she was holding, which is now tattooed with deep purple crescents.

"You're insane," he says, and she does her best to ignore him. Then, after he's stared at her a little longer: "God, your *hair*."

She says, "What about it?"

"How does it always look so *good*? It fucking kills me."

Paul

Paul fumbles in his pocket for a cigarette, but quickly remembers that he's with Mark, who hates it when he smokes. Instead, he locates a lone piece of gum and pops it in his mouth.

"It's just so *bouncy,* is the thing. Even in this humidity it's just so bouncy."

"It didn't look that bouncy to me," Mark says.

"Her hair's always been like that, though. Even when we were kids. She must get it from her dad. He must have bouncy hair. Because, I mean, look at Alice. Look at me. It practically looks like someone crowned us both with mops."

"I think you have very nice hair."

Mark's not paying attention. Instead, he's looking up and down Shaftsbury Avenue for a taxi, of which there are none. Less than none, it seems. In fact, Paul thinks, the street's crammed with so many people and so few cars that he suspects they'd have better luck finding a rickshaw, or hitching a ride on some strapping Londoner's back, than hailing a cab. And yet, still Mark appears determined—he's got his hand shoved into the air like a hitchhiker—so Paul indulges him; he stands by his side and chews his gum.

"I wonder if we should have stayed," he says, suddenly thinking about the end of dinner. Eloise snatched up the bill and invited them all over to her flat for coffee and scotch. Alice and his mother had agreed to go—but then, Donna's also staying there, and Alice has the unfortunate duty of being a bridesmaid. Before Paul could even weigh the option, though, Mark had declined on behalf of both of them.

"We've got plans to meet a friend of ours," he'd said, matter-of-factly.

Eloise had stared at Paul, and the only thing he could think of was how the restaurant's low lighting, coupled with the spectacular volume of her hair, created the impression that her head was exploding.

On Shaftsbury Avenue, Mark pauses from his taxi hunt to turn and gawk at Paul.

"You're kidding, right?"

"She's just trying so hard," Paul says, a little astonished by how quickly he's leaping to his half sister's defense. "If having a glass of expensive scotch in her palatial apartment makes her happy, it seems like it's the least we could do."

"She's an awful snob."

"Oh, come on." Paul smiles and kisses Mark's cheek. "You're only saying that because she managed to out-snob you."

Mark pulls away. "No, I'm saying it because she's insufferable." He straightens the lapels on his blazer. "Besides, my God, Paul. She practically assaulted you. I'm surprised she didn't draw blood when she grabbed your arm."

Paul rubs his wrist. The little crescents still remain. "She was just excited," he says. "I mean, like I said, she's trying so hard."

"Are you listening to yourself right now? She abuses you, Paul. She bosses you around, and she abuses you. Sometimes I think you actually like being pushed around. Christ, look at how Goulding treated you."

Paul's puzzled. "I threw a mannequin at his head. I broke his nose."

"Only after he treated you like a halfwit pack mule, no doubt. You truly are a glutton for punishment."

A cyclist swerves toward the curb and nearly crushes Mark's foot. He curses.

"Yeah, ha, look who I date."

But Mark's still screaming at the errant cyclist, who's disappeared behind a bus. When he's finished, he turns to Paul, red-faced, and huffs. "What'd you just say?"

"Nothing. Forget it." Paul thinks. He takes a breath and says, "Maybe we should just go home."

"You're being ridiculous."

"I'm serious, Mark. You're in a bad mood—"

"I'm *not* in a bad mood."

"—we're already late, and there are literally *zero* cabs in this city. And besides, what are we even planning on doing? We're just going to end up getting drunk in a crowded bar, which is what we do every Saturday night at home, anyway." He kicks a piece of gravel off the curb. "I'm exhausted, too. Maybe we should just go home."

On the opposite side of the street, two women spill out from a pub door. One of them drops her purse; her friend laughs and stumbles backward.

"Five minutes ago you were practically begging me to go to your snob-of-a-sister's house," Mark says. "And now, when we're on our way to meet Alcott and actually do something fun, you tell me that you're tired and you want to go home?" He spots an open cab turning onto Wardour Street and he nearly throws himself in front of it. Craning his head around to face Paul, he calls out, "When did you become so boring?"

Is he boring, though? If that's the case, it's certainly not due to a lack of thinking, of considering, on Paul's part. In fact, if anything it's *because* he's plagued with this tendency to mull things over that he frequently finds himself in a state of overwrought paralysis.

"Here you are." Alcott hands him a vodka soda. "Bottoms up." He winks. Next to Paul's left shoulder, an old Spice Girls song warbles on a stand-alone speaker. This, from a country that produced the Sex Pistols and the Rolling Stones.

He must become different, Paul thinks. He can't allow this dreadful ambivalence to dictate his nondecisions—his *boringness*—any longer. He needs to start making choices. Start acting. Throw more proverbial mannequins in the faces of sadistic psychotherapists, so to speak. He must show Mark that, despite what he might think, Paul is not dull. And he must do it defiantly. But how? What's the first step toward unshackling himself from, well, *himself*? For starters, he'll drink this vodka-soda as fast as he can. Then he'll order another one, and he'll drink that one even faster. A little lubrication, a little loosening up, might do him some good, he figures, particularly as he enters this new Era of Not-Thinking. Besides, Mark hates it when Paul drinks too much, which is, currently, a perfect excuse for drinking too much. And then what? He'll dance. Yes. Rather than concern himself with how he moves his hips (awkwardly, like he's squeezing between two chairs), or how much he's embarrassing Mark (a lot), or the state of the bar's music (terrible: the Spice Girls have stepped aside for S Club Seven), he'll wend his way through the crowd of twinks to the dance floor, where he'll bask in the comfort of knowing that regardless of the country gay bars everywhere are all more or less the same. The only thing he has to do first is get out of his own way.

He sips his drink and takes a breath. Exhaling, he imagines his old ambivalent self, fleeing his body.

"Let's leave," Mark says.

"Wait, what?"

"Alcott says this place is awful tonight, and I agree." Mark finishes his beer and leaves the bottle on the bar. "He knows of some other place. We can walk there."

"But I was just going to—"

"Come on, Paul. Finish your drink."

Christ, Paul thinks once they've made their way outside, he's being especially dickish tonight. With a silver lighter, engraved with something in Latin that Paul can't read, Alcott lights a cigarette, and Paul must resist the very real urge to tackle him to the ground and snatch the thing from his long, British hands. What *has* gotten into Mark, though? Eloise had embarrassed him—that happened—and while Paul had assured him that his sister's slight wasn't intentional, privately he knew the truth: Eloise hadn't taken to Mark. She thought he was a phony. This in itself doesn't surprise Paul: Eloise is a subtle bitch—which, in his opinion, is the worst kind of bitch a person could be. What *does* surprise him, though, is how mixed his emotions are toward Eloise's judgment of Mark. On the one hand, he's fiercely loyal to his boyfriend, despite how douchily he's currently acting, and wants, desperately, to eviscerate Eloise, to give her a piece of his mind. On the other hand, for the first time he finds himself suddenly curious about his sister's opinion. How, exactly, is Mark a phony? In which categories of class and culture does she find him lacking? What specific *breed* of awfulness does she attribute to him? Because if he's being totally honest, he suspects that whatever she thinks of Mark, whatever her judgment of him may be, he might, for the first time, actually sort of agree with her. He *is* kind of awful—and not just momentarily, but generally, perpetually. For the first few years of their relationship he did a commendable job of keeping his awfulness at bay, of convincing people that there was another side to him, and that his undesirable qualities only came out when he was tired, or annoyed, or hungry. Lately, though, it seems to Paul that Mark's stopped giving a fuck, that enough of the Prestons and Crosbys and Alcotts of the world have responded positively to his douchiness that he's no longer concerning himself with what it means to be a decent human being. These are obvious truths, he knows, but he feels suddenly that he's confronting them for the first time, and he dreads the nagging existential doubts they're bound to leave in their wake.

But oh, God: here he is, thinking himself into a standstill all over again.

He stands behind Alcott and gulps up a redemptive cloud of second-hand smoke to calm his mind.

"Right then," Alcott says, flicking the cigarette into the gutter. "Here we are."

He leads them into a dim bar with mirrored walls and a low, baroque chandelier. The room is sparsely populated—only a few men occupy the barstools scattered around the curved black bar—and its walls are painted with silver fleur-de-lis whose petals interlock to create dizzying and unpredictable patterns. Paul blinks and, quickly recalling his mission to dispel Mark's notion of him as boring, he announces that he'll be buying the first round of drinks.

"The cocktails here are delicious," Alcott says. "Very inventive."

"What'll it be, then?" Paul does his best to sound carefree. *Jocund.*

Mark says, "Why don't you just surprise us, Paul."

The drink list is daunting: over eighty cocktails divided into one-term, self-conscious categories: *bubbles, risky, foreign, medieval.* He scans the menu, flipping through the pages, his eyes tripping over words like *coriander* and *cloudberry.* He mustn't look too long at it, Paul knows, lest he find himself paralyzed by choice, and so when the bartender asks him what he'd like, Paul tells him three Orange Willys, even though the only ingredient he recognizes is gin. Between his two hands he balances the three drinks, all of which are the color of dusty, smoggy sunsets, and by the time he's reached Alcott and Mark, he hasn't spilled a single drop, and although Paul's duly impressed with himself, the two men are too engrossed in a whispered conversation to notice.

Paul sets the three coupes on the table around which Mark and Alcott are huddled and says, "What are you talking about?"

Mark's head shoots up. "Nothing. Forget about it."

Alcott rolls his eyes and laughs. "Oh, come on, Mark. He's not a child." Then, glancing down at the cocktail, he says, "An Orange Willy, eh? Bold choice."

"What aren't I a child about?" Paul asks.

Alcott grins at Mark; Mark frowns at Paul.

"I've brought us a little surprise," Alcott says. "Just to make the evening a bit more interesting."

"What kind of surprise?" Paul sips from his drink: it tastes like fermented orange cough syrup and burnt rosemary.

"Have you ever heard of mephedrone, Paul?"

"No, I don't—"

"You Americans." Alcott laughs. "So unimaginative when it comes to your drugs. If it's not coke or hash or heroin, it might as well not exist. Hmm . . . I'd forgotten how . . . *chemical* this drink tastes. In any event, mephedrone. A lovely stimulant that makes its home in the amphetamine and cathinone classes. Typically snorted, it carries a high not entirely dissimilar to ecstasy or cocaine. For years it could be bought, legally, as plant food—"

"Plant food."

"Yes. Plant food. But then, well, you know how these things go: some bloke up in Manchester took a little too much and ended up cutting off his own thumb before stabbing his mother eight times. The authorities stepped in, made the drug illegal, and ruined the fun for those of us who are capable of holding our substances in a more responsible fashion."

Paul swallows another mouthful of Orange Willy. Viscous syrup coats his mouth, his throat. "And you said it's called mephedrone?"

"Yes," Alcott says. From his pocket he produces a small plastic baggie, the sort that Paul's used to seeing filled with coke, except the substance here is light brown, the color of weak coffee mixed with too much milk. "A lot of folks call it Meow Meow, but frankly I can't imagine a *chavvier* name, so I stick to mephedrone."

Discreetly glancing over his shoulder to ensure no one's watching, Paul takes the baggie from Alcott. The drug's not as fine as coke; instead, it clumps together in rocky crystals.

"You've got to crush it up, obviously," Alcott says.

"And you say it's like ecstasy?" Paul tries to remember the last time he did ecstasy.

Alcott nods. "A bit. With the mental acuteness of blow."

"Oh." Paul grimaces. "Blow gives me the worst hangover. It makes my soul feel like it's drained, or something. And the *headache*. Jesus."

He starts to pass the baggie back, when Alcott says, laughing, "Oh, come on, Nervous Nelly. Don't be such a bore!"

Paul looks over at Mark, whose glass is empty and whose eyebrows are arched, knowingly, glibly.

"I'm *not* a bore." He snatches the baggie back. "Where the fuck is the bathroom?"

"It's on the other side of the looking glass." Alcott digs into his pocket. "Here, take my key."

"The looking glass?"

He points to one of the mirrors along the wall, this one framed in chipped gold paint.

"Push that mirror open—it's actually a door. On the other side there's a small back bar. Next to it you'll see signs for the bathroom."

Paul does as Alcott instructs—he leans his weight into the heavy glass—and, after the door groans and swings open, he emerges into an even dimmer room, this one entirely empty, with the exception of a sole, lonely bartender, dicing up cilantro beneath the faint green glow of a banker's lamp.

"Loo?" he says, glancing up.

"Er, yeah."

The bartender nods toward a corner of the room, where there's a row of three identical stalls. After locking himself in the one farthest to the left, Paul scrambles in his pocket for the drugs. Two sconces are affixed to the wall on either side of the sink, but the light they throw is anemic, so instead he huddles around a candle that reeks of patchouli and inspects the mephedrone. He shakes the bag so the chunks gather at the bottom, and he's reminded of how this moment was often his favorite part of doing coke, back when he did it more frequently than he should have, during those wilderness years of his early and midtwenties: the standing-alone-next-to-a-cheap-scented-candle-in-a-bathroom-with-which-you're-quickly-becoming-too-familiar-wondering-if-you're-taking-too-long-wondering-if-the-cilantro-dicing-bartender-will-start-to-suspect-that-you're-doing-a-little-more-than-taking-a-piss. That's not to say he didn't like the instant the drugs kicked in, that devastatingly beautiful split second when he swore he could feel his arteries tighten and his mind burst open with clarity. The problem, though, was that as soon as he felt that moment he simultaneously began to anticipate its inevitable death; he saw before him the twilight of the high where instead of feeling phenomenally interesting he started worrying that he'd made a terrible—and predictably boring—decision.

"You're bad at doing drugs," Alice said to him once, when he explained all this to her. "Some people are good at drugs, and some people are bad at drugs. You're bad at drugs."

He disagreed. "No. People who are bad at drugs start doing them in their thirties, and then talk about them with the same immature excitement that we had about stealing Dad's vodka when we were teenagers."

Alice shook her head. "No. Those people are just tacky." She repeated herself. "You're bad at drugs, Paul. I'm bad at doubles tennis, and you're bad at drugs. It's nothing to be ashamed of—it's just the way it is."

Watching the light from the candle cast shadows across his fingers, he still disagrees with her. He's not bad at drugs so much as he appreciates them in a different way. As opposed to deriving his high from the substance itself, Paul's tastes are finer, he tells himself, more refined; he appreciates the preparation, the chase, the anticipation. That sliver of time when he can be sure of his decision without having to concern himself with its consequences. But then, what was he supposed to do: give Alcott a full bag of the stuff and say that the *thought* of snorting it was enough? How dull, he imagines Mark saying. How *boring*.

Using the toilet seat as a makeshift table, he uses his credit card to crush the mephedrone. The more he works it, the whiter the crystals turn, and Paul questions, briefly, the merits and pitfalls of inhaling such a chameleonish substance. But before he can think any longer, he pries open the baggie and plunges the long end of the key into it, scooping up a healthy pile of speckled dust. The first bump he does is borderline unbearable: it burns worse than cocaine, and instead of blow's familiar gasoline-y drip, Meow Meow (can he call it that?) tastes and smells like artificially sweetened stale piss. Still, after snorting a few gulps of air to clear his sinuses, he convinces himself to snort a second bump, and then a third. He wants there to be a noticeable dent in the stuff by the time he slips the baggie back to Alcott. He wants them to see just how fun he is.

It's 4:07. No. Now it's 4:08. From the orange couch in Alcott's living room, Paul watches another minute blink by on the clock above the stove. Alcott sits next to him, his arm draped over his shoulder; on the other side of the coffee table, Mark drinks from his beer. A half-finished cigarette burns, neglected, in an ashtray. *The Very Best of Fleetwood Mac* has been playing for the past twenty minutes, and they're all doing their best to ignore the lyrics to "Gypsy." Paul wonders what time the sun comes up in London. He wonders if the Thames turns blue at the first light of dawn, or red.

How many bars did they go to once they left the Looking Glass? Four, Paul counts. Or: three bars, and one dance club. A place with strobe lights and a moody fog machine, where Alcott started getting handsy with Paul (pushing his groin against his thigh as they danced, slipping his fingers through his belt loops, working his palm up under his shirt, etc., etc., etc.) while Mark made an extended trip to the bathroom. Paul had done more Meow Meow, but he considers his decision to be one fueled by self-preservation, as opposed to pleasure seeking. Twenty minutes after his initial three bumps, a jolt of euphoria shocked him, much as Alcott said it would, and Paul found himself smiling involuntarily, and saying fascinating things, and wanting, more than anything else, for everyone to just *be friends*. He knew he was buzzing, and he could tell Mark was becoming mildly irritated, but the prospect of shutting up, of not sharing everything that he was feeling, struck him as *actually* impossible, and so to help temper that impossibility, he ordered himself two more vodkas and some tequila. It turned out, though, that he overshot that decision—about thirty minutes later he nearly fell asleep in the back of a cab—so when they arrived at the next bar, he promptly found an unoccupied stall and cut himself a line of not-insignificant size, just to level himself out. The rest of the night followed a similar seesaw pattern, with Paul and Alcott and Mark snorting and drinking and groping in search of an acceptable high until, sometime around three thirty, the mephedrone disappeared and Alcott couldn't get a hold of his dealer.

"The bloody son of a bitch," Alcott said, furiously staring at his phone after trying the man for the seventh time. They were standing on Hollen Street, three blocks from where Paul and Mark had eaten dinner earlier in the evening. "What else could he possibly be doing?"

A minute later, Alcott proposed that they return to his flat and drink whatever he had lying around while they waited for his dealer to return his call.

And now what? 4:08 flips over to 4:09, and it becomes clearer and clearer that Alcott's dealer—a Mancunian called Jose—has called it a night.

Mark finishes his beer and looks at Alcott. Alcott smiles and looks at Paul. Paul does his best to look at neither of them, and in the process looks at both of them.

They've been doing this for the past fifteen minutes, ever since they finished the sambuca stashed behind the coffeemaker on the top of Alcott's fridge. Passing the baton of furtive looks, Paul thinks. It reminds him of the gym he used to go to in New York, where old married men would spend hours in the steam room, staring each other down, giving each other peeks of what lurked beneath their towels. A few times after he had finished working out Paul had joined them, under the pretense of needing to sweat out some imaginary cold. Beyond the sadness of the experience, what struck him most acutely was its sheer tedium: here were a bunch of dudes staring at each other—literally, staring at each other for an hour—without actually ever doing anything about it. *For God's sake,* he remembers wanting to scream, *just whip it out already. We all want the same thing, don't we?*

And indeed: Don't they? Honestly, though, Paul's not sure. He knows what Mark wants—he's hardly been subtle about it. And he suspects that Alcott's gunning for the same, multilimbed outcome. But what about him? What about Paul? He doesn't want Mark to think that he's won, but if this thing happens, Mark's sense of victory will be impossible to prevent. But then, his desire to prevent his lover from feeling a sense of accomplishment seems like a petty reason for not pursuing an experience. That desire, though, which is very real and which Paul admits he should probably address at some point, skirts the more pressing issue, the more pressing question: *What does Paul want?* Objectively, sex with two (or more) people sounds fun. The logistics might prove to be a little stressful, but still—fun. To say otherwise would be to lie. Wendy was right about that. So, yes, from a purely primal sense, this is something that Paul wants. Yet obviously it's not that easy; Paul's not a purely primal being. None of them are. They are all cursed with the ability to reason what unreasonable consequences might ensue if they end up sleeping together.

He has a headache. He hopes against hope that Jose calls back.

More than anything, he thinks, he wants to be done with it. With all of it: the parsing out of *why* Mark wants this; the dissecting of *what* prevents Paul from having Mark's confidence; the infinite permutations of *what if* and *how about*; the millions of outcomes that he can't stop himself from imagining. He just wants it all to be done.

The song switches over to "Second Hand News" and, in what Paul will later remember as one of his more graceless maneuvers, he leans over and shoves his tongue down Alcott's throat. He's not sure if the drugs and alcohol have blunted his ability to appreciate nuance, or, alternatively, if this is just the way things are, but he's surprised to detect very little difference between drunkenly kissing Alcott and drunkenly kissing Mark. There's the same eager pressure of lips, the same frantic exploration of tongues and teeth. Paul feels a hand work its way up his knee, and then his inner thigh, before Mark gently pulls Alcott away and starts to kiss his neck. Paul's initial impulse is to cry out: *Here my boyfriend is, sucking on another man's Adam's apple!* But then he remembers that approximately two seconds ago, he kissed Alcott—that, when it comes right down to it, Paul started all of this—and so to stop Mark midhickey would be to betray a level of inequitable jealousy that, while very real, even Paul is uncomfortable voicing. So he lets Mark continue exploring Alcott. He lets him peel off Alcott's jeans and kiss the inside of his thighs and wiggle a few fingers beneath the elastic band of his underwear. Unsure of what he should be doing during all of this (moaning, even though he's not the one being touched? Providing Mark with some canned suggestions, some encouragement? Neither strikes him as the right option), Paul struggles to take off his own pants and, after nearly falling onto the coffee table, finally kicks them to the floor. He's impressed by the gusto with which Mark is presently inhaling Alcott, and tries to remember a time that his boyfriend gave him such an enthusiastic blow job. But this leads him back into that same murky jealousy he's trying to convince Mark that he's shed, and so instead of focusing on how Alcott's head is thrown back, or how his eyes are closed, he tries to think of something else. He wonders, for example, if anyone would like a glass of water.

It's Alcott who eventually pulls him into the fray, grabbing Paul by the back of his neck and shoving his face toward Alcott's crotch. At first it's crowded: Mark's still attacking Alcott's dick, so Paul awkwardly maneuvers himself onto the floor in order to get himself within tongue-length of the action. Once he's there, and once he's found a position that's not too uncomfortable on his knees or lower back, he does his best to emulate Mark's vigor—or, actually, to surpass it. Now that he's got part of Alcott in his mouth, and now that Mark's chin is knocking against the top of his head, he becomes quickly aware that, unlike most blow jobs he's given, this one has turned into a fierce competition. His mouth too stuffed to actually say anything, Mark lets out a low, performative groan, and Paul realizes that he's yet to make a sound. Does Alcott now worry that Paul's not enjoying himself as much as Mark is? Does he think that Paul looks at licking his crotch as some kind of chore?

He frees his lips for a moment.

He says, in a voice an octave lower than normal: "Your balls taste great."

Mark grinds his knee into Paul's ribs to shut him up, then comes up for air. Paul hears the wet pop of lips against skin; his vision limited to Alcott's groin, his inner thighs, the light hair sprouting on his belly, he assumes that Mark has resurfaced to kiss Alcott, leaving Paul to continue the job at hand alone. And so Paul does: with Alcott now totally fair game, he gets on his knees and swallows as much of him as he can, determined to best Mark's efforts. He's doing well, he thinks, taking special care to avoid the little faux pas that characterize Mark's oral abilities (too much spit, not enough hand. Teeth). That's not to say all this isn't strange, because it is— *it's really fucking strange*—but he's doing what he can to make the most of it, to enjoy himself.

Behind Paul, Mark uses one hand to tilt his hips up and the other to press down hard on his lower back. Before he has time to turn around, he feels pressure against his ass and then an unmistakable and familiar jolt of pain.

"*Jesus*, Mark," he says. "A little—"

But Mark just pushes Paul's face back down.

Although he's currently too preoccupied to at least consciously consider such things, later Paul will reflect on this moment. He'll wonder, primarily, about what's going through Alcott's mind. If he considers himself an intruder, or more of a guest star. If he's turned on by observing, firsthand, the cruel and subtle intricacies of Paul and Mark's relationship, or if he's too wholly consumed by pursuing his own pleasure to notice the finer details.

Right now, though, there's no time for that. Right now, he's too busy focusing on the irregular pace at which Mark is fucking him.

He's thirsty. He should have gotten a glass of water when he had the chance.

There's a silence in which all he hears are the strange, squishy sounds of sex. Then: the first four chords of "Gold Dust Woman."

"Come here," Mark says, pulling out of him. Paul starts to stand, but Mark holds him down. "No. You stay where you are."

Mark repositions himself farther down along the couch, where he watches with a sort of crazed possession as Alcott slips into Paul.

He's concerned about the condom situation (namely: there isn't one), but it also gets him off, in that shameful way he imagines most gay men experience when they realize they're flirting with the thin boundary between sex and death. So he tries not to think about it; he tries instead to concentrate on noticing the differences between Mark and Alcott's styles, their ways of finding and losing rhythms.

But then it stops. Before "Seven Wonders" even reaches the bridge, Alcott pulls out and crawls up to the couch, where he sits next to Mark and starts jacking off.

"Come on up here," he says to Paul, and Paul does. Because, really, what other options are there?

He doesn't know how long they sit there. At least through the rest of "Sisters of the Moon," and the entirety of "Family Man." Occasionally they'll reach across a leg and touch one another, but mostly they touch themselves. No one actually climaxes—among the three of them, not a single person comes. Rather, at some point during "As Long as You Follow," Alcott says that he's got to piss, and excuses himself. Five minutes later, when he still hasn't returned, Mark goes in to check on him. He comes back moments later and tells Paul that he's fallen asleep.

"He's passed out naked on his bed," he says, dryly.

Paul bites his lip. "Well, that doesn't mean we can't finish . . ."

Mark scratches his left knee. He doesn't smile. "I don't think I've got it in me," he says. "Must be the drugs."

"Oh."

Paul looks down. The hair on his lower abdomen and thighs is coated with sweat and lube. Suddenly he wants, more than anything, to be clean.

Coming over to him, Mark digs through the heap of discarded clothes for his underwear.

"Get up," he says. "Help me make up the couch."

Alice

_____

July 6

She can't see her toes. The robe they gave her to wear after her massage is long enough that it bunches around her heels, and she nearly trips on it as she shuffles, spaced out and bleary eyed, from the treatment room to one of the recliners in the spa's lounge. A walking terry-cloth pillowcase—that's what she imagines she must look like. An attendant asks her if she'd like a glass of cucumber water, and she says yes because she thinks she's supposed to, and as she waits for the girl to return with it she traces the spa's logo embroidered on the robe's belt. The room's dimly lit, and cold, and this latter point puzzles her; in a place where people spend most of their time naked, or at the very least covered in a paper-thin sheet, shouldn't there be a little heat? On the other side of the room, next to a vase holding a lone orchid, sit two other women, flipping through copies of *Tatler* and British *Vogue*. Alice doesn't recognize them—they aren't members of the bridal party—but she does notice how they've both got their legs crossed in front of them, instead of folded up beneath their chins, and so she quickly corrects her position.

The attendant gives Alice her water. She sips from it and smiles. She knows she's supposed to like it—she knows it's supposed to make her feel relaxed, or rejuvenated, or youthful, or something. Still, staring at the cucumber slice floating among the cubes of ice, all she can think of is the shitty salad bar on Wilshire where she usually gets lunch during the workweek. From a collection of hidden speakers, water trickles through imaginary brooks. Reeds blow in electric winds. Zen is carefully and laboriously digitized.

Where is Eloise? Where are the other bridesmaids? A minute ago she heard a door open and close, and then the soft shuffling of slippered feet, but no one materialized in the waiting area; still, the only company she's got is the pair of *Tatler* readers. Maybe that's for the best, though, Alice thinks. Maybe it's better that she spends some time alone. The past four hours have been exhausting, and the massage—forty-five minutes of being pummeled by a Finnish Vikingess called Majia—did nothing to change that. She needs a rest, a breather, a pause. A break from conversing with Eloise's friends—an act that feels more akin to moonwalking on a tightrope than talking.

There are three of them, and they're nice enough. And when they're not being nice, it's out of ignorance, as opposed to some classist form of malice: this is what Alice needs to keep reminding herself. She'll admit, when she first met them at eight o'clock this morning at Eloise's flat, their names—the *sheer things that they called themselves*—almost sent her running for the hills. Minty, Henny, and Flossie. Christ—she knew they were nicknames; that they stood for slightly more normal things like Henrietta, or Florence, or Matilda, but *still*. How could they introduce themselves with straight faces? How could they spend an hour with their parents without breaking down in tears? Without shouting *Good God, what were you thinking?* Shaking their hands and kissing their cheeks, Alice could feel the bemused shock creep across her face, but she stopped herself at the edge of becoming transparent. This was not how she wanted to start the day.

Because the night before, sitting alone at the bar at Claridge's, she'd reached the unfortunate and dreadfully boring conclusion that she needed a change of attitude. She was humiliated by how she'd acted since arriving in London. Storming her room's minibar; gorging herself on eggs and buttered toast until she made herself sick, only to then wipe spittle from her mouth as she reached for a slice of bacon; employing gluttony as an act of retribution against her sister—that was just the start of it. There was also that dinner two nights ago—the one that Eloise planned at that awful, crowded restaurant in Soho. An hour and a half before they were all scheduled to meet, Alice found a hole-in-the-wall pub half a block away, where she fortified herself with two bourbons and a Klonopin. At the time she considered it a necessary move: this was the first time she was seeing her family—her *whole* family—in three years. There was bound to be some inevitable awkwardness (Paul seeing Donna; Eloise seeing Paul; Paul seeing everyone), and Alice considered getting too blitzed to feel that palpable discomfort to be a matter of pragmatic strategy.

The plan backfired. She hadn't anticipated having to down another bourbon once she arrived at the restaurant—Eloise had stressed how important it was that everyone showed up on time. But she did, and she suspects that was the drink that tilted her over the edge. At dinner she nearly passed out in her soup, and whenever anyone asked her a question, the most she could manage were monosyllabic responses. When she woke up foggy and cotton mouthed the next morning, the only things she could squarely remember from the evening were the knowing, dickish looks that Mark had shot her from across the table.

Today will be better, she tells herself again, fishing the slice of cucumber out from the cup and crunching down on it. Today she'll act like an adult. And so far the plan has worked out well. Or, if not well, then at least okay. She does worry that she made a fool of herself during the day's first scheduled event—a private yoga session that Minty had arranged at a studio in South Kensington. The instructor, a bald, sinewy man named Linus, kept coming around to correct her poses. Whereas Eloise and her friends glided through their sun salutations and crow poses and downward dogs with gelatinous flexibility, Alice's body seemed hell-bent on being uncooperative. "Breathe into it," Linus kept telling her, as he pressed his palm against the base of her spine. "Let the breath guide you." And each time, Alice did: she'd exhale long, and hard, and loud, as she imagined slugging the son of a bitch in his smug, enlightened face. The whole thing was made doubly problematic by how boastful she'd acted before arriving at the studio. When Flossie (was it Flossie?) asked her if she'd ever done yoga before, she scoffed and explained that in L.A. yoga was performed on the beach, at sunrise, most mornings before work. "I just hope I'll get as good of a workout," she said. "On account of there not being any sand."

And then, an hour later, there she was: knocking Minty over as she toppled out of her tree pose.

No one said anything—this was England, after all—and really, they didn't need to. Once class had finished, and the women had showered and changed and settled down with tall glasses of beet juice, Alice intercepted enough clandestine glances to provide her with at least a year's worth of humiliation. At first she thought she was being paranoid. After she mentioned that she was staying at Claridge's, and she caught Henny raising an eyebrow at Minty, she tried telling herself that she was being overly sensitive and childish; that she was acting like she did during freshman volleyball, whenever she missed a strike and Chrissy Sherman laughed at her. But the looks kept coming. Minty winking at Henny; Henny gently nudging Flossie in the ribs; Eloise staring into the purple mess in her glass, doing her best to feign ignorance. Soon, Alice found her paranoia aligning a little too perfectly with reality.

When they had finished their juices, a receptionist from the studio announced that a town car was outside waiting to take them to the spa, whenever they were ready.

"We've arranged for a bottle of prosecco to be waiting for you in the backseat," she said.

Minty thanked her, and everyone stood.

"Is this when we put on penis hats and slip dollar bills into a stripper's G-string?"

Alice looked around: no one was laughing. Instead, each of the women offered her own peculiar version of a pained smile and filed out toward the car.

"Strippers and penis hats? Honestly, Alice," Eloise said, when they were the only two left in the room. "Sometimes it's like you've made it your mission in life to embarrass me."

That had stung, so much so that Alice was inclined to strike back, but she stopped herself. And looking back now, as she chews and swallows her cucumber, she's glad that she exercised some restraint. Because if she had lashed out in retaliation—if she had, for instance, told Eloise that her friends were farces of fucking people with made-up fucking names— well, where would that have gotten her? She'd be left wallowing in a hole of her own making, a hole that she'd spend the next twelve hours trying to climb out of.

Lunch is prix fixe in a private room at the Ledbury, and when it's finished Alice is still starving. The portions weren't exactly small in size (though a confit leg of pigeon hardly inspires delusions of decadence), and there were five of them—six, even, if you count the petit fours the waiter brought out at the end. Still, very early on it became apparent to Alice that this would be a lunch of picking, as opposed to eating. Salads of almonds and green beans and peaches were dissected and rearranged, the ingredients lined up and scattered. The same went for the salmon in tomato butter, and the pork jowl with fennel and mousserons. When the baked meringue graced the table, Alice didn't even bother to lift a fork.

For all their aversion to solid food, though, none of the women seem to take issue with the prosecco. Since she climbed into the shotgun seat of the town car that brought them to the restaurant (there was no more room in the back), Alice's glass, along with everyone else's, has hovered somewhere between half full and spilling over. Initially, she was relieved by the addition of booze. In the disastrous aftermath of yoga she feared that the rest of the afternoon would be dry, and characterized by the sort of responsible and health-conscious activities that she's spent much of the past decade avoiding. After her third glass, though, she began to grow nervous. She'd already screwed up once with that stripper comment, and all she'd had to drink at that point was a glass of blended beets. Who knew how badly she'd blow it after the fifth, sixth, seventh glass?

"You can't *possibly* claim that she's got an ounce of taste," Minty says. "For God's sake, did you see what she wore two weekends ago at Goodwood?"

"It's easier than one might think to make that sort of mistake with mauve." Henny leans back in her chair and drapes a long, bare arm over the back of the empty chair next to her. Of the three of them, Alice finds her to be the most intimidating. She's not the most talkative of the group, but when she speaks, it's with a bored, lazy authority. Reaching up, she unfastens the pin that's been holding her bun together, and dark hair tumbles well past her shoulders. "Besides, babe, if we're working off the proposition that a *single* case of erroneous judgment in selecting a sundress confines one to a lifetime of bad taste, you would've been a goner in the fourth form."

Flossie leans forward. "Remember that terrible *plaid* number, Mint? The skirt with those awful green tights?"

"It was before my growth spurt." Minty clinks her wedding ring against the stem of her glass. "It was *more* than the mauve, Henny, and you know it. That hat she was wearing with it looked like an omelet. A big, bloody omelet."

Henny runs her fingers through her hair and cranes back her long neck.

"You're just cross that Simon ended up with Lucinda, instead of you."

"UM, I BEG YOUR PARDON, DO I LOOK CROSS?"

Alice glances over at Minty, who is presently flipping her left ring finger at Henny. At its base, pinched up against Minty's sizable knuckle, is one of the bigger diamonds that Alice has ever seen.

"I can't travel with it, you know," Minty says, cocking her head and gazing at the gem. "Last year Thomas took me to Tulum. Not for any special occasion, really—just *because*. In any event, I had to leave it in a safe at Coutts. Anyway, Lucinda's got a face like a feral cat. And she's from Nottingham."

"For fuck's sake, Minty." Henny holds her champagne coupe by its wide bowl, instead of its stem. "*Please* try not to be such a terrible bore."

"I hardly see what's boring about Tulum."

Alice doesn't know what to say, though she's sure she should say something. The only comments she's had to offer so far have been bland critiques of the food that's been served—food that none of them have actually eaten. Every time she's on the verge of saying something else, though, of putting her neck out and *contributing*, she stops herself. She worries that whatever it is she's thought of to say might stop all conversation dead in its track.

Still, despite her better judgment, she says, "Tulum's the best," and everyone stares at her.

"You've been?" Minty asks, and Alice tries not to be too hurt by the incredulity in her voice.

"A few times, yeah. I . . . I lived in Mexico City for a few years, actually."

"Fascinating. Simon loves D.F." Minty looks around for the bottle of prosecco. "Why'd you leave?"

Alice reaches down and begins picking at a loose thread on her napkin. She can feel her face turning red. "Uh, well—"

"She just missed me *too* much," Eloise says. Beneath the table she reaches over and squeezes Alice's leg.

"Anyway, Mint," her sister says, "what were you saying about Simon?"

"Oh, just that he doesn't need reasons to take me on holiday."

Flossie groans. "What are you going to tell us next? That he whisked you off to Lapland for Christmas, and that's the reason you sleep with him? Because he flew you Club Europe to meet the real Father Christmas? It's just all so terribly pedestrian."

"Simon only flies first." Minty adjusts her ring and purses her lips. She's near to a retort—Alice can tell—but Eloise stops her.

"It's a lovely ring," she says. "And Lapland is gorgeous in December. So," she continues, trying to diffuse whatever tension remains, "who's going to Tilly's shoot the first weekend in September?"

"I suppose I am," Flossie says. "Though the Cotswolds can be so tedious."

Eloise shifts her chair so she's facing Alice. "You'd love a shoot. They're fun."

Alice smiles. "Is Tilly the name of the model?"

There's a brief moment when the women do their best to be polite, but it fades quickly, and just as quickly they dissolve into laughter. Alice feels her nostrils flare. Looking down, she sees herself, distorted, in the reflection of her knife.

"That's positively *adorable*," Henny says. Leaning forward and speaking softly, she explains, "No, darling, it's not a *fashion* shoot. It's a *proper* shoot."

She pantomimes holding a rifle, and Flossie about falls from her chair to the floor.

On the other side of the table she can see Eloise shift in her seat, uncomfortable, wanting to save her again. Alice prays that she doesn't. She prays that Eloise just lets them laugh.

"It makes perfect sense that she'd think it's about models," Eloise says. "Alice is a big player in Los Angeles." She smiles. "She works at one of the most important big data companies out there. Last year *Forbes* ranked them as one of the most innovative firms to watch in the United States."

"Oh?" Henny lifts an eyebrow.

"Yes," Alice says. "I do."

Minty tucks her blond hair behind her ears and tops off her glass. "I went to Los Angeles once. Dreadful place unless you like the beach, which I find to be absolutely awful. All that *water*." She takes a sip and smiles at Alice. "I hear plenty of people find it positively lovely, though."

"Well, I—"

Eloise interrupts her. "Hopefully she won't be there for too much longer, though." She winks at Alice.

"Oh?" Minty says. "Considering a move?"

Again, Eloise answers for her. "We're *hoping* she'll agree to come to London. Ollie knows of a new job in town that's absolutely perfect for her."

Alice stares at her sister. This morning, when Eloise first told her about Ollie's proposal, Alice—with as much grace as she could muster—quickly declined the offer. Eloise had stared at her, confused, as if Alice had suddenly sprouted a second head.

"But why?" she'd asked.

"Because I like Los Angeles. Because I'm just starting to thrive there," Alice had responded.

"Will you at least consider it?"

"Sure." Alice blinked, and counted two breaths. "There, I considered it."

"*Al*ice."

"Look, I like where I'm at, all right? So . . . thanks, but no thanks."

She knew it was pointless. For starters, she could never explain her relationship with Jonathan to her sister. The real problem, though, ran much deeper than that: Eloise couldn't comprehend Alice's life, which bore such little resemblance to her own.

Minty tucks an errant strand of hair behind her ear. "How thrilling! What's the job?"

"Some film thing," Alice mumbles.

"Oh come on, Alice." Eloise pours herself some more prosecco. "It's not just some film thing. It's a distributive analytics job for a new production company that one of Ollie's classmates from Sherborne has started. Xavier Wolfson's his name. Using data from old box office receipts to decide which foreign markets might respond best to his films, and then going out and selling them to those distributors. I bet you'd get to travel to the most fascinating places."

Henny adds, "Side note: I know Xavier Wolfson and he is *fucking fit*."

"Anyway, it would be perfect for Alice, what with her experience in big data. Also, she's worked in film before. In Mexico City. And she studied it at UCLA. Her thesis on misogyny in Latin American cinema almost won the undergraduate prize for her major. She's brilliant."

Flossie reaches across the table for the bottle of prosecco and knocks over a glass of water, which no one moves to clean up. She refills her coupe and sips a scrim of foam off the top.

"I like my current job," Alice says. She wishes she could crawl beneath the table. Find some crack in the floor and disappear.

"Crunching numbers in front of a screen all day? Alice. Come on. In any event, here's to my sister—" Eloise raises her glass. "And the possibilities that *might* await her."

The women clink their glasses, and Alice excuses herself from the table.

In the restaurant's bathroom she checks to make sure she's alone before she splashes cool water on her face and dries her hands on a cotton towel. What the fuck does Eloise know? she thinks. So maybe working in big data isn't the life she'd always imagined for herself, but look where it's led her: to Jonathan, to something approximating love, to the possibility of escaping the entrapping loneliness that's defined her life since she left Mexico City. Her sister thinks that she's saving her, that she's rescuing Alice from a life that she deems unworthy. She's reminded of the dress Eloise sent her years ago, for her junior prom, and how furious she'd become upon opening the package, and trying on the dress, and seeing how perfectly it had fit her. She remembers wanting to throw both her fists through the mirror; instead, she cut the gown's thin, expensive straps and sent it back to New Haven in the same box.

"It's the same fucking thing," Alice says to herself, and her voice echoes. Eloise the Angel, Eloise the Divine, Eloise the Saint, sweeping in to save a life that doesn't need saving. Sweeping in to remind Alice just how much more capable she's always been.

She wonders how long she can stay here before they start to notice that she's gone. Alas, she's hardly shut off the faucet before Eloise comes in and locks the door behind her.

"Alice—"

"You didn't have to do that."

"Do what? Talk about how nice it was for Ollie to think of you for this job?" Eloise leans against the sink. "Alice, you're *good* at film. You *like* working with film. You should at least talk to Xavier about the job." She adds, "It's like you're punishing yourself for what happened in Mexico by chaining yourself to some awful job that you could give two shits about."

"I happen to like what I've got going in L.A.," Alice says. "You made me look like a goddamned idiot out there."

"I'm sorry if I don't believe you." Eloise looks down at her fingernails. "Alice, why can't you accept that I'm just trying to look out for you? That I'm just trying to help?"

"Well, stop. Okay? Just *stop*." Alice tosses the towel into a woven basket. "Because you're ruining my fucking life."

"That's an awful thing to say."

"Oh, stop acting so surprised."

Someone tries to open the bathroom door, rattling it a few times on its hinges.

Eloise pushes herself away from the sink. "I can't win with you, Alice. Do you know that? I can't ever win. I try, and I fail. I try, and I fail."

"You're breaking my heart."

"You know what? Fine. Just . . . *fine*. You can go to hell."

The rattling against the door continues, punctuated with brief, nervous knocks.

"You don't get it," Alice says. "You just don't fucking get it."

"You're right," Eloise says, throwing up her hands and heading for the door. "I don't. Unfortunately, though, I'm starting to suspect you're the only one who does."

Minty flicks the butt of her cigarette into Regent's Canal, and Alice watches as the thing bobs in the gray-green water. Two hours ago, she wouldn't have pegged any of these women as smokers—now, though, it's a rarity to see any of them without a cigarette, save her sister, who Alice knows wouldn't be caught dead with one. In some respects, it makes her feel better, seeing them let their hair down, seeing them act uncouth. At the restaurant, she had a minor panic attack deciding what fork she should use to eat her salmon, but now here's Minty, nearly stumbling over the railing of the long, skinny barge that they've rented—a barge that's meant to comfortably host twelve people, but that obviously isn't big enough for the five bitches currently patrolling its decks.

They boarded the boat in Little Venice, just east of Paddington Basin. From there they floated through Maida Vale, past the neighborhood's hodgepodge of old Edwardians and Victorians, aligned like hordes of sleepy, constipated sentinels. Each side of the canal is lined with trees whose leaves blend together to form a canopy that's not quite thick enough to provide shade; when they emerge from the Lisson Grove Tunnel, an errant branch nearly smacks Alice in the face. As they inch along, Minty lights a fresh cigarette and Alice watches commuters ride their Boris Bikes along the paths that rib the canal. They mostly look absurd, with their knobby knees jutting outward in sharp, uncoordinated angles. While the barge is waiting to pass through the Hampstead Road Lock, Flossie complains about having to spend an intolerable amount of time in Camden ("anything longer than a cigarette"), and Alice finds herself suddenly missing Los Angeles. She'd trade anything, she thinks, to be stuck in traffic on the 405, or waiting in line behind some Beverly Hills housewife at Gelson's. Anything to be back in a world that's filled with things that she knows how to hate.

She considers calling Jonathan. It's been two days since they've spoken (she tried phoning him yesterday—twice—but each time her call went to voice mail) and right now, especially right now, she thinks that she'd give about anything just to hear his voice. But then, what would she say to him? That Eloise is trying to get her to move to London? That she suspects her half sister's actions are as guided by her own selfish generosity as they are by guilt over not having been there five years ago, when Alice lost her child in Mexico and she needed Eloise the most? That all these awful details about her past she suddenly wants Jonathan to know? Wants to tell him how when the doctors removed her little girl and the baby didn't cry—didn't blink, or breathe, or grasp at the world—Alice convinced herself she was just sleeping, and that any moment she'd wake up? That she's currently sitting in some backwater channel of London, watching grown women—women who've mastered the art of making her feel small—flick cigarettes at feeding ducks?

The barge glides under the Kentish Town Bridge. A breeze robs a nearby cherry tree of its blossoms. Alice won't call Jonathan, she decides. He'll call her back—she knows he will—and she'll tell him everything then.

"Alice."

Eloise wraps her arm around Alice's waist and rests her head on her shoulder. She smells like expensive shampoo and champagne and exhaust.

"Alice, Alice, Alice."

An errant strand of Eloise's hair floats into Alice's mouth. She removes it.

"What, Eloise?"

"I'm sorry."

"You're drunk."

"I am not." She giggles. "Okay, maybe I am a little. But that doesn't mean I'm not sorry about what I said."

When Alice doesn't respond, Eloise lifts her head and says, "Did you hear what I said? I said that I'm sorry, Alice. Please don't be difficult."

"I heard you." Alice swallows. "Thank you."

Eloise relaxes and replaces her head.

"Are you having a lovely time?"

"The loveliest."

"I'm glad to hear that. My friends adore you."

"That's a load of bullshit."

"It is not." Eloise sighs, exasperated, and Alice feels her breath, warm and sticky, on her shoulder. "I know they may seem like a handful," she says, "but they really are good people."

Alice opts against pointing out the obvious to her sister: that if you have to describe a person as *good*, then chances are she's not. And yet, she finds little comfort in knowing that she's likely lived her life without earning such a characterization.

"Anyway," Eloise says, "I wanted to tell you something."

"That you've somehow entered me into the running to be Britain's next prime minister?"

"You're awful." She pinches Alice's thigh.

Flossie hollers something at two men jogging along the canal. They both flex their underfed biceps, and Henny shakes her head, disappointed.

"What is it?" Alice says.

"I just . . . I feel like there's been a wedge between us or something, and it's because I wasn't there for you in Mexico five years ago. And it's something I've been meaning to bring up to you for a long time, and I'm sorry that I'm just doing it now."

She's known the entire afternoon that this moment was looming, ever since Eloise grabbed her knee beneath the table at lunch and saved Alice from laying bare her sadness to the circling pack of wolves. She knows she should be thankful. She knows she should have reached down and taken hold of Eloise's hand, and squeezed it in return. Done something to signal that she recognized and appreciated how her sister had just saved her. She didn't, though; her body didn't let her. Her rage toward Eloise's perfection, toward her *kindness*, was too all encompassing. Instead, she brushed her sister's hand away and crossed her legs.

They reach St. Pancras Lock, and the boat stops. Gates close, and water spills on all sides of them. Alice feels as if she's rising and falling at once.

"Don't worry—" she begins to say, but Eloise cuts her off.

"Because I feel awful about it. I've told you that before, but I want to say it again. I let you down, and I've never stopped feeling awful about that."

The boat lurches, and Eloise stumbles back. Alice grabs her wrist to stop her from falling.

"Anyway," Eloise says, steadying herself. "That's all I wanted to say. That, and that I love you."

Alice doesn't say anything; she just stares forward to the point where, past the lock, the canal vanishes behind a shallow curve.

Mark

Mark blows a wisp of steam from his cup of coffee and watches as cars queue at a traffic light on Bermondsey Street. Paul had been cajoled into running errands with Eloise, and so he's alone, occupying a single seat at a table meant for four, at a nearly empty café two blocks from Alcott's apartment. He's pleased to be by himself, though; since arriving in London a week ago, he's hardly had a single moment of privacy, and now, more than ever, he needs the headspace to hear himself think.

Had Friday night met his expectations? No. But then, what had his expectations actually been? He'd consciously tried to rid himself of any preconceived notions of the event before it happened; he knows from experience that the key to happiness is setting a low bar. But still, even with rather opaque ideas of what it would be like, it wasn't what he had allowed himself to fantasize. Expectations aside, what amount of *utility* had been derived from the event? This is a question that's more difficult to answer.

With his spoon, Mark pokes at the yogurt parfait that he ordered along with his coffee, mixing soggy bits of granola into a blob of apricot compote. Once he's made a mess of it, he sets the spoon down without taking a bite.

Paul hadn't enjoyed himself. He claims that he did—in fact, since Friday he's put on quite a show of asking when they'll have a chance to give the whole thing a second go-round—but Mark knows better. After Alcott passed out and Mark and Paul set up the sofa bed, Paul had been restless. While Mark feigned sleep, Paul tossed and turned, and eventually got out of bed and padded over to the kitchen. With one eye open, Mark watched as he opened and closed the refrigerator, drank a glass of water, and, finally, dialed a number on his phone.

"Uh, hi, Wendy, it's Paul Wyckoff," Mark heard him say. "I know it's late there and you're sleeping and you won't get this message until tomorrow morning . . ." Paul spoke into his chest to muffle his voice. It wasn't working—Mark could still make out the awkward moment when he started to cry. "Oh, Wendy. I think I've made an awful mistake," he said. "A really awful mistake."

Mark sips his coffee and watches a young man tumble from his skateboard.

There have been more calls since then. More calls to Wendy. At first Mark found this phenomenon curious; if he insisted on rehashing his anxiety, why call a germophobe in Philadelphia, as opposed to, say, Alice? The more he thought about it, though, the more he supposed it made sense. After all, who else was there to better empathize with Paul's paralyzing logic than a woman who lost her mind every time she had to take out the trash?

As for himself, he'd had fun. There were moments when Paul's performance was less than spectacular (Mark cringes thinking about his stilted voice tripping over the phrase *your balls taste great*), and when Mark felt a strange competitiveness emanating from him, but as a whole he's pleased. It satisfied the newness that he's been desperately craving, the desire to shatter the monotony of monogamy that he finds so wholly suffocating.

He thinks again of the moment he pulled out of Paul and instructed Alcott to take his place. How thrilling that had been! The exhilarating notion that he, Mark, was controlling two men so fully and completely; determining who experienced pleasure, and when!

"How's the yogurt, sir?" a waitress asks him.

"Inedible," Mark says.

"I, uh—"

"I'll take some more coffee, though."

Would Paul be willing to be so controlled again? To submit so fully to Mark's sexual orchestrations? Despite his bravado during the past forty-eight hours, Mark suspects not. There have been too many hollow proclamations. No, he and Paul are headed in different directions. Friday night made that fact clear and now, watching the waitress refill his mug, Mark is even more convinced of the rightness of the decision to leave Paul. He needs someone with a sexual appetite that's as modern as his is. Someone who hasn't thrown all his emotional stock into the concept of intimacy, only to cheapen it by equating it with monogamy.

He thinks of Alcott, and of how easily he'd given himself over to the events of Friday night. There'd been no mental hairsplitting, no infantile second-guessing; rather, mouths were kissed, pants were removed, and that was that. The morning after, there hadn't been any awkwardness, any unnecessary small talk. Instead, they drank coffee and ate cereal and read the paper with the same ease as the previous morning; only Paul chattered incessantly. Put another way: Alcott is game in a manner that Mark finds alluring and that Paul could never hope to emulate. Granted, there are also physical dimensions to Alcott's attractiveness that Mark feels obliged to recognize. The way sweat seemed to highlight the crevices of his musculature, for instance, or how his ass flexed as he had his way with Paul. But it was more than that, Mark reminds himself; it's not just some bodily lust that draws him to Alcott. It's a meeting of minds, a sense that he's found someone who understands and shares his evolved worldview.

Christ, he thinks. Listen to yourself. *A meeting of minds.* Is he *falling in love* with Alcott? He snorts and nearly spills his coffee. Falling in love with Alcott: it's an absurd proposition; despite the closeness he feels towards him, he hardly knows the man. And even if there *is* an ounce of truth in it (he will admit that he's had a difficult time *not* thinking of him since Friday), it would be wrongheaded and impossible to equate what he's certain he *now* shares with Alcott to what he *once* shared with Paul. Because what had that been? Puppy love, really. The sort of doe-eyed infatuation that causes men in their twenties to abandon important life plans. There's nothing inherently wrong with that kind of love, Mark figures, so long as one's view of it matures to account for the nuances and complexities of one's needs. The problem with Paul, of course, is that his view of love has never matured. He's still stuck in an uncertain adolescence, a perpetual state of unknowing where he's only comfortable when his own needs are subsumed by someone else's. Alcott, on the other hand . . .

Mark looks down into his coffee cup. Flecks of ground beans float along the milky surface. He thinks of a few mornings ago, when Alcott flicked soap away from his bare thigh, and he smiles again.

"It's a possibility, though," Paul says.

"I can't keep having this conversation."

"Admit that it's a possibility, and I'll stop."

"I'm not admitting that."

Paul rests his elbows on the guardrail of the Millennium Bridge. Below them, the Thames swirls in loops of brown and gray. A tour boat disappears beneath their feet.

"You're acting like I don't have a right to be worried," Paul says. "But I think I have a right to be worried. I mean," he lowers his voice here, "he fucked me without a condom, Mark."

Mark instinctively reaches out to rub Paul's back, but stops himself short of actually touching him; he doesn't want to convey conflicting messages, particularly given what he's brought him here to say. Behind him, two tourists snap a series of photos, and Mark wonders if he's in them—if the back of his head features prominently in shots of the British Parliament.

Paul continues, "I could have AIDS."

"You don't have AIDS."

"It would be HIV, I guess. But still, it's a possibility."

"It would only be a possibility if Alcott were positive, which he's not."

Paul scrapes a marred spot along the metal railing.

"Do you know that?" he asks. "Have you asked him?"

Mark's patience burns low, and he considers chastising Paul for his ignorance. Again, though, he exercises restraint. The last thing he wants is for Paul to run and tell their mutual friends that Mark put him in harm's way—that he threatened Paul with disease—before leaving him. Better to hedge his bets, Mark thinks. Better to suffer through a little more empathy so as to save some face in what will inevitably be a face-decimating few months.

"I haven't," he says. "But I can if it'll make you feel better."

"No, don't. Oh, God, please don't. I'd never get over the humiliation." Paul sighs. "I'm such a hypochondriac."

"It's endearing."

Mark looks left. Sun reflects off the Shard in broken slivers of light. For once, London's skies are cloudless.

Paul says, "No, it's neurotic. Do you know that after I kissed my first guy I went and got tested?"

Mark can't fathom how many times he's heard this story. He masks his annoyance by reminding himself that this is the last time he'll ever have to suffer through it.

"I vaguely remember you mentioning that," he says.

"I was sixteen, and I went to Boystown with this kid from my soccer team. Scott Reardon. Anyway, Scott got so drunk on the frozen slushies at Sidetrack that he puked in his mom's Accord, and I spent the whole night in the corner of some bar with a thirty-two-year-old French Canadian."

"That's right. It's all coming back to me."

"Every day for the next week I called the AIDS hotline. The one that the CDC runs. You know what I'm talking about?"

"I do."

"Anyway, I'd tell whatever poor son of a bitch picked up that I had this friend who made out with a guy, and who was worried that he might get sick. And then they'd give me this whole runaround about how low the chances are of getting HIV like that, and how it would require that both guys had, like, bleeding open sores in their mouths." Paul rips off a shred of fingernail with his teeth and flicks it into the Thames. "Still, though, they'd never actually say it was impossible. I'd try to get them to say that it was. I'd ask the question in, like, twenty different ways. Still, they'd stick to their line: *there have been no reported cases, and the likelihood is very, very low.* Which, I mean, obviously wasn't good enough for me; I still stayed up at night wondering how I was going to tell my mom and dad that I was gay *and* that I had AIDS in the same conversation."

Silently, Mark tallies what details are left; he maps out how many plot turns he must endure before Paul's story reaches its merciful end.

"So I got tested. After two months of total misery, I told my mom that I had to go back to Chicago for some research paper, and I went to a free clinic in Boystown, a block away from the bar where I made out with the French Canadian. The woman who took my blood was this hippie earth mother named Kat. While we waited for the results—it was one of those ten-minute things—she sat me down in her office and gave me little packets of lube and talked to me about wearing condoms during oral sex, which, I mean, *can you even imagine?*" He adds: "I actually went back to see her every time I was home from college. Two weeks ago she added me on LinkedIn."

Mark nods. He says: "I think we should end things, Paul."

Below him, another boat passes. He glances down at the tops of a hundred heads.

Paul's silent. He stares at Mark wide-eyed, his shoulders bunched up around his ears.

Mark recalls all the words he practiced reciting the night before, the delicate balance of his reasoning and rhetoric.

"I care about you," he says. "Deeply. Very deeply, incidentally. But we're two different people. We've grown into two different people."

Of all the canned phrases he's prepared, this is the one in which he believes the most. They have changed, they have grown—or Mark has, at any rate. Indeed, what's surprised him the most over the past three days is how swiftly his categorization of Paul has changed. Alcott's presence has reminded Mark of how intoxicating new lust is, and has cast his fraternal love for Paul in a dull, bloodless light. If anything, Paul has become a barrier: he's the guy who Mark regrettably asked to dinner, and with whom he's thus obliged to dine, even though the only person he's actually interested in talking to is the waiter who winks at him every time he refills his water glass.

"But I . . ."

Paul's voice cracks, and Mark's muscles tense: Paul mustn't cry. That's a fate that Mark was actively trying to avoid by bringing him here, to the Millennium Bridge, one of the busiest pedestrian walkways in the city. He'd hoped that the scrutiny of strangers would keep Paul in line. Besides, he figured that monumental events should take place at monumental locations. And for Paul, this afternoon is sure to become a monumental event.

"But what about Friday night?"

Paul is pleading now, and Mark wants nothing more than to shake his shoulders, to tell him to stop. He wants to tell him that the most important thing now is to show a bit of dignity, for Paul to think of his future self looking back on this moment without shrinking from shame.

"We both know that you did that for me," Mark says, coolly. "You were trying to make me happy and prove yourself."

"Fuck you for saying that. I wanted to do it." Paul's choking back tears. He speaks as though he's been in a terrible car accident, emerging from a state of shock. "And even if what you're saying is true, why isn't that enough? Why isn't wanting to make you happy enough?"

"Because that's not how things work."

Mark watches as the gravity of Paul's misfortune crests over him. Finally, he cries—softly at first, but then he sobs. Yet, while Paul mourns the destruction of something communal, something vital and shared, Mark's experience is more akin to explaining the death of a pet to a child. Logically, he understands the source of Paul's unhappiness, but that's where their common ground stops. Paul's pain has grown too foreign to elicit Mark's empathy.

"Are you in love with Alcott?" Paul asks. His blond hair is matted against his forehead, and Mark realizes that he's sweating.

"Stop it."

"Tell me."

"Of course not. I just—I've come to the conclusion that we conceive of relationships in different ways." He searches for the explanation he crafted earlier. "It wouldn't be fair to manipulate you into some version of a coupling that you weren't comfortable with."

Paul refuses to listen. "Is that why you're leaving? Because of him? Answer me that."

"Paul, please don't cause a scene. You're better than that."

"Isn't this what I said would happen?" His voice isn't accusatory: it's defeated. "Didn't I say that we'd do this thing, and that it would end in tears? That you wouldn't be able to resist the—what the fuck did you call it?—the *newness* of it?"

"I'm not going to answer that question," Mark says. "I'm not going to dignify it. I care about you; I'm going to save you the embarrassment."

"I can't believe this is happening." Panic creeps into Paul's voice. "Could I have been better? On Friday, I mean? Is this all because I wasn't that great at . . . at getting fucked by Alcott, or something? Because I can be better, Mark. It was my first time with all that stuff, and the drugs certainly weren't helping anything, and I—"

"Paul." Mark sighs. People have started to watch them. Not ostensibly— a crowd hasn't gathered—but still, he's caught the discreet turning of a few heads. Some raised eyebrows. He was really, really, really trying to avoid this. "This is just what I want."

"But what about what *I* want? Since we moved to Philadelphia it's been entirely about what you want. Why, for once, can't it be about what I want?" He's close to shouting now, and tears soak his face. His distress tugs at Mark's prick—seeing Paul upset has always been a turn-on—and Mark does his best to resist the very real urge to have sex with Paul; to find somewhere discreet and fuck him one last time.

Calmly, he asks, "And what is it that you want, Paul?"

"To be with you! To keep living our lives together! To keep watching you cook, and listening to your stories about your students, and going to Maryann's with Preston and Crosby. To just . . . to just keep loving you."

"You hate Preston and Crosby."

"That's not the fucking point!" he screams.

Mark buries his face in his hands and shakes his head. He says, "This isn't how this was supposed to work out."

Paul's quiet for a moment. He sniffles once, and then asks, "What did you say?"

Mark takes his hands away from his face. "I said, this isn't how this was supposed to work out."

"Oh, it wasn't?" Paul wipes his nose with his shirtsleeve. "Geez, I'm sorry to hear that. Would you like to start over then?"

"That's not what I meant, Paul."

"Then why don't you tell me what the fuck you *did* mean, Mark?" He's still crying, but his devastation seems to be giving way to a heated anger. Mark had anticipated that this might happen, but now, seeing the rage in Paul's eyes, he's not sure if he's entirely comfortable with the shift. At least a few minutes ago he could still fantasize about the possibility of breakup sex.

He says, "I just . . . I just mean that this is starting to get uncomfortable. That's all."

"For *you?*" Paul says—shouts—incredulously. "Because the last time

I checked, you weren't the one getting dumped *in front of an audience on the London Bridge* four days shy of your sister's wedding, just because you weren't *quite* willing enough to have a stranger's dick in your mouth."

"We're on the Millennium Bridge. The London Bridge is in Southwark. And please, Paul. Keep your voice down."

"No!" Paul shouts, and people around them turn their heads. "Fuck you, Mark. I won't keep my voice down. You don't get to tell me that, do you hear me? You don't get to tell me that ever again."

Eloise

July 8

Mark suddenly dumping Paul is costing her six hundred pounds. She figured that out last night after Paul called, crying, to tell her that they'd broken up, and that there'd be an empty place setting at the wedding, and that he, Paul, needed somewhere to stay. She doesn't care; she would've happily paid double that amount to not have that son of a bitch there. In fact, she'd be fine giving Mark twenty thousand bucks if he promised to never speak to Paul again. But then, she stops herself: she's always considered it tacky to think about all the things she'd do with her money, so long as no one else was watching.

She watches as a car across the street tries to parallel park between two black sedans. Ollie left half an hour ago—he had an early-morning meeting—and after following him out to their building's front stoop to say good-bye, she decided to stay, to sit and bear witness to the morning unfurling itself. She's not properly dressed—she's wearing an old Yale shirt and a pair of running shorts—and if anyone she knew were to walk by, she'd be mortified. Still, she stays where she is, blowing into her mug of coffee to cool it, even though it's already grown lukewarm. She wants to be here when Paul gets here—she figures that's the important thing. She doesn't want him to have to climb the stairs up to her flat (and away from Mark) alone.

She hopes he showed a little strength: that's what she's been thinking all morning. When Mark dumped him, she hopes Paul showed a little strength, and told that prick to fuck off. She knows, though, that's likely far from what actually happened; probably, Paul had caused a scene. Something's happened to her brother recently, though she can't quite articulate what. To put it vaguely, he's become curiously unhinged since his father's death (she closes her eyes as she remembers the funeral and the awful secret her mother told her); it's as if Bill's passing robbed Paul of whatever necessary fiction he'd been using to keep his life together. The fact that he endured dating Mark for so long is evidence enough to convince Eloise that something crucial has shifted, but there are other signs, as well. In the few times she's seen him over the past three years, she can't help but sense that he's blindly groping for something—an explanation, someone to blame, a metaphorical or literal lifesaver. Just—*something*.

He's so quick to anger now, she considers as she pulls her knees closer to her chest. Take the other night at Dean Street Townhouse, when he'd chastised Donna for harmlessly referring to Mark as his *friend*. The old Paul would've never reacted like that; the old Paul would've made an offhand comment, would've laughed at himself; the old Paul had a sense of humor. Now, though, it's suddenly become impossible to say or do anything without offending his sensibilities in some convoluted way. He's subscribed, she'd argue, to a policy of unabashed and unapologetic victimhood. She does her best to convince herself that the old Paul is still in there, somewhere; that, beneath the layers of shit and shame that have accumulated, her little brother's hiding, waiting to emerge. She thinks back to how fun, how *easy* he was in high school, when Bill was still alive. For better or worse, she hadn't been around much then—she was living her own life in New Haven—but she's still keenly aware of the mythologies that emerged from those years. The family stories that Alice and Paul continue to tell and retell. The same stories that leave Eloise feeling like she's destined to forever be on the outside looking in.

Paul's taxi pulls up in front of the apartment, and she sets her coffee down and gets up, wiping dust from her shorts.

"Hi, Paul," she says, once they're both out of the car.

He glances up at her, but doesn't say anything. Instead, he turns to Mark with an expectant look. She wants to run down to him and tell him to stop, to save himself the humiliation of having to beg. She doesn't, though, for as awful as Mark is, she knows that running to Paul's rescue would only compound his humiliation. And so she stays where she is at the top of the stoop and looks on as they lock heads in some hushed, private conversation. What draws Paul to Mark? Or, perhaps more appropriately: What *drew* him? While she knows she's predisposed to be a little biased (Paul is, of course, her brother), she can't help but think that he is, objectively, a better person: better looking, better intentioned, better behaving (mostly). And yet, still there's something that prevents him from recognizing his own worth, or from seeing himself in the same light in which Eloise (and presumably others) see him. Still there's something that makes him believe he doesn't deserve better.

Mark tries to reach down and grab her brother's bag, but Paul won't let him; he hauls it over his shoulder and climbs up the stoop. Once he reaches Eloise he tries to wordlessly slip past her, but she stops him.

She kisses his cheek and squeezes his arm and says, "The couch is all made up," before allowing him to retreat inside.

A moment later, she hears her front door open and close.

From where he's standing on the sidewalk, Mark clears his throat. "Well."

"Well," Eloise says, looking down at him. She folds her arms across her chest; the A in YALE gets pinched between her breasts. "I guess we won't be seeing you at the wedding, then."

"That's not looking likely, no."

He stares at her intently, as if he's expecting her to say something else. As if he's been fantasizing about confronting her since she humiliated him at the restaurant the other night. She's above this, she tells herself; she's above granting him that satisfaction. That doesn't mean it's easy, though, resisting the very real urge to say something so crippling as to leave him second-guessing himself for months to come. And God, could she do it. Looking back at his smug, shit-eating grin; at the tacky summer scarf he's got looped loosely around his neck—God, could she destroy him.

"Right then," she says. "Can I help you get a cab back to wherever it is you're staying?"

He searches her face. *That's it?*

"No," he says. "It's just that—no, I don't need help getting a cab. Thank you, though."

Disappointed, he turns and steps out into the street and shoves his fists in his pockets.

Fuck it, she suddenly thinks. She waits for him to wave down a cab and duck inside of it before she calls out, "Mark."

He leans forward to say something to the driver, and then rolls down the window.

"Yes?"

"I hope you're better off," she says, thrilled for a few glorious moments that she still knows how to be a bitch. "I know Paul will be."

She tries not to smile. She's unsuccessful.

Paul lies on a love seat in the living room, with his feet dangling over one of the armrests and his head and neck bent at a painful angle against the other. His eyes are closed, and when he hears Eloise close the front door he pulls his left arm across his face.

"You can move to the couch, you know," she says. "It's longer. You don't really fit on that thing."

Paul doesn't say anything—he just buries his nose deeper into the cushions.

"Oh, come on, Paul. Get up."

She reaches down to stroke his head, but he bats her hand away.

"I don't know what I'm going to do," he says.

"Have you eaten anything?"

"I'm not hungry."

"How about something to drink, then?"

He buries his nose in the pillow again, which she takes as a *yes*, so she pushes herself off the love seat and goes to the kitchen for a glass of orange juice.

As she opens the refrigerator, she hears him yell, "Where's Mom?"

"She's at the National Gallery," Eloise says as she fills a glass. "She wanted to see the Turners, so I had Alice take her."

"You sent her away, is what you mean."

Eloise thinks for a moment, then opens the freezer, where there's half a bottle of Grey Goose. Uncorking the top, she pours about a shot glass's worth of vodka into Paul's juice.

She calls back, "What, you're telling me you wanted her around when you got here?"

"No," Paul says. She returns to the living room and, as he sits up, she hands him the glass. "I guess not."

"Don't worry about it. She understood."

This isn't the whole truth. Earlier this morning, when Eloise had told Donna that Mark and Paul had broken up and that Paul was coming to stay at the flat, she'd insisted on canceling her plans for the day.

"He'll need me," she'd said. "He'll need his mother."

Gently, over the course of poached eggs and a pot of coffee, Eloise convinced her otherwise. Or, if not entirely otherwise, she at least convinced her to leave. She stopped short of explicitly explaining to Donna that she was the last person Paul needed; that, after waging a cold war with his mother for close to three years, falling into her arms after failing at love would be the cruelest kind of defeat. Instead, Eloise told her that Paul needed space. He needed to cry without someone hovering over him, and surely that was something she understood.

Paul takes a sip of his orange juice. He swallows it, and shivers. "You put vodka in this."

Eloise sits on the love seat next to him. Their knees touch.

"I figured it was the least I could do."

He looks into the glass, at the shreds of pulp slowly separating, sinking to the bottom, and then takes a longer drink.

"There's something wrong with me," he says, swallowing.

"There's not, Pauly. He was an asshole."

"He may have been an asshole, but there's still something wrong with me."

She pulls his head to her shoulder and runs her fingers through his hair. She wants to say something, but she can't. Comforting her siblings—a task that, as the eldest sister, she knows falls squarely on her shoulders—has always confounded her. On the one hand she wants to fix them, to save them, to pull Paul and Alice up and out of the messes they've made. On the other hand, though, she worries that her own gilded life somehow prevents her from empathizing with them as deeply as she should. More than that, she worries that her siblings' *perception* of her life puts her at an inevitable and insurmountable disadvantage: she *has*, and that means she *can't*.

Paul finishes his orange juice, and she thinks of the things Alice said to her in the bathroom during the hen do. *You just don't get it, Eloise. You just don't fucking get it.*

Maybe they're right, she thinks, as she slumps farther into the couch and Paul starts to cry. Maybe I just don't get it, and maybe I never will. After all, here's Paul, her little brother, weeping on her shoulder, and she can't think of a damned thing to say. She knows what she *should* tell him. She *should* give him some pep talk about being okay, about everyone being okay. She should talk about how awfully banal breakups are, and how that fact is actually entirely humanizing. She should remind him how heartbreak is a universal emotion; how everyone, everywhere, has experienced what he's feeling at this exact moment, and in that way Paul, through his pain, is becoming part of something larger than himself.

The problem is that it'd all be a lie. She'd be rehashing a speech she gave to a suitemate at Yale whose boyfriend broke up with her in the middle of freshman year. Some girl whose name she can't remember. The fact is that Eloise has never been dumped. She's broken up with people, sure, but it's always been amicable, at least on her end; and now, watching her brother cry, she suddenly suspects the only people who share her holistic and delusional perspective on heartbreak are people exactly like her—people who've never actually been heartbroken.

The only thing she can do, she realizes, is let him cry—let him cry and, when he asks if he can smoke a cigarette out of her bathroom window, answer with an empathic *yes*.

"In fact," she says, "don't worry about going to the bathroom. Let me just get you something to ash in."

She goes to the kitchen and returns with an old mug.

"Won't Ollie be mad?" Paul looks up at her with red eyes. "About the smell, I mean."

"He'll understand. Besides, I think I've got some air freshener under the sink."

He lights his cigarette and collapses into the love seat. Eloise sits next to him, pulling her feet up and holding her knees to her chest. The sun coming through the windows illuminates streaks of dust on the coffee table in front of them.

"What if I'm unlovable?" he says. Ash falls onto his shirt.

"Oh, come on. Of course you're lovable." She reaches over to brush hair out of his eyes.

"You don't know that. The only thing you've ever been is loved." He blows out a long, thin cloud of smoke.

"That's not true."

He doesn't answer her—she wasn't expecting him to. Instead, he says, "Or maybe it's not that I'm inherently unlovable. Maybe it's that I make it too difficult to keep on loving me." More ash falls to his shirt. "I think I've somehow become my own worst enemy."

"Mark was an asshole, Paul."

"I think that's probably true."

"So you should be happy that you're done with him."

He's only halfway through his cigarette, but he drops the rest of it into the mug, stubbing the butt against the cracked porcelain.

"Unfortunately, I don't think that's the way it works," he says.

"It is if you want it to."

"God," he says, his voice cracking, "I wish I knew what it was like to be you."

PART THREE

If a man's character is to be abused, say what you will,
there's nobody like a relative to do the business.
—WILLIAM MAKEPEACE THACKERAY, *Vanity Fair*

Paul

"I can't fit back there."

Paul looks into the backseat of the Peugeot, cupping his hands on either side of his eyes as he presses his face against the window.

"A fucking Chihuahua couldn't fit back there."

"Well, this is the car that Mom's rented."

Alice glances down at her phone before slipping it into her purse, discouraged.

"*Well*, go tell her to get a bigger one."

"Too late," Alice says. She's wearing dark glasses that hide half her face. "This is the last one they've got."

Paul stands up straight again and wipes sweat from the back of his neck. Slough spreads around them on all sides, the British equivalent of the same Midwest suburbs where he and Alice wallowed away eighteen years of their lives. A plane of gray duplexes and strip malls, dotted with ancient brick houses and the occasional medieval church. He looks across the Hertz parking lot and counts the number of full-sized sedans he sees.

"There are sixteen other reasonably sized cars here," he says. "And that's just on this side of the rental office. Who knows what sort of glorious minivans we might find on the other side."

"They're all rented." Alice leans against the Peugeot.

"Every single one of them."

"It's vacation season, Paul. Everyone's driving to the beach. They need cars."

"Well, *I* need leg room. And I'm grieving."

When Alice doesn't respond, he asks, "Why is this thing in Dorset?"

"I don't know." Then: "Ollie went to school down there or something."

"The British and their goddamned traditions. We went to school next to a cornfield in Illinois. You don't see us planning our weddings there."

Alice scrapes something from underneath her fingernail. "You don't see us planning our weddings, period."

Paul fills his cheeks with air, then exhales. "How long is the drive?"

"Google Maps puts it at about two and a half hours. But that's without traffic."

"*Two and a half hours?* Aren't we already pretty far south, and isn't England smaller than New Jersey?"

"Take it up with Google."

Paul watches as Donna emerges from the rental office, a road atlas of England tucked under her left arm. She's wearing khaki pants, a light blue camisole, and a pair of sensible shoes—the kind that are sold at places like Talbots and Eileen Fisher under the dubious pretense of being fashionable, while also serving vague and unnamed orthopedic functions. Aging is a sudden process, Paul thinks, as his mother navigates a minefield of cement parking barriers. And despite her best efforts, Donna suddenly got old.

He turns to Alice. "Can I at least have a Klonopin?"

"You know I stopped taking that shit years ago," she says. "Ever since that weekend in Carlsbad."

"Sure you did."

She rips her glasses off her face. "And what the fuck is that supposed to mean?"

"Here's Mom."

Donna stops a few feet from them. She looks at Paul, and then Alice, and then forcibly smiles, as if she's paying due respect to her executioners.

"It's going to be a gorgeous drive," she says. "And before she left yesterday, Eloise gave me the names of a few places we can stop for a drink, or lunch. They're all supposed to be positively charming."

"Positively charming," Alice parrots.

"What?"

"You've been spending too much time around Eloise."

"I—"

Alice stops her. "We should go. There's already going to be a ton of traffic." She opens the passenger-side door, pushes down the shotgun seat, and motions grandly to the sliver of space in the back of the car. "Your chariot awaits, Paul."

Contorting his way past seat belts, a roller suitcase, and Alice's purse, Paul folds into the rear of the Peugeot. He loathes himself for giving in so easily to his sister's demands. More than that, though, he loathes how quickly and seamlessly he slips into his old childhood role. He loathes how quickly and seamlessly they all slip into their old roles: Donna trying to be *nice*, despite the fact that *nice* became an impossibility years ago; Alice veiling her disdain as she makes peace by bossing people around; Paul allowing himself to be tossed around like a rag doll because it justifies his contempt. He pulls his knees up to his chest—there's nowhere else to put them—and wonders what Mark would say.

"Here, Alice," he hears his mother say outside the car. "Take the keys."

"What do you mean take the keys? Why would I need the keys?"

From the backseat Paul watches as Donna walks around to the left side of the car, where Alice is standing.

"I'm not going to drive this thing," Donna says. "The steering wheel's on the wrong side."

"What makes you think I'd be any better at it?" Alice removes her sunglasses again. Her cheeks are red, which makes the faint freckles that dust her nose burn like sunspots. She's got her blond hair pulled back in a ponytail, and she brushes a few loose strands out of her face.

"You're from L.A.," Donna says.

"What's that have to do with anything?"

"You drive on the 405."

She squeezes past Alice and claims the passenger seat. Reaching back, she pats Paul's knee.

"I'll navigate," she says, pointing to the road atlas in her lap.

"Oh, no." Alice slams the passenger door shut and shakes her head as she circles back around to the driver's side. "No, no, no," she says, opening her own door. "God knows when that atlas was made. I've got the map pulled up on my phone. Paul can navigate as we go."

"I'm fine doing nothing. Really." He shifts, trying to find a comfortable position for his legs, which now, in the backseat of the Peugeot, seem longer than they ever have before.

Alice tosses her phone at him, and it lands squarely in his lap.

"You literally just have to follow the blue dot," she says. "No one's asking you to blaze a trail, for Christ's sake."

The hole in his life that Mark left creates a hollow pit in Paul's stomach, but strangely it's all the small actions the breakup will eventually necessitate that cause a million pangs to prick his ribs. There are so many knots to untie as they work to separate their lives, and loosening each one will require a phone call, an e-mail, a text. Who will keep the apartment? Mark, likely, though maybe that isn't such a bad thing. Paul's tired of Philadelphia—of people overlooking the mediocrity of its restaurants; of its obsession with a whitewashed and mythical history. Yes, he could use a change, particularly now that he's been (1) sacked from his job and (2) ceremoniously dumped by his boyfriend. What better time to hack away at the ties that bind? But where should he go? There are, of course, hundreds of places. Thousands, really. Picking up and leaving for any one, though, would require—*will* require—the same awful and impossible steps. The buying of cardboard boxes. The emptying of closets and cupboards. The division of goods and wares. The artifacts, so to speak, that must be salvaged from a fire. Stained pillowcases and half-burned candles; two coat racks and a love seat that's not quite long enough to accommodate two grown bodies. A mail receptacle they never hung, a crafty little thing that had been given to them as a housewarming present: a box with two smaller containers, one for Paul's letters and one for Mark's.

"A his-and-his sort of thing," their friend Audrey had said, when she'd presented them with it.

Now what would he call it? In the event that he got to keep the receptacle—and he hoped he would; like everything else, he wanted it—how would he explain those twin boxes to people? What's more, what would it look like with only one of the boxes stuffed with letters? Lonely, Paul thinks, lonely and unbalanced.

They're stopped in bumper-to-bumper traffic on the M3, a few miles north of Woking, and it dawns on Paul that he can't feel his toes; his legs are hiked halfway up his nostrils, which has cut off circulation to everything below his kneecaps. He tries wiggling his toes, and when that doesn't work he decides to let it go. Wincing through a wave of pins and needles, he fantasizes over what Mark might say if he called him up to tell him that he'd suddenly become a double amputee; that, thanks to a torturous few hours that he'd selflessly spent in the back of a Peugeot, surgeons had to saw off everything below his knees. He thinks of the look that would be on Mark's face—a mix of horror and pity and sympathy—and for a moment he gets giddy. But then he tells himself that he's better than that—or, if he isn't, then he wants to be—and forces himself to look out the window, where a long scar of vehicles, minivans and caravans and coupes, gashes south toward the English Channel.

He counts how many heads he can see in the cars that surround him, and then he wonders about the thoughts festering and multiplying inside of them. He wants to know if he's the only person on, say, this mile of the M3, who's been dumped in the past seventy-two hours, or if there's some other kindred, miserable asshole stuck in the backseat of a car. But even if there is, and even if they could sit on the curb and air their wounds, what good would it do?

Heartache, he's come to realize, the devastation of being chewed up and spit out, is an individual and isolating experience. Why else would there be a million different idioms in just as many languages that tried, always unsuccessfully, to describe it? If there were some common, shared experience, language would have already accounted for that. It would have streamlined the feeling into something concise and translatable, like water, or food, or air.

"You're going to take a left in about four kilometers," Paul says.

Twenty minutes ago, after some initial bickering, Paul, his sister, and his mother agreed to stop for lunch at one of the places Eloise had suggested, some Ye Olde Inn ten kilometers off the main road in the New Forest.

"You mean I'm going to exit the M3 and *then* take a left." Alice glances at him in the rearview mirror.

"Yeah, sure."

"No, not *yeah, sure,* Paul. I have no idea where I'm going. I need specific directions."

In the passenger seat, Donna begins flipping through the road atlas.

"Hold on." Paul zooms in on the map. "It's like none of these roads even have names."

In the past twenty minutes, the traffic has opened up; they aren't freely moving, but there is enough space now between the cars for Paul to see a series of lazy bucolic hills to their right and a thick green forest to their left. On Alice's phone, the blue dot jitters, correcting and recorrecting its position on the map.

"I think the road that you want is called Old Forest Lane," he says. "But just . . . just give me a second."

"That road isn't on my map," Donna says.

Paul squints. He just wants the goddamned dot to stop moving for a second. "Your map was published alongside the Magna Carta," he says. "The roads have probably changed."

"It's the 2005 edition." Donna holds up the atlas so Paul can see its cover. "Certainly things haven't changed that much?"

"Get that thing out of my face."

Now she's handing it back to him.

"Maybe just look at it, sweetie? Just to double-check what your phone is saying?"

Traffic stops again, and Alice nearly rear-ends a minivan. Donna drops the atlas, and it falls between Paul's knees. Behind them, someone honks.

"Oh, geez."

"I don't need to double-check it. It's a satellite. Satellites don't need to be double-checked."

Alice thuds the steering wheel with the heel of her hand. "Can someone just *please* tell me where I'm fucking going."

"The next exit," Paul says. He's not sure if that's right, but he can't stand the prospect of prolonging this discussion regarding the merits of GPS with his mother any longer. Besides, each of the one-lane roads leading into the New Forest seems as good and worthless as the next, and he imagines that they all lead to the same, predictable destinations: a cow blocking traffic, a village of thatched roofs, a gastropub that's been serving the same watered-down ale since before the American Revolution.

"Take the next exit—yes, this one—and then bear left."

They crawl down a lane walled in by thick shrub hedges. Above them, branches of elms wrap together to form leafy tunnels perforated by pinpricks of sunlight. Hugging the steering wheel, Alice balances her sunglasses on top of her head and leans forward. The road's hardly straight—every hundred yards or so it inexplicably and carelessly banks around a sharp corner of nothing, and it's only blind faith that promises Paul that they won't smash into something head-on once they clear the curve. After ten kilometers they emerge into a small hamlet, an afterthought of a village with a few houses, a gas station, a chemist's, and a smattering of other single-story buildings. Alice parks the car in a gravel lot behind a pub, and once Paul's extricated himself from the back of the Peugeot, he tells his sister and mother that he'll meet them inside in a few minutes.

"Are you sure?" Donna asks; Alice has already gone inside.

"Yes." Paul does his best not to sound irritable.

He waits for her to leave and reaches into his pocket for a pack of cigarettes. Fishing one out, he lights it and leans against the car. Mark used to hate it when he smoked. Not because of the smell, or for how it was crippling Paul's health, but because he thought it looked trashy.

"There are smokers you know, and smokers you don't know," he would say. The smokers you know—or, as Paul thinks now, the smokers Mark thought he knew—were people like Audrey Hepburn and Clark Gable, people who managed to turn puffing a cigarette into high, erotic art. The smokers he didn't know were Paul and everyone else.

"Honey?"

Hearing his mother's voice, Paul moves to drop the cigarette, but Donna stops him.

"Oh, don't worry about it," she says. "In fact, you mind if I have one?"

"Yes," Paul says.

"Yes, I can have one, or yes, you mind?"

"Yes, I mind. You're trying to turn this into a moment."

"I'm not sure I know what that means." Donna scuffs at the gravel with her toes. "Alice forgot her wallet. And I wanted to check on you."

"I'm fine," Paul says, exhaling a thick cloud of smoke. "I'll be there in a second."

Donna pulls him to her and kisses his forehead. "Oh, Pauly."

"What did I say about calling me that?"

"I know how hard it is," she says.

Across the street, a small pickup truck pulls into the gas station. Pigeons coo atop sloped roofs.

"You don't, though," Paul says. "Your husband *died*. He didn't just up and leave you in the middle of a foreign country. It's not the same thing."

"I wasn't talking about your father."

"Who, then? Henrique?" He ashes his cigarette and stomps sparks into the earth. "He was a prick. Good riddance."

Donna sighs, dramatically, and Paul's blood boils.

"All I'm trying to say—"

"I know what you're trying to say," Paul says, "and please—I'm begging you—just keep it to yourself, okay? Do me a favor and just *keep it to yourself*."

Dropping the cigarette to the ground, he adds: "The only person I want to talk to is Dad, and he's fucking dead."

He first catches sight of the coast around three o'clock when, on account of some roadwork, they're forced to take a detour on the A338 and dip through Bournemouth. He's staring straight forward to ward off carsickness—the fish and chips and beer he had for lunch are somersaulting in his stomach—so when they crest one of the gentle hills that carve through the English southwest, he's able to see it immediately, the sea. It lacks vastness, is the first thing he thinks. It doesn't have the sort of oceanic interminability that he's used to. Rather, this—all this blue and gray and dull green water—somehow feels reasonable, digestible. Maybe it's because he knows that France is right there, just out of eyeshot, or maybe it's because right now, crammed in the back of the Peugeot, suffering through Alice's Fiona Apple album for the umpteenth time, he knows that vastness is something that he lacks the mental capacity to confront.

"How gorgeous," his mother says, and neither Paul nor Alice says anything in response.

His mother's right, though, Paul thinks. It is gorgeous—it really is. Lush open fields sloping toward gunmetal beaches. Sheep dotting hillsides like wisps of cotton. The sun glinting off the surface of the water. It's not the blazing glory of a California sunset—that fiery magnificence whose beauty lies in its ability to convince you each night that the world is ending. No, he thinks, there's something subtler going on here, something less intrusive. A polite and very British reminder that gorgeous things are out there and happen every day.

"Thomas Hardy country," Alice says.

Paul blinks. "Never read him."

"That's a lie. We had to read *Far from the Madding Crowd* in the tenth grade."

"I know. I didn't read it. Bought the Cliffs Notes."

"*Tess of the d'Urbervilles?*"

"Skipped that one, too."

Alice looks at him in the rearview mirror. "What a disappointment."

Paul ignores her. At lunch she twice interrupted him by taking out her phone, and once she stormed away from the table, *sans* excuse, to make a call. He's irritated—today is his day to be in a foul mood.

He looks out the window, back to the sea.

Mark was an asshole, right? Particularly at the end? Yes, Paul tells himself. He was. Objectively, Mark was an asshole. Why, then, can't Paul seem to believe that? Why, in the past seventy-two hours, has he been dead set on revising the history of their relationship, on wiping clean the terrible and sadistic ways Mark treated him? It's not due to a lack of effort; he's lost track of how many times he's replayed that scene from the Millennium Bridge, of how many times he's recited Mark's words, zeroing in on his cold, compassionless voice. But every time he does that—every time he's on the verge of convincing himself that, maybe, this breakup is a good thing—he'll stumble upon some other memory. He'll recall those heady days when they first moved to Philadelphia and Mark's insecurities overshadowed his own. When Paul would hold Mark's head in his lap and stroke his hair as Mark rattled on about what it was like to be young and inexperienced in one of the country's best economics departments. Paul would respond with what he knew Mark needed to hear—that he was brilliant, that it was only a matter of time until his colleagues realized that—and Mark would pull his face down to him and kiss him and tell him how crazy, how absolutely fucking crazy, he'd go without him. Invariably, the next day Paul would come home to find lamb roasting in the oven; he'd trudge in after another terrible day with Goulding to an apartment filled with the woodsy scents of rosemary and sage. "Hell," Mark would say, wiping his hands on his apron. "It's the least I could do." And there was, of course, more: in the middle of the night, for example, when he thought Paul was asleep, Mark had a tendency of kissing the back of his neck, of gently mussing his hair. During the last six months, these moments grew few and far between—Paul was more likely to find Mark snoring with his back turned toward him than gently kissing him—but still, for some vexing reason, he can't help but give them a disproportionate amount of attention. They grow and fester, these pleasant memories, forming indelible cancers that belie Paul's despair. What he wouldn't give, he thinks, to be wholly convinced of Mark's dickishness. To be rid of this nagging doubt rooted in happier times.

"Where am I going?" Alice says. "It looks like the road splits up here."

"Hold on." Paul struggles to get her phone out of his pocket. "I think you want to stay on the A338."

"That's not what my map says."

"Mom, I thought you put that goddamned thing away. We don't have a lot of time here, Paul."

"Hold *on*."

Freeing the phone, he opens the atlas. "Yeah, just stay on this road."

He makes a silent note that Alice doesn't thank him, and as he's moving to slip the phone back into his pants, it buzzes quietly in his palm. Looking down, he sees a new message from Jonathan: *I TOLD YOU TO STOP CALLING ME.*

What should he tell her? That he now knows the source of her irritation? That her boss-cum-lover has rejected her? That, like Paul, she's being spurned and discarded, written off as subpar? He's filled, suddenly, with a violent empathy for Alice, with a need to protect her from the awful fucking love mess that's weighing him down.

With a quick sleight of hand, he deletes the message and watches it vanish from the screen.

Donna

It's a spectacular house, she thinks, looking at the accommodations that Eloise has found for her, Alice, and Paul: an old dairy farm called Tender-way Glen that's been retrofitted and converted into a posh vacation rental. But then, what else should she expect from Eloise? Donna smiles: she taught her well. In addition to the property's main house, its square lawn is flanked on one side by a smaller guest cottage, and on the other by a series of un-used cow stalls, sheltered beneath a sloped tin roof. Beyond the property line, to Donna's rear, extends a broad meadow of wet, green grass, where there's a flock of sheep, which make it their business to baa at the wind.

Soon, she'll need to get in the shower; in a few hours, they've got to trek over to the Kings Arms, a restaurant in Dorchester, for the weekend's welcome cocktails, a precursor to tomorrow night's rehearsal dinner and Sunday's wedding. Besides, she's been standing here, staring at the house, for about ten minutes, ever since she set her suitcase down in the master suite and announced to her uninterested children that she needed a bit of air. And that was true—she did need air—particularly after being cooped up in that car for three hours, smelling the fish and cigarettes on her son's breath. But she also came out here for some space to breathe, and blink, and generally just exist without fear of her children's incessant scrutiny. When did they become like this? she wonders. For how long have they been ascribing secret meanings and clandestine messages to each and every thing Donna does? She wants to tell them that she's not that deep, that she no longer has the energy to be manipulative or conniving. She wants to tell them that, sometimes, a sigh is just a sigh.

She can't, though. She couldn't possibly. Because to do so would be to provide them with a whole new set of words and actions to analyze and deconstruct. She can hear Alice now: *In saying that a sigh is just a sigh you're actually admitting that it's something much larger than that—you're basically proving my point.* Christ! Donna thinks. How exhausting it must be, seeing the world and the people in it not for what they are, but rather as conduits for a language of nefarious messages. Had she taught them to think like that? Likely, she wagers. Yes, somehow, her children are her own fault.

And Paul. Poor Paul. Selfishly, she had been hoping that his breakup with his boyfriend (she can scarcely remember the man's name) might afford them an opportunity to reconnect, but now she doubts the likelihood of all that. Still, her son's in pain, and that breaks Donna's heart. It's difficult not to think of him as a wounded child who needs his mother during moments like this. Instead of seeing him as a grown man, she can't help but think of her son as the teenager who bleached his hair or pierced his ear—the boy who was forever searching for ways to escape who he feared he might be, but who always managed to stumble back to himself again.

But then, what else can she do but delicately let him know that she's here, ready to listen, and hold, and coddle, should he ever allow himself to need her? And oh, God, she knows she can't blame him for this, but she'd just about screamed when he said he wanted to talk to his father. She'd had to leave Paul in the parking lot, crushing his cigarette into the gravel, lest she risk running her mouth and telling him what she really thought: that his father died a bigot who understood compassion about as well as he understood tolerance, that the only advice he would have had for Paul would be to change everything about who he was.

"St. Charles," Ollie's father says, and Donna strains to hear him above the din of the cocktail party—the mix of music and voices and ice knocking against glasses. "That's a bit of a ways outside Chicago, is it not?"

Ollie's mother looks at her husband and then at Donna. She smiles, meekly.

"It's really not all that far, and it's still very cosmopolitan," Donna says. She adds: "I also know London quite well."

"There you have it! Sounds like you three have already got a lot to talk about." Ollie kisses Donna's cheek and squeezes her shoulder, and Donna smiles back at him, taking in his big, puppylike eyes, his floppy hair, his lanky good looks. She's fond of him. She was when she first met him in Chicago four years ago, but now she feels that fondness growing. He's likable. Plain and simple. Just like Eloise.

"Now, if you'll excuse me," Ollie says, "I've got to go have a word with security. Seems that there are some young men who've taken to climbing the lampposts outside, and I've got a dreadful feeling the suspects are none other than my bloody groomsmen."

The three of them—Ollie's parents and Donna—all laugh. Ollie shrugs and leaves.

Now feeling unprotected and exposed, Donna turns back to her soon-to-be in-laws. In one hand a gin fizz sweats against her palm. She'd originally planned to wear the blue tunic tonight, but at the last minute decided to go with something simple instead. An old silver A-line that had always given her luck. Maybe that had been a mistake.

"I've never been to Chicago," Ollie's mother says, after what appears to be much consideration.

Everyone nods.

How long must she stand here? Donna wonders. On one hand, she wants to flee, to escape into the throngs of Eloise's friends and assorted in-laws to find some abandoned table where she might fade into the background. On the other, though, she knows she's obliged to stay and make conversation with Ollie's parents, no matter how dreadful and vapid that conversation may be. She has to laugh at their jokes, to frown at their minor complaints, to agree with their politics, even if she finds them vulgar. Worst of all, she knows that they're bound to her by the same set of obligations.

Ollie's father looks over his shoulder toward the kitchen, where a steady stream of waiters bearing trays of prawns flows out into the restaurant. *Really*, Donna wants to say, *you can go. We don't have to do this.*

Thankfully, just as she's about to ask something about the price of gas in Dorset, Eloise grabs her arm from behind.

"Mind if I steal you away for a moment, *Maman*?"

"Ollie's parents and I were just starting to get to know one another."

"It'll only be a second, I swear."

She smiles at Ollie's parents and begs their pardon.

"I'll bring her back shortly," says Eloise.

Relieved, they both tell her not to worry.

Eloise leads Donna toward a second bar near the rear of the restaurant, where it's less crowded, and where she can finally hear herself breathe. Of the three tables in the room, two of them are empty, occupied only by crumpled-up napkins and half-empty glasses. At the third sit a man and a woman—Eloise identifies them as a cousin of Ollie's and his moody wife—engaged in a heated conversation, their heads bowed together. Along the south wall there's a single window, and through it Donna can see sea-borne mist start to encircle the trunks of the trees on the restaurant's small lawn. It's a moonless night and, save a few courageous stars, the sky's an inky black.

"What is it?" Donna asks her.

Eloise grins.

"Wait here," she says.

Donna does as she's told, sitting at one of the free tables. Happy to be off her feet, she slips her heels off and rubs the sole of her left foot, where a dull ache throbs. Looking out the window again, she watches as lights in the stone houses of Dorchester flicker on and off. As much as she tries not to, she can't help but concern herself with the impression she made on Ollie's parents. Had they thought her provincial? Simple? Crass? She's irritated that she cares. Moreover, she's irritated that they know that she cares. And she knows that they do; she'd seen it in Ollie's father's face, when he asked her about St. Charles's proximity to Chicago. He'd nearly laughed when she said "cosmopolitan."

Or maybe she's making it all up.

She takes a larger gulp of her gin fizz and holds the liquor in her mouth until she's got no choice but to swallow it or be sick. Where has her daughter gone? she wonders. She thought she wanted to melt away into a wallflower when she was talking to Ollie's parents, but now that she has her solitude, she feels alone, exposed. Watching the couple argue at the table across from her, she decides that she wants to be back among the throng; she wants to disappear amid other people. Yes, she'll go search for Eloise. She'll go find her daughter.

But then, just as she's standing, she hears her name.

"Donna?" a deep, accented voice says.

"Oh," she says, her heart in her throat. "There you are."

Alice

_____

The hair on the back of her neck stands on end, and she wonders how easily she might nab one of the bottles of champagne chilling behind the bar to her left. She bites her lip: one of the bartenders is trying to seduce a woman twice his age, aware, surely, that her husband is standing hardly two feet from them; the other barman, a fat Welsh guy with a ruddy face, has just escaped off somewhere. In the dining room she hears the clinking of a knife against a glass, but then, this is no surprise; since they arrived two hours ago she'd hardly been able to take a breath without being interrupted by one of Eloise's friends, clambering over herself to prove her worth and adoration for the bride. Through strands of flickering tea lights Alice can see her sister's face, beaming and intoxicated by the praise being heaped on her, on Ollie, on their ability to create something so perfect and enviable, to forge it through *the sheer strength of their love*.

She needs that champagne.

The woman's husband gently pulls her away from the seductive bartender, and the ruddy Welshman returns; her hopes for a full bottle squandered, Alice settles for two flutes of champagne. Out on the lawn, a few guests have ventured out for cigarettes, and above them the smoke hangs in the humid air. In an hour, their ranks will grow; the fathers who now look at their sons disapprovingly will stumble out and try to bum a fag.

It's different than younger weddings she's been to, Alice thinks, the ceremonies she attended right out of college, the first few of which marriages are just now starting to crumble in divorce: there wasn't the standard bum rush for the bar at the beginning of the evening, the tittering excitement of everyone getting dressed up together for the first time. No, this wedding—her sister's wedding—has a distinctively thirty-something vibe to it. That's not to say the people around her, the Hennies and Flossies and Poppies and Minties, aren't looking to get fucked up. They are, they definitely are, and they'll pay for it in the morning. But they've clopped over this well-worn territory before; they know how to at least cultivate the impression that they're pacing themselves.

Confronted with such unabashed happiness, she suddenly feels like she's going to be sick with anger. Where the hell is Paul? she wonders. She needs him. She wants to rest her head on his shoulder and to see her defeat reflected in his eyes.

Outside, away from the smokers and the toasts and the ruddy Welshman, Alice kicks the tire of a Fiat, then yelps as the pain radiates through her toes to her knees. She remembers back in May, sitting on the phone at her office, trying to broker a truce between Paul and Donna. She was nice then. Good. Sure, one could argue that in acting as mediator she was advancing her own interests just as much as anyone else's, but still, at least altruism was a pleasant side effect of her selfishness. How then, in a matter of a few short months, has she pulled such an abrupt 180? How has she become such a monster?

She looks down at the dress she's got on—it's the same one that the rest of the bridesmaids are wearing. (Eloise had bought the dress for her—but then, of course she had.) Watching Henny and Flossie float around in theirs,

Alice wants to tear hers off. Wants to throw it down to the cobblestone streets, stomp on it, and run, screaming in her underwear, through the claustrophobic alleyways of this awful little town. Instead, though, she kicks the wheel of the Fiat again, this time relishing the pain. Then she limps over to one of the cabs that Eloise has hired to take guests home in an hour, when the party's scheduled to end. Slipping the driver a ten-pound note, Alice tells him to take her back to the farm now, please, even though he's technically off duty. She's afraid of what she'll do if she stays here, she realizes.

She's become, suddenly, afraid of herself.

The farm, Tenderway Glen, sits at the base of a long, though not necessarily steep, gravel hill, and as the cabdriver approaches it he tells Alice that he can't take her all the way to the house, but rather must leave her here, on the side of the main road.

"Got to be back in twenty minutes, and I reckon trying to turn around down by the house will take me nothing short of an hour."

"But there's plenty of room to turn around down there," Alice pleads. "And really, it's not that far. It just looks like it because of the field, and the way the hill curves around that hedge."

"Don't know what to tell you, miss. I've got paying guests waiting."

"But *I'm* a paying guest."

"Surely you know what I mean."

She doesn't, but she gets out of the cab anyway and slams the door. Before the road slopes down the hill to the house, it passes by a small field where, this morning, a company section of the Boys' Brigade set up camp for a weeklong jamboree. On the acre of unruly grass they've erected pup tents, and passing them Alice sees the flicker of flashlights. Charred driftwood and charcoal cut through the mossy scent of wet grass, and as she picks her way past a naked flagpole, she hears young voices whispering beneath the domes of one of the tents. Are they talking about her, she wonders? Did one of the boys, sneaking out for a piss, see her emerge from the cab, her dress hiked up around her knees, her heels dangling from her left hand? And if that's the case, what are they saying? Are they swapping stories about where this gorgeous mystery woman is going, about why she's floating down to an old dairy farm in a cocktail dress at nine o'clock at night? Or do their predictions inch closer to the truth? Are they imagining Alice closer to what she actually is: tired, half drunk, annoyed with her shoes, disappointed in herself?

She doesn't go into the house. For starters, she doesn't have a key, but also the thought of being alone in such a large space, surrounded only by other empty rooms, sickens her. So, instead, she sits down on an empty bucket in one of the concrete cow stalls that face the house's lawn. It's been a while since they've been used, she imagines; the stall itself smells more like fresh paint and concrete than cow dung. She likes it, though. She just likes that the stalls are here. She likes her ass pressed up against the tin bucket, and the sensation of her feet against the cold, stark floor. She likes looking into the rambling mess of trees and weeds and hedges beyond the perimeter of the house. She likes hearing the sheep baa.

She reaches into her clutch for her phone and calls Jonathan.

He picks up on the third ring. "Jesus Christ, Alice."

"You're telling me." She leans back against the stall's wall and feels the concrete scratch against her skin. "I've had a terrible night."

"I told you to stop calling me," he says, and she sits up straight again. "Why the fuck are you calling me?"

"What? You never told me that." Her heart feels as if it's been pumped with helium. "Jonathan, what are you talking about?"

"I texted you earlier today. Alice, you've got to stop calling me. Marissa knows. She figured everything out. She's threatening to leave me and take my kids."

"Oh, God. Um. Okay." She fumbles. "That's awful, but, uh, I mean, weren't you saying things weren't going well, anyway?"

"Married people have problems, Alice. That's just called *life*. I'd be fucking crazy to ever leave Marissa, but now she might leave *me*."

"But, Jonathan, when we were getting tacos, you said—"

"Look, forget what I fucking said, all right?" he hisses. "God, I can't believe this is happening."

Alice stands up and begins pacing in the stall. "That's impossible, though."

"It's not." He sounds pissed. She imagines him standing in his office overlooking Wilshire, his arms raised about his head as he shouts at her, the glass door blocking out the noise. "It's *not* impossible, because you insisted on posting your every goddamned move on Facebook and Twitter and Instagram and God only knows where else."

An owl perches itself on the house's chimney, and, somewhere in the ink-black field, a dog barks.

"And guess what," Jonathan continues. "Marissa's not some fucking idiot. All she had to do was see your *thirty missed calls* on my phone, check out your Facebook page, and then look at our credit card statement. And now—*fuck*, Alice, do you know what you've done? Do you know how much you've fucked me over?"

"Wait a second," she says. "*I* fucked *you* over? What, I tied you down and insisted that you screw me? I demanded that you have an affair? I'd like to remind you that *you* were the one who followed me into the supply closet and—"

"You knew damned well what you were doing."

Should she be sorry? Should she be feeling empathy for him, right now? She wonders if she could, even if she wanted to; she wonders if she's lost the capacity to empathize.

"It's not my fault you married Nancy Fucking Drew," she says.

"Fuck you, Alice."

"I had a miscarriage."

"What?" His voice lightens, hovering somewhere between shock and panic. *I'm despicable*, Alice thinks. "When?"

"Five years ago."

"Oh, for fuck's sake."

She starts crying.

"I'm sorry, Alice, I really am, but that's got nothing to do with me."

"Do you know where I am right now?"

"I've got a meeting in two minutes. I've got—"

"I'm sitting in a cow stall in England, Jonathan. A cow stall that's probably never been used, but was built to make rich people believe that they're staying in a farm that people actually used to use. I'm sitting here in a fucking gown that my sister bought for me. A gown that all of the other bridesmaids are wearing. These *awful* women whose one goal in life seems to be making me feel like shit. My sister hardly spoke to me tonight, and my mother—literally the person I've been trying to prop up for the past three years—was more interested in flirting with her ex-husband, this guy who absolutely fucked her over, than in spending time with me." She's sobbing now. "About a hundred yards away a group of preteens from the *fucking Boys' Brigade* just watched me walk barefoot down a gravel hill after saying their nightly prayers. And—"

"I've got to go, Alice."

"Wait."

He doesn't, though; he just hangs up, and Alice throws her phone against the stall's wall. It doesn't break—it bounces off and falls back to her feet, its screen now bearing a small, hairline crack. The distant dog starts barking again. The owl on top of the chimney cranes its neck around, and takes flight. Alice watches it beat its wings against the night, then vanish somewhere in the tangled branches of a tree.

"Goddamn it," she says, picking up her phone. "God*damn* it."

She runs a finger over the crack, and as she's doing so she hears shoes crunching against the house's gravel drive. Standing up, she sees her brother's silhouette, lit dimly by the porch light.

"Heyo," he says, spotting her, and she wonders how much he's heard.

"Hi."

"What're you doing over there?" He wobbles a bit before finding his balance.

"Nothing," she says. "Just listening to the sheep."

"Bet that's the first time in your life you've ever said that." Paul grins.

"How long have you been standing there?" she asks him.

"About two point five seconds." He sneezes. "You see all those *boys* up there? In their little tents?"

"Yeah," she says. "Just acting like a bunch of boys." She wipes the wetness from underneath each eye. "Why aren't you still at the party?"

"I couldn't be there anymore," he says, scratching his cheek. "It was making me too depressed. All those people in love. I hate those people."

"Yeah, well."

Paul rubs his eyes and cranes his neck from side to side. He's untucked his shirt, and now the tails of it hang loose and wrinkled at his side. It's too big for him, Alice thinks. It looks like it belongs to a set of pajamas.

"Mind if I join you?" he asks.

She looks on either side of her. "There's only one bucket."

It doesn't matter, though; he steps into the stall and sits, cross-legged, on the floor.

"What happened to your jacket?"

"Left it there, I guess," he says. "Were you crying or something? You look like someone slugged you in the fucking face."

How much should she tell him? she wonders. On one hand, she wants to lay herself bare and confess to her epic decline—a fall that could be described as Icarian, had she ever actually been close to the sun. She wants to confess to Paul how, two weeks ago at Claridge's, she snorted enough Klonopin to seduce a woolly mammoth before gorging herself on a thousand pounds' worth of room service. She wants to say how, two minutes ago, Jonathan slapped her with a scarlet letter before telling her to fuck off for good. But then, on the other hand, she doesn't think she can stand another ounce of familial judgment, not from Eloise, or her mother, or, most of all, from Paul. She imagines what words of wisdom he might have for her: that she made her own adulterous bed and now she's got to sleep in it; that, as a victim of a recent breakup, he can only imagine what the wife is going through; that this is the problem with heterosexuals—they extol the importance of marriage, only to go and do shit like this.

So all she says is: "It's over with Jonathan."

"Is that why you broke your phone?"

She looks down; she hadn't realized she was still holding it, the crack catching fragments of the porch light.

"Yes," she says. "I guess. Or, I don't know. It was one of the reasons."

He lays his head in her lap, and at first she doesn't know what to do. She straightens her back and watches as he closes his eyes. She stays still for a moment, listening to the sheep baa, and finally relaxes. She reaches down and brushes his hair, damp with sweat and humidity, from his eyes.

"He sort of sounded like a douche, anyway," Paul says with his eyes still closed.

"He said I ruined his life."

"You don't ruin anyone's life. People do that on their own. People ruin their own lives."

She wants to start crying again, but she can't. For whatever reason, the tears won't come. Instead, she listens to the crickets out in the field.

"He basically called me a whore."

"Yeah? And what is he, then?"

"I think . . ." Alice says, "I think just for once I want someone to be on my side. Like, unequivocally and unconditionally on my side, even when I'm obviously so fucking wrong."

Paul shifts. He makes a pillow with his hands and slips them under his head. She can feel his fingers, hot and clammy, on her knees. He squeezes her leg and sighs once.

"Mark and I had a threesome," he says.

"Wait, *what?*"

"In London. With that Alcott guy." He adds, "Mark wanted to, so I did it."

"The one who looked like a porcelain doll with a dick?"

He sits up. Faint impressions of knuckles form dull craters on his cheek. "Yeah. That one."

Alice laughs. She buries her head between her knees to try to contain herself, but she can't—she just keeps laughing.

"I'm sorry," she says. "Oh, God. I'm so sorry."

"I let him fuck me, Al, and now I probably have AIDS."

She reaches out and sweeps her hand through his hair again. *"Pauly,"* she says, and leans forward to kiss his cheek. "You do *not* have AIDS. Scabies, maybe, but that's just an inconvenience."

He doesn't laugh.

Pulling herself together, she asks him: "Is this why you guys broke up?"

"I don't think so," he says. He kneels on the cement and sits back on his heels. "I think Mark broke up with me months ago, and this was just a reason to finally end it."

Alice braces herself on the side of the bucket, then lowers herself to the floor. Resting her head against Paul's shoulder, she gazes at the stall's wall of uneven concrete, and then beyond it, through the sliver of space between the stall and the ceiling, and finally at the deep indigo of the sky, the dusting of stars stretching over the English Channel.

"I wonder why this shit always happens to us," she says, and presses her cheek against his neck.

"I don't know . . ." Paul says. "I guess because we let it."

Donna

July 10

At nine o'clock in the morning Henrique knocks lightly on the front door, and even though she's been ready for the past two hours, Donna invites him in and says that she'll be ready in a moment; she's just finishing her coffee.

"Would you like some?" she asks him as he sits at the kitchen table.

It's warm out—muggy—and condensation clings to the base of the windows.

"No, thank you," he says, smiling, and she tries to stop herself from blushing.

She finishes her coffee, which is now cold, in near silence. Every so often, either she or Henrique makes an innocuous comment about something they can see—the state of the house (*lovely*), the weather (*humid*), the overgrown lawn (*needs a good mowing*)—but mostly they just listen to each other breathe. Watching him watch her, she presently wonders if this—their day together—is smart thinking. Last night, in the glow of tea lights and too much champagne, the prospect of a reunion struck her as a terrible idea, but terrible in that magical, thrilling way that she knew she was powerless against. Now, in the light of day, she fears that she's set herself up for disappointment. An afternoon of tripping over each other. Of scratching open wounds that she's spent too many years nursing.

"*Es-tu prête?*" Henrique says.

"*Oui.*"

Should she tell her children she's leaving? No, she thinks. Probably not. They need their sleep. Last night when she returned home, she found them both passed out on the sectional in the living room, the TV blaring some reality show about young people in Essex. Paul's head was resting on Alice's knees, and her hand was set on his neck, like she couldn't decide whether to pet him or strangle him. Donna had tried to wake them both up so they might move upstairs to their beds, but with little luck; when she poked Alice in the shoulder, all she did was grumble and readjust herself. So she let them stay there, exactly as they were, drawing maternal comfort from the fact that, at least when they're unconscious, her children seem to legitimately care for each other. And she figures it's only reasonable that when she came downstairs this morning she felt a dull but predictable disappointment in discovering that they had separated, left the couch, retreated to the isolation of their own rooms.

"*D'accord,*" Henrique says, standing. "*D'abord, je crois qu'on—*"

"Ha, uh," Donna laughs. "My French is a little rusty. How about we stick to English for the day?"

He kisses her cheek. "Of course."

This is a lie, she thinks, but only a small one, and one that's hardly malicious. The truth is her French is fine. Still, she feels that speaking English gives her a bit of power in what would otherwise be a powerless situation. Besides, she doesn't want Henrique to know how much practice, how much time, she's put into maintaining her French. She doesn't want him to get any ideas about her preparing for anything. Because what, after all, would she possibly be preparing for? This? Today? The moment Henrique realizes his mistake and comes sweeping back into her life? Oh God, she thinks. She hopes not. She hopes she's not that naïve, that foolish.

Quietly she shuts the front door and follows Henrique out to the gravel driveway, where he's parked his rental car, an electric-blue Audi convertible coupe with the top already down. How gorgeous, Donna thinks, which is followed instantly by Christ, my *hair*. She spent nearly an hour on it this morning, combing it and recombing it, trying to hide the gray with the blond. Maybe she should run back inside, she thinks. Grab a scarf or a handkerchief. Something she might wrap around her head to keep things in place. But then—for what? She's not exactly young anymore, and at sixty-three she's liable to look more like some old Russian babushka than Marilyn Monroe on a leisure drive.

No, she thinks, as Henrique opens her door for her. She'll let the wind do its work and just hope for the best.

"So, where are we off to?" she says, buckling her seat belt.

He winks at her. "It's a surprise."

"I feel terrible that we're not at Ollie's parents' house helping to set up for tonight."

He starts the car. "You shouldn't. Eloise told us to explore today. She asked us not to help."

"She's just saying that."

"And we're just doing what she says."

They climb the hill, the gravel crackling beneath the wheels of the car, and pass the Boys' Brigade jamboree. As they wait to turn left on to the main road, Donna watches in the rearview mirror as two boys in uniform unfold the Union Jack and send it up the flagpole. Behind them, three of their mates are clipping wet bathing suits to a clothesline. Then Henrique turns, and they're gone.

He drives too fast—she had forgotten this from their marriage—banking around blind turns like he's the only man on the road, hardly slowing down as they pass by a stopped truck with its hood open. The wind howls so loudly on either side of Donna that she can't hear herself think, let alone Henrique talk. When they reach Dorchester they're forced to slow down, lest Henrique career through a roundabout or smash into one of the cheap vacation-wares storefronts that line the town's anemic roads. But it seems that as soon as they enter the town they're out of it again—these cities don't sprawl in the same way that Donna's used to, at least not here, in the southwest; she feels the car lurch forward as Henrique shifts into fifth; she ventures a quick touch of her hair and abandons all hope.

They travel west on the A35, slowing down again as they pass through Winterbourne Abbas, and speeding up once they leave behind the town's ancient limestone walls. Resting her arm against the windowsill, Donna watches as the countryside stretches out around them: shallow hills of unimaginable green; ramshackle and futile fences zigzagging toward oblivion; the occasional tree, sprouting up from nothing, tossing shade in all directions at once. Aesthetically it's not that different from her home in Illinois, but somehow, here in England, all this bucolic laziness stems from a more exotic, enticing place. She could stare at these hills for hours.

But why? she wonders. How can a sheep in Dorset capture her imagination in a way that a cow in St. Charles can't? She resists attributing her intoxication to Henrique, though she fears he may have something to do with it. She wants, desperately, to believe that their outing is innocuous, the acting out of a diplomatic accord between two people who used to be married. Instead, though, she's got this awful excitement fluttering around her stomach. This schoolgirl inkling that causes her to wake up two hours early, to steal glances, to worry about her hair. And for what? So she can fall in love with him all over again, here on the A35? So he can reach down and pull her out from the ache of widowhood? So she can open herself up, only to be shot down? No, she instructs herself. *No.* As mesmerizing as the sheep are, as seductive as Henrique is, she's smarter than she was when she was twenty-three. She knows how to protect herself, even if it means committing to another two decades of loneliness. She repeats the mantra she's always told her children, and for the first time she tries believing it:

Never expect someone to change, because he won't. If you don't love some-one at his worst, you shouldn't bother loving him at all.

At the B3071 they bear south, zooming through Coombe Keynes and Burngate before arriving in West Lulworth, a smudge of a seaside village smelling of fish and algae and ice cream cones. They park in a crowded lot near the visitors' center, and before Donna can get out of the car to stretch her legs, Henrique lays a hand on her bare knee and says to stay put, that he'll get the door for her.

"Oh, really, you don't—" she begins to protest.

"No, no." He smiles. "I insist."

"Well, then. All right."

She waits, and watches in the rearview mirror as he circles around the trunk of the car. He looks like he's ready for a cruise, she thinks. Slim khaki pants paired with a white linen shirt unbuttoned to the sternum. Strappy, Jesus-ish sandals that she can't imagine are comfortable, particularly on these rocky, barely paved roads. The wind blows gray hair away from his sun-kissed forehead.

Donna folds her hands in her lap and waits.

"*Mademoiselle,*" he says, swinging open the door and offering her his hand.

She doesn't take it. She stands up and flattens the creases from her pants.

"So what are we doing here, anyway?"

He lightly takes hold of both her shoulders and spins her around to face a small shack. In front of it is strewn a small armada of plastic sea kayaks, along with a collection of fiberglass paddles. Looking up to the shack's tin awning, she sees a handpainted sign: SVEN'S KAYAKING AND COASTAL EXPLORING. The letters shrink as they fight for space at the sign's end. Donna panics.

"Henrique," she says, turning to face him again. "I don't really think this is for me."

"Nonsense. Everything is for you. Besides, I've already made a reser-vation."

There's hardly a crowd gathered around the shack. Aside from a pair of Germans lathering sunscreen across their doughy bellies, only one man is present: a leathery fifty-something in board shorts and nothing else who Donna assumes to be Sven.

Still, despite her efforts otherwise, she's flattered by Henrique's thoughtfulness.

"You made a reservation?"

"For a private tour," he says.

"In boats?"

"In *kayaks*."

"With Sven?"

Henrique shakes his head. "No. Sven, he is only the owner." He points to the grizzly board-shorts wearer. "That, I think, is Kenny."

"I didn't realize they made Kennys in England."

He rubs her arm and kisses her cheek again. "I've missed you."

She lingers by the car as Henrique trots over to Kenny. Maybe she's been too selfish, she thinks. Maybe this desire of hers, born in Paris, for something exotic and elegant and chic is nothing more than materialism dressed up as culture. She thinks of Bill. He had his shortcomings, certainly, but maybe she was too quick to dismiss him after his death; sure, he may have turned out to be a closet homophobe, but he would have known better than to ask her to go kayaking.

She forces herself to join Henrique, and when she gets there she's immediately greeted with a limp handshake from Kenny, who smells overpoweringly of Banana Boat sunscreen and grease.

"Must be Donna, then," he says and smiles, revealing some basic approximation of teeth. "Lovely."

"Yes," she says, wondering how rude it would be to wipe her hand off against her pants. "Lovely."

"Right, then. Mis-sur Lafarge gave us all your information when he phoned this morning, so we won't be needing you to fill out any forms. Just a few t's to cross and i's to dot and we'll be on our way. If I could just get you to sign here"—she does—"we can get you all squared away with a wet suit."

"I'm sorry. A wet suit?"

"You'll freeze your knackers off without one!" Kenny laughs, and Donna holds her breath. "Don't be fooled by the color of the water," he says. "It may look like you're in the Caribbean, what with all those greens and blues, but that's on account of the chalk in the soil. The second you dip a toe in you'll remember you're still in England."

"I see." She turns back to glance at Henrique, who's already taken off his shirt and is spreading zinc oxide across his nose.

"Now, Mis-sur Lafarge gave us your size—"

"He did?"

"So we've got a suit all ready for you in our changing room. If you'd just be so kind as to follow me, I'll show you to it."

Kenny directs her past three long benches to the rear of the shack, where a curtain hanging from the ceiling separates a small room into two smaller cubicles. In one of the cubes is Donna's wet suit, dangling from a rusted nail pounded into the wall. Next to it stands a mirror.

"I'll leave you to it, then. Just come on out when you're ready," Kenny says, closing the curtain behind him.

Donna removes the wet suit from the hanger. Inspecting the tiny openings where she's meant to squeeze her arms, her legs, her neck, she's sure there's been some sort of mistake. A Cabbage Patch doll couldn't be expected to fit into this fistful of neoprene, let alone a sixty-three-year-old woman. How much did Henrique tell them she weighs? Seventy-five pounds? Eighty? My God, she thinks. Two months ago she was standing in a dressing room at Nordstrom's worried that she looked unpresentable in a purple dress, and now this . . . this *wet suit.* What was the salesgirl's name? The one in the black pants with the terrible tattoo? She can't remember now, and it's hardly the point. Briefly she considers calling Kenny over and asking him to bring her a larger size. But then, what if Henrique heard her? What if he saw Kenny rummaging through his bin for a suit that was more appropriate for Donna, something roughly the size of a manatee? Would he suddenly lose interest? Realize that she's not the nubile young thing he met thirty years ago? Call this dreadful kayaking trip off? The sheer prospect of it has her sweating through her blouse, which is the exact thing she told herself she *must not let happen*: she *must not let him seduce her*. Her daughters' reincarnation of feminism was meant to solve these problems, she thinks. In the sixties women were freed from the home; now, they're meant to be free from men. And yet, here she is, standing barefoot in a shack in Dorset, wondering if her ex-husband—a man who left her for a Spanish au pair—will think she looks fat. Really, Alice and Eloise must try a little harder.

"Oh, fuck it," she says, and rips the wet suit from the hanger.

To her delight, it slips on easier than she expects. There are a few moments where she's got to stuff herself into it, where she's got to pull, and pinch, and stretch, and cajole, but for the most part the suit's forgiving; it works with her in wondrous and surprising ways.

"How's it going, love?" Kenny shouts through the curtain.

"Just another minute," she shouts back.

A long zipper runs down the back of the suit, from the base of her neck to the top of her ass. Reaching around, she takes hold of the frayed lanyard attached to it and tugs. As the suit zips, she feels it compress her body, flattening any lumps into solid, sturdy plateaus. Her body now confined, she ventures a breath, and the fabric expands and contracts against her rib cage. She looks like a seal, of course—this much is confirmed when, breath held, she turns to face the mirror—but then, she suspects (hopes?) that most people do when they're clad only in black neoprene.

"Donna!" Henrique bellows once she emerges. "How gorgeous."

"Oh, shut up, Henrique."

He, to Donna's dismay, looks fantastic. Whereas Donna's suit merely contains her body, Henrique's accentuates his. The brand name stenciled across the suit's front stretches across his chest, giving the impression of muscles that she suspects disappeared decades ago. Long, ropy legs suddenly seem taut, athletic. Even the suit's color—black, with off-white streaks on each side of the torso—teases out the gray in his hair in irksome and flattering ways. The brief, elusive confidence she felt moments ago fades.

She stands by and watches as Henrique helps Kenny load the kayaks onto two rolling trolleys, which the three of them then begin to guide down a steep pedestrian walkway toward the beach. The tourists around whom she helps Henrique maneuver the boat seem conspicuously undisturbed by her presence, and she wavers back and forth between wanting to thank them for being polite and hating them for not joining in on the joke with her. She wants them to confirm the craziness of all this. To laugh with her and at her, and to agree with her that, above all else, this is absurd. They don't, though. They just go on buying towels, and beach balls, and ice cream, and rubbing suntan lotion on their pink arms.

The beach to which Kenny directs them sits on the south end of a large, oval-shaped cove. A few sunbathers have ventured out onto the sand, which is more a field of pebbles than a proper beach. For the most part, though, people stand at the end of the small road down which Donna has just trekked, staring at the shore like it's a circus act that they sense should excite them, but that, in reality, just confuses them. Kenny and Henrique haul the kayaks off the trolleys and drag them past a rotting skiff and a few knots of seaweed, right up to the water's edge. Donna pads after them, dodging a toddler in diapers making failed castles out of rocks.

"Right," Kenny says. He's slipped on a life jacket, and he tosses two others to Donna and Henrique. "A few quick safety announcements, and then we'll be on our way."

She struggles to get the life jacket around her shoulders, then gets her arms caught in its nylon straps. Once she's finally figured it out, she clips it across her chest.

"Water's typically pretty calm," Kenny continues. "So won't do much good to be worried about waves and such." He cracks his neck and puts his hands on his hips. "In the event that you do get tossed around a bit, don't panic. Just stay calm and ride it out. And if you *capsize*—"

"That could *happen?*" Donna asks.

Kenny raises both of his palms, like he's pleading the fifth on the ocean's behalf. "The sea can be a mighty mistress, Donna."

"But, like, how many times has that happened? Has someone . . . flipped over?"

"Oh, just a handful per week."

"Per week."

Kenny laughs and grabs hold of her shoulder. "Don't worry, love! The water won't kill you. If you flip over, you just climb back on. Like this." He belly flops on to the kayak and wiggles his way toward one of the seats. "Then, you just flip around. Like you're a pancake."

"Like you're a pancake," she says back to him.

From behind her, she feels Henrique wrap a hand around her waist. "I'll help you."

The water bites her toes, and she gasps. Gently, Henrique pushes the kayak into the surf, and she wades out with it, guiding it, steadying it, holding her breath as the ocean seeps and swirls in the space between her skin and the neoprene.

"You get in first," he says, "and I'll keep it upright."

"Okay," she tells him. But how? Should she throw one leg up first, then the other? That seems like the most graceful way to go about it, but she doubts her flexibility. What, though, are the other options? She turns to look for Kenny, to see if she might glean some tips from watching him, but he's already twenty yards offshore, paddling in lazy circles.

Pressed and at a loss, she throws herself across the boat's bow, lying there for a moment like a felled pterodactyl.

"Bon," Henrique says. *"Bon,* now just roll over. Yes—yes, that's it. Right. Now . . . oops, don't fall out. Okay. Yes. Now, here's your oar. Hold on to it tightly! I'm getting in."

And he does. And they're off. It's slow going at first; they can't quite seem to find a rhythm, and because Henrique is stronger than Donna, it's hard for them to keep to a steady, straight course behind Kenny. He's got to readjust their trajectory constantly, paddling twice on the left side, then on the right, which elicits in Donna a great and untiring guilt. She wishes, desperately, to be a better kayaker.

Miraculously, though, once they break free of the cove and the break-water, Donna hits a stride and they begin gliding through the water with an acceptable, if not graceful, ease. To their right, chalky cliffs plunge toward jagged spits of beach, their white faces reflecting off the still sea with blinding clarity. A few yards ahead of them, Kenny babbles something about prehistoric history and the Jurassic period, about fossils wedged for eternity into the cliffs' soft walls. Donna does her best to ignore him; she doesn't care about brachiopods or ammonites. She wants only to enjoy the warmth of the sun against her neck and the blissful sound of her paddle cutting through the water. She wants to watch the light ripple across the surface as she flirts, however guardedly, with the idea that Henrique might still love her.

They round a rocky point and find themselves in a small, isolated cove. Overhead, gulls circle, rising and falling on the wind's currents. With his paddle, Kenny points to a spot on the cliff where emerald grass forms a stark contrast to the white chalk.

"We've got a peregrine falcon nest up there," he says.

"Oh?" She's surprised by her interest. "Where?"

"A bit hidden. But if you look closely, you can make out a small indent in the cliff wall, right under that patch of grass. They've stowed themselves away in there."

"I can't see it. Are there a lot of them around here?"

"One of the few in the area, I'm afraid. Almost completely killed off during the First World War."

Henrique says, "It's always the Germans."

"Matter of fact, in this case it was the English." With two deft strokes he spins the kayak around so he's facing them. "Little buggers were killing too many carrier pigeons coming over with messages from the Continent. The war ministry started paying farmers a pretty penny to poach them."

"You're kidding," Donna says.

"Afraid not," Kenny says, and shrugs. He adds, "Sort of makes you wonder about how shortsighted we can be."

Donna squints at the wall in search of the nest, suddenly skeptical. Soon, though, she gives up. Kenny's story has caused her to lose interest in the falcons; she's never been comfortable with allegories.

They thread their way out of the cove and continue their westward route, hugging the coast. In front of them, miles ahead, the cliffs begin to merge with the turquoise sea, and the sky dips to meet the impenetrable green of the land. The view's so clear, and the colors so lush, that it's hard to believe that they're in gray, dreary England, rather than on some far-flung Mediterranean island. It's hard to believe that this—that all of this—is on account of chalk in the cliffs' soil. It's a fascinating thought, she thinks, just how deceptive beauty can be, and she's proud of herself for having it. Dipping her paddle into the water, she's tempted to turn around and share her notion with Henrique. That moment passes, though, and she doesn't. She's worried that if she speaks out loud, the idea might then become ludicrous, and that the magnificence of the moment will turn dull. Yes, she'll keep it to herself. She'll stare forward instead, keeping her gaze fixed on the point where the colors collide, as she imagines Henrique smiling behind her.

Ten minutes later, just as Donna's triceps begin to burn and she worries her arms might fall off, they round another craggy point and come face-to-face with a giant limestone arch, running parallel to the coast. Easily one hundred feet high, one of its ends plunges into the water of a shallow bay while the other connects to the shoreline. As they paddle through it toward the beach, shadows darken the water beneath them.

"Durdle Door," Kenny says.

"Sounds like something out of Harry Potter."

He ignores her. "Constant erosion of the limestone band that stretches there—at the western end—is what caused the arch. UNESCO's named it a World Heritage Site. To the east there, that giant beach we're looking at is Man o' War Bay. 'Durdle' comes from the Old English 'thirl,' which means 'bore' or 'drill.'" He adds, "Did a report on it back in the fourth form. Got myself an A."

Donna's not really listening. She's staring up at the striated layers of limestone, wondering how the English could give something so beautiful such an absurd and mockable name.

Once they've passed through the arch and they're closer to the beach, Kenny spins around to face them. "Who's up for a little surfing, then?"

Donna twists around to look at Henrique, who shrugs.

Kenny laughs.

"No, no," he says. "I just mean on the kayaks. You can stand up and paddle it like it's a surfboard." Leaping to his feet, he demonstrates, performing a few loose circles. "See? Perfectly safe. Could do a bit of yoga while you're at it, if you'd like."

"No, thank you." Donna rests her paddle across her lap.

"Donna's an excellent surfer," she hears Henrique say.

She turns to him again, this time knocking the paddle into the water. Leaning over, she snatches it up.

"I've never surfed a day in my life."

"Nonsense," he says. "I bought you those lessons in Biarritz."

"No, Henrique, you didn't."

"I did so! With that Australian instructor with the terrible accent. Afterward we had sangria by the casino."

Thinking of Maria Elena, she can feel her lips starting to curl. "You're confusing me with someone else."

"Surely you're mistaken."

Donna whips her head around and faces Kenny. "All right," she says. "Tell me what I have to do."

"'Atta girl! So, first you're going to want to—"

She doesn't wait for him to finish. Inspired by rage, and jealousy, and defiance, she plants both of her feet on the kayak's floor and stands straight up.

This is a mistake, she realizes. The kayak sways violently beneath her uneven weight, and as Henrique reaches out to steady her, she topples over and plunges into the water. The cold knocks the wind from her, and sea-water floods her ears and nose. Kicking and flailing, she resurfaces and spits out a mouthful of salt.

"DONNA!" Henrique is shouting. "HANG ON!"

"Oh, for Christ's sake," she says. The life jacket lifts and presses against her ears. "I'm fine."

"I'm coming in after you," he says, swinging his legs over the kayak's edge.

"That's really not necessary," she says.

It's too late, though. Henrique throws himself from the kayak, and the splash from his impact crests over Donna, reclogging her ears, nose, and throat with brine.

"Really," she says as he doggy-paddles over to her. "I'm fine."

"You're certain?" His hair hangs in his face.

If she stretches out her legs long enough when she kicks, she can feel her toes scratch against the sea floor. "Yes."

She wants to sink, to disappear, to bury herself in heaps of wet, rocky sand.

Their abandoned kayak floats back toward the arch, and Kenny instructs them to retrieve it before it drifts away on some strong current.

"Just drag it on over to the beach," he yells, still standing. "We were going to stop there, anyway."

Henrique swims out toward the boat. Now used to the cold, Donna dunks her head beneath the surface one final time before paddling toward the shore. After a few meters, she risks planting her feet on the floor. Rocks—some smooth, some not—press against the pads of her feet, and the incline up the beach is so steep that she has to lean forward as she walks, lest she tumble backward back into the surf. On two separate occasions, a wave knocks into the back of her knees and nearly sends her flying face-first into the rocks; both times she manages to steady herself. She thinks: small blessings.

She finds a spot on the beach where the slope begins to flatten out, and she plops down on the rocks. The wet suit clings uncomfortably to her thighs and armpits; she regrets ever letting Kenny convince her to put the damn thing on—she would've preferred to just freeze. Pulling the neoprene away from her skin, she lets whatever water was trapped beneath it flood down her ankles and across her toes. Henrique schleps the kayak halfway up the slope and collapses next to her. Sweat mixes with the seawater on his cheeks.

"You know damned well that I never went surfing in Biarritz," she says.

Kenny picks through the smooth, wave-worn rocks in search of fossils. Next to him, on a blue, oversized towel, a mother prepares sandwiches for her two screaming children.

Henrique says, "Really, I didn't. I'm sorry if I've forgotten and I somehow hurt you."

She studies him, trying to uncover some twitch that might betray his sincerity—a smile, a sideways glance. There's nothing, though; his face is clear, blank.

"Of course you hurt me," she says.

"We were kids."

"What—kids can't hurt each other?"

"What do you want, Donna?"

"An apology would be a start."

He chews on this and flexes his jaw. His face, she thinks, still looks like it's composed of a series of interlocking triangles—a combination of sharp, definite lines that, even now, she finds infuriatingly attractive.

A gull squawks before diving headlong into the sea, and Henrique says, "Our little Eloise is getting married. How exciting. I was worried it wasn't going to happen."

"Because she's thirty-five?"

"Elle n'est pas jeune, exactement."

"I think it's good. It's smart. Getting married too young can be a disaster." She adds: "She learned from her mother's mistakes, I guess."

Henrique stands up. "This was a bad idea."

Donna reaches up and takes hold of his wrist; she doesn't want him to leave and is fearful that he might. "Oh, come on," she says. "There's no need to be dramatic."

"What is it that you want from me? To sit here and listen as you abuse me for something that happened thirty years ago?"

She doesn't answer, mostly because she knows he's right, and she's too ashamed to admit it out loud. Yes, that is what she wants: to chastise and blame Henrique for what's befallen her over the past three decades. She wants to strap him down and recount, in excruciating detail, the history of her life in St. Charles with Bill; her nights watching *House Hunters International* with Janice; what it's like to have your fifteen-year-old Volvo break down on the side of I-88. And as much as she wants to tell him about all that, she also wants to tell him about the slow, always-there ache of being alone; of losing one husband to circumstance and the other to death, and realizing that while she may not have had the best luck when it comes to love, bad luck is better than no luck at all.

And then she wants to start all over again, to retell it all, and make damned certain he understands it.

But again, she doesn't say any of that. Instead she tugs on his wrist, coaxing him back to the rocks. Because, she figures, the only thing worse than Henrique not feeling guilty would be Henrique not being here at all.

He sits down again, and she tightens her grip.

"I'm sorry," Donna says, eventually. "That was uncalled for."

"It's fine. I understand."

Kenny picks up two rocks, turns them over in his hand like they're poker chips, then tosses them into the sea.

She feels her throat closing up, and she swallows hard. "I'm still . . ." she ventures, "I'm still happy to see you."

"*Ouais. Moi aussi.*" He buries his toes beneath a small pile of stones. Being so close to him now, she considers how suddenly fragile he appears. In the glint of the sun, and the wet suits, and her own insecurities, Henrique had seemed timeless—aging, but still somehow locked in that youthful state with which she'd fallen in love. But here, on the beach, there are bags, shadows, that darken his eyes. His lips are thin and chapped, and loose pockets of skin form divots in his neck. She wonders what would happen if she were to reach out and take his hand. She wonders if she'd be any more capable of saving him than she's been at saving herself.

Then he says: "What is it that you want, Donna?"

She lies down flat and stares up at the cloudless sky, exhausted by the realization of a fantasy thirty years in the making. "Oh, I don't know, Henrique. I don't know."

He lies back as well, and props himself up on his elbow. He's rolled the top of his wet suit down to his waist, and evaporated water has left swirls of salt across his chest.

"What don't you know about?" he asks her.

"Some of it." She throws her arm across her face, shielding her eyes from the sun. "No. All of it."

She feels him reach out and run his fingers through her hair. He takes a few strands and rolls them between his fingers. Gently, he pushes her arm away from her face and leans over to kiss her.

"How about we take it slowly," he says. "Slower than when we were kids."

Gulls continue squawking overhead. The sea laps against the shore, beating limestone blocks into hollow, forgiving arches. Henrique dips down to kiss Donna again.

"Yeah," she says. Licking her lips as he pulls away, she tastes salt and peppermint Chapstick. "Okay."

Eloise

July 10

There's a problem with the tea lights, and Eloise decides it's best to take care of it herself. Dreadful, but not wholly disastrous. In short: her wedding planner, an expat American named Katie whose capabilities Eloise now realizes were woefully oversold, bought the wrong ones. Instead of arriving this morning at Ollie's parents' estate with three thousand Richmond votive unscented *white* ten-hour-burning candles, she showed up with three thousand Richmond votive unscented *crème* ten-hour-burning candles. When Eloise pointed out the flaw, and mentioned how the crème might clash with the white furnishings and the white linen tablecloths and the white lilies and the white *everything else she had fucking ordered*, Katie merely shrugged; she suggested that the flames from the candles would likely distract the guests, and that chances were they'd never notice the difference in color.

"I'm sure your other clients might not notice," Eloise had said. "But I'm not hosting a wedding for the lowest common denominator."

Which is why she now finds herself here, parking Ollie's father's Range Rover in a small lot in front of a party supply shop off Hound Street in Sherborne—the town where Ollie spent fourteen romantic and idealized years as a public-school boy. The town where, if everything goes as planned, tomorrow she'll become a romantic and idealized wife. Mr. Horwood had been nonchalant this morning when he tossed her the keys.

"Need three thousand more tea lights?" he said. "Isn't that always the case. Here. Take my car."

But that's just his nature: a casualness that makes Eloise think either that he loves her or that he's fucking with her. No matter if it's the latter, though—she loves him. Loves his bushy gray mustache, his gin blossoms, his general ease—a lassitude that's happily out of place in such a buttoned-up country. The Admiral. That's what they all call him, at least. A throwback to when he served as an officer in the Royal Navy. He never actually rose to such a high rank, at least according to Ollie; to hear her fiancé tell it, his father never made it past captain before he retired from service to take up work as a private military contractor in Rwanda.

"Why do you call him Admiral, then?" Eloise had asked him. This was on their second date.

Ollie had shrugged and finished his pint. "He just likes the sound of it, I guess."

Eloise loved this—the reasoning struck her as nothing but solid.

"And what was he doing in Rwanda?"

Ollie smacked his lips and licked away a spot of foam. "Unclear. All I know is that when he came back it was at the request of the British government. Something about an arms deal."

"How old were you?"

"Twelve? No. Thirteen. I'd just started third form at Sherborne."

"Did your mom go with him?"

Ollie laughed. "No, ma'am. She stayed back and looked after the house."

Of course she did, Eloise thinks now, locking up the Range Rover. Jane Ainsworth scarcely has the disposition to work in the front yard of

Horwood Hall on a hot day; she'd hardly do well in sub-Saharan Africa. Her soon-to-be mother-in-law's a small woman, a mousy five foot two, with shoulder-length gray hair and sensible, ignorable features. In dealing with Eloise she's deferential, always asking Eloise for her opinion or permission. It's a dynamic that initially disquieted Eloise—shouldn't she be the one trying to win Jane's approval?—and now mildly irritates her. Particularly with all these wedding preparations, more than anything else Jane has been in the way; she rises early in the morning to brew coffee for the household, then stands back, waiting for instructions as people maneuver themselves around her. Yes, granted, Eloise and Ollie are paying for most of the wedding expenses—they are, after all, thirty-five years old—but would it kill Jane to have an opinion? To put her neck out there and criticize the flowers, or the marquee, or one of Eloise's other aesthetic choices?

"Consider yourself lucky," Flossie had said to her when she first complained about Jane. "You're the only person I know who doesn't have a dreadful mother-in-law."

"It's like dealing with a corpse in a doily" had been Eloise's response.

She locks up the Range Rover and walks across the lot to the party supply store. Opening the door, she hears the faint tingle of a bell. She orients herself and tries to find the cashier. The shop is longer than it is wide: seven aisles of shelves stocked high with tchotchkes and knickknacks: themed cocktail napkins and Mylar balloons and plastic utensils that she imagines have been sitting there since Britain went to war over the Falklands. Wandering down the center aisle, Eloise picks up a miniature plastic model of Sherborne Abbey, the church where, tomorrow, she's to be married. Accidentally she pushes a small button next to the abbey's nave, and the whole thing lights up like it's being napalmed. From some hidden dwarf speaker, the "Hallelujah Chorus" begins.

"Jesus Christ," Eloise says, startled, and puts the thing back.

She continues on to the cashier's desk, which has been left unattended, and rings a small silver bell. After counting to ten, she reaches down to ring the bell again, but just as she's about to do so an impish woman in purple chiffon emerges from the shop's back office.

"Hullo there," she says. Her eye shadow matches her dress, and her cheeks have been rouged to a lethal shade of pink. Eloise catches whiffs of Rochas Femme and Earl Grey tea. "How can I help you?"

She readjusts her purse on her shoulder. "Hi, yeah, I called an hour ago about the candles."

"Of course." The woman smiles. "The three thousand white votives."

"Yes, those."

"Just one moment."

She slips away into the back office, and Eloise breathes, relieved. When she called, the woman—Polly, Eloise thinks she said her name is—assured her that they had the candles, all of them, and that they'd be here waiting when she arrived. But past experience has taught her that those types of promises are less than certain. There's truth in that tired old adage about doing things yourself—if planning a wedding has taught her one thing, it's that. Take this candle mishap: If she could, she thinks, she'd make the goddamned votives with her own bare hands. She'd buy the wax, cut the mold, fire 'em up. She can't, though—someone's coming to do her hair in two hours—and so the whole thing's become a tragedy of delegation. Blessed are the incompetent, she thinks. For they shall inherit the earth.

Polly reemerges holding a single box.

Eloise balks. "I said three thousand."

Polly laughs and sets the box on the counter. "The rest of them are round back, by our service entrance," she says. "I thought it would be easier if you brought your car there so we might load them into the boot, instead of trucking them through the aisles."

"Right. Of course." Eloise nods. *Polly's just trying to help.*

"Thought you might want to peek at one of the boxes, though. Just to make sure they're the right ones."

"That's kind of you."

Polly's fingers are stacked with rings—big, bulbous pieces topped with faux sapphires and emeralds—so opening the box's cardboard lid is slow going. She gets it eventually, though, and when she does, and Eloise peers past the tissue paper inside, she worries she might vomit.

"Those are crème," she says.

"Are they?" Polly looks on the side of the box, which is unmarked. "No, dear, I'm almost certain they're white."

"Polly—"

"It's Patty. Patricia."

"*Patty.*" Eloise reaches into the box and plucks out a votive. With her other hand, she digs into her purse for an old receipt. "This is white," she says, holding the paper up. Then, she holds the votive at eye level, so the old bird can see it clearly; so she can appreciate how loathsome and filthy and entirely *un-white* it looks. "These candles are fucking crème. In fact, those are the same fucking crème candles that we returned to you an hour ago."

Patty clears her throat and smooths her chiffon. "I really don't see the need for that sort of language."

"I need you to tell me you see the difference."

Eloise leans across the counter, still holding the votive in one hand and the receipt in the other. She thrusts them forward, and Patty recoils.

"Do you want them or not?"

"*Tell me you see a fucking difference.*"

"There's a difference!" Patty screams, and Eloise backs off. Once Patty's confident that she's escaped harm, she sighs. "My *word.*"

"I'll take all three thousand," Eloise says, putting the receipt—and the candle—in her purse. Crème candles are better than no candles, she decides, and at this point, the universe hasn't given her much of a choice. "I'll pull my car round back."

When she arrives back at Horwood Hall, Jane is in the front garden, staring helplessly at her roses.

"I was so hoping they'd bloom before the wedding," she says, and Eloise slams the Range Rover's door.

"I don't know what to tell you, Jane." Eloise keeps her sunglasses on.

Jane sighs and turns her back to the budless bush. "Did you find your candles?"

"More or less. Look, I need you to do me a favor."

The color fades from Jane's face, and, panicked, she reaches down to pick up an errant leaf that has floated down from the wych elm that looms over the house's driveway. "Oh?"

"Yes."

"Of course." Jane's voice cracks. "Anything."

"I need you to distract Katie."

"The wedding planner?"

"Yes. Her." A car passes by and honks. Jane and Eloise both wave, and Eloise continues. "I need you to keep her occupied and in another room while I bring these candles inside and have them set up."

Jane folds the leaf in half. "I can't imagine why you—"

"Jane?"

"Yes, dear?"

"This is very important to me."

And it is. Because what sort of authority would Eloise maintain if Katie were to see her setting up the very candles that not two hours ago Eloise asked her to return? She knows, though, that she can't explain that to her mother-in-law. Rather, she has to say that it's important and leave it at that. Any nuance that she tries to convey will be lost on Jane, who she suspects doesn't understand the necessity of saving face.

"Well, if it's important to you . . ." She slips the leaf into the pocket of her gardening coat.

"It is."

"I suppose I'll see what I can do, then?"

"Thank you."

Eloise watches Jane slink back inside, then sneaks around to the back side of the main house, where preparations for the rehearsal dinner are under way. On the lawn dividing the house from the family's old stables, men in uniforms work to erect three bars and twenty-two high-top cocktail tables. Eloise walks up to the one closest to her and, noticing how uneven the table's linen cloth is, straightens it. Beyond the stables is the estate's abandoned barn, a gorgeous, half-dilapidated thing that, tomorrow night, will be transformed into the wedding's marquee. Using it had been her idea. After an afternoon of touring Sherborne's dingy pubs and stale event halls in search of a suitable reception location, she floated the idea of the barn to Ollie over negronis on his parents' back patio.

"It could be really gorgeous," she'd said, watching the sunset throw shadows across the barn's splintered roof.

"It's filled with hay. We'd have to have it swept out." He added: "And there aren't any lights in there. Someone would have to find a way to hang lights from the ceiling."

Now, looking past the cocktail tables toward the barn, she thinks: Should I check on the chandeliers?

Her planning, though, is interrupted; Ollie sneaks up behind her, wraps his arms around her waist, and kisses her cheek.

"Hiya," he says.

She smiles and bats his hands away, just as he's starting to work his fingers up her shirt.

"Hiya."

"Looks beautiful."

She puts her hands on her hips and flexes her back. "It's getting there. Did you check in with the caterers like I asked?"

"I did."

"And?"

"Enough canapés to feed us until Christmas. Was Candlegate solved? You know you've got that poor American girl crying."

"You're kidding."

Ollie grins. "I'm not. Mum's making her some tea right now."

Eloise nods, satisfied with Jane's distractive abilities. Then, remembering the larger issue of the votives, she sighs. "It wasn't solved," she says. "The goddamned store in Sherborne only had crème candles."

"Think we should call off the wedding?"

"You think I'm being crazy."

"I think you're being detail oriented."

"That's a euphemism for crazy."

"You're not crazy." He brushes his hair away from his eyes and kisses her forehead. "Come on inside, though. We've got to leave for the church in an hour, and the Admiral's made gin and tonics. A little fortification before we practice our waltz down the aisle."

She turns back toward the lawn, and the stables, and the barn. Two of the cocktail tables are off center, and the last bar still needs to be constructed. Also: she hasn't seen a single lily yet.

"Sounds lovely," she says.

"Hey, you." Ollie pokes her shoulder. "You okay with all of this?"

"Yeah, of course."

"You can tell me if you're not, you know. I'm liable to go nuts and perch on top of the abbey with a machine gun, but you can tell me."

"I'm more than okay with it. I'm thrilled." This time, she brushes his hair out of his face. "You need a haircut. Go start in on the gin. I'll be there in a second."

He trots back inside, and she wanders out onto the lawn. Behind her, the limestone of the house bleeds red against the late afternoon light. Bending over, she picks up a twig and begins to tear away the bark—anything, she figures, to keep her hands occupied. The ground's still wet—she can feel her heels sinking into it when she stands still—and she worries about whether that will be a problem before she forces herself to stop. She can't keep doing this. She can't keep going over every possible thing that could go wrong.

Framing the perimeter of the lawn are the long strings from which half the lit votives will eventually hang. The other fifteen hundred will illuminate paper lanterns dangling from the branches of the property's elms. No one will notice the candles are crème instead of white. And if they do, fuck them; they should be enjoying the free wine, instead of inspecting the color of her votives. So yes, fine—Eloise is being crazy. Not just detail oriented, but certifiably crazy.

Unfortunately, this has been a feeling to which she's become more and more accustomed. Lately, there have been a few nights when she's found herself second-guessing her decision, and they've shaken her. She reminds herself, though, that they've only occurred during the two weeks when her own mother and siblings have been here, in England. And that makes sense; that's reassuring. Who wouldn't be apprehensive about starting a family after seeing how Alice behaved at her hen do, or witnessing the spite with which her siblings spoke to their mother? Who in their right mind would want to get married and have children, only to have those children turn around and spit in their face? She's quick to catch herself during these moments of panic, though, reminding herself to look at Ollie's family and the easy respect they have for one another. And she tells herself that for her that's not far off: only three thousand tea lights and a walk down the aisle away.

And perhaps there's hope for her own family, too—she must keep reminding herself of this. Earlier today, as she was driving to Sherborne, she received a text from her mother saying that she and Henrique were having a wonderful time. Okay, fine—the communiqué was a bit more guarded than that (*wonderful* was never once used), but Eloise could read between the lines: Donna was happy to see Henrique again.

She's also made significant headway with Paul. First, she helped to rid him of that awful boyfriend—maybe not directly, but surely her coldness toward Mark at dinner had played some sort of role in effecting the split. And thank God she had the good sense to do that, she nearly says aloud. The prospect of having to attend family gatherings with that farce of a man was enough to send her screaming for the hills. She thinks back to a few days ago when Paul had called her to ask, sheepishly, if he could stay at her flat. Incrementally, her brother has been warming to her—or at least she senses that he has—which, she hopes, bodes well for the next few days. Last night, when she was drunk, she asked him if he'd give a few remarks at the wedding reception. At first, he'd looked at her incredulously.

"You mean, like, a *speech*?" he'd said.

"Yes. A speech."

When she awoke this morning, though, she was terrified that she'd made a horrible mistake—that somehow he'd find a way to humiliate her, or their mother, or both of them. But now, remembering how she had let Paul cry in her lap after watching Mark pull away in a cab, she allows herself to be cautiously optimistic. Debts need to be repaid, and he owes her this. He owes her a goddamned speech.

From the house, Ollie calls to her. The ice in her gin and tonic is melting.

Ollie

He pulls aside the curtain and looks down onto the lawn, where the rehearsal dinner is already in full swing. Guests—most of whom he knows, some of whom he doesn't—gather around high-topped tables as black-tied cater waiters bob between them. The sinking sun turns the gray bricks of Horwood Hall lavender, and the branches of the trees that line the lawn stretch their arms into endless shadows. He often forgets how much he loves coming home; when he's living his life in London it's so easy to write off Dorset as a bumbling backwoods, a place that's fine to visit, but that he'd just as soon relegate to the confines of his past. Standing here now, though, it's impossible to imagine ever doing such a thing—instead, he finds himself nostalgic for the southwest's idyllic pace. Let the rest of them have London, he thinks, pulling the curtains wider apart. The traffic clogging up anemic alleyways that lead to nowhere; the persistent and suffocating smog. Sidewalks filled up with people who never look anywhere but past you, their eyes cutting through you like you're nothing but smoke and mist. Buildings built on other buildings, towers of steel and glass that reduce history to foundation in the crudest sense of the word. The relentless and insatiable appetite of a city whose ambitions are too large, too ravenous, for the quaint island that houses it. Yes: *fine*. Let them have it. Ollie, though? He'll take Dorset; he'll take the southwest, yokel-stocked backwoods and all.

On the far end of the green, beneath the leaves of a knotty old wych elm, he spots Donna, his future mother-in-law, huddled over her purse. Above her a thousand tea lights cause the elm's leaves to shimmer in a gorgeous cascade, but Donna's not paying them any mind—she's too busy with whatever's occupying her hands. Probably rolling a joint, Ollie thinks, smiling.

Two nights ago he pointed out to Eloise that her mother had become a certified pothead, and she'd been terribly offended.

"Knock it off, Ollie," she'd said. They'd just arrived at Horwood Hall and were unpacking their bags in Ollie's childhood room, where he's presently standing, spying on the proceedings unfolding below him. "That's an awful thing to say."

"Why?" He'd laughed. "I think it's brilliant that she managed to smuggle a few emergency joints through customs. Besides, didn't you smell her when we had lunch at the Shard? I thought I was liable to get a contact high just by giving her a hug."

"I asked you to please stop," Eloise said, hanging up a dress. And so, he did. He set down the shoes he'd just retrieved from his suitcase and walked over to hug her from behind, holding her until he felt her muscles start to soften.

Hiding behind the trunk of the elm, Donna leans over and licks something. Absolutely a joint. His smile broadens.

He lets the curtains fall back and tries to remember, against the odds of all the champagne he's had, why it is that he came up to his old room in the first place. Something about fetching a book. Yes, that's it: his old German exercise book from lower sixth form. His mother had invited his old

German teacher from Sherborne to the wedding (they belonged to the same gardening club, as Ollie understood it), and five minutes ago Frau Winkler had cornered him and asked him if he had any of his old work lying around.

"Your declension work was lovely," she said, her breath smelling like vodka and butterscotch candy. "You managed to screw up in the most gorgeous ways. Really, I've just got to show Jane."

He looked over at his mother, smiling shyly behind Frau Winkler, then said, "Let me see what I can find."

In his room he scans the titles on his bookshelf—an old copy of *Canterbury Tales,* Ovid's *Metamorphosis,* three Hardy Boys novels, a bunch of other shit he's never read—until he finds a small black notebook with his name and GERMAN scrawled across its cover. He knows that he should be surprised that he still has it—he's cleared out this bookshelf more times than he can remember, keeping only the titles that either (a) are intellectually impressive or (b) have sentimental value—and yet he's not. He has a knack for having what people need, and, in this case, Frau Winkler needed his lower sixth German notebook. It's a strange talent he's had ever since he was an infant (his mother likes to talk about how, as a newborn, he always seemed to sense her moods, often predicting her needs before she knew them herself), and which he became consciously aware of as a teenager. People needed someone to have a pint with—he was there. People needed someone with a joke—he had one. It's for this reason, he suspects, that so many people call him *likable,* that tag that he used to associate with *boring,* but that now, after having met so many insufferably *interesting* people who are dreadfully *mean,* he's proud to have earned. People like being around him. They like that he's not the smartest guy in the room, but that he's not a dolt, either. They like that they can safely expect him to succeed, to be impressive but not threatening, without pinning their hopes for the world onto him. In other words, they like that he's easy. They like that his life is easy.

And it *is* easy—almost embarrassingly so. This used to be a fact that caused him great consternation. Once, when he was fifteen, a fifth-former from the girls' school had told him that he would never understand what it was like to suffer.

"Everything's been just *given* to you," she'd said. He was sitting with her and a few friends on the rugby pitches that separated the boys' school from the girls'. Her father, a Russian oilman, had just been thrown in prison in Moscow, and she was sobbing. Her name, he thinks, was Tatiana. "You're gorgeous, and rich, and don't have any siblings to contend with, and you're captain of the football team even though everyone knows Thomas Dodge is the better player." Ollie looked at Thomas; Thomas looked down. "So just face it, Ollie, when you tell me that *everything will be all right,* you're lying, because you don't actually know what it's like for things *not* to be all right."

This notion that his own coddled life was preventing him from under-standing the plights of others pained Ollie greatly. It threatened, in so many ways, his own likability, the sole part of himself that, at the very unsure age of fifteen, he was absolutely sure of. For the next year he did every-thing he could to pop the bubble in which he'd been accused of living. At night, while his friends were sneaking cigarettes behind the abbey in town, he stayed in his room and struggled through books that might, somehow, open his eyes to a world that had heretofore gone unseen. God, the things that he read during those twelve months! *Things Fall Apart. The Joy Luck Club. Notes of a Native Son.* They were moving, surely, but also so terribly *sad.* Halfway through Kate Chopin's *The Awakening* (a book that was, he admits, already pretty slim), he decided it was probably best to just give up.

The thing that he figured was most important was that he was good, and kind, and above all else likable. People expected him to be easy—they expected him to be happy, and fun, and always ready for a good time; all those things that he felt he already naturally *was* without having to cringe over tragic literature—and so those would be the things he would focus on being.

And it seems to have worked out, he thinks now as he tosses the German book up into the air and catches it. After Sherborne he'd gone to Oxford to read economics, a subject in which he received passable (if not outstanding) marks, and which interested him just enough to hold his attention. From there, he moved to London, where, with the help of an old naval buddy of his father's, he landed a job in the analyst program at Barclays. Much as before, his life during these nascent stages of adulthood seemed to follow a path of negligible resistance. He received promotions, raises; his financial security was such that he never had to live with a roommate. He knew he'd never become a managing director at the bank—his reviews were always impressive, but very rarely stellar—but that didn't cause him any lost sleep. He saw the work it took to climb to Barclays' upper echelons, and it was work that, quite frankly, he knew he wasn't cut out to do. Perhaps more accurately, that he wasn't *willing* to do. Occasionally, he'd remember the things that Tatiana had said to him; he'd recall the scathing tone with which she berated him, and he'd feel a lingering shame. These moments, though, weren't too dreadfully difficult to mediate. There were enough charity dinners and galas and auctions happening at any given moment in London, and he found that all he need do was shell out five hundred pounds for a ticket to one, and partake in whatever picturesque version of Good it was selling, to alleviate a solid dose of that Tatiana-bred guilt. The events also had the added benefit of being, well, *fun*; they gave him an opportunity to wear his tuxedo, and get sauced on champagne, and cavort with his mates, a group of people who apologized for the trappings of their upbringings by making a deliberate show of them.

It was at one of these events (he can't remember which one—they bleed together, like most of his twenties) that he first met Eloise. He knew after two years together that he wanted to marry her. Like so many decisions in his life, this was one that he didn't think about particularly hard, or for particularly long. While they may not have been a perfect match (she got annoyed with his partying; he got annoyed with her getting annoyed with his partying), he was starting to suspect that perfect matches didn't actually exist, anyway—at least, not when two sentient people were involved. In this way, he concluded, they were likely the best that either one of them was going to find, and thus the prospect of forgoing her and trying to find a relationship that was in some way a little *closer* to perfect only to later realize he'd let something wonderful go . . . well—one in the hand, as they say.

Besides, he thinks now, as he descends the stairs from his room to Horwood Hall's kitchen, he loves her. He loves his life with her. A month ago they met for the second time with an adoption agency (an adoption agency! If only he had Tatiana's address), and the very real potential of beginning a family together had him nearly combusting with excitement. *A son!* he kept thinking to himself, as the woman across the desk from them—a dowdy northerner named Fern—explained endless reams of paperwork. *A son, a son, a son!* In the cab on the way back to their flat, he hadn't been able to stop shaking his leg, so gripped was he by excitement.

"You've got to stop doing that," Eloise had said to him, resting a hand gently on his knee. "You're driving me nuts."

"I'm sorry." He stopped shaking and gripped his thighs to hold them still. "This is all just so exciting."

"It is." She smiled, warily. "Still, I just . . . I don't know."

He leaned over and kissed her cheek. "It's going to be great."

"Danke!" Frau Winkler kisses his cheek and takes the notebook from him.

"Bitte," he says, grinning broadly. Having forgotten the rest of his German, and gripped with a very present need to escape the Frau's butterscotchy breath without appearing rude, he says, "If you'll excuse me, word is the speeches are about to start, and I worry if Eloise has to sit through Bixby's toast without proper fortification there might not actually be a wedding tomorrow." The Frau laughs; Ollie's grin widens, and he winks.

Turning, he nearly knocks over the cello player that they'd hired for the evening—a striking, raven-haired beauty in a black dress and a gold necklace who Eloise met four months ago while she was planning a dinner for Mission: Breathe. Ollie raises an eyebrow and mouths *oops*; the girl smirks and lifts both eyebrows in response. As she readies her bow against the instrument's strings, Ollie steals a peek at her ass and steps out onto the lawn.

He did want to find Eloise—that wasn't a complete lie—though he has no idea when the speeches are set to start, or if there are to be speeches at all (there's meant to be; after the fourth round of canapés circulate, Andrew Bixby is indeed expected to propose a toast. Andrew Bixby, though, is hardly reliable, particularly when free champagne's involved). Really, he wanted to find her simply to be with her. His friends often mocked him for this sort of romantic sentimentality; most of them had been married for a few years already, and they constantly harassed him for his desire to *start the rest of his life* at the expense of his *freedom*.

He finally spots her on the opposite end of the lawn, where she's standing with her siblings. She's talking to Paul, and she looks tense—her shoulders are up near her ears—and this, again, makes Ollie smile. He likes Paul. He knows that lately she's found him trying; she speaks often about a monumental shift that happened in Paul at some point during the past three years, this transformation from the brother she thought she knew into a neurotic, narcissistic stranger. Ollie doesn't know about all that—he didn't grow up with Paul (but then, neither did Eloise, really), so he hasn't got much of a frame of reference. He thinks Paul's funny, though. Hilarious, even. Fifty percent crazy, maybe, but Ollie knew enough sane people already. Besides, crazy could be fun, particularly when you only had to encounter it during holidays. And even then, didn't he have a right to be a little bit nuts, what with his dad dying having basically disowned him? Sure, Eloise has said that Paul doesn't know the things his father said about him; she's said that Paul can never know. But then, how reasonable is that assumption? Ollie's not the brightest—he freely admits that—but he suspects that if he were in Paul's shoes, he'd know. He'd just have to. There's never not-knowing a thing like that.

(Thinking of all this now, as he watches Eloise speak to her brother, Ollie congratulates himself on what he said to her when she recounted the whole sordid history between Paul and his father; how he told Eloise that if they adopted a gay son, he'd embrace him and love him from day one. He makes sure to mention this in passing to Paul whenever they're with each other—just that he's okay with gay people, and all. He thinks that it's important.)

Alice, though. Eloise's sister. She's a tougher one to crack. The few times that they've all been together it's seemed to Ollie that he can hardly glance at Alice without catching her glaring at him. Eloise has assured him that his fears are misguided, and that his paranoia is a product of his own thinking—"If she hates anyone," she told him, "it's me." For whatever reason, though, this has done little to assuage his misgivings. Eloise had mentioned that she suspected Alice loathed her life in Los Angeles, and so he'd nearly tripped over himself getting her that job with Xavier Wolfson's production company. Whenever he saw her, he unleashed his usual charm offensive—the smiles, and jokes, and compliments that had won over so many skeptics in the past. And yet, still she seems dead set on freezing him out. It drives him insane.

He continues to watch as a caterer, a lanky red-haired kid in a coat two sizes too big, offers Eloise and her siblings glasses of champagne. Paul reaches for one, but Eloise bats his hand away.

Despite his frustrations with Alice, despite all the confusion she causes him, he knows that Eloise's relationship with her brother and sister is infinitely more complicated. He tells himself that this complication is normal, and that as an only child he's in no position to understand it. His parents had done a remarkable job shielding him from the uglier parts of familial life—he never did know what his father had actually been doing in Rwanda, or why his mother often spent her nights holed up alone in her room—and for this he was both thankful and scornful: on one hand they facilitated, indeed helped craft his formidable and unwavering bliss; on the other hand, they've left him feeling terribly isolated from the anxiety Eloise feels toward

Paul and Alice. She speaks of them—she's always spoken of them—with the same mash-up of conflicting claims: they are the only people who understand her, and the people who understand her the least; she needs to speak with them immediately, and she'd be lucky to never speak with them again; she craves their affirmation—more than anything in the world—but once she gets it, she doesn't know what to do with it.

Straightening his tie, he begins to pick his way through the crowd over to them. He stops, though, when he sees that Eloise has beckoned his parents over; Jane and the Admiral haven't spent much time with Paul or Alice, and he wants them to be able to know one another—to *like* one another—before the ceremony tomorrow.

Within moments, though, his hopes are dashed: Paul says something, and Jane looks down.

Eloise grabs her brother's arm and begins dragging him toward the kitchen.

He arrives just in time to see her push Paul against a cupboard and yell, "What the actual *fuck*."

The caterers scatter to the far corners of the kitchen and busy themselves by rearranging rows of *gougères* on their trays. Ollie considers intercepting Eloise (and saving Paul), but stops himself just short of doing so; he doesn't know the language of familial discontent. Instead, he hangs back and watches, uncomfortable with his own presence but unable to pull himself away.

"The, uh . . ." Paul sounds sauced. Contrite and apologetic, but sauced. "I guess I overshared."

Ollie pictures a puppy, its tail hidden between its trembling legs.

"You *guess*? You *guess*!?" Ollie shudders. Rarely has he found himself the target of Eloise's ire, though that doesn't stop him from sympathizing with those who did.

"I'm . . . I'm sorry if I embarrassed you," Paul says.

"I can't imagine why you think you might've embarrassed me, Paul. Could it be because you opted to tell the story of your first threesome to my future in-laws? To *actually use the phrase* 'fucked from behind' with a woman who hasn't had sex since Thatcher was prime minister? Or, I don't know, is it because you thought it wise to condemn *the entire institution of marriage* on the eve of my wedding? Or, wait, wait, I've got another total shot in the dark: *maybe* it's because—"

Ollie tries not to think of Paul in sexually compromising positions, which only leads him to think of his mother in equally lurid ways. He stifles a laugh—Eloise hasn't seen him yet.

"I said I was sorry."

"Sorry because you've turned my wedding into some horrible movie? Sorry because—"

"Please stop, Eloise."

Hearing Paul's voice crack, Ollie winces.

"You're a selfish prick, Paul," says Eloise. "You've always been a selfish prick."

"Oh, *I'm* the selfish prick." Paul's voice picks up, and Ollie once again considers stepping in. "Last time I checked, I wasn't the one who cited some bullshit work excuse when my own sister had a miscarriage and needed me."

"I can't believe you're still lording that over me."

"I'm not lording anything over you, Eloise. It's the goddamned truth. You've always acted like you're too good for us, like you haven't got time for us. I mean, *fucking hell*—you sit on a trust fund that you're *literally doing nothing with* while Alice goes twenty thousand dollars into debt."

"What, I'm supposed to bail her out? I'm supposed to feel guilty and charitable because Alice can't act like a responsible adult? Ollie got her a *fucking job opportunity* in London, and she threw it back in my face."

"My *GOD*! You just don't *get* it, do you?"

"I DON'T KNOW WHAT IT IS THAT I'M SUPPOSED TO FUCKING GET! YOU'RE BLAMING ME FOR THINGS I CAN'T

CONTROL!" Suddenly conscious of the people around her, the caterers pretending to ignore her, she lowers her voice. "Why can't you just be *happy* for me?"

"Because you make it too goddamned hard. You've never understood us," her brother says. "You've never even *tried* to understand us. You were our holiday sister. We called you that, you know? Our holiday sister. The whole school year, while we were fighting over who got to drive Mom's *Volvo* to the movies on a Saturday, you were . . . Christ, I don't know . . . *eating fondue* in the Swiss Alps. And okay, sure, you were around for Christmas, and sometimes Thanksgiving, and *maybe* a few weeks at the end of summer, but that's *it*. That's all we'd ever see of you. We'd just be getting back from Tampa, and you'd fucking *waltz in* from Saint-Tropez. And the whole time—*the whole goddamned time*—you'd try to act like we were all exactly the same."

"Who understood you, then, Paul? Tell me. Because at this point, that's looking like a pretty impossible task."

There's a pause, and then Paul says: "Dad. My dad understood me. While Mom was too busy worrying about all the shit she gave up when she left Henrique, *Dad* was there for me. He got me."

"Dad."

"Yeah. Dad."

One of the caterers uses the brief silence to escape the kitchen. The door swings open, letting the rest of the party in, then slams shut.

"All right, Paul, how about this: your father, who you worshipped, whose opinion meant *everything to you*, died hating you."

Ollie closes his eyes.

"You're a fucking cunt, Eloise."

"Maybe," she says. "But that doesn't change the fact that the one person who *you* claim understood you went to his grave never wanting to see you again. No—don't turn away from me. Don't you *fucking* turn away from me. He hated you, Paul. You told him you were gay, and he hated you. Said he didn't want to see you again until you changed. Until you stopped becoming yourself."

"Yeah? Then why'd he never tell me that?" Paul's crying now.

"Because Mom didn't let him," Eloise says. "I'm telling you right now, kid, if you roll your eyes at me *one more goddamned time*, I'm going to rip 'em square out of your face."

She continues: "Are you listening? *Mom didn't let him.* She told him that if he so much as *looked at you wrong* she'd divorce him and tell both you and Alice why she was leaving. So he kept his mouth shut, and so did Mom, and they went on like that until he died, just so you could be protected from the truth."

There's a second brief silence, and the door opens again: crickets dissect the night, and on the other side of the house the cello moans.

"So how about that," Eloise says. "The woman you've spent three years torturing is the same one who saved your life."

Ollie thinks: *Fuck.*

Paul

His sister's lying. She must be. His father had been his ally, a source of certainty amid what was otherwise a jumble of female ambivalence. He didn't miss a single one of Paul's high school soccer games, and when Paul played in college and his team had a match somewhere in the Midwest, Bill would often drive five, six, seven hours to watch Paul take the field. He cried when Paul graduated, and tried to convince him, in his own stoic way, not to move to New York.

"Why do you want to go all the way out there?" he'd said. "You've got everything you need right here."

How would they keep up their tradition of going to Pete's for a full rack of ribs on Saturday afternoons if Paul were living a thousand miles east? How would they go on one of their long, itinerant drives, those nomadic wanderings past suburbs and strip malls and into the belly of Illinois's heartland? Still, Paul left. He had to. He had to find a place where he could start the process of unknowing the person he'd been pretending to be. When his dad dropped him off at O'Hare, Paul promised that he'd call twice a week, and it was a promise that he kept, right up until the Saturday morning in April when he phoned to tell them he was gay.

It wasn't a big deal—those were the first words out of his mother's mouth, and he believed her. It wasn't even a deal, at all. Christ, they probably already knew and were just waiting for him to tell them on his own terms. That's what his friends in New York told him, at least. *Parents always know*. His father had been more or less silent as Paul blubbered through the confession, but that in itself wasn't all that surprising: Bill was a quiet kind of guy. He'd just wanted to give Paul room to talk, room to explain himself.

But then: oh, the insidious sting of truth as it crawls into the light. Because now, as he weaves together memories of his father, discrepancies arise that had previously gone unnoticed: Bill declining Paul's invitation for ribs when he was visiting for Christmas, claiming some unmemorable excuse—high blood pressure. Bill standing up from his blue La-Z-Boy and leaving the living room whenever Mark phoned during the holidays. Bill returning every other call, then every third, then every fourth. Bill losing interest, fading away.

The moon throws shadows that splice up the field in pieces. Paul presses the heels of his palms to his eyes.

How could he have ignored all this so willfully? How could the truth be so arbitrary as to subject itself to the whims of his own idealizations? Is knowing what people think of you really such a deceptive negotiation of self, a bartering between the knowledge that you have and the knowledge you choose to accept? Because now he wants to know what his father said about him during those last deceptive years—he wants it all laid bare and gruesome before him, like a corpse, decayed and dissected. Bill belonged to a club—not the best one, he couldn't afford that, but a fine one, filled with like-minded men. Paul wants to know what Bill told them, how his dad talked about him after he knew. How many times was he called a disappointment, he wonders; how many times had Bill received the sympathy of others, simply because Paul existed? He wants to dig his dad up from his grave, tie him down, and ask him every question he's thinking at once. But then—no. He doesn't. Not really, anyway, because the answers that he's looking for don't exist. They rarely ever do.

"Hey, Paul."

Ollie stands over him, his broad silhouette blocking out the moon. Paul scoops up a handful of gravel from the house's driveway and transfers it from one hand to the other.

"Hey," he says.

Ollie shoves his hands in his pockets.

"Everything all right, then?"

"Just getting some air," he says, and looks back across the field.

"Right. Can get, uh, ha, can get a bit stuffy back in there. That kitchen's pretty tight."

"Have you got a cigarette?"

"What's that?"

"A cigarette."

Ollie nods, as if he's suddenly understood the language Paul's speaking.

"A smoke! Right. Yeah, hold on." He digs in his pockets and pulls out a bent Camel Straight, which Paul takes, and a matchbook, with which Paul lights up.

"Your sister'll kill me if she knows I'm smoking, but, ha, hey. Last night of freedom or something, right?"

"Thanks," he says, and exhales. "Shouldn't you be getting back to your guests or something?"

An airplane passes overhead, its lights upstaging the stars, and Ollie rubs his head.

"Yeah, probably," he says, but doesn't move.

Paul holds the cigarette in front of him and watches it burn. It's stale—he wonders how long it's been stashed away in Ollie's pocket—but all he can think is that he hopes it lasts forever, because when it's over he has to go back to worrying about the mess he's made.

"How long were you standing in the kitchen?" he asks.

"Oh, me? Not long. Just came in to see how the *gougères* were shaping up and saw you and Eloise talking. Probably about five seconds."

He's lying, which means he heard everything, Paul thinks. Suddenly, he wants Ollie to stay.

"You coming back in?"

Paul watches smoke drift skyward. "Not for a while, I don't think."

He feels a tap on his shoulder. When he turns, he sees Ollie is holding out a five-pound note.

"There's a pub about two kilometers down the road. I'll go inside and call you a cab," he says. Then: "And, Paul, she means well. I know sometimes it doesn't seem like it, but I swear to God she does."

The Thirsty Lion is a forgettable, prosaic place, which suits Paul's mood. Exposed wood beams and dank green walls. A long wood bar and a rectangular dining room with mismatched vinyl chairs. Above the cashier, a casual coat of arms. The smell of beer and Lysol—an army of cleaning solutions fighting an uphill battle. Peter Gabriel's "Solsbury Hill" warbling on the room's single speaker. He orders a whiskey.

There's a part of him that's still furious at his mother. She *deceived him,* goddamn it. She conned him into thinking one thing in order to shield him from another; she treated him like a child. Had he just known what Bill had said, how his father had felt, he could have started some process of healing. At the very least, he could have avoided being eviscerated by Eloise in a country from which he can't wait to escape. His mother had robbed him of that opportunity, though, and had taken it upon herself to decide what was best for him. It was an exercise in parental tyranny, he thinks to himself. Plain and simple.

And yet, curiously, his rage, the white-hot indignation that's fueled him for the past three years, is fading fast. Because once he strips away his knee-jerk anger, his contrarian disposition, how terrible had Donna's decision actually been? How justified is Paul in vilifying her? She had lied—that much is true. It was a lie of omission, but it was still a lie. But the intentions of that lie were purer than any truth he can presently conceive: to protect him from his own ruin, a propensity for self-destruction that she understands better than he ever will himself. Eloise was right: she had saved him. It was a salvation based on false pretenses, but does that necessarily make it any less real? Was he not spared regardless? Can you smoke in this place? He looks down the long stretch of bar and doesn't see a single ashtray. He sucks on a fistful of peanuts instead.

God, he's been awful to Donna. If he could disappear into the glass in front of him, he would. Just crawl beneath an ice cube and let the whiskey wash over him. He closes his eyes and thinks of how certain he'd been of his anger toward her. "She erased Dad from our life, so I'm erasing her from mine"—those had been his words to Mark, the reductive and solipsistic foundation for his righteousness. How many of her calls had he let roll over to voice mail? How many of those voice mails did he delete before listening to them? During the holidays he never opened her Christmas cards; he threw them into the trash with pamphlets of Best Buy coupons and direct-mail ads from real estate agents. Whenever Alice passed along news about her—that she was remodeling the kitchen, or that she was spending the weekend in Indiana—he consciously forgot it. A sudden, drunken epiphany: Paul can't account for two years and eight months of Donna's life; two years and eight months estrange them.

He's already drunk, but that doesn't stop him from ordering a second whiskey as he tries to anticipate the next song on the pub's playlist. Sting and the Police, he wagers. "Roxanne." Closing his eyes, he listens and holds his breath. The silence lasts a second shorter than forever, and finally he hears the song's first few notes. Elton John's "Rocket Man." Foiled again.

Taking his phone out of his pocket, he drops it, retrieves it from the filthy floor, and squints at the screen. The images are blurry, and he tries to focus through the boozy fog. He wonders if he should call Mark. The day before, as they were driving to Dorset from London, Alice had made him promise that he wouldn't; she knew it was something he often did.

"You get drunk, and sad, and you call people," she'd said. They were at a gas station, filling up the Peugeot. "Just . . . don't do that this time around. In fact, give me your phone."

"Knock it off."

"You're going to do it."

The pump clicked; the tank was full.

"I am not," Paul had said.

"You will, and you'll regret it in the morning. It'll just be another story for Mark to tell."

Now, swaying on his stool, typing and retyping his password into his phone, he thinks, What the fuck does she know? He needs to talk to someone, someone who knows him, and Mark *knows* him. They were together when his dad died, and Mark watched Paul grieve. Yes, he thinks. Mark. He's the right person to call.

He's seeing double, so he closes his left eye and concentrates on finding his contacts. Scrolling down, he finds Mark's name.

A woman's shrieking laughter diverts his attention, and he drops his phone again.

"Shit," he slurs, and glances over to where the sound is coming from. The woman laughing looks to be about his age. She's an English rose type—delicate features, with a lithe, boyish body in a slim blue dress. A man's arm is wrapped around her waist, and he's kissing the spot where her neck meets her shoulders, and Paul's got to blink twice and rub both his eyes before he can put two and two together and realize that the man is Henrique.

Henrique. Wait, he thinks. And then: *shit.* Because Henrique is supposed to be with Donna—yes, this much he knows. And more important, he should be at their daughter's rehearsal dinner. He drags his mind through the sludge and tries to get his bearings, his sense of who's currently being wronged and whom he should currently hate. Donna had spent the day with Henrique, and came back flushed and excited. And now he's here, sliding into second base with some cut-rate Kate Moss, while Donna wanders around an old British manse, munching on lukewarm cheese puffs, alone.

No, Paul decides. Firmly: no. His mother's suffered through enough without having to contend with a replay of Henrique's philandering. And besides, if anyone has a monopoly on fucking her over, it's him.

He stands, wobbles, and regains his balance before steeling himself. Paul has made a decision. Paul is a man possessed.

"Excuse me."

He jabs a finger into Henrique's shoulder, and Henrique detaches himself from the girl's neck. Paul's drunk, but his double vision can see the first bruised marks of a hickey.

"Yes?"

"What—what do you mean *yes?*" Paul focuses on appearing stern and disappointed, and on not slurring.

Henrique blinks. "Paul," he says. "I didn't recognize you. Why aren't you at the party? You look unwell."

"And who's your—your friend?"

"*Paul.*" Henrique leans forward and puts a hand on Paul's shoulder.

"Don't touch me."

"Let us call you a taxi. You're drunk."

"Yeah? Well, you're an asshole."

A single couple occupies the pub's small dining room, and they look up from their menus.

The English rose clears her throat and tucks her clutch beneath her left arm. "Maybe I should go," she says.

"You stay right where you are," Paul says, blocking her way. "I won't be long." He turns, once again, to face Henrique. "*You're an asshole.*"

Henrique straightens his lapel and licks his lips. "Your mother and I had a lovely day," he says.

"Not that lovely, evidently."

"Are you going to let me finish?"

Paul raises an eyebrow.

Henrique continues.

"We *had a lovely day*. But sometimes these things . . . they don't work out."

"Yeah?" Paul rocks back on his heels, and then forward onto his toes. "Does she know that?"

"I—I'm sure she'll understand once she does."

Paul tries to decipher what song is playing. He listens for recognizable chords or lyrics, but the sounds are all blending together into a mess of clanks and strums and crashes.

He wipes his nose and says, "She deserves—*deserved*—better than you."

"Excuse me?"

"She's a good lady." He shoves his finger at Henrique again, this time burying it into his sternum. "The *best* lady. And *she deserved better.*"

Henrique knocks Paul's finger away. "Oh-ho! Better, you say!? She deserved *better*? And what does this 'better' look like, Paul? No—don't walk away. Please, tell me this. What does this *better* look like? Does it look like you, Paul? Or Alice? Is that what your mother deserved? Because . . ."

But his voice becomes just another sound in the knotty maze of the music, so Paul stops listening. He watches Henrique's mouth move, but he relieves himself of all responsibility for making sense of what he's saying. Instead, he does the only thing he deems logical—the only thing that, in his compromised state of consciousness, where reason is reduced to dos and don'ts, to eithers and ors, makes absolute sense: he whips out his dick and starts pissing on Henrique. He had to go anyway, he figures, and what better place to go than this.

The English rose screams, but Paul doesn't stop; he believes it's always better to finish what one's started. Soon, though, he senses a greater commotion gathering around him: the bartender, rushing out from behind the bar; patrons shouting, pointing; a chair being knocked against a stuffed stag head; and finally, Henrique's fist, clocking him squarely on the left side of his jaw. He feels the vague and far-off chatter of his teeth rattling and of the room spinning away from him; as white glacial light closes in around him, Henrique's piss-soaked suit sinks farther and farther into the distance. He falls backward, then, as his vision becomes a pinprick of something resembling the truth. And within it all—thanks be to karma, or to a God Who Understands, or to that strange and imperfect force that governs when sunflowers bloom in August and when lilies die in fall, there's a final and unexpected touch of grace: in the split second before Paul's head smashes miserably into the cold wood floor, the lights— blissfully—go out.

Alice

"I don't think I've ever bailed anyone out of prison before."

Alice shuts the door of the Peugeot, buckles her seat belt, and slips the keys into the ignition. But she doesn't start the car.

"I'm sure that's not true. And it's not prison. It's jail." Paul leans his head against the window and gazes forward at the small, squat police station where he spent the night. Alice can still smell the whiskey on his skin; she's pretty sure he's still drunk.

She says, "You're right. Sophomore year of college I bailed Jackie Rubenstein out of jail in West Hollywood after she handcuffed herself to a lamppost on Santa Monica and Robertson. But that was different. Jackie was protesting changes to the water rights legislation in the Central Valley. I should have said that I've never bailed someone out for peeing on a man."

The clock on the dashboard reads 8:05. She's due at Horwood Hall in an hour to get her hair and makeup done with the rest of the bridal party, and she still hasn't showered. Paul just keeps staring at the window. A bruise is starting to bloom along the right side of his jaw, where Henrique clocked him.

"No one's going to press any charges," Alice says. "I mean, you got drunk and pissed on someone in a country that's full of drunks who piss on people. The woman at the front desk in the station hardly batted an eye about the whole thing. This is standard fare for these folks."

"Fuck," he says, and rubs a hand over his face, like he's trying to erase it.

"You'll be okay."

Finally, Alice starts the car.

"Did you hear what Eloise said?" Paul asks.

"I did."

She thinks back to last night, the rehearsal dinner, when Eloise approached her. Alice had been huddled over an empty cocktail, digging through her purse for a Klonopin, when her sister grabbed her arm and dragged her into a bathroom. *I think I just did something terrible,* she'd said.

They'd spoken about it again this morning. At a quarter to six, just as the sun was beginning to crest the low eastern hills, Eloise had crept into Alice's room at Tenderway Glen and woken her by gently shaking her shoulder.

"What the—" Alice blinked and rubbed her eyes.

"I have a key," Eloise said, and then climbed to the other side of Alice so she could lie down next to her and stare at the ceiling. "I'm worried about Paul. He's not in his room."

"He's probably just licking his wounds somewhere." She was still half asleep. "Does Mom know you're here?"

"No." Eloise reached behind her for a pillow and held it over her face. Releasing it after a few seconds, she said, "Do you really think he's okay? I can't believe I said all that to him. God, I hope he's okay."

"I mean, what he said to Ollie's parents was insane. But yes. I think Paul is okay. We're basically just surrounded by a bunch of sheep. What could possibly happen to him?"

"But still, what I said was awful." She picked a feather from the pillow and turned it over on her palm.

Alice said nothing. Instead, she watched as a sliver of light stretched across the room's western wall. As it grew, she thought of what Jonathan said to her two nights ago, how he'd written her off completely. She thought of her phone, currently balanced on the windowsill—a two-inch-thick piece of wood—because that's the only place in the bedroom where she gets any service, and, until she finally fell asleep last night, she was still toying with the notion that Jonathan might call back to apologize.

Jonathan. She replayed their conversation again, turning it over in her mind until the words lost their meaning. She remembered the part where he implied that she was some sort of whore; she remembered loathing herself enough to believe him. She squeezed her eyes shut.

Before she could stop herself, she said, "Do you think I might be able to talk to Ollie about that job still? Just to find out more about it, I mean. Like, does that offer still stand?"

"I don't see why not."

"Well, I'd like to, if it's okay with you."

"You don't have to do that for me."

"That's not why I'm doing it," Alice said.

"I thought you said you liked L.A."

"I was kidding myself. It's an awful place. I'm tired of the beach."

"Ollie—both of us—we just . . . we thought it would be a good fit, you know. No one thinks you're not capable—"

"I know. I realize that. I'm grateful."

They lay there on the bed together for a few minutes longer, afraid that if they rose they'd disrupt the mutual understanding of each other into which they'd just stumbled. And now Alice suspects they would have kept on lying there—not speaking, just listening to each other breathe—right on through that afternoon's ceremonies had Paul not called (collect) to inform Alice of his whereabouts.

"You can go back to your normally scheduled wedding," Alice said once she hung up the phone. "Our brother's just in jail."

Back in the Peugeot, she cranes her neck from side to side and squints into the sun.

Next to her, Paul says, "Thanks for coming to get me."

"What was I going to do, let you rot away?"

"I couldn't call Eloise," Paul says. "And Mom . . . oh, God . . . " He trails off.

Henrique hadn't needed to call anyone; he had a thousand pounds in the breast pocket of his blazer and had been able to arrange for his own release. Paul, though, had only had the five quid that Ollie had given him outside Horwood Hall, which he'd already used on the taxi that brought him to the Thirsty Lion—where, incidentally, he'd left his tab unpaid once he was arrested.

Paul asks her, "And did you know about Dad? Had you known?"

Alice turns the car off again. She knew he was going to ask, she was just hoping that they'd already be somewhere along the highway when he did so she could feign concentration on driving and avoid the sort of authenticity the conversation demanded. Had she known? It's an excellent question to which she's certain her brother deserves an answer. Yes. She had. Not explicitly—Alice learned last night that Donna had only told Eloise—but that didn't matter; theirs was a family that communicated most effectively via the implicit, anyway. If anything, she was surprised at her brother's willful ignorance.

"I think . . . I think I figured it out," she says. "I'm sorry."

Paul chews on a fingernail and spits it out the window.

"I've been so terrible to Mom," he says.

"We both have."

"Does she know about Henrique and that girl?"

Alice shakes her head.

"I'm not sure."

"She can't know," Paul says. "At least not yet. We have to—I want to protect her from that." He adds, "I just want her to enjoy the wedding."

"Okay."

Paul slumps down in the seat.

"I was going to call her instead of you. To pick me up, I mean."

"I think it's good you didn't."

"When she does find out, she's going to be devastated."

"I hope not," Alice says. "But yes, probably."

Paul leans forward and presses his forehead against the dashboard.

"Oh, God."

Alice reaches forward and grabs his shoulder.

"Hey, look at me," she says. "*Look at me*. What you did?" She nods toward the police station. "What you did for Mom?"

Paul looks at her. His eyes are all veins.

"You did a good thing."

Paul

The Wedding

Sherborne Abbey traces its roots back to A.D. 705, when Saint Aldhelm arrived in Dorset with his educated and cosmopolitan brand of Christianity. Still, people who concern themselves with the vague and foggy past of the church say there's every reason to believe that some other pile of bricks stood in the abbey's place before his arrival; some testament to a Celtic and barbarian form of worship.

If they're right, if some earlier church did exist, then Aldhelm got rid of it. In the same way sixth-century Christians conveniently turned the Parthenon, that improbably gorgeous tribute to Pallas Athena, into a temple for the Virgin Mary, Aldhelm insinuated himself into religion's epic tradition of reappropriation. Appalled by the barbarism he saw among Dorset's shallow hills and hollows, he wrote off the backward breed of Christianity being practiced: sacraments wantonly breaking stoic rules of orthodoxy; toothless locals celebrating Easter in July. And so he, at the behest of his superior, one King Ine of Wessex, took it upon himself to build a cathedral.

None of that original building exists anymore. In fact, the Saxon architecture around the abbey's western door was actually taken from a building that postdates Aldhelm's reign as bishop of Sherborne. That doesn't mean the structure isn't old—two of the chapels were built in the thirteenth century, and the choir was finished sometime in the 1400s. Still, none of it can be traced to when Aldhelm first rode into town. Since then, thanks to a series of political maneuverings and redistrictings; to royal christenings and marriages and—in the case of Henry VIII—divorce; to the sort of backroom decisions and betrayals that turn England's idyllic countryside into a chessboard, the abbey has changed. Now, like much of England, it's as much a mausoleum as it is anything else, a crypt that holds a country's disintegrating foundations as a relentless and horrific future barrels in.

And apparently, Paul thinks, it's a future without air-conditioning. He glances back down at the wedding program, on the back of which is printed this brief sketch of the abbey's past—a history that he's read and reread no fewer than ten times. He fans himself with the thick card stock, but it only makes him hotter. He checks his watch. He's trying to ignore his hangover; he's trying to be a good sport, but what the fuck: the wedding was supposed to start fifteen minutes ago.

He wipes sweat from his forehead and the back of his neck. Five minutes earlier, a small commotion broke out in the back of the church, and when he turned around he saw an elderly woman being led outside, her fascinator lying impotent and forgotten on the stone floor. *Fainted from the heat*, he heard someone say from where he was sitting, in the pew at the front of the church. And Christ—he believes it. He can't remember the last time he was so hot. On the drive over to the church he heard a BBC report on record temperatures sweltering all over the country. Really, it's this goddamned morning suit. No man should be required to wear a waistcoat *and* a morning coat with tails down to his ass on a day when you could fry an egg on the sidewalk. He dries his palms on his trousers, which are pin-striped and cut from thick, scratchy wool. Like pajama pants, he thinks. Ones I'd never be caught dead in.

Turning around, he looks toward the church's entrance, past rows upon rows of similarly miserable men and women. He scans the pews, searching for Henrique, and gives up when he can't find him. Probably fucking the twenty-year-old from last night in the rectory. Paul lifts an eyebrow; he shouldn't be crude, at least not here. He's not religious, but his natural inclination for guilt takes over whenever he's in church.

A drop of sweat works its way down his spine and settles near the top of his ass. He turns back around.

The string quartet in the north aisle of the nave cues up Chopin's Nocturne in E-Flat Major for the fifth time, and Paul closes his eyes, lets himself, and his hangover, get lost in the pockets of the wide melody. He sinks down and rests his neck on the back of the pew; when he opens his eyes again, he's staring at the ceiling. There's an instant when he's sure he's going to be sick—the abbey's fan vaulting is that dizzyingly intricate, that spectacular. Lines spread out and converge again like hands folding, and in the spaces that those lines create Paul sees tiled mosaics, blocks of deep blue and crimson and green and gold.

He checks his watch again. Another five minutes have ticked by, and there's no sign that anyone plans on starting soon. No priest; no groom; no Pachelbel's Canon. Where the hell *is* everyone? he thinks. It makes sense that Alice isn't here, given that she's a bridesmaid. But what about his mother? What about Ollie's mother? What about fucking *Eloise*?

He hears footsteps echoing in the north aisle of the nave and sees Donna scurrying past the string quartet. Nearly knocking over the cellist's music stand, she stops to apologize, then keeps moving.

"What's going on?" he whispers once she's slid into the pew beside him. Peeling himself away from the pew, he feels his shirt cling to his back. "I'm melting in this goddamned suit."

"I don't know." Donna's cheeks are flushed, and Paul can see faint paths where sweat has streaked her makeup. "She's just—she doesn't want to do it."

"Doesn't want to do *what?*"

"This!" Donna juts her chin toward the altar and then dabs at her forehead with a handkerchief. "She says she doesn't want to go through with it." Then, in case Paul didn't understand her: "She's saying she doesn't want to get married."

"Does she know that people are *literally fainting from the heat* in here? An old lady collapsed on the floor. Ruined her goddamned fascinator and everything."

"Ollie's aunt is fine. I saw her outside drinking water. And please stop saying 'goddamned' in church."

"Well, does Eloise know?"

"Of course she knows." Donna folds the handkerchief and slips it into her purse. "But right now she's got other things on her mind."

"Well, what are we supposed to do in the meantime?" he asks his mother.

Donna says, "Wait. I tried talking to her, and Alice is out there now. In the meantime, there's nothing we can do but wait for her to make up her mind." She adds, with less than perfect conviction, "It's her decision, after all."

Paul stares forward toward the stained-glass window on the east face of the abbey. He squints at the figures, at the light that gives them life: Mark, Luke, Matthew, and John, talking shop with a few saints. He wonders, briefly, what it would be like to be stuck in one of those windows; to perish each time the sun went down, only to be reborn into the exact same conversation the very next morning.

The quartet plays the final notes of the nocturne. This time, no one bothers to clap.

"Excuse me," Paul says, standing. He buttons his morning coat.

Donna takes hold of his sleeve.

"Where the hell do you think you're going?"

"I'll be right back."

Before he leaves, he leans down and kisses her cheek.

The sun streams through the trees that frame the abbey's perimeter, leaving shadows across the lawn. Paul blinks at the brightness and, feeling again that he might be sick, considers ducking back into the solemnity of the church. In the air hang traces of lavender and lilac, and as he breathes them in, he steadies himself and steps out onto the grass. He doesn't immediately see Eloise, or Alice—in front of him is the small drive that circles up to the north end of town, and then beyond that Half Moon Street, with its cadre of squat pubs and shops. He walks a bit farther, down a set of ancient stairs and toward those same shops, past some invisible barrier where the distant murmurings of the Nocturne in E-Flat Major are suffocated by the general discord of the town, and that's when, finally, he sees her.

Eloise sits on a bench behind a low stone wall, out of view of the church. She's alone—Alice must have returned to wherever the bridesmaids are being held, circling in their holding pattern—and next to her lies a bouquet of lilies, their petals drooping down toward the sidewalk. Across the street from where she's sitting there's a pub with an outside patio, and Paul watches as people drink sweaty glasses of beer and light cigarettes and check their phones, oblivious to his sister's presence. Looking down on her from where he's standing, he notices that she's watching them, too, and he wonders if she's thinking the same thing he is: that it would be so easy to join them, to order a few drinks, to say *fuck it* and make friends with a new bunch of assholes who don't know them and how awful they've managed to become.

He tilts his neck from side to side, feeling the joints crack and pull, and he walks the rest of the way to the bench.

"Hi," he says, when he's close enough for her to hear.

Startled, she turns and sees him.

"Oh, God."

Unsure of how to respond, he sits down next to her, moving the bouquet to the ground.

"You must be loving this," Eloise says.

Paul shakes his head. "I'm too hungover to be opportunistic."

Across the street at the pub, an empty pint glass falls from a table and shatters into pieces.

A woman in khaki capris, a Westmoreland terrier tucked beneath her left arm, unlocks one of the souvenir shops. A place called Sherborne Mews.

"What are we doing out here, Eloise?" Paul says.

"I don't know."

"You'd better damned well know. It's your wedding."

"I don't know if I can do this, Paul."

A plane flies overhead, cutting a cloud in two.

"Oh, no," he says. "*No*. You don't get to rent out a church that was considered old when *Henry the fucking Eighth* was around. You don't get to *haul your whole family* across the goddamned *ocean*. You don't get to make our *entire lives about your happiness* just to say that you *don't know*."

She looks down. Her shoulders are bare, and in the sun her skin has begun to freckle.

Paul continues, "I mean, people are on the verge of death in that church, Eloise. Have you been in there? Have you felt how hot it is? *Hell* is cooler than that church is today."

Her cheeks tremble, and he notices for the first time that she's started to cry.

"Christ," he says.

She dabs beneath each eye with the back of her index finger, and her nostrils flare.

A cab crawls down Half Moon Street and slows in front of them. Paul waves its driver on, and then watches as it turns around a low brick wall.

"I was so awful to you last night," Eloise says.

Paul nods. "You were. But then, I also talked about getting fucked in front of your in-laws. We're even. Eloise, come on. Let's get this done."

Paul moves to stand, but she stays seated, so he lowers himself back down again. The wool trousers press against the backs of his thighs in damp, warm patches.

"I told my dad to leave," she says. "I said I didn't want him here after what he did to you and Mom."

"I pissed on him. If I'd pissed on me, I'd've slugged me, too."

"You know that girl wasn't even a guest? She was some cook from the catering company. He met her when he was waiting for the bathroom next to the kitchen." She scratches a spot behind her ear. "I lied to Mom. She asked where he was today, and I told her he was running late."

"I think that was a good call," Paul says, and he genuinely means it. "Keep the body count low. Now, let's go."

She doesn't budge. She just sighs, and rolls her shoulders back, and stretches her long neck from side to side. Paul watches as taut skin stretches over vertebrae. Down some distant medieval street, a car honks.

"Do you remember the Warners?" she asks him. "The neighbors who lived over on Bluebird Court in St. Charles? There were four kids—Nick and Robbie were the boys; Jill and Heather were the girls."

"Yeah, we called them Aryan Youth. Said they were fueled by sunshine and superiority instead of food and water."

"I loved them."

A june bug crawls a few inches away from the toe of Paul's left shoe. Reaching his leg out, he lightly nudges it, and it rolls over on its back.

"I still trade Christmas cards with Heather, actually," Eloise says.

"You're kidding."

"They all still live in Chicago. Within blocks of each other." She leans forward and rests her elbows on her knees. New folds appear in the dress's skirt. "Heather says they all get together for dinner once a week."

Paul licks sweat from his upper lip. "Those poor, wretched things."

Eloise sits up straight again and turns to face him. "I thought that's what this was going to be, Paul. That's what's so crazy. I thought that this wedding was going to turn us into the Warners. You and Alice always had each other, and I never had either of you. I thought that this was going to change all that. Like, suddenly we'd all stop acting like such idiots and start loving each other and, fuck, I don't know, take a family portrait in matching shirts at the brunch tomorrow."

She's crying a little harder now. Paul folds his hands together and looks down at the june bug, which is still struggling on its back, its legs flailing in six directions at once. Its underbelly glows iridescent in the sunlight.

"That's never going to happen, Eloise."

"But why not?" She says this louder than Paul suspects she intends, and her voice ricochets off the buildings across the street. At the pub, drunk Brits turn their heads. "I'm serious," she pleads, now with her voice lowered. "Why can't we be like that? Why can't we be like the Warners?"

"Because we're *not* the Warners. That's just . . . that's not who we are, okay?"

He reaches forward and turns the june bug upright again. Fazed, it scrambles in erratic circles before hiding in the shade beneath the bench.

"And besides," he says, "I bet they all hate each other, anyway. I bet they all go home at night and tell their spouses how awful their siblings are, and then drink a bunch of wine and feel guilty about it and cry themselves to sleep." He brushes his hair out of his face. "At least we have the dignity and respect for one another to do all that in public."

A man flicks a cigarette from the pub's patio out into the street.

Pigeons flock to the abbey's belfry, and their coos echo in great iron domes.

Eloise says, "I think you're wrong. The Warners have got it figured out. Somehow they've managed to hold onto something that we lost. I mean, you should read these Christmas cards, Paul."

"Yeah? Maybe you're right. Maybe they really do all sit around on Sunday nights and make tacos and play Pictionary and do whatever the fuck else people like the Warners do." He goes to fish in the pocket of his morning coat for a cigarette before remembering that the morning coat has no pockets. "But we're not them, Eloise. You get that? That's not our tribe. And we can sit here and bitch about it and blame Mom and Henrique or whoever else because we aren't compelled to call each other every time we, like, bake a batch of cookies, or we can appreciate that when it matters, we'll do what's right by our family."

"We'll piss on someone."

"Sure, whatever, we'll piss on someone."

She reaches down for the bouquet, and Paul sighs.

"This is why I'm leaving," she says. "This exact reason is why I'm not going through with this."

Paul snatches the bouquet from her and hugs it to his chest. One of the lily petals snaps from its stem and floats down to the sidewalk.

"This is batshit," he says.

"No, Paul, it's not. Listen. Did I tell you Ollie wants to adopt a kid? Well, he does. He can't wait to be a dad, he says. We've already started talking to some agencies. I've been going along with it, but the whole thing makes me sick to think about. Because—no, don't interrupt me. Just *listen*. Think about it: If I go in there, if I go through with this and marry Ollie, and in a year, let's say, we adopt a child, you know what's going to happen? I'm suddenly going to have a family of my own. *Great!* you say. *Everything you ever wanted! Everything the rich boarding school brat has been pining for!* And, okay, maybe I thought that. Up until, like, a month ago. Because guess what, soon that kid's going to grow up. Soon Ollie and I will start fighting. Soon, I'm going to find myself in Mom's position— tied, *by blood*, or you know, whatever, *adopted blood*, to these people whose job it is to disappoint me. I mean, fuck, Paul. I can't even bring *this* family together at a goddamned wedding! Think of what I'll do with a family of my own!" She shakes her head and wipes away more tears, this time using her whole hand. "No. I can't fail like that again. I'm sorry you flew all the way here. But I just can't fail like that again."

Paul looks directly at her. He grabs her shoulders.

"Of course you'll fail!" he yells. "Everyone fails!"

"The Warners didn't fail."

She's sobbing now.

"FUCK THE WARNERS! Eloise, look, you'll be disappointed, okay? Love disappoints. It can't help itself. That's why . . . I don't know, that's why Ingrid Bergman gets on the plane and leaves Casablanca, or Maude takes all those sleeping pills at the end of *Harold and Maude*. But what are we supposed to do? Stop trying? Preemptively say *fuck it* because we know everything invariably ends? That's bullshit. You hear me? *Bullshit*. Love may disappoint, but that doesn't absolve us from the duty of loving. Of trying to love."

Eloise covers her face with her hands and breathes into her palms. The abbey's bells chime, and, disheartened, the pigeons flee their roost. It's two thirty.

"I don't think you believe yourself," she says.

"You're right. I probably don't. At least not right now. But I'm going to. One day, at least. That I promise you."

A cloud passes before the sun, and for an instant the world darkens.

"So what do I do?" she asks.

Paul looks at her—at her clear and desperate eyes—and realizes that she means it.

"I've got no idea," he says. "But I think you've got a better shot than most of us, and you'd be a fucking idiot not to try."

Somewhere in the distance, far from the bench on Half Moon Street, they both hear their mother's voice calling their names. It's soft at first, but as she approaches them it grows, filling the space between them.

Paul stands and helps Eloise to her feet. A tendril of blond hair hangs in her face, and he pushes it behind her ear.

Eloise nods, slowly at first, but then with increasing gusto. "Okay. Yes."

She looks back toward the church, and now says, "I think I'm ready."

Beyond his sister and the stone wall, Paul sees Donna trudging across the grass. Alice trails behind her, jogging as she yells at their mother to wait, her heels dangling from her left hand.

Upon hearing them, Eloise turns as well. Paul watches as she stares at them, and he wonders what she's thinking: if she sees love or a letdown; salvation or inconvenience. Reaching down, she gathers up the train of her dress and begins trudging up to them, working her way across the broad swath of grass. He stays behind for a moment, and as his sisters and his mother vanish behind the abbey's arches and spires he stares upward, past his blinding hangover, to a point in the distance that he can't quite grasp. A bit of infinity where blue bleeds to white, where absence and hope collide. He thinks of the beautiful, gut-wrenching future awaiting them, and the claw marks they've left in everything they've given up. He thinks of all the times they've faced the world on two steady feet, and all the times he knows it will knock them over to the ground. Mostly, though, he thinks—he forces himself to think—that for today, at least for today, they'll all be okay.

Acknowledgments

This book is indebted to the generosity, humor, talent, and time of so many wonderful people. And I'm going to do my best to name them here.

As always, the brilliant Richard Pine and Eliza Rothstein have worked tirelessly on my behalf. Thank you for taking my calls and keeping me in check.

James Melia is, frankly, a terrifyingly good editor, and an equally impressive drinking partner. Without him, this book would be a stack of pages in a drawer somewhere. Thanks also to the superb team at Flatiron Books: Amy Einhorn, Colin Dickerman, Bob Miller, Marlena Bittner, Greg Villepique, and all the rest. You've taken better care of me than I possibly deserve.

When it comes to being a genius reader, unflappable friend, and all-around mensch, Peter Schottenfels is second to none. Thanks for reading every word (often twice).

Special thanks, also, to other early readers: Irini Spanidou, Chris Rovzar, Ali Bujnowski, Beth Machlan, Max Ross, Molly Schulman, Peyton Burgess, and Zach Patton. Your advice and guidance are present on every page.

Topher Burns: Thanks for asking me who I hated at the wedding.

Steph Myatt: Thanks for *having* the wedding.

Mac McCarty: Thank you for your love, compassion, and patience on nights when I did nothing but type. It's difficult to imagine what life would look like without you.

Finally, I owe momentous thanks to my family. Mom, Dad, Reid, Katie, Sam, and Henry: You keep me just the right amount of crazy, and I wouldn't have it any other way.

ABOUT THE AUTHOR

Grant Ginder is the author of the novels *This Is How It Starts* and *Driver's Education*. He received his MFA from NYU, where he teaches writing. He lives in New York City.